MW01122625

Books by Lizzie Newell

Sappho's Agency
The Fisherman and the Sperm Thief

Coming Soon
The Tristan Bay Accord

The FISHERMAN

and the

SPERM THIEF

By Lizzie Newell

lizzienewell.com
Anchorage, Alaska

9138 Arlon St., Ste. A3-625
Anchorage, Alaska
99507

ISBN: 978-1-942528-05-0
eISBN: 978-1-942528-06-7

Version 2.0.1

In memory of Marcy Gentemann, who encouraged me to write but unfortunately died before I published any of my books. She is greatly missed.

Acknowledgements

Pat the Rat Wendt for brainstorming and for his perspective as a sailor and as a former baker aboard a Navy ship. Pat told me to never bake blueberry cobbler on high seas. I also received many of my best ideas while listening to him play music in Café Amsterdam and in bars in Anchorage, Talkeetna, and on the Kenai Peninsula. Drunk fishermen who dance while wearing rubber boots can be inspirational.

This story also came into shape in response to conferences and conventions including: North Words Writers Symposium, Kachemak Bay Writers Conference, Norwescon, Emerald City Writers Conference, RWA National Conference, and Wiscon. Faculty and attendees gave me valuable suggestions that formed this book.

Thank you, Rebecca Goodrich, for telling me the book wasn't complete, and to my writers group who told me the hard truth and sent me back for more rewriting: Brooke Hartman, Kellie Doherty, Tam Linsey, Michael Robbins, Louise Willis, Molly Gray, and Bill Swears. The suggestions made what was a novella into a novel. Thank you, beta readers Gwen Nirschl, Mary Wasche, and Susan Niman. Finally, thanks go to Cassie Cox of Red Adept Editing.

Succubi

A TECHNICIAN LIFTED A vial from a rack of phlebotomy samples. The rack contained blood taken from several fishermen recuperating in the hospital.

The technician's partner leaned against a lab bench, her tawny arms crossed. "You're never going to find a good man that way."

The technician admired her Minora partner's duskiness, her skin infused with melanin as if a warm brown dye had washed through her and left behind rich deposits in her hair and eyes. They were a moon couple, Majora and Minora, two women committed to each other. To have children, a moon couple traditionally partnered with a sun couple, a man and a woman representing the sun and the earth.

"My hobby." With a pipette, the technician transferred a droplet of blood to a DNA sequencer. "The perfect father for our children." Finding such a man was nearly impossible, but the technician enjoyed the thrill of the hunt.

On a nearby wall, the five hands of a clock-calendar pointed to divisions of the hour, day, year, and periods of both moons, not yet in alignment. The Majora technician and her Minora partner still had time before the spawning tide year.

Her partner snorted a laugh. "Oh, yes. Discovering an altruistic man through his genes."

"Not altruistic. Loyal!" The technician touched the screen, initiating analysis. "Noah characteristics breed true."

The partner ran her fingers through her curly black hair. "The Noah eugenics project failed."

"Maybe it didn't." The technician set aside the pipette.

"The project was disbanded. The breeding stock couldn't be controlled."

"And why couldn't Noah studs be controlled?" The technician waited as the machine ran its tests and algorithms. "I'll tell you—because they were loyal and wouldn't abandon their children. See, the characteristics breed true."

"Suppose you find such a man. What makes you think he'll cooperate when the other one wouldn't?"

The technician shrugged. "He preferred men, and that made him sinking difficult to seduce." The courtesan she'd hired to acquire the sperm had failed and returned the fee.

The partner laughed. "Searching for a four-leaf clover."

The technician kissed her Minora. "I'll find one for you, my love."

CHAPTER 01
The Stud

TEAKH RECLINED ON mounded pillows. A woman spooned behind him, her fingers twining in his hair and her lips on his nape, nibbling along the welts of his neuro scars. Other hands cradled his chin. The second woman kissed him, her teasing lips soft. And a third woman knelt beside his splinted ankle. Her bowed head spilled auburn hair in a cascade that tickled his thighs.

Oh Danna! Oh Danna! He mumbled, "I've-I've never..." How could he admit to being a virgin? A dozen-nine years old and he'd never been laid.

"That's all right. We'll take care of you."

Struggling against engulfing passion—or was it lust?— he observed details: oval nails, a hint of eye shadow, glossy hair—auburn, brown, and curly black. Courtesans maybe, but he'd never met even one courtesan, let alone been pleasured by three. These beauties were no ordinary dock prostitutes, not with every curve of pink or brown-tipped breasts and satin thighs perfect.

"I didn't get your names," he said.

"Beautiful stranger, names are unnecessary," one of them said.

The Noah Code gave highest honor to those who assisted strangers in need—anonymous charity. But other than the dull pain of his injured ankle, he wasn't in great need, and sex didn't normally constitute necessary assistance. Still, he spoke the traditional words of gratitude for charity rendered.

"Honor is yours."

"We'll make you comfortable."

They settled him in the softness of the bed and resumed their ministrations. The three beauties hadn't asked permission from his clan matriarch. As for theirs, what clan held their records? His seed was not his to share. Clan Ralko owned him. Oh, they claimed him as kin but gave him nothing. Founder them! The auburn-haired beauty straddled him. He admired her slim waist and the flare of her hips. Her hands cupped her breasts as she arched her back and moaned, her enjoyment unmistakable.

Her skin glowed with a bright sheen as if dusted with copper. Above the rich red-brown hair of her mound, a tattoo of an angel fluttered with the undulations of the woman's midriff. Instead of legs, the angel tattoo had two fishtails curving outward like tendrils.

As if Teakh were a primitive sea sponge, he was about to scatter his sperm to the tide. He wouldn't, shouldn't, yield to animal desire, but pleasure flooded him. Impossibly, he loved all three women, loved them as Poseidon loved triune Amphitrite. To him they were sirens, irresistible.

Teakh had always hoped and expected to love one person only, as had his mother. Flouting her clan, she'd remained devoted to his father then to his father's memory. She'd often stood on a rocky headland, gazing out to sea, awaiting his return.

The sirens held Teakh in their thrall. Ah, yes. The tattoo wasn't of an angel but of a siren, one of the winged women who sang mariners to their doom.

Hands caressed between his legs—whose hands, he didn't know or care. He saw only the beauty who rode him, her glossy hair falling forward, curtaining both her face and full breasts. Then he was being kissed, intoxicated by her sensitive mouth. Heady with passion, he returned her kisses, enjoying the smoothness of her teeth, the softness of her lips. Sliding into warm wetness, he surrendered his hopes and dreams to the woman he decided to call Angel.

He and the women moaned in unison as they brought him to climax. The three were virtuosos and he was a less-than-perfect instrument, but they coaxed him to the heights of performance. He arched against Angel and, with a surge, ejaculated.

"Magnificent." She panted.

Spent, they all kissed him. He drew them close, embracing all three, nuzzling dark-ginger hair and enjoying Angel's wild, musky scent. And he wept—wept for the loss of himself as his mother had seen him and for the loss of his parents, both years dead.

Angel patted his cheek. "What's wrong?"

He had nothing to cry about. Depths! If this were the treatment for a broken ankle, he'd trip on the companionway ladder more often. Bent on extinguishing a grease fire, he'd rushed down to the galley and misjudged the last step.

"Nothing," Teakh said, but in succumbing to lust, he'd thrown away his mother's expectations. Was the taste of bliss worth it?

The woman with curly black hair spoke. "We'd best get him back to the hospital. He'll be missed."

They helped Teakh pull on his shirt, worked his trousers over his leg brace, and fastened his vest. He pulled on his one boot. They gave him his crutches and assisted him to stand.

Angel brushed her lips against his cheek. "I'll go with you."

"But you'll be seen," one of the others said, maybe the brown-haired woman. "Better he goes alone and through the back door."

Angel smiled and shrugged. "We've already been seen together."

That morning, he'd met Angel making her charitable rounds at the hospital. She'd asked about his medical evacuation. He'd claimed he wasn't a hero, and she'd laughed. They'd hit it off.

Teakh swung his crutches forward. "I'll be all right." He hoped he'd be all right. He was as new to getting around on crutches as he was to feminine favor.

A fine mist of rain spattered Teakh's face as he hobbled along the lane, passing house-front businesses. His crutches thumped the damp boardwalk. Women glanced up from planning frames placed behind the windows so they could watch the lane while working on accounting or engineering or the like.

Two pedestrians turned toward Teakh and stared. Truth be told, every head swiveled toward him, seemingly talking about him. But they couldn't have known what he'd been doing in private. There was nothing wrong with accepting the invitation of a woman during the waning moon anyway. He'd broken no laws or taboos. For all they knew, he'd only gone to get his pants repaired. Why would they care who he was? His life vest bore no indication of clan. The color, once a serviceable orange, had faded to a shade of salmon—pale dog salmon at that.

At the waterfront, men in slickers worked, cleaning decks and tinkering with propulsors. The tide had receded, and the piers now floated lower than they had in the morning. A junk scow was in, loading recyclables. A kittiwake glided, wings cupping an updraft, its mew high-pitched and plaintive. A hose gushed as a man in coveralls sprayed a boat hull. The men paid him no unusual attention, just a normal bob of the head or the greeting: "What are you about?"

Teakh gave the standard response. "Observing the tide."

That was the truth. The statement had many meanings, including engaging in recreational sex only at the proper phase of the moon. Three women dallying with one favored man at such a time was common and accepted, even expected. Dancing was traditionally done in quads, a moon couple and a sun couple. It had to be that way since women outnumbered men. Oddly though, the three beauties had avoided being seen with him.

A man pushing a wheelbarrow laughed. "Observing it nicely, I'll warrant. Or is it the girls observing you?" He winked. "I hear they're casting for you."

So strange, this sudden feminine attention. Despite the shortage of men, women were generally picky, and Teakh was a poor relation in his clan. The name of his father's clan was unknown, and Teakh's mother had died over a dozen years ago.

At the hospital, he nodded a greeting to the nurse on duty. He entered the room he shared with Cooky, now awake and sitting up with bandages on his arm and the side of his face. The two men, injured during the same shipboard fire, had

6

been evacuated and lodged together. The window beside Cooky's bed had been dimmed against the afternoon light, but the esskip lagoon and emergency landing could still be seen through the hazy glass.

Cooky gave Teakh a lopsided grin, half of his beard singed off. "Have a good time?"

"Aye." Teakh smiled. "Thanks."

"Thanks? What for?"

"Didn't you—" He'd assumed Cooky had arranged his encounter with the three beauties to remedy Teakh's virginity. Few on Fenria shared his mother's expectation of monogamy. No, a true mariner had a girl in every port.

"If I could get a woman like that, do you think I'd send her your way?" Cooky said.

"Three of them," Teakh said. He'd accompanied Angel from the hospital to her friend's house. The friend had a companion. The visit had stretched to include lunch then to discussion of Teakh's preferences regarding kissing. They'd ended up in the bedroom.

"I'll be sunk," Cooky said. "Some fellows have all the luck."

And that brought Teakh back to his question. Why had they gone for Teakh, an unkempt fisherman too clumsy to safely use a fire extinguisher?

He lay on his bed and activated it to elevate his foot, then he used his neuro to access the Network. He couldn't exactly search for women by hair color, and "angel tattoo" merely produced bycatch of body art and tattoo parlors.

Might as well get some other work done. Teakh hoped to establish himself as a fisheries detective, so using his neuro, he brought up video records as if to his mind's eye. Eyes closed as if he were dreaming, he viewed images of silvery pollock being pulled from the sea. Gulls screamed. He felt the boat rocking and a fresh breeze. The winch whined as it pulled the net over a squeaking block. Silver bodies spilled into the hold. Teakh focused his attention on the writhing cascade. He watched for bycatch mixed in with the target species.

A man shouted, and the camera wrenched away from the spilling fish. Two fishermen in slickers and rubber boots stood on the deck.

One lifted a finger in an obscene gesture. "Sink you, Seaguard."

This could be a prank, but more likely it was an attempt to slip illegal catch past the cameras. Teakh laughed. Fishermen were always attempting to dodge regulations, while Seaguard tried to catch them doing it. He played the game from both sides, never letting on to Cooky or their shipmates that he had a Seaguard neuro and played for the other team.

A fisherman produced a harmonica and bowed to the camera. "Here's for you."

He blew a chord, and his mate belted out a filthy ditty, the exploits of Jack Tar and his dondering dandy dickledoo. The performance ended with catcalls and hoots of laughter. The ruse was an old trick—get the enforcer focused on the bawdy antics so he'd miss what was really going on.

Teakh watched the rest of the video record in slow motion, often pausing and rewinding, searching for illegal catch that was surely there. He shifted to the other deck camera and watched again. Damn, those guys were good. Maybe their catch was entirely legal; maybe it wasn't.

He checked the records against displacement and movement of the boat, recorded at the time by underwater sensors. That seldom yielded much. He yawned. For the most part, detective work was tedious to the extreme.

"Hey! Wake up!" shouted Cooky. "Got visitors."

A nurse had entered through an open door. Two other women peered from behind her.

"Is that him? The man with the bandages?" one woman asked.

Cooky straightened up.

"No. The other one."

"He sure doesn't look like much."

Cooky grinned. "Who's the stud now?"

"You are," Teakh said. "Hey, girl. My friend here thinks you're sweeter than pie."

The women giggled, and the nurse shut the door behind her.

"We'll have none of that." The nurse advanced on Cooky and pulled the privacy curtain around his bed.

Cooky peeped out and wiggled an eyebrow. "She's changing my dressing. How good is that?"

That was Cooky, always seeing the bright side. So why were women interested in Teakh and not the more experienced Cooky? If sympathy was part of it, Cooky's injuries were worse. He had a nice full beard, or it had been full before the fire. Teakh's body was scrawny, and his sparse beard needed a trim.

Teakh went back to auditing fishing videos, attempting to find salmon hidden in cascading pollock.

The door opened. "I demand an explanation!" Aunt Dyse barged in and advanced on Teakh's hospital bed. "Oh, my dear boy, what happened to you? Are you feeling better?" She patted him, pawing at his shoulder. "What are you about?"

Aunt Dyse had never cared much for him. Her attention was the strangest of all.

"Uh, the tide," Teakh said.

"I've heard. Now tell me it's not true"—Dyse pulled up a chair—"that you were with a woman?"

"I stopped by her place," Teakh said. Aunt Dyse had no need to know what he had done in private.

"Are you sure? I won't have a bunch of hags stealing from our clan."

"She mended my pants," Teakh said. "Did a good job of it too."

"How about your seed? Where were you while she was sewing? What were you wearing? Or were you still in those pants when she did the job?"

Now that was an intriguing idea, lying in the lap of Angel as she bent over him, her needle nearly pricking his thigh. But while her companions had entertained him, she'd used a sewing machine. Then she'd used a sketch pad to draw pictures of Teakh.

"What does that matter?" he said. "The Poseidon-damn moon is waning." No child would result from his activity.

"Your seed is the most valuable thing we own." Aunt Dyse rubbed her hands. "That *you* own. We've received word that you have the Noah Code."

What was she talking about? Surely not the twelve precepts of Noah. "Auntie, I don't have a copy on me." Teakh swung his legs over the side of the bed. "But I can recite if you wish. 'Observe the tide, and you will survive. Assist those in need.

Honor to those who assist strangers. Highest honor if the stranger be an enemy in need. Be prepared. Respect—'"

"The code is in your DNA."

Teakh shook his head. He supposed that if nucleic acid were treated as a four-letter alphabet, scripture could be written in a person's genes. But why? Such a text could only be read with a DNA sequencer. "The Noah Code is a lot easier to read in flagtile letters. Anyway, if it's in my DNA, I still have it. No theft occurred."

"It's not written in your DNA but programmed into you. Nephew, you've been bred, engineered even, to follow the precepts of Noah, instinctively altruistic and loyal. You are the Noah Code."

So that was the reason for women staring at him. Word had got out about his genetics, and the women thought him some sort of freak.

A guffaw issued from the other bed. "Lad, you sure have them shined."

What a sick idea, to suggest he was the result of a demented experiment. "Some joke," Teakh said. "How'd you get everyone to play along?"

"Not a joke." Dyse straightened. "For generations, scientists have sought the genetics of the perfect father, a man who puts the needs of women and children before his own. A man innately monogamous and altruistic. They tell us that's you."

Not only sick but delusional. Surely they didn't know how he earned money. "Me? I'm a fisherman when I can get the work." He passed himself off as a fisherman while investigating fisheries fraud and blackmailing poachers. For Danna's sake! He'd just had sex with three women without knowing their names. Enjoyed it too. Like depths he was monogamous.

"I don't believe it either." She shrugged. "Doesn't matter. We play this right, and we stand to pull in a good haul, make a bundle."

Sink it to Poseidon! Teakh wasn't altruistic. His investigations weren't philanthropy. Seaguard chiefs wouldn't go after the petty stuff, even after it took hours or even days to identify, so Teakh regularly went after poachers without notifying local

Seaguard. He was fair, letting folks know of information in their favor, but he asked for money in exchange for withholding evidence from authorities.

"And what do I get?" he asked.

"What do you want?"

This was new. She'd never before cared about his wants and needs.

"How about my own esskip?" Teakh said. Almost every member of the Seaguard owned or had access to such a flying boat. Traditionally marine craft was purchased for a man by his mother or sister. Teakh's mother was dead, and his sister, a student less than a year his senior, couldn't afford such a gift. Without the necessary watercraft, Teakh couldn't patrol as Seaguard.

He'd made do by auditing catch records, doing background checks, snooping around docks and processing houses, and collecting fees on his own. He'd purchased a small drone aircraft for surveillance. He'd even moved beyond his own clan's territory, working as a freelance fisheries detective. That was the title he gave himself. He hoped to develop a clientele among Seaguard enforcers in need of outside consultation. Whoever had labeled Teakh instinctively altruistic was seriously mistaken.

"You'll have your esskip," Aunt Dyse said. "But promise me"—she jabbed his chest—"never give away your seed. You talk to me before you go anywhere with a woman. We can't sell what you're giving away."

Who he had sex with was none of her damn business. Furthermore, he'd give Angel anything she wanted. If by chance she bore his child, well, that was how sex worked.

"Nothing happened," he said. Women sometimes became pregnant during a new moon in a neap tide year, but it was unlikely.

"Make sure of it." Dyse stood and stormed out of the room. Her voice came from beyond the door. "Thieves have stolen our clan property. Your protection of my nephew is completely inadequate. We demand restitution. Good Danna! He could have become ill. You call this a hospital?" She popped back into the room. "Nephew, pack your gear.

I'm taking you away from all of this."

"I can't leave Cooky," Teakh said, delaying in the hopes of a chance to see Angel one last time.

"You're so sweet," Dyse said. "Always looking out for your friends. Sacrificing yourself to save another from the flames." Anyone could use a fire extinguisher, and most would likely use it less awkwardly and more effectively than Teakh had. Dyse flounced into the hallway.

"Sorry about my aunt," Teakh said.

"Go on," Cooky said. "Got some good nurses changing my dressing. I'll heal up. I might miss the entertainment of watching you fight off the girls, but I'll be fine."

"Well, then." Dyse glanced back into the room. "Get your gear."

"I have matters to attend to first," Teakh said.

"Do it over the Network." Dyse stood at the door.

"My comset is lousy," Teakh said for Cooky's benefit.

"I can't imagine what would require your physical presence. Actually, I can, and so we must leave."

"I'm getting a prosthetic splint," Teakh shouted. "It'll arrive in a few days." The splint would work in conjunction with his implant, speeding healing and supporting his leg while he walked normally.

Dyse waved off the issue. "Never mind that. We need to go now. You'll heal just fine without it."

"What if I refuse to go?"

"I've been appointed as your guardian. I'm only looking out for your best interest."

Sink her! If not for his sister, he'd outright refuse. The clan backed her student loan. He collected his other boot, held together with silvery repair tape. Carrying it awkwardly, he crutched into the bathroom for the toothbrush, razor, and comb provided by the hospital, the razor still unused on his growing beard. He stuffed the toiletries and extra underwear into his spare boot and was ready to go. His dummy wallet comset was in his pocket. He didn't even have a parka.

Dyse glowered and accepted the boot. Teakh couldn't carry it while on crutches.

"Hail you later," Teakh said.

"Tide carry you," Cooky said.

Teakh hobbled after Dyse, who carried his incidentals as if they were the rotting carcass of a thorny sculpin.

CHAPTER 02
Dojko

T HE BLACK ESSKIP floating in the harbor sported a scarlet
band, Clan Ralko colors. Clouds had lowered and drifted
as mist in the fjord, obscuring the blue-green mountainsides.
Beside the esskip loitered Cousin Gorbus, also in black picked
out with scarlet piping. The craft's wings were folded against
her fuselage. Her high tail bore a Ralko call-sign prefix in
bright flagtile letters.

Teakh approached Gorbus. "Hi, cousin. What are you about?"

"Giving your sorry ass a ride. Hear you're now a big stud.
Think you're too good for the rest of your kin?"

Teakh shrugged. "For the likes of you."

Teakh had been the kid without an uncle, then the man
without an esskip. Gorbus and the other Ralko boys had
leered and made catcalls at his sister, considering her fair
catch, not truly clan. But most reprehensible in Gorbus's eyes,
Teakh had been a good student, excelling in biology.

News of his valuable genetics would only make the
situation worse. Teakh didn't share much genetic material
with the rest of Clan Ralko, maybe none at all. His
grandmother had been ingathered, and his mother had
refused to partake of a shared clan husband, or to share her
own. In a society with a shortage of men, this refusal could
only be seen as greed. For her possessive jealousy, she'd
been branded cold and selfish.

Clattering crutches askew, Teakh crawled into the three-
seat cockpit of the ground-effect craft.

"Take the middle," Dyse said.

So with his crutches tucked beside the seats, Teakh sat directly behind the pilot, cousin Gorbus. Dyse sat in the rear seat. Sandwiched between the two, enclosed in the small cockpit, Teakh had a view of Gorbus's neuro scars through his stubbly hair.

Dyse demanded, "Give me a channel."

Teakh fastened his seat harness then, with a mental shrug, adjusted his neuro. He transmitted, *Auntie, that's rude.* His unit transmitted subvocal speech, so he could communicate without his lips moving. The discussion remained silent, provided the recipient also had a neuro. Dyse did not. Instead she used a comset clipped to her shoulder. Her voice boomed while his whispered from her unit. Gorbus would be subjected to half the conversation.

"We shouldn't distract the pilot," Dyse said. The woman had no respect for Seaguard protocols, which prohibited vain use of Seaguard channels.

Seemingly indifferent to the discussion, Gorbus cast off and stepped aboard. The canopy closed, and the esskip pulsed slowly out of the marina, passing the junk scow close enough for Teakh to see the recyclables heaped on her deck and to read the name PZ *Idsir.* His stowed crutches digging into his elbow, Teakh sighed.

Clear of the harbor breakwater, the esskip turned and scooted across the bay before rising on step and extending its wings. The craft went airborne and flew only meters above the sea, riding on the cushion of air between outstretched wings and the ocean surface.

Staring at Gorbus's stubbly head and glossy scars, Teakh realized he'd most likely never see his three sirens again. He'd planned to discover their identities, but Aunt Dyse had come after him as if he were an escaping milch goat. She'd drag him back to Ralko Village, a miserable cluster of dwellings that had never been home. His chance was slipping away like the blurred water beneath the wings of the craft.

He wouldn't despair. A good detective knew how to make the most of his contacts. He closed his eyes as if he were sleeping and hailed Cooky.

You know the girl who sewed my pants? he transmitted. *I want to thank her, but I didn't get her name or address codes.*

She helped you out, did she? Cooky chuckled, his laughter natural. An ordinary mariner, Cooky used a comset, no implant. *And you're not giving her the honor of anonymity?*

The second precept of Noah was to assist those in need. The honor was all the greater if both recipient and donor remained anonymous. Still Teakh wanted to see Angel again.

Well, she was really nice and—

Cooky snorted. *In your boots, and with a gal like her, I'd do the same. Set your net, I would.*

Was Teakh's intent so obvious? *Will you ask around for me? Find out who she is?*

I'll see what I can do.

Honor. Teakh's investigation had begun. He shifted in his seat and spoke aloud. "So what's this all about? Auntie, why are you suddenly getting maternal on me?" Dyse might be rude, but he wouldn't be.

"An opportunity," Dyse said. "What do you think of becoming a stud?"

Not a career he'd ever considered. He wasn't sure if a stud actually had sex or merely donated sperm for artificial insemination. "What exactly does a stud do?"

"Not much," Dyse said. "Just get women pregnant. I'll arrange negotiations, payment, and all of the liaisons."

"So I'm paid for sex?" Teakh crossed his arms, nausea in the pit of his stomach. "And you're my pimp?"

"Not exactly. We're selling your genetics. Your services are gratuitous."

"How often do I get to have sex?"

"For you, I'm thinking of high fees for a premium product. Your children will be a limited edition, so to speak."

He'd always wanted to be a father, but not for a few years yet. Maybe after he'd established himself as a real detective. "How many children?"

"Well, we'll need to coordinate with the tides. If you do one woman at a time, once a month, you could sire twelve babies per spawning cycle. But I'm thinking that's too many. Maybe three or four per cycle."

The great prophet Catherine Smith had taught that children should be conceived in cohorts spaced three years apart and synchronized with the conjunction of the two moons. If he followed Dyse's plan, Teakh would have sexual encounters in flurries followed by three years of celibacy, unbearable years without Angel or any other woman.

"We'll have to work out the best pricing structure," continued Dyse. "Too many, and we'll have to drop the price per liaison. Too high a price point, and our product won't sell. But then sometimes high sells best. It's a tangle."

"I'm not selling my children," Teakh said.

"We'll find the best possible mothers for your offspring," Dyse said. "And they'll pay for the privilege of bearing them. Society needs your children. With enough nice guys in the gene pool, cooperation becomes the most successful strategy. I appeal to your innate altruism."

"Kinkill! Society can sink itself," Teakh said, loudly enough for Gorbus to overhear. He didn't want Ralko Seaguard ribbing him for being saintly, and he didn't intend to cooperate with Dyse.

She laughed. "You're perfect. How about sex with a different woman every twelve-night?"

That didn't sound good at all. In terms of frequency and quality, your average married man could do better.

"How much do you want?" Dyse asked. "Name your price."

Gorbus snickered.

Teakh craned to direct his words over his shoulder. "No!"

"Perfect. The trick is to convince you that our plan is in the best interests of your children. I know it is."

"They aren't born yet." Teakh clenched and unclenched his fist. "And I may never have children."

"How about in the best interest of your sister?" Dyse's laugh grated. "Despite the shameful behavior of your mother, we took both of you in."

"Keep her out of this."

"Some money would go a long way toward finishing your sister's studies and starting her in business." Dyse tapped his shoulder. "Her genetics are nearly as fine as your own. She could attract a good husband. No need to decide now."

Teakh fell silent, not transmitting or speaking. He watched the water rush below the craft, and the subtle adjustment of the wings as they adapted to speed, chop, and wind direction. What did he want? What was the right thing to do? Did right and wrong matter in this?

"I prefer to marry," he said. Actually, he'd prefer marrying all three of his beauties. He'd sleep with them in a big pile every night, watch his wives become full with pregnancy, be there when his children were born, raise his children, and stand by them when they became parents themselves.

"You can," Dyse said. "Later. Try this career for a few cycles, then settle down. You'll have your pick of women. Marry several of them if you wish."

Surely he could discover the names of the three, and maybe at least one could tolerate him in her life. Pray to Danna that one would be Angel, the earth to his sun.

But he was a fool. For Angel, the encounter had most likely been a spur-of-the-moment fling. Teakh was a captive to instinct, a male animal responding to a receptive female. A pretty girl smiled at him, and he was caught in her snare. Yet in Angel's smile, he'd seen something more than that. She'd genuinely liked him.

Blue icebergs drifted in the ocean. Cooky hailed, his comset transmitting the background chatter of the hospital. *Teakh, my lad, I asked about your girl. She's not from here. No one recognized her.*

Maybe Teakh could find the identities of the other two. *Got anything on who she might be staying with?*

Nope. Here and gone in a day.

The news of Angel's short visit both narrowed and broadened the possibilities. She must have arrived in the village by ferry, aircraft, or boat. Idylko Seaguard would have flight plans and manifests.

Thanks. Let me know if you find out anything else.

Will do.

Teakh could request manifest records, claiming he'd been seduced and his seed stolen. Possibly this was the truth. By such means, he might learn Angel's identity, but not win her love.

18

Anyway, his request for records would get back to Clan Ralko, and he didn't want that.

Teakh dropped his head on his hands. The leads on the other two women and the cottage remained. He should have been more observant. Depths! He'd slipped up at the very time alertness was most crucial.

A painting above the bed had been of a male nude rendered in oil, and there'd been bondage cuffs in place. The women had offered to restrain him. He'd turned them down. Was the cottage used as a place for lovers to meet in private?

He straightened. The mist-shrouded fjords slipping past the canopy were unfamiliar.

"Where are we going?" Teakh asked. He'd assumed they were headed home, that he'd return to living in the Ralko men's house. He'd sit with the great-uncles jawing about the old days, and he'd glance over fishing videos and occasionally laugh over the rare prank. When he grew bored with the routine, he'd run off again and go freelance. He'd work undercover, passing himself off as a fisherman, lumper, or longshoreman, whatever he could get.

"I've arranged training for you," Dyse said. "We've only a year to get you ready. Fortunately you were born in a neap year, or we'd miss the upcoming spawning cycle."

Teakh sighed. Against all tradition, he'd been conceived between spawning cycles. That detail of his conception had also been held against him. "What if I don't want to be a stud?"

"I know it's hard for men to make up their minds," Dyse said, "but you'd better not turn this opportunity down. Keno Dojko has generously agreed to accept you as a protégé in his stud-training program. You should be grateful."

A bit of income would help until he established himself as an investigator, but he hated being beholden to Dyse or anyone else.

They flew northwest for over an hour along a fjord until a village hove into view. Homes, harbor, and warehouses strung out along the shore were backed by dark mountains veiled in mist. The esskip splashed down and taxied toward a breakwater of dark riprap. Above it jutted the superstructure of fishing boats. Teakh identified trollers, seiners, and pot boats for crab and shrimp. Slowing, the esskip rounded the breakwater and pulled up to a floating pier. The canopy opened, and Gorbus leapt out to tie off his craft.

Through the drizzling rain, a couple walked toward them along the pier. The woman wore leggings and a hooded smock. Clad in a rain parka, tan pants, and waterproof boots, the man with her appeared to be an ordinary mariner.

"Auntie, you want me to stick around?" Gorbus asked. "Play chauffeur to lover boy?"

"Lover boy yourself." Teakh extracted his crutches from beside the seats.

Dyse spoke over his head to Gorbus. "Please remain here until our business is concluded."

Hauling crutches, Teakh crawled from esskip to dock. Dyse clambered out after him.

"Iris here." The woman bowed, her hood thrown back from dark glossy ringlets. Teakh estimated her age as in her third dodecade. She indicated the man beside her. "This is Keno, my brother."

The man bowed as well. His short hair was dark and thick and his beard neatly trimmed.

"Dyse Ralko." Dyse bowed. "And my nephew, Teakh."

Teakh bobbed his head in a semblance of a bow, the best he could do while balanced on crutches.

"Please come to our place for a hot drink and bite to eat," Iris said.

"Here." Gorbus tossed Teakh's boot, and it thumped on the dock, trailing tape and spilling toiletries onto the wet planks.

The man—Keno?—picked it up and led the group along the pier. Teakh checked his implant for record of the exchange. The man's name was indeed Keno. Teakh stumped along behind Keno and Iris, doing rather well until faced with the wet dock ramp. With the low tide, the walkway from floating pier to harbor front had taken on an abrupt angle, and the entire incline was slick with rain.

Keno stopped. "You need some help there?"

Head down, Teakh considered the size relationship between his crutch ends and the openings in the grating.

How stable would his crutches be on the rungs fastened on one side of the ramp?

"I can take one of those. Free up your hand," Keno said.

Teakh gave up a crutch and placed a hand on the wet railing. Bracing himself between it and the other crutch, he hopped up the ramp. The crutch end slipped, and he grabbed for the railing with both hands. His arms jerked, straining in their sockets. The crutch rattled down the incline.

He started to slide as haphazardly as the wayward crutch. So much for valuable genetics. He couldn't even get himself from a dock to a village waterfront. Keno grabbed him, arresting his fall.

"I can do it." Crawling would hurt. Sink it all! If only Dyse had let him wait in Idylko for that prosthetic splint.

"Here." Keno put an arm around Teakh. "Lean on me."

Together they staggered up the ramp. Iris and Dyse viewed their progress from the top. Gorbus and at least two men working among the boats watched as well.

A fisherman stooped for the crutches and brought them to Teakh. "Hospitality."

"Honor," Teakh said.

They continued along the waterfront past fuel tanks, the harbormistress's office, and a boatyard, then they turned uphill. Teakh stumped along as best he could, arms and shoulders burning, crutch-pads rubbing his ribs raw. They climbed a steep lane into the village, passing housefront businesses and a village common. Higher still, they approached a housefront with a sign in the window announcing: Iris's Salon. Body Waxing. Braids. Barber Services. Haircuts and Styling for Women and Men.

They passed the beauty shop but stopped before an adjoining building, a cluster of nearly windowless hexagonal blocks. Gables, cupolas, and peaks jutted above the roof, protecting clerestory windows. Tucked against this structure, as if an afterthought, was an ordinary business front. Interior louvers blocked the view into street-level windows.

Keno opened the door, and they went inside. A square table had been laid with a white cloth. Bowls and a heated soup tureen waited on a sideboard. Keno pulled out a chair.

Etiquette dictated Teakh seat Dyse, but encumbered by crutches, he couldn't. So Keno stepped in, seating Dyse first then turning to help Iris and Teakh.

Rain pattered in the street as Iris distributed the soup. She and Dyse took their time, making small talk, complimenting each other's taste in clothing, and trading comments about the lovely weather, which was always spoken well of no matter how inconvenient. Teakh endured, sipping his broth in silence.

When he was in Ralko, Teakh had lived in the Seaguard men's house. His room had formerly been a closet stuffed with old furniture and ancient telecommunication equipment. The place was lit by one window which had a view of an elevator shaft interior, and the light blinked every time the car passed. The quilt his mother had made covered his bed, and his sea chest remained at the foot. Teakh had liked his room, but he wanted only one thing from his quarters—his remote-control drone. If he had Gull with him, he'd send her to investigate Angel, but he'd left Gull dormant inside a locked case, and that case was packed in his sea chest.

Iris pushed back her chair, and her gaze scanned Teakh from head to foot. "So this is him. The Noah man. Rather young."

What could Teakh say to that?

"You've seen his genetic profile." Dyse wiped her hands on a napkin. "He'll mature nicely in the next year, just in time for the spawning tide."

"Aye. We received the lab analysis and have given it a preliminary review. It's a miracle you found him," Iris said. "In a hospital! Nearly dead from a fishing accident. To think of putting a Noah man on a fishing boat."

"We didn't know," Dyse said.

"Clearly," Iris said.

Teakh planted his hands on the table. "Let's get this straight. The injury to my ankle is a hairline fracture. And it's my choice to work as a fisherman."

Dyse waved her napkin. "Always thinking of his sister. He behaves exactly as his genes predict, sacrificing himself for others. His apparent immaturity? Part of the genetic complex."

Teakh grimaced.

"Ma'am," Iris said, "you might speak of your nephew with some respect." Surprised that she'd come to his defense, Teakh straightened, but she went on. "He's a true rarity. You do understand he'll be difficult to work with. Noah men are notoriously persnickety as far as virility goes. With maturity, they often develop sexual dysfunctions."

Teakh rose awkwardly, steadying himself with a hand beside his soup bowl. "What?" His sexual performance was none of their drift.

Dyse patted his arm. "Sit down. It's not truly a dysfunction but a valued characteristic. Noah men tend to have difficulty ejaculating. It gets more pronounced with age."

Teakh cleared his throat.

Keno leaned forward, forearm on his knee. "It's like this— you got to take a little longer for sex. It makes the woman happy. She'll have multiple orgasms and thank you for it. She'll come back for more, and so will you."

Iris gave Teakh a knowing smile. "He needs a patient partner, one who understands him and his unusual needs. This need keeps Noah men from straying to other women. As a result, their partners' children have a high survival rate. He's a great stepfather."

Teakh stared at the window louvers and through the slits at the rain-washed lane. What a bunch of shine. He'd had no problem with delayed ejaculation.

"Good thing we got him young," Iris said. "He's still got testosterone running the show. In a few years, oxytocin will take over. Likely he'll be unable to perform with strangers." She pushed herself back from the table. "Well then, our rare Noah man, let's take a look at you."

What did she mean by that?

"Oh, you're shy. Go into the other room and undress. Keno can help you. Then return."

Nudity hadn't been a problem with his three beauties, but now his so-called aunt was looking on? Teakh ducked his head.

"Ma'am, just don't look at him," Iris said. "It'll be fine."

"It's not." Teakh decided to leave. He'd just walk out. He stood but tipped the chair.

What the depths! What did he have to lose? Teakh hobbled into a small room set up with a bench, a mirror, and a robe hanging on a hook. Seated on the bench, Teakh closed his eyes.

"Are you well?" Keno asked through the door.

"Just tired," Teakh said. He silently articulated his sister's name, hailing her. *I'm in Dojko. I don't know how long. Do me a favor. Go to my room for Gull. Mail her to me here in Dojko.*

Sorry, I'm traveling, Sis said. *I'll send her when I get back to Ralko Village.*

How long will that be?

End of the twelve-night.

Teakh signed off. He'd have to get Gull some other way. He stripped off his vest and shirt. Keno came in and helped him remove his pants, working them off from around the brace. Keno offered the robe, and Teakh slipped it on.

They returned to the front room, and Dyse averted her gaze. Iris leaned back, her head cocked. Teakh tried to drop the robe, but it tangled around the crutches. The entire mess clattered to the floor.

"He's got a nice package." Iris reached out. "May I?"

"No." Teakh tottered.

Keno put a steadying hand on Teakh's shoulder.

"So bashful," she said. "Good size and shape, not too big or too small. Can't say as much about the rest of him. Teakh, would you please turn around? I want to see you from the back."

Dyse was watching again. Teakh's face burned. The women surely could see it. He complied, mostly to hide his face.

"He could use some muscle development," Dyse said. "I expect your training program will remedy that shortcoming."

"And his posture," Iris said. "What has he been doing? He's hunched over like an old man. Or maybe like a dog kicked too often."

"He's been treated well," Dyse said.

He'd never been beaten, if that's what she'd meant, but he'd never been truly welcomed in Clan Ralko.

"Can you straighten up some?" Iris asked.

Teakh tried, standing on one foot, a hand on Keno's shoulder.

"Posture. The first thing we'll have to work on. Thank you, Teakh. You can get dressed now."

With Keno's help, he returned to the dressing room and put on his clothing.

"I want a cut of his fees," Iris said from the other room. "He'll be a challenge. He might not be able to do it at all."

Teakh moved with care, listening to the women's assessment of his worth as he pulled on his pants.

"He'll probably wash out," Dyse said, her voice distinct beyond the curtain. "I'll give you a flat rate."

"But if his career takes off, it'll be big. Big money. I'll take the risk."

"Flat rate. He's scrawny. Bad posture. Painfully shy. It'll be a miracle if he can do it." That was the Dyse he knew, an avaricious woman who had nothing good to say about Teakh but who would do anything to win a bargain.

"He's already a miracle," Iris said. "You pay his room and board, and I'll lay my bets on him as a stud." Her opinion seemed more favorable, but surely she also worked the bargain.

"Think we can succeed where the Noah Project failed?" Dyse asked.

"I'm betting he's the results," Iris said. "Genetics such as his don't happen by accident. He just happens to have the exact genetic profile sought by the project. Entirely too serendipitous."

"But he's always been Ralko," Dyse said. "Born in Ralko waters to a Ralko mother."

"Likely his father was from that project," Iris said. "Possibly his mother's father as well. Noah studs are difficult to control. They prefer to pick their own partners. Actually, given the quality of Teakh's genetics, Noah men, his father and grandfather anyway, may have proved better at picking mates than the geneticists. Still, Noah men are lousy at staying alive. They tend to sacrifice themselves helping others. If we're lucky, we might keep him going for a cycle or two. By the way, how did his mother die?"

She'd died of an illness—nothing heroic about it. Teakh sat on the bench and rested his head against the wall.

"Stubbornness," Dyse said. "Refused to seek medical care. He'll probably do the same."

"More likely he'll refuse to cooperate," Iris said. "That's what happened with many of the subjects in the Noah Project.

25

He's still a sweet boy. We'll make the most of it."

Sweet? That wasn't a word Teakh applied to himself.

"His entire family is obstinate and willful," Dyse said.

Sink her. As far as he was concerned, she and the rest of Clan Ralko could sink to Poseidon. According to her, his entire genetic patrimony was a curse. If it led to this embarrassing meeting, then it was. Teakh positioned his crutches and heaved himself up, ready to put an end to their dickering.

"A Noah characteristic," Iris said. "They do what they believe to be right regardless of the consequences."

"From what I've witnessed," argued Dyse, "they take morality into their own hands, exalting their own egos."

"That may be, but their innate tenacity and loyalty has great value. Let's get him listed with Kordelko Auctions."

Teakh pushed back the curtain and cleared his throat. Dyse started.

"Excuse me," Iris apologized with a nod then waited for Teakh to seat himself.

He hesitated. Now was his chance to walk out the door.

"What are you doing?" Dyse asked.

"Leaving." His sister was traveling as part of her studies and so wasn't in Ralko. He'd have to get Gull himself.

"Just where are you going to go?" Dyse asked. "Gorbus won't give you a ride, and neither will anyone else. Lord Ralko knows about you. He'll issue a Seaguard bulletin."

"That's completely unnecessary," Iris said. "No one is compelling Teakh to stay."

Dyse frowned. "Please. Sit down. At the very least hear her out. Iris and Keno have an excellent reputation."

"I'm listening," Teakh said.

Iris nodded. "Our plan is for you to stay with us. Keno will be your trainer. He's a therapist and can work on your physical fitness. He's also experienced as a stud and can show you the ropes."

Keno straddled a chair. "It's a performance. You've got an audience of one, and best make her happy. There're usually onlookers as well, witnesses. You've got to get accustomed to being in the spotlight."

"Do you want to do this?" The concern in Iris's eyes seemed

genuine. "You can leave at any time."

What other options did Teakh have? Sit hunched in the men's house while sorting through video records of dying fish? Counting herring? Estimating the size of juvenile halibut? Iris and Dyse thought he'd wash out anyway. If nothing else, he'd get room and board without having to actually live in Ralko Village. Teakh lowered himself onto his chair and stowed his crutches beneath it. He still wanted Gull.

"We're anxious about security." Dyse's eyes shifted as her gaze traveled over window blinds, the front door, and the buffet as if criminals lurked in the cupboards. "My nephew may have already had a run-in with the succubi. They're swarming like hagfish to a trapped salmon. They must have known about his genetics before even I was informed. Less than two days in the hospital, and they got to him."

"So the suckies are after you?" Keno said with an affectionate shove.

Suckies? He hadn't heard that term before. Succubi were mythical women who came to men in their dreams and stole night emissions. Boys were told stories of how succubi would filch semen out of condoms thrown casually aside. In such tales, the evil women used the fluid in diabolical experiments.

"I won't tolerate those hags around my sweet nephew," Dyse said. "I'm relying on you, your clan, to safeguard our investment."

"Both our Seaguard and village police provide excellent security," Iris said.

"He should not be left alone with a woman, any woman." Dyse shot an accusing glance at Iris.

"You don't seem to trust Teakh," Keno said.

Dyse raised her chin. "He's young and impressionable."

"No mythological bogeywomen are out to get me," Teakh said.

"They aren't mythological. Just common criminals using a romantic name for themselves."

"I can take care of myself," Teakh said. "I'm a dozen-nine years old."

"Can you?" Dyse turned to Iris. "His forebrain isn't fully developed. Men aren't capable of rational planning anyway.

Left to their own devices, they spend money on booze and recreational sex, even to the detriment of their children and their clan. Men must be sheltered from their own base instincts."

Iris cleared her throat. "If Teakh is truly a Noah man, he's not a victim of those instincts. He'll spend his money rationally, as a woman would."

"I don't really believe that," Dyse said.

Keno crossed his arms, displaying well-built biceps and shoulders.

"We're just as capable of planning and preparation." Teakh smiled, his voice modulated. "And sometimes a man has a good reason to buy a drink or—" He stopped himself. Or to cavort with succubi.

Dyse frowned. "I expect my nephew to have close supervision while under your care."

"Ma'am, we can provide training and consultation, but we aren't jailers," Keno said calmly. "If you don't trust your nephew, take it up with him."

Without much appetite, Teakh crumbled a cracker. Iris and Dyse continued sipping broth until the discussion wound down and the soup was nearly gone.

Just like Gull, locked inside a sea chest, Teakh was trapped. He needed Dyse to go into his room to get the device. Then he'd have to trust Gull to the mail.

He folded his hands, took a breath, and spoke. "Auntie, I need a favor. I've got an ornithopter in my room in the men's house. Could you please send her to me? She's in a case inside the chest at the foot of my bed." Dyse would have to agree to a request made in front of others.

CHAPTER 03
Keno's Gym

KENO GAVE TEAKH a tour of the place, a complex made up of the gym—Keno's business—next door to the beauty salon run by Iris and her wife. The gym was a cluster of interconnecting rooms containing exercise equipment and racks of gleaming free weights. A cacophony of music pulsed, different selections competing: surge, bongo-bee, and shout. In the dining room, screens on a wall listed a work roster and a menu with bread, chowder, and salad slated for supper. Keno still carried Teakh's boot.

"We all pitch in with chores." Keno nodded at the roster. "Take your pick."

Teakh leaned on a crutch. The tasks included sweeping, cleaning mirrors, folding laundry, clearing the dining room table, and the like, jobs performed in the Seaguard by boys too young to patrol with their uncles. He sighed. He'd escaped the Ralko men's house kitchen only to fall into more household tasks. Most of them he couldn't even perform, not while hobbled by crutches and a brace.

"I guess I'll take laundry folding," Teakh said. It seemed like work he could do.

The room contained a large dining table as well as several card tables and a sideboard with mugs, a hot water urn, and a toaster oven.

"Kitchen is that way." Keno indicated a door. "We have major meals catered, but you're welcome to fix yourself a snack. There're usually leftovers if you have a hankering for midrations." He stood by the sideboard. "Your aunt seems to be a problem."

"Aye," Teakh agreed.

"You don't have to take that shit from her. If you don't want to be a stud, just say so."

"I haven't made up my mind," Teakh said.

"Fair enough." Keno left the dining room, and Teakh followed

In the weight room, to the thump of bongo-bee, two men worked out. One used a bench press and the other did crunches. Both men were stark naked. Teakh averted his eyes.

The weight lifter, showing no embarrassment, sat up. "Pretty Boy, what's with the clothes?"

Keno grinned. "New fellow."

The man bobbed his head. "Welcome to Pretty Boy's gym. What are you about?"

"Observing." Teakh cursed his obvious discomfiture. "I mean, observing the tide."

Keno smoothed over the awkwardness. "We're all brothers here, regardless of clan, so we use nicknames."

"Hairy." The man tapped his furry chest. He had an even coverage of hair over his entire body. "And you must be One Boot." His glance dropped to Teakh's ankle brace. "Or maybe Cripple."

"Watch out." Keno held up Teakh's slashed boot. "You might get stuck with it. Pretty Boy." Keno glanced skyward.

How had Keno earned that moniker? Possibly Keno was good-looking, but with his beard and solid musculature, he wasn't what Teakh considered pretty, nor did he look like a boy.

The man at the bench press patted his sculpted belly. "Ripple here."

Beyond a wall of windows, overlooking an indoor pool, a man swam laps, his long gray beard and hair streaming in the turquoise water.

Keno flicked his thumb in the swimmer's direction. "Tunes there. Short for Neptune."

All of the men were older than Teakh. If he stuck around, would he become like them?

Keno continued giving the tour. In a studio, to the strains of a tidal chant, a man inverted himself in a handstand and remained that way. Mirrors covering the walls confronted Teakh with his own sorry image—a scrawny fisherman on crutches, his lank hair tied back with a string. And, he had to admit, a fisherman with lousy posture. Another man flexed his muscles, the mirror reflecting his sculpted physique.

"Limber and Pector," Keno said.

Both men gave nods of acknowledgement.

Keno led Teakh into a quiet dormitory wing. "You can lodge here." He opened a door to a hexagonal room with a couch and two built-in beds. The bunks had storage underneath and were flanked by charging niches and closets. "Take your pick of berths."

Teakh stepped inside. "Nice place." Deluxe, actually, when compared to a cramped berth on a fishing vessel. Teakh would still prefer to be in Idylko with a chance of seeing Angel.

Keno set the boot beside a bunk. "You should know we don't wear clothing in here. That's why it's called a gymnasium."

Teakh didn't relish lifting weights with his gear flopping for all to see. "I was wondering."

"That was a joke." Keno grinned, his teeth even in his neatly trimmed beard. "Actually, the policy keeps clan rivalry to a minimum. Anyway, saves on laundry. The hamper is over there. We collect sheets and towels twice a twelve-night."

Teakh flicked his thumb toward a berth. "Do I get a roommate?"

"Not for now. You may have to buddy up later. If need be, the room can sleep three."

Teakh dropped himself on the couch, relieved to take the weight off his foot. Daylight glowed through light wells and high windows, natural lighting in accordance with the Noah Code. *Allow darkness. Keep holy the new moon.* A nearby door most likely led to a bathroom and toilet, but Teakh's arms ached, so he didn't get up to look.

"I've left the door codes open for you. Lock up if you want." Keno glanced around the room then cleared his throat. "Something else you should know about, an oddity of mine."

Teakh raised his eyebrows. Oddities could be secrets, and secrets were power.

"Let us be forthright," Keno said. "I'm experienced as

a stud, and in my prime, I commanded a good price, but I prefer men. I can do women, but given my druthers..." Keno glanced away. "I know how to behave myself."

If Keno considered Teakh's scrawny body attractive, he was odder than even Teakh. "I prefer women," Teakh said and moved a firm round pillow from behind his back.

"A good thing," Keno said. "Occasionally my little friend gives me away, a disadvantage of nudity."

"How about the other fellows?" How did they react to Keno's preferences? Surely they weren't all homosexual.

"They have their own tastes. We respect differences."

"Each of us has our quirks," Teakh said, unsure if he could live with this strange crew.

"Features," corrected Keno. "From what I understand, yours are quite unusual."

"So they tell me."

Dyse had claimed Teakh was inherently generous, altruistic, and self-sacrificing, but even she didn't believe it. One of his aunts had labeled him clinically insolent. Others had called him a smart-mouthed brat. That was before he'd learned to keep his opinions to himself. Regardless of the relationship between selfishness and altruism, Teakh knew himself to love beautiful women and to enjoy pleasing them.

"I've got an appointment at the clinic," Teakh said. He'd made it as soon as he'd arrived. "Healthwyv agreed to fit me in. Can you tell me where it's at?"

AFTER MEETING WITH the village healthwyv, Teakh crutched himself back to the gym. She'd recommended hydrotherapy supervised by Keno, and she'd told Teakh to wear the brace for another three twelve-nights. Otherwise she'd given him a clean bill of health. No strange diseases remained as a memento of the rendezvous with his three beauties.

Teakh collapsed on the couch in his quarters. Might as well get some work done. He hailed a kinsman in Ralko. *Got any catch records for me?*

Chief doesn't want you auditing, sent his kinsman, his transmitted words crisp.

Eyes closed, Teakh imagined his kinsman in the distant Ralko men's house, maybe in the command room. More likely he was in the hangar, doing maintenance on his craft. *Why the depths not?*

Didn't say. I'm guessing it's because you've got, uh, other responsibilities. Cousin, I wouldn't mind your job. Pretty cush. What do you say?

Wouldn't know. Haven't started yet. I can't work on shipboard or dockside with my busted leg, and Dyse won't advance me a stipend.

You've got room and board.

Food and shelter. A man needs more than that.

His kinsman chortled. *And you got it coming your way.*

Teakh signed off. Food, shelter, and sex. Sure, those were the basics, but pocket money came in handy, especially when it came to treating women well.

If only he could ask Angel what she wanted of him. Yet if she cared about him, wouldn't she have arranged for them to meet again? Maybe he'd left before she'd had the chance. Tomorrow, she'd visit the hospital only to find him gone.

He sat up and composed a note by dictation.

> *Hailing Idylko Hospital,*
> *Please relay message to...*

How would he identify the three women? He struck out the note and began again.

> *Hailing Idylko Hospital,*
> *Relay my thanks to the woman who rendered me hospitality during her charitable rounds.*

Danna! Asking for the name of a charitable benefactor violated several precepts of Noah.

> *Please let her know that I've removed to Dojko Village and am doing well. Permission given to forward her messages to me.*

33

There. If she came looking for him, she'd at least know where he'd gone.

Broken ankle fisherman. Sending.

He leaned against a bolster and recalled the three beauties in Idylko Village. The windows of the cottage had all been shuttered from the inside, same as the front of Keno's gym. Were his beauties bathing? All three of them kissing in a tub, their limbs entangled?

Keno hailed from the door, breaking Teakh's reverie. Teakh transmitted to release the lock and said, "Come on in."

Keno remained in the hall. "Better undress for supper." He had a whistle and comset fob on a lanyard around his neck, nothing else.

Teakh reached for his crutches. "Proper evening attire?"

"Aye. Here, proper attire is none at all."

"Give me a moment." Teakh transmitted to shut the door. He removed his vest and shirt then worked his pants off over his brace. Wearing undershorts, he put his vest back on and fastened it. With a thought, he transmitted the door open.

Keno stood in the doorway. "You gonna drive me crazy going around half naked like that." He guffawed. "Those boxers don't go with the vest. The vest doesn't go at all."

"I always wear this." Teakh patted the faded orange fabric. The Noah Code: *Be prepared.*

"You can't be going around the only man in body armor. The lads will be thinking you don't trust them."

"It's just an ordinary life vest." Fishermen commonly wore life vests while working.

"Aye. It's also a flak jacket, and the boys know it."

"What's the elevation of this place?" Teakh deadpanned. "Might get a tsunami."

Keno threw his head back and laughed. "And you might be paranoid. How old is that vest, anyway? By the look of it, you inherited that relic from Jamie Noah himself."

Teakh grinned. "It works. No shine." The Noah code prohibited excessive displays of status and wealth.

"Ah, you inherited that idea from Jamie Noah. But it'll attract plenty of attention here. Lose the vest."

Keno had a point. Teakh shut the door. He hung his vest in the closet and left his quarters wearing only his brace. Accompanied by Keno, Teakh crutched into the dining room, acutely aware of his exposure. Maybe that was the point. Naked, men were equal in their vulnerability. Most of them wore comsets strapped to their arms or on lanyards. Teakh was the only man present with an implant. He ought to have brought his fake comset.

Wells in the ceiling let in the light of a waning day. Wainscoting reached to hip height. Other than the clock-calendar and screens displaying the chore roster and menu, the walls were unadorned and painted a simple, austere beige.

The men sat at a dining table, leaving over half the seats empty. At the sideboard, Teakh filled a bowl with chowder and balanced a roll of crusty bread on his plate. He then considered the problem of getting his meal to the table.

Hairy pushed back from his own meal and helped out. "I'm trying to figure out your shtick."

"My shtick?" Teakh said and lowered himself onto a chair. "That's not what I call it."

"All of us have our type of clientele." Hairy pushed aside a comset fob to pat his own furry chest. "I tell you, women like a hairy man, something to get their fingers into."

"Your clients are strange," Pector said from across the table. "Smooth as a baby's butt, that's what they like."

"That's because Iris waxes you," Limber said. "Ouch!"

"Iris is a cruel woman." Pector smiled, a wicked gleam in his eye.

"Then there's Tunes, specializing in threesomes—he forks them with his trident," Limber said. "His clientele is a bit more mature."

"Discerning," shot back Tunes. He was a striking man with his flowing gray hair and well-built musculature. Teakh wasn't sure if the hair had gone prematurely gray or if Tunes maintained remarkable physical fitness.

"The moon couples like him." Pector winked. "They think he's fun."

A traditional dance quad consisted of two couples: one couple a man and a woman—the sun couple—and the other couple two women—the moon couple.

"Sure thing. I can do three at once," Tunes said, surely referring to all three women in the quad.

Teakh sipped his chowder while the banter flew.

"Shine off. One shot? And all three pregnancies take? Better to do one after the other with a rest in between."

"Was that three women? Or three couples? That would be six! He thinks he can do half a dozen. Not a trident, a six-shooter!"

"Moon couples like Pretty Boy too, but his clients are younger. Hey, Pretty Boy! When are you getting back in the spawn?"

The men looked toward Keno, but like Teakh, he kept eating without giving an answer.

"But for really strange, there's Limber's girls," Pector said. "Spawning asana. Lord of the Fishes. They think he's some ancient guru."

"Normal women go for the basics, a nice solid abdomen." Ripple patted his washboard.

"So what's the new guy's shtick?"

"Don't know yet," Keno said.

"Maybe Crippled Fisherman," suggested someone. "They can offer him hospitality."

"Too rough for Pretty Boy's clientele, but he might clean up."

Keno wiped his hands with a napkin. "First thing is getting that ankle healed. We'll worry about the rest later."

"That's it—we'll call him Ankle." The suggestions flowed, each man contributing.

"Anklebiter."

"Broken Leg."

"Charity Case."

"Pity."

"Neap," offered Teakh dryly, referencing minimal tidal fluctuation and the unconventional timing of this own conception.

Hairy laughed and cuffed Teakh. "We like you. You've got that silly tuft of fur in the middle of your chest. Do me a favor and don't wax it off. You'll figure out your shtick."

Despite the lack of clothing, the studs were about the same as longshoremen jawing in a tavern. Teakh settled back and worked the banter, encouraging the bragging and letting the studs strut their stuff while he gleaned useful information. Listening with an occasional appreciative nod, he received an education in the structure of the reproductive business, an industry served by three kinds of sex workers. There were donor studs, mostly amateurs, who produced semen for artificial insemination. Hairy described donor studs as men jacking off in a closet.

Assistants, professional men and women, lent a hand to donor studs or inseminated women using donated seed. But the most highly-paid sex workers were the cover studs, men with the bodies, the technique, and the genetics to use their own seed for inseminating women directly.

"They love us," Pector said. "Crowds of women screaming, trying to cop a feel. They pick out a special girl and pay you to do her. Maybe a couple of girls. The most beautiful in the village, and they can't get enough of you. Nothing better than that. Except doing it every night."

"Don't sell yourself cheap, Peckerhead," Limber said. "Donate sperm, and you'll flood your own market. Best get yourself a niche and a reputation for rarity."

"Thank you, Limpy. Limber is so rare he's not getting any. Now, me, I've got what most women want, and I charge a reasonable rate. Give them a good show. Make a lot of women happy. Not as much per woman, but I do quantity," Pector said.

Hairy shook his head. "Every woman wants to feel special, that she's the only one."

"Make a lot of women feel special. That's the golden combination," Pector said. "And I got it."

Hairy explained to Teakh, "Cheap insemination studs can produce every day, year round, year in and year out. But no one will buy that much splat. We cover studs perform only in accordance with the tide—full moons in the spawning years. Not in the neap tide years, not in the dark of the moon."

Teakh wasn't entirely sure how the men supported themselves during neap tide years. Possibly they earned enough to carry them over, or they worked side jobs. He planned to leave the gym before he found out.

The banter rolled.

"Full moon and women go into heat."

"We know that, Peckerhead."

"Assisting is fine. Pull in some extra money. You can actually raise your value that way."

"But you're doing men or using someone else's seed."

"You can just assist. No insemination intended."

"For money," Pector said. "That's prostitution. For fun is no one's business but your own."

"Still, got to be careful," Limber said. "Protect your reputation."

After supper, when the table was cleared, leftovers stowed, and dishes put away, the men cleared out of the room.

Keno stood in the doorway. "Are you attending?"

Teakh gathered his crutches. "What?"

"Tidal observation. You're welcome to attend or to observe on your own. We gather morning and evening."

Teakh fingered the welts hidden under his hair. Some believed awareness of the tide to be the sacred responsibility of the Seaguard and of the Seaguard alone. Apparently Keno didn't ascribe to that ideology.

Following Keno, Teakh hobbled into the studio. Fading evening light filtered from clerestory windows onto men seated cross-legged on mats. Some used round cushions identical to the throw pillows on his couch. The room had no other windows, no view of ocean or of the setting sun.

All of Teakh's life, he'd been taught to observe the tide. As a child, he'd mumbled the date and stated if the sky was clear or cloudy. He'd noted wind direction, lunar phases, time of sunset, and the position of the moons. Little of that could be seen from the nearly windowless room with only the gray light directed by the high windows.

"Here we observe the tide within." Keno placed a mat and a cushion on the floor for Teakh and helped him lower to the ground.

He sat awkwardly, one leg under him, the other outstretched.

"Try this." Keno offered him a small three-legged stool.

All music had been turned off, and the men meditated in silence. Keno settled on his own mat. Not one man peered outside to observe the actual sky or ocean. Attempting to copy the others, Teakh closed his eyes. Now what? What weather could be observed with eyes shut?

He saw near-blackness with purple and chartreuse spots that drifted and merged randomly. Bored with the patterns of his own retinas and with nothing else to do, he silently recited all twelve precepts of the Noah Code. As he floated in thought, the flavor of a dream bloomed—a woman swimming, her auburn hair drifting unbound, skin copper-touched but pale. She entwined about him, her legs sinuous tentacles. A mouth between them sucked gently, pulling him into her. He surrendered, yielding to her hunger, feeding her with his own being, and he was consumed. The warmth of an erection pulsed in his loins.

He opened his eyes. The other men remained deep in meditation. Teakh cast his thoughts in a direction potentially less embarrassing, cataloguing species of flatfish.

After closing prayers, the gathering broke up, and men retired to their quarters. Most doors were left open with shows playing on screens and men talking. Teakh went to his room and sat on his bed, his arms and shoulders as sore as his ankle.

Hoping Angel had responded, he closed his eyes and checked his mail. A text message from Idylko hospital had come through.

> *Hailing Broken Ankle Fisherman,*
> *We are unable to relay message as no one at this hospital regularly makes charitable rounds. Idylko Hospital. Sending.*

The walls let through the muted music and dialogue of an audio play.

He gave Cooky a hail. *What are you about?*

A bit slow here without you around, said Cooky.

I'm in Dojko. All set up in a stud-training program.

Didn't know a fellow needed training in that. It's simple enough. Wham! Bam! She's pregnant.

Seems there's strategy to it. My aunt is packaging me up, marketing me as if I were fish paste.

Positioning, Cooky said. *The girl's got to be willing before a fellow can do the deed.*

That girl, the one who sewed my pants. If she stops by, give her my address codes.

Get her in position, eh?

I might have left something behind. We went to a house up the lane. Maybe I left it there. Teakh hadn't seen the cottage from the front. How would he describe it?

And just what did you leave?

His heart, but Teakh wouldn't say so.

CHAPTER 04
Swimming

THE DUSK OF twilight pressed against the high windows of Teakh's new quarters. He hadn't spoken with his sister much in the last few days, not since his emergency evacuation from the ship. She would be worried and might not approve of his encounter with Angel. He sighed and gave her a hail.

Teakh here, he sent. *Still awake?*

I'm in the bunk room of a student hostel. Her voice whispered in his head, but her cheap comset transmitted the rustle of bedding. She didn't have a neural implant. The surgery, performed on children, sometimes led to death or disability, so it was considered unsuitable for girls.

Where are you at? she asked. On her side, a door clicked shut.

Teakh stared into the darkness, profoundly alone even while hearing his sister's words in his thoughts. *Dojko. Keno's gym. I'm training to be a stud.*

Aunt Dyse told me. Sis yawned. *Is this what you want?*

Teakh affected a jocularity he didn't feel. *Why not? Got the genes.*

Aye. Aunt Dyse told me we're Noah, bred to be altruistic, and that your Y chromosome matches Jamie Noah. So our great-great-great-something way-back grandfather wrote the Noah Code.

Teakh sent a burst of laughter, the sound an electronic imitation. *Can you beat that? Descended from a myth.*

It makes sense, Sis said seriously. *How Ralko treats us as outsiders and the way we lived apart. Those years in the estuary fen. Do you remember Papa?*

Teakh peered into the dimness of the room. The couch and other bunk were hidden in inky shadows. *Not very well.* The recitation had become a shared ritual.

I recall, she said. *He wore seaboots, and he'd lift me up in the air. Was he Seaguard?* Teakh recalled only a comforting presence, someone large and safe.

I don't know. Don't even know his clan. He'd visit for a while, then go, and Mama would cry. She loved him very much.

Teakh added his part of the story. *And he loved her.* Then Papa hadn't come again. Mama either shut herself in the cabin or stood looking out to sea as if she expected a ship to clear the horizon. Tears sprang to Teakh's eyes. He was grateful for darkness hiding his sorrow and his shame that he had thrown away love.

I need to see you, Sis said. *To know you're well. You're all I've got. But right now it's late, and I'm tired.*

I'm sorry to bother you. Teakh signed off and stared into the evening darkness. Mama had caught a fever, maybe from insects in the marsh or maybe because the cabin had been primitive, with no running water and with an outhouse for a privy. Then Sis and Teakh had been taken to live in Ralko Village.

Conceived in a neap tide year and only ten months younger than his sister, Teakh had been a misfit among Ralko boys. They had taunted him for speaking like a woman until he'd learned to talk like them and to blend in. Now he'd come to a new place, one just as alien and loveless. Again he was being asked to conform.

IN THE MORNING, the men greeted the rising sun and invoked the tides, bowing to each of the cardinal directions. Seated on a cushion, Teakh flexed his fingers, stiff from using crutches.

Invocation complete, the men meditated, except for Teakh, who downloaded the weather report. He synchronized his breath with the others, inhalation and exhalation rising and falling like waves breaking on a beach, but in his mind's eye, he saw not transcendent visions, not even of Angel, but isobars on a satellite image. Fearful of embarrassing himself, he kept his thoughts locked on barometric pressure, wind speed, and height of the seas.

The men rolled up their mats. Music now blared from the weight room.

Teakh gathered his crutches and approached Keno. "What's all this about? I witnessed no tide."

"The tide is here." Keno placed hand to heart. "And here." He moved a hand to his belly and inhaled, his breath sighing noisily.

Such breathing sounded a bit like surf, but if Teakh had a tide within, that force had a single aim, one he had no wish to explore while surrounded by other men.

Training began in earnest after breakfast. Keno led Teakh through a series of poses and breathing exercises, all of them adapted to sitting and lying on a mat.

"Your hamstrings are too tight." Keno tossed a strap to Teakh. "Use this."

Teakh lay on the floor, the strap looped over the ball of his foot.

"You should do this every day," Keno said. "Got to have some range of movement in your pelvis, keep those girls happy."

"That hip thrust is everything," commented Hairy in between push-ups.

Keno slapped Teakh's leg. "Knee straight. And keep it active. Tighten those leg muscles."

They worked on kneeling backbends with Keno spotting. "Don't forget to breathe," he said.

Teakh's muscles quivered with effort. Depths! He was Seaguard, not an eel. Teakh wiped sweat from his forehead. "What does all this breathing have to do with anything?"

Keno tossed him a towel. "Your breath is your spirit, the tide of your being. Observe."

What a useless heap of entrails. Such navel-gazing wouldn't lead to survival, and it certainly wouldn't bring in any money. As for impressing girls, he'd done just fine, thank you, without observing the smoothness of his own inhalation.

At noon, food waited on the dining room sideboard: onions, peas, and carrots cooked with groats, cod fillets, and a dessert of steamed pears—all of the food healthy and plentiful.

After the meal, some men cleared the table. Others swept floors, wiped down mirrors, and checked supply inventories or pool chemistry. Teakh's name was on the chore roster as Gimp with the assignment of folding laundry. He dutifully straightened napkins.

Once linens had been stowed in the buffet, Keno directed Teakh to the lap pool, a single lane of blue water. Tiled walls muted the pounding music, although the men could still be seen working out beyond a window between the weight room and office.

"I don't know how to swim." He didn't particularly want to flail around with Keno and the weightlifters looking on.

"Thought you were Seaguard," Keno said.

"Don't need to swim if you've got a life vest." Teakh's formative years had been lived in an isolated cabin in a marsh, and the nearby water had been too cold, too shallow, and too muddy for swimming.

Keno's laughter echoed. "And you're the one who's supposed to instinctively follow the Noah Code."

"Where does it say 'learn to swim'?" Teakh leaned on a crutch.

"It says 'Be prepared.' Says 'Educate children.' That means know how to swim so you can teach your children how."

Teakh grunted. Insects in the marsh had been fierce—leeches too. Better to explore by using robotic toys while staying sheltered from the bugs. "No one taught me."

"I'm your uncle then." Keno cuffed Teakh. "Some fellows just throw kids into the pool and let them thrash around. I won't do that to you. Don't think I could. So you'll have to jump in yourself. Thing is, you already know how to swim. You just need to believe it. Judging by your build, your body floats. Most people do. So you keep your head down, kick a bit with your feet, and tip your head to the side to breathe. Keep everything down except your mouth. Want a bit of propulsion? Paddle with your arms or kick."

Keno dove in and propelled himself with strong strokes, swimming the length of the pool. Nearly at the other side, he plunged out of sight and came up, direction reversed. At Teakh's feet, Keno shook water from his hair. "Like that."

No way could Teakh duplicate any of it. "How do you do the turn at the end?"

"Show you later, after your ankle heals. Now get in the pool. I don't care if you dog-paddle. Just get in."

Swimming, unlike breathing exercises, had utility, and the skill couldn't be all that different from flying his remote-control bird. Teakh sat on the pool edge to remove his brace, then he lowered himself into the water. He shivered. If he were a bird, he'd fluff his plumage to increase warmth and floatation, but exposed human skin had no such protection.

"Listen up," Keno said, his head above the bright water. "Here's what you do. Hold on to the side of the pool and make like you're lying on your belly. It's like a bathtub. Just relax."

Teakh submerged his head, an odd experience since his implant array included an ambient sonar pickup. With his eyes closed, he still saw the dim shape of the pool. Keno appeared in green, his hands glowing as they sculled.

"You're floating. Yes?" Keno's hand planed through the water, trailing glowing movement.

Teakh wasn't, not the way Gull floated, bobbing high on the water. He was unprepared—no life vest, no wetsuit, no boots—and ashamed. He set his hands against the smooth tile of the pool wall and gave an experimental jump.

"Like you mean it," Keno said. "You'll float. Put a leg out. Let the other drift up to meet it. When we were kids, we used to kick water at each other."

Teakh slammed his left foot on the water surface and doused Keno.

Keno dashed droplets off his face. "You got it. And me too."

Teakh grinned. If nothing else, Keno was a good sport.

"Okay, now just float," Keno said. "Take one hand off the wall and scull with it. Push that water down."

Teakh got a mouthful of salty water and pulled his head up, coughing and sputtering. He held the lip of the pool. "It's not like flying."

"Flying through the water."

Teakh shrugged.

"Been using remote-control aircraft, I reckon," Keno said. "A lot of Seaguard do. I'll teach you the breaststroke, maybe butterfly. That'll feel more familiar."

"Maybe," Teakh said. Keno was right. Teakh's drone was an ornithopter, and when flying the device, it seemed Teakh became a bird.

Keno glanced at the large wall clock, the hour hand nearing the three. "The tide. I'd best go to work." He hauled out of the pool.

"What?" Teakh said, hoisting himself out as well. "Where are you going?"

Keno toweled off. "I'm village swim coach."

Teakh sat to strap on his brace, eager to get out of the windowless gym. Oh, it had windows, but not ones a fellow could see out of, and the unchanging view of naked men grew tiresome. "Mind if I come along?"

"Sure. But hurry it up."

The village team was already suited up and in the pool when Keno and Teakh came through the door of the rec center. Keno called the kids together, explained the day's workout, and had the team in the pool for warm-up laps. Blue-and-white floats divided this pool into multiple lanes, a change from the single-lane lap pool at the gym.

Keno flicked a thumb toward a locker. "Got extra swim trunks, if you want."

"No thanks." Teakh would only embarrass himself further by floundering around, unable to swim even as well as an eight-year-old.

Excusing himself, he went outside to get to know the locale. The rec center shared a plaza with the clan meeting hall and the house of the grand matriarch. The monumental stone gnomon of a sundial cast its shadow on the pavement, a reminder to observe the tide. Sacred to Danna, the gnomon of a sundial pointed toward her in her manifestation as the North Star. The weather had cleared, but clouds drifted in the sky, and a light wind blew, an afternoon land breeze.

Teakh passed through the plaza and crutched to the harbor, the haunts of fishermen and longshoremen. He could take the ferry back to Idylko Village or hop a freighter and work his passage. The tops of his crutches rubbed his side every time he swung them forward. The situation was damn sinking frustrating. If he couldn't carry anything, how could he work?

He trekked along the waterfront, his passage slow, encumbered by the crutches and ankle brace. Signs in windows advertised housefront businesses, including a bachelor store. That might be a good place to pick up some clothing for wearing around the village, if he only had some money.

At the next housefront, a sign advertised SALTY HOUND TAVERN. It seemed Teakh had discovered the local watering hole. Leaning on one crutch, he slid his arm through the other, grasped the door lever, and pushed. Now to get his arm back over the crutch. He tottered.

A man inside opened the door farther. "Here you go."

Teakh gave a nod of thanks. "Honor."

"Ya new here," the man said, phrasing his comment politely.

"Aye."

The man helped Teakh to the bar. The bar top displayed not the usual news articles under glass and digitally updated but graffiti, years of comments and names carved into the wood.

"Well, pull up a seat." The man waved to the waitress. "Hey, Loopy, a beer for the stranger."

Loopy leaned forward, full breasts filling her bodice. "What'll you have?"

"Onion rings." So much for the healthy food at the gym. He matched his cadence to the speech of the fishermen. "And apple juice. Sparkling. In a beer glass."

The man chuckled.

"Doctor's orders," Teakh said. He seldom drank. Needed a clear head for his work, mining gossip for leads on criminal activity.

"Broken leg. What a hag."

"Real bad." Teakh patted his brace. "Right in the middle of the crabbing season too."

"That's bad. Tell you I busted my toe once, kicked a foundered deck cleat. Kept on hauling nets." The man launched into chronicling his various accidents, injuries, and how long they'd taken to heal.

Loopy delivered the onion rings, a bowl of sauce, and the drink. Teakh leaned back, sipped his soft cider, and kept the story rolling, nudging it with a question here, an exclamation there. He never knew where those monologues might go, and most folks appreciated a good listener. Teakh and the man shared the onion rings, dipping them into the bowl of sauce, tangy with vinegar and chopped pickles. While tasting the crisply coated rings, Teakh made notes, dropping information into a matrix held in his neuro, practicing his chosen profession, undercover fisheries detective. To catch lawbreakers, he set his net wide, damn wide. This man seemed about as honest as they came.

"You can call me Jamie." Teakh offered the name of his mythical ancestor in place of his own.

"Jamie? You shine a bit high, boy. Chuck Dojko here."

Teakh laughed. "Jamie Noah."

"Lad, you're a shiner." Chuck shook his head. "Like you wrote the Noah Code."

"Why not?" Teakh raised his glass. "Might as well steal from the very best."

When the onion rings were gone, the depleted sauce sculpted with deep grooves, and the beer and cider had been drained, Teakh knew a goodly amount about Chuck and had the information catalogued and tagged in his records. Chuck worked as a deckhand aboard his cousin's boat, the *Bekra Irene*. Chuck, in turn, knew next to nothing about Teakh.

TEAKH STUMPED AWAY from the bar. He sat on a bench near the harbor and hailed Cooky. *You still in the hospital?*

Aye. Can't go back to work yet, and my clan hasn't sprung me either. They're not sending an esskip for me. So it's wait here, then home on the ferry when I'm well enough to travel. Say, skipper wants to know where to send your stuff. I reckon you won't be coming back as crew.

Reckon not. Teakh gave his mailing address. *Got anything on those girls?*

Most likely Cooky was sitting up in bed, or maybe he was now pacing the hospital room. *Nah. If the nurses know who they are, they're not telling me. Idylko standing together. What did she take from you?*

A small item.

They don't want you or me to know who those girls were. I done my best.

Teakh stood and hailed Keno, letting him know he was on his way back to the gym. He crutched up the lane, returning to the place he couldn't bring himself to call home.

Relaxing in his quarters, Teakh made another search for information, this time for house rentals in Idylko and for women offering sexual services in the Idylko vicinity. Nothing that came up matched the cottage or the three women. If he could get back to Idylko, he'd retrace his steps and find Angel, but he was stuck in Dojko with a broken ankle and not much money. Even less than that. The account he shared with his sister was in the red and bleeding interest. Gull remained locked in his sea chest. Teakh flopped onto his bunk. Helpless!

CHAPTER 05
Junk Barge

TEAKH HOBBLED ALONG the waterfront, his crutches thumping the boardwalk and vibrating with his frustration. He'd been a fool, a sinking fool. He'd met the woman of his dreams, so what the depths was he doing in Dojko, living with a bunch of sweaty musclemen?

He sure didn't want strangers watching him make love. Keno had explained the sordid business. To market his services, Teakh would have to get it up reliably in front of witnesses. The activity would be filmed—recorded for posterity, founder it all!

Teakh took a breath and straightened. Regardless, he would follow the precepts of Noah. *Observe.* He looked over the moored boats floating in the harbor and the slip, which had been vacated by vessels going out to the fishing grounds. He saw that a junk scow was in—the PZ *Idsir.* Had he seen that vessel in Idylko, making its rounds? A man stood at the rail of the ship. If Teakh were that man, he could regularly visit his threesome. Angel's burnished hair had smelled clean as an autumn breeze. As he turned away, he heard a splash. A blue tote floated past the pier, the side of the box marked with the letters Papa and Zulu.

The man aboard the ship hefted a second tote. "Take this job and sink it!" He heaved the lidded tub. It plummeted into the harbor.

Another man rushed up on deck. "What the depths are you doing?"

"I'm not taking any more hag slime."

The jettisoned tote sank with a bubbling sigh.

A man wearing a captain's cap, braid on the brim, stormed out of the deckhouse. "You're off my ship!"

"Well, I quit," shouted the man. "You're a kin-killing lubber."

"Your cooking is crap," the captain shot back.

Was this the opportunity Teakh needed? A tote bumped against the floating pier. The tide was higher than it had been the other day, and the ramp wasn't nearly as steep. The former cook came out of the deckhouse, hauling a duffle, and stomped down the gangway. He passed Teakh, who bobbed his head in a semblance of a bow.

"If you want to know," growled the cook, "that skipper is tighter than the skin on an eel. Fratricidal lubber! There's no pleasing him."

Teakh would give it a shot. What the depths!

He'd work on the junk scow, if only for a few days, just long enough to get to Idylko. Teakh planned to present himself aboard the ship as clanless, so the trick would be convincing the captain to take him on without references. Heedless of the danger, Teakh stumbled down the dock ramp, his crutches skittering on the slick metal grating. If someone else didn't get to it first, he'd recover the ship's gear and have an in with the captain.

Teakh knelt on the pier and reached his crutch toward the box, but it drifted farther away. He lay down, reversed his crutch, and dragged the arm brace against the lid. *Come on! Come on!* He hooked the crutch over the top of the tote and tugged it toward the dock. He raised one end of his prize to edge of the pier and dragged the tote ashore, then he flipped off the lid. The box contained sacks of potato flakes, dried onions, cabbage, and flour.

He hailed the junk scow. *Captain, I've got a container here marked as belonging to the PZ Idsir. I'm on pier one if you'd like to retrieve it.*

Honor, said the captain, the transmission crackling.

I understand you're in need of a cook. You're in luck. I got two years' experience in a galley, and I'm ready to sail. That experience had been bussing tables and washing dishes in the Ralko men's house. *I'm going to need some help carrying the container.*

51

Our sailing time is in a quarter of an hour.

I'm ready to go. At the gym, Teakh had only toiletries, a damaged boot, and a bathrobe. He wanted this job and wouldn't delay.

Two crew members tramped down the gangway. "That ours?"

"Aye." Teakh stood up straight. "And I'm your new cook."

The mariner's gaze dropped to Teakh's foot. "You?"

"Busted my ankle, but I can still get around a galley."

Teakh followed the two up the ramp and onto the ship.

"Galley is this way."

They went into the deckhouse and hauled the tote down a ladder. Teakh threaded an arm through both crutches, braced himself on the handrails, and lowered himself on one foot. The men dropped their load and left Teakh faced with open cupboards, dishes piled in the sink, pots encrusted with burnt food, and a cleaver stuck in the wall. The place smelled of rancid grease.

While the crew shouted on the deck, casting off from the pier, he set to work. Soon the junk scow would pull into Idylko, and he'd see his beloved Angel. He'd be well away from the homosexual gym owner and his sweaty stable. Leaning against a work surface and standing on one foot, Teakh scraped carbon from a pot and scrubbed with gusto. His luck had turned.

He hailed Keno. *I've shipped out. Got a job.*

You planning on coming back?

Can't say. If you could avoid telling my aunt, I'd be most obliged. I do appreciate your expertise, but I'm thinking the life of a stud isn't for me. Teakh worked on a crusty pan as he transmitted.

You're welcome to come back any time. Do me a favor. Keep up with those exercises. Your ankle will heal quicker.

I'm not going to be swimming for a while.

Do what you can.

The captain arrived in the galley. "So you're the fellow who thinks he can cook. Got a name?"

Teakh straightened, scrub pad in hand. "Jamie."

"Clan name?"

"Jamie Clanless."

The captain chuckled. "Figured as much. You can't do

much worse than the last fellow, and he was kin. I don't know what to tell his mother. Having no clan avoids that little problem. Show me what you can do."

Teakh gulped. The clanless had no legal recourse, and with the boat underway, he couldn't leave. But even without pay, he'd reach Idylko, and that was fine by him.

"What do you have slated for the noon meal?" the captain asked.

What did Teakh have on hand? He spied the cabbage heads in the open tote. "Coleslaw and..." He hadn't yet looked in the refrigerator. "My specialty." He grinned. "I'll rustle up something."

"Looking forward to it," the captain said. "Half past eleven. Be punctual. We run a tight ship."

"How big is the crew?"

"Two-dozen. The afternoon watch eats early, half past eleven. Supper ready at half-past five with midrations in the fridge. Breakfast, same time in the morning."

Teakh didn't have much time. How much cabbage would feed two-dozen men? He looked around at the heaps of pots and dishes. "Captain, I'm thinking I won't be able to get this cleaned up by noon, not without some help."

"I'll send someone," the captain said and mounted the companionway ladder.

Teakh opened cold storage and peered into bins and unmarked containers. How long had the food been in there? What was it? Here was a job for a fisheries detective. A container of baked white fish was most likely cod. He lifted the lid and sniffed. The smell wasn't exactly fresh, but he didn't detect any putrefaction. It seemed to have been preserved in brine. His menu was shaping up: coleslaw and leftover cod, maybe cod cakes.

Teakh slapped the fish on the table then went to the pantry for bread crumbs. The shelving held canned soup, canned herring, powdered eggs, and multiple packages of hardtack, but no bread. Hardtack would have to do. Teakh located a wooden rolling pin from a drawer and dumped the crackers on a baking sheet.

A short mariner with a grizzled beard arrived. He spat

a wad of sunflower hulls on the floor. "Cap'n sent me."

Teakh eyed the wad. "If you could get going on cleanup, I'll get lunch fixed."

The helper tied on an apron. "Think you can cook to please the old man?"

Teakh grunted and continued crushing crumbs with the rolling pin. He didn't plan on being around long enough to find out. "Do you happen to know how long that fish has been in the fridge?"

"We had cod yesterday," the mariner said. "And the day before. And the day before that. We're getting mighty tired of salt cod."

"We'll get this eaten up, then I'll cook something else." Teakh dumped fish and crumbs into a bowl. "What kind of route does the ship follow?"

"Around in circles. Idylko, Dojko, Ordako. Oh, and Kosura. Tatumuko, Itaskako, Pontako, and a bunch of other two-fish clans. Then the same thing over again. Gets about as tiresome as cod."

"So when will we reach Idylko?" Teakh added powdered eggs and stirred the mess together.

"We should be back at the end of the month. We left there a few days ago." The assistant set to work on the pots.

Depths! The scow was going in the wrong direction. Teakh should have looked into the ship's route before signing aboard. He would have to pass himself off as a cook for an entire month. The captain's opinion actually mattered.

Teakh formed a patty. "You know anything about succubi?"

"Just the usual." The man guffawed. "Stories to scare teenage boys."

Teakh made another patty and lined them up on a baking sheet. "Ever met one?"

The man shook his head. "Can't say that I have. Next thing you know, there'll be stories about stealing snot and earwax. You could clone someone from fingernail clippings, you know." He cocked an eyebrow. "My opinion? It's all to get boys to clean up after themselves. Or maybe to stroke their egos." He winked. "You think your swimmers are worth anything?"

"Maybe."

"Bring it on, ladies. Steal from me. Stroke my ego." Grinning, the man scrubbed with enthusiasm.

Teakh washed the cabbage and sharpened a knife.

At half past eleven, when the first of the crew members arrived for the noon meal, Teakh had pans of coleslaw and hot cod cakes. He wiped his hands, pleased that he'd gotten the food out on time. The crew filed past the buffet window. At a quarter past noon, they'd eaten the cod cakes and nearly all of the coleslaw.

"Where's the food?" the captain bellowed. "What is this? Snacks? Dainty hors d'oeuvres?"

"Got more coming," Teakh said, opening a can of herring. His hip ached from standing on one leg, but he chopped and dressed more cabbage.

When the crew had cleared out, Teakh consolidated the coleslaw and stowed it for midrations. He hauled himself out of the galley, again using his arms on the handrails. The deck was heaped with recyclables and secondhand goods.

A deckhand called out, "Hey, Cooky, what are you about?"

"The tide," Teakh said, unaccustomed to the name being applied to him instead of his friend. "And I'm in need of a stool." Surely the scow had some sort of chair among the household goods heaped on the deck.

"Don't think we got one of those. What do you need it for?"

"I got a problem with a broken ankle," Teakh said.

The deck hand gestured with an electronic noteboard. "Take a look around."

Limping between bins of scrap and heaps of machinery, Teakh searched for furniture. The armchair with the stuffing coming out wouldn't fit down the companionway, even if he could figure out how to carry it. He'd make do with a packing crate and the help of the deckhand in getting it down to the galley.

SLUMPED ON THE crate, Teakh hailed Cooky. Teakh couldn't handle this job on his own, no getting around it.

You'll never guess what. I'm now a ship's cook. Got the job today. How are you going to get around with that busted leg?

I'm pretty good at standing on one foot. Teakh wouldn't let on that he ached all over. *Got some questions for you.*

Teakh balanced on his crutches to count cans, sacks, and jars, identifying the foodstuffs and relaying the information. Cooky made recommendations on menu and supplies. The freezer contained more cod but little else. Cold storage had the remainder of the coleslaw, but no milk or eggs. The pantry was chock full of powdered milk, potato flakes, hardtack, and canned goods.

While they worked, the ship pulled into Ordako. Teakh scrambled up on deck. On the quayside, customers waited with boxes and bags of used items and recyclables. Crew members weighed and priced items. Shoppers came aboard to snoop through bins and shelves of secondhand goods. The ship offloaded pallets, shipping crates, and bales of aluminum for reuse and recycling.

Teakh hailed the captain. *I've inventoried our food supply. If you'll release me the funds, I'll buy groceries.*

I'll be doing all the buying, said the captain. *Send me a list. I'll take it under advisement.*

Sending. Teakh transmitted the requested list. *I've already inventoried supplies. Sir, I'm knowledgeable and experienced in purchasing fish. I believe I can get the best price.*

Frozen and dried is cheaper and more reliable, said the captain. *Cook what I buy.*

By evening, the groceries hadn't arrived. Teakh heated and served canned soup. His foot, hip, and arms ached. He still had leftovers to stow and dishes to wash. He peered into the pantry, planning breakfast out of the food on hand.

Exhausted, he set his neuro alarm and nearly fell into his berth, a narrow bunk in a compartment shared with other dozing men. He fell asleep to the drone of engines and the sighing snores of the junk crew.

His neuro jolted him awake to darkness broken only by the dim glow of a red nightlight. His hands were stiff and clawlike. They hadn't hurt like that since his first fishing gig. Now where were those sinking crutches? He felt for them in the dark.

56

Bleary-eyed, with an arm threaded through the damn crutches, he flexed his fingers then hauled himself up the ladder to the deck. Under starlight, he inhaled cool night air and saluted Danna the Northstar, always steady in her guidance. Then he bowed to each of the cardinal directions.

The sky was clear. He licked a finger, held it to the breeze, and noted that the wind blew out of the northwest. He attempted exercises then crutched across the deck and went below. In the galley, he flicked a switch, and light blazed. Teakh squinted at the fixture, which was missing a red filter. Depths! The unshielded light violated the precept against excessive light and wreaked havoc with nighttime vision.

Midmorning, after breakfast, a mariner came into the galley with groceries. Teakh opened the tote. The supplies inside had little relation to his list—no bread, just more flour. He'd specified fresh fish, but the tote contained dried salt cod. Teakh groaned.

"Captain insists the food stores better this way." The mariner rolled his eyes. "The lads on the crew would like better grub, but anyone who complains is off the ship. That's what happened to the last cook. And the one before."

If Teakh wanted to keep his job for a month, he'd best keep his mouth shut and revise his menu.

AFTER THREE DAYS, the grueling schedule took its toll. Teakh struggled with proofing bread dough as well as cooking and planning menus. He used up the frozen cod, canned herring, and chipped pork product. Handicapped by the captain's stinginess and his own broken ankle, he barely had enough time to wash up before preparing the next meal. His tidal observations and exercises remained brief. He didn't even have a change of clothes. That morning, he'd tried to clean up with a sponge bath. If his rank odor bothered him, it surely put off the crew.

Teakh peered into the pantry. He'd have to work with what he had: packages of dried fish. He tasted a strip of leathery flesh, as salty as an old boot washed up on a beach and about as smelly. How the depths was he going to cook this mess? He hailed Cooky. *How do I fix salt cod?*

Bacalao. Now that's about as traditional as you can get. If you do it right, it takes hours.

What's bacalao?

Ancient dish, a sort of stew. It dates back to Earth at a time before refrigeration.

So how do I fix it? The fish is like shoe leather.

Cooky chuckled. *Tomatoes, potatoes, maybe some peppers, onions. But first soak the cod.*

Teakh thanked Cooky and signed off. He had dried onions but no tomatoes or peppers. He frowned. Cod cooked with dried onions didn't make for much of a meal, but he had beans. They needed to be soaked as well. For bread, how about dumplings? He'd cook it all in one pot, save on cleanup and baking.

He measured out beans then opened packages of cod and laid the fish on top of the beans in a pan of water. With the meal underway, he went on deck to take a look around. The junk scow cruised through gray waters between distant mountainous islands. He went below and set the beans and cod on the stove to simmer. As noon approached, he mixed flour, baking soda, and water. He dropped the dough by spoonful on top of the bubbling stew. At half past eleven, the first of the crew arrived. Teakh balanced on one crutch and ladled out the meal.

The captain took a bowl, sniffed, and wrinkled his nose. "What's this?"

Teakh straightened. "Bacalao stew, sir."

The captain poked at a bean. "Like depths. What did you put in here, turds?"

"Beans, sir. I cooked what we had."

The captain plunked his bowl on the table. He stirred his stew then screwed up his face. He tasted then spat. Beans spewed across the table. "Poseidon! Get me water!" He spat again. "You! You!" His finger shook. "Off my ship."

"It can't be that bad," Teakh said then tasted the stew. The beans remained crunchy and littered with strips of leathery flesh, the whole mess unbearably salty and the dumplings were dense and gummy. He forced himself to swallow. "Sorry, sir. I'll bring out dessert."

"You're no cook," the captain sneered. "Just where was your galley experience?"

"We served a large crew." Teakh kept his chin up, his face stony.

"And you served them this?" The captain stabbed a finger toward Teakh's chest. "Tell me, where's your comset?"

Teakh held out his dummy wallet unit.

"That piece of junk?" The captain snorted. "What kind of mariner uses that as a comset? Your transmissions are a bit too crisp. I reckon you're either a complete lubber or you're Seaguard. It's about the same."

Teakh had never been able to afford a really good imitation of speech. His neuro was programmed with the tone and timber of his speaking voice but not natural breath patterns. "No, sir."

"I seen you up on the deck early in the morning. Observing the tide, eh?"

"I'm religious." If Teakh boldly maintained his pretense, maybe the captain would let the issue slide.

"Like depths you are. You've got a Seaguard implant. You've used it often enough to gripe. There's only one reason Seaguard would pass himself off as a cook—you're a felon. Who'd you murder?"

Teakh's anger boiled. "Who are you calling a murderer?"

"Killed with his cooking," shouted the mate. "That's the murder weapon. Beans." The crew laughed. "Deadly flatulence."

"Get off my ship," the captain bellowed. "You're a liability."

"I'll fix something else," Teakh said. He'd planned on serving canned peaches for dessert.

"You'll go to your compartment and stay." The captain tapped his comset. "Bridge. Make for the closest port."

"How about Suziko?"

"Closer. Pull over."

"That would be Deception Point."

Poseidon's trident! The captain planned to strand Teakh in complete violation of hospitality. Every man was entitled to food, water, and shelter.

"You can't do this," Teakh said.

"Oh, yes, I can. You're on my ship under false pretenses. And with your so-called comset, you can hail the Seaguard any time you want. They can deal with you. Mate, escort this lubber to his quarters."

"Let's go." The mate grasped Teakh's arm.

He shook it off and squeezed the grip of his crutches. The deck tilted as the ship turned. Teakh stumbled.

The captain rolled his eyes. "Seaguard renegades." He picked up the pot and went toward the galley. "I'll do the cooking. Where's the damned food?"

"You wouldn't release the funds," Teakh said. "Tide carry you."

He sat on his narrow berth, head in his hands, even farther from Idylko and Angel.

CHAPTER 06
Marooned

A WAVELET BROKE ON the beach, splashing over formerly dry cobblestones, a good indication of a rising tide. Teakh held out his hand to the sun, shading his eyes and using his fingers to estimate the position of the sun along its daily path. Oh yes, he could observe the movement of the tide and the passage of the sun, but that did Poseidon-damned nothing, not without a vessel and a chart.

The *Idsir* pulled away, growing smaller until, dwarfed by mountainous islands, it was swallowed by the vastness of the ocean. Waves hissed against the shore, and a gull cried. The waves rumbled and hissed with the shifting of gravel and sand, the distinctive sound of that particular beach. Teakh kicked at a stone. Marooned. The captain had sinking marooned him, all because of a pot of stew.

He assessed his situation. The rocky shore sloped up to a shear bluff. A smooth stretch of mud where a stream had cut its course bore the three-toed footprints of birds. His own tracks were a series of single footprints flanked by the circular depressions left by crutches. No other human prints marked the expanse. The windrow of kelp and bladderwrack deposited at the high-water mark contained not even a single scrap of human trash.

Founder the captain! Teakh had his neuro, but by using it, he'd reveal himself as Seaguard to whoever patrolled these waters.

Teakh tried to guess his location. What clan controlled

Deception Point? Kosura? Itaskako? He rubbed his ear and recalled which of the local clans had ongoing disputes. About all of them. Dig deep enough and every clan harbored grudges about unfair fish allotment, failed rescues, jilted lovers, or plain cussedness. When disputes escalated into pitched battles, Seaguard took the brunt, attacking neighboring Seaguard. An unidentified man with a functional neuro stranded on a beach would seem damn fishy. They'd suspect he was a spy or saboteur sent by a rival clan.

The stream provided fresh water, but of dubious quality. For food, Teakh could collect mussels and dig clams with his knife. Shelter remained the major problem. Eventually he'd need help. That was, unless he could cobble together a raft out of driftwood.

He sighed. With no other viable options, he accessed the emergency channel and hailed. *Mayday! Mayday! Mayday! Stranded. Deception Point.* Waves lapped the shore, tumbling the gravel. *Mayday! Mayday! Mayday! I'm stranded and need transport.*

Teakh held his breath. What had the captain told them about the Seaguardsman passing himself off as a cook?

This is Seaguard command, came the response.

He exhaled and sat on a brine-bleached log, its roots a skeletal tangle. *I've been marooned. Request hospitality.*

What's your need? The voice came across crisply, a sure sign of a neuro.

I've got no food, no water, and the Poseidon-damn tide is rising.

Are you in immediate danger?

Teakh picked up a smooth stone. *No.*

How's your vessel?

He flung the stone underhand. *She sailed off and left me.*

Stand by. Patrol will be along as soon as we can fit you in.

Teakh would have to wait, not knowing what sort of treatment he'd receive. Those who requested hospitality couldn't specify how it was given. Shelter could be nearly anything, and food didn't have to taste good. A wary clan could make hospitality damn unwelcoming. It could be worse than undercooked beans. Weevil-infested bread remained a possibility. As long as he was out of danger and had sufficient food and water, local Seaguard could do whatever they wanted.

The sun moved across the sky until shadows grew long. Some gulls winged past. He amused himself by skipping stones then thinking of Angel. Between imagined satin sheets, he tasted the sweet moisture of her lips, stroked her silken thighs...

When the hail came, the sun was three fingerwidths from the western horizon, and Teakh was cold. He didn't have a parka. An esskip skimmed toward him.

Seaguard here. I'm supposed to pick you up.

Teakh jumped to his feet, waving one crutch.

I see you, came the transmission.

With a flapping of wings, the craft splashed across the wave tops and settled on the water. The craft, navy with silver stripes, bore a tail number with the prefix Papa Delta Kilo, Clan Tatumuko. Didn't they have a dispute with Pontako?

As the esskip glided toward Teakh, the canopy opened. The pilot shouted, "Ahoy!"

"Honor," Teakh shouted.

"Come on. Get in."

Unsteady on his crutches, Teakh splashed through the surf, waves topping his boot and soaking his leg brace.

"You injured?" shouted the pilot.

"Busted ankle."

The esskip glided forward, and the pilot reached out a hand. Teakh steadied himself against the side of the craft and handed the crutches to the pilot. The man's life vest was Tatumuko silver and navy. Out of politeness, Teakh would make a pretense of not knowing Pilot Tatumuko's clan name. With the man's help, Teakh hauled himself aboard.

"That a recent injury?" Tatumuko asked.

Teakh fastened his seat harness. "A few days ago."

The canopy closed and the pilot said, "Word is you're a felon."

"Where did you hear that?"

"Captain of PZ *Idsir*."

Depths! The captain had been talking with Tatumuko Seaguard, probably making sure the locals knew where to find Teakh but making it hard on him at the same time.

Tatumuko turned. "Listen here, stranger. My kinsmen are tracking my location. Harm me, and no one is going to pluck your carcass out of the sea. It's cold, and it's deep."

"I'm not a felon."

Tatumuko shrugged. "Claiming hospitality, you could be anyone. We assume the worst."

"Seaguard," Teakh said, addressing Tatumuko respectfully, "I just want to get off that beach. I'm not planning to hurt anyone."

Tatumuko scowled. "Be sure of it. I'm in constant communication with our Seaguard command. Our chief knows exactly where we are."

"Where are you taking me?"

"You're not the one to be asking. We'll provide necessary hospitality and no more."

That could be bad. Teakh hunched in his seat. He articulated the name of Clan Ralko ready to make the hail, then paused. Aunt Dyse would arrive with Gorbus to haul Teakh back to Dojko, and she'd do her best to make sure he never left again. Lord Ralko could attach a watch notice to his name, worse than shackles. No, Teakh would forgo any mention of Clan Ralko. He'd take his chances with Tatumuko.

Sculling the craft's wings, Tatumuko backed away from the beach then turned and took off. They flew in silence until they neared shore and a scattering of houses behind a floating pier. A clump of men clad in navy and silver waited on the quayside. The canopy retracted, and the pilot stepped out. The crowd of Tatumuko Seaguardsmen stared at Teakh.

"This is him," Tatumuko said.

A stout man stepped forward. "Stranger, under hospitality, we're obligated to provide you with food, shelter, and emergency care. You may not dictate assistance provided or ask the identities of those who assist you. You have the right to remain anonymous."

They were going to do this by the book. Kinkill!

"Do you understand the conditions and accept hospitality?" the man asked.

"Aye," Teakh said. He had no other option. What could he say?

The group of Tatumuko men led Teakh from the waterfront, past a few cottages, to a shack and opened the door. "You stay here."

The interior contained a mat and a blanket on a concrete floor. Daylight lit the cell through a high, barred window. In one corner, a bucket stank of urine.

Teakh halted. "The village brig?"

"We have no way of knowing if you're a danger to the village or not," his Tatumuko jailer said.

"I've done nothing wrong," Teakh said. "The captain didn't like my stew. That's all."

"You're free to leave provided another clan vouches for you."

"How long will that be?" Teakh asked.

"Having names of contacts would speed the process. Do you know of any clan who can vouch for you?"

Teakh shook his head. He didn't want Ralko involved, and he hadn't even met Lord Dojko.

"This is a small village," the jailer said, "and you've put us in a bind. We will not endanger our women and children."

The locals weren't happy about having him in their village, and they'd eventually need the brig for a real criminal. In a few days, they'd realize he was harmless and let him go. He'd wait it out. If Aunt Dyse knew of his predicament and had her way, he could lose his freedom completely. She'd try to get him blacklisted as an outlaw.

The door closed with a clang, and Teakh slumped on the mat. He could hail anyone he wanted, for all the good it would do. Cooky had no money. Nor did Sis. Neither had influence with Seaguard lords or clan matriarchs, the kind of people whose word was gold. As for his paternal clan, he'd never even known Papa's name. The cold floor pressed through the thin pad. The cell darkened with twilight, then night.

Villagers brought him water and a bowl of mush, which they slid through a slot in the door. The mush didn't have weevils, but it sure was bland.

Teakh relieved himself in the bucket. The day dragged on.

Wind whistled under the eaves, then rain pattered on the roof. Wrapped in the blanket, Teakh ran multiple searches on the Network for Angel and found nothing. His butt hurt from sitting, and his legs were cramped. Danna! He might have been better off stuck on the beach. He hoisted himself up and paced. Two swings of the crutches brought him across the cell. Two swings brought him back.

He hailed his sister. *Teakh here.*

What are you about?

The tide. Not much else, he sent. He sure as depths wasn't going to let on to his sister about his incarceration. She'd worry, and there wasn't anything she could do to help, but she wouldn't be put off so easily.

Don't shine me, she said.

I'm not.

Sure, you are. I can tell it in your transmissions.

How could she tell? His neuro imitated speech but didn't convey the full emotional timber of a human voice. He shook his head. She just knew him too well. *I've left the gym.*

Did you tell Aunt Dyse?

No. I got a job on a junk barge and left.

Sis fell silent, and Teakh shivered in the cold cell.

She spoke. *Dyse has been talking to Lord Ralko. She's calling for a Seaguard bulletin on you.*

Founder it all! What kind of bulletin?

She's to be informed of any change in your location. Sis snorted. *She's claiming you're a valuable clan asset.*

Damn shine, sent Teakh.

Lord Ralko isn't going along with it, so now she's taken it up with the Ralko Mothers Council, asking them to pressure him into issuing the bulletin.

Good Danna! If Dyse found out about his incarceration, she'd have all the ammunition she needed. Lord Ralko would put out the bulletin, and every member of the Seaguard would be obligated to report his whereabouts and activity. His neuro would be used as a tracking beacon.

I'm not her property, he sent.

I'm sorry.

He signed off and sat hunched on the mat. Ralko Seaguard men often banded together, but the mothers' council was the real power. They voted and approved funding. Stuck in the Tatumuko brig, he could do nothing. Teakh was dependent on the goodwill and fortitude of elderly Lord Ralko.

Teakh's attempts to pace in the tiny cell were futile as a distraction. Maybe he'd try some of Keno's exercises—

anything to keep his mind off debate in Ralko.

He removed his brace and rubbed his foot. Spreading his toes, he tensed his muscles then shifted to his other foot. He lay on the mat with the blanket over his torso and extended a leg upward to stretch his hamstrings. He worked through Keno's sequence of backbends, twists, and static poses.

Finished with the routine and somewhat warmer, Teakh sat on the mat, closed his eyes, and turned inward, not to the Network but to his own interior darkness and his breathing, regular and even.

Observing such nonsense wouldn't get him out of this cell or get him any closer to Angel. He opened his eyes to his stark surroundings. He needed a clan, or someone with status, to vouch for him. If Teakh had actually spent some time with Angel and her companions, their clan lord might put in a word for him, but Teakh didn't even know their names. That left Dojko. Keno hadn't pressured Teakh one way or the other, and the trainer had a sense of humor. Keno it was.

Teakh hailed. *Gimp here.*

What are you about? The transmission contained the background noise of banging weights and Hairy's choice of jarring bongo-bee.

I'm having a bit of trouble, Teakh said. *I hired on as a cook aboard the* Idsir.

The Idsir? *That captain goes through cooks...*

I know, Teakh said. *He marooned me.*

How long did you make it as a cook?

Three days.

Keno chuckled. *Not bad.*

Local Seaguard picked me up. Clan Tatumuko. They think I'm some sort of criminal, so I'm in the village brig. They're asking for assurances that I'm not a safety risk. You'll have to speak with Lord Dojko.

The brig? Keno said. *What for?*

Serving stock cod and beans. My dumplings were gummy. I used baking soda instead of baking powder.

This is a first. Only man in my training program to be jailed for bad cooking.

Teakh reluctantly sent a burst of synthetic laughter. *Actually, Captain thought I'd come aboard under false pretenses. Some sort of grudge against Seaguard. He might be trying to hide something himself, but I don't really care if he's underreporting the amount of aluminum collected or whatever. I didn't get a chance to poke around.* Very likely the garbage scow outfit was engaged in tax evasion. Hiring the clanless was a common way to get around clan fees.

I'll give Lord Dojko a hail, Keno said. *The chief owes me a few favors, and he might have a good laugh.*

It's not all that funny, sent Teakh. *I'd prefer to keep word of this from my kin.* The news might be enough to turn Lord Ralko against Teakh.

Understood. We need to protect your reputation as a stud. Keno chuckled. *I'll hail Lord Dojko. We'll send someone to pick you up.*

Teakh couldn't care less about his marketability. Soon as his leg healed, he'd ship out again, and he didn't want his location broadcast. *If you can get him to vouch for me, that's all I need.*

Watching the scrap of sky visible through the bars, Teakh waited on the mat. His days of pain while trying to cook on crutches had been for nothing. He was going right back to the gym. His hope of finding Angel receded like the ebbing of the tide.

CHAPTER 07
Girly Pictures

KENO HELD OPEN his office door. "Let's talk about your training. Come on in."

After a shower and a good night's sleep in a comfortable bed, Teakh felt much better, although his shoulders still ached. He hobbled into the room. Two armchairs faced Keno's planning frame. The desk-sized screen could be tilted upright. Teakh relaxed on a chair and set his crutches aside.

Keno tipped the screen to vertical. "Here's what we've got." Remote in hand, he took the chair beside Teakh. "We're not all that far behind schedule. I've got you working on flexibility, stamina, muscle definition, body awareness, and physical therapy for that ankle. We still need to bring you up to speed on physiology and on the legal aspects of the business. When I send a man to a client, I'll be damned sure he knows what he's doing."

The comment hit a sore spot—Teakh's cooking—but he made a joke of the situation. "No cod stew then?"

"Not for a lady. We're billing you as a top stud, and I expect you to perform as one—that is, if you accept the job."

Teakh grunted. He sure didn't feel like a top anything, not after the last twelve-night.

"I'm giving you an assignment, a pleasant one." Keno pointed the remote. "Before a man can please a woman, he's got to know how to please himself."

Teakh picked at his brace. He already knew what pleased

him—Angel. A stack of images appeared on the screen. "Every man is different," Keno said. "For some men, it's tactile. For others, it's intellectual, a combination of ideas. For most men, it's visual. So are you an ass man or a breast man?"

Teakh liked all of Angel, no cutting her up into parts.

Keno raised an eyebrow and said, "We've got a full library of pictures, both still and video." He brought up an image of a woman peering through long eyelashes over a bare shoulder. "See what turns you on. For now, don't worry about what's possible or acceptable. If you have a thing for bathing in custard or reciting poetry while hanging upside down, so be it. Whatever makes your narwhal breach."

"Bathing in custard?" Teakh asked. "How many eggs do we put on the shopping list?"

"You're the wise guy." Keno grinned and closed the images. "Seriously, this is something you'll have to do on your own. I've put together a sample. Nothing extreme. No weird poetry. Take a look, pick out your favorites." Keno tossed the remote, and Teakh caught it. "Go ahead and use my office. I'll be out in the gym. Give me a hail if you need anything." Keno collected a noteboard. He went out, shutting the door.

Teakh set the remote on the table. His neuro could control the screen and worked just fine. He settled back in the chair and flipped through Keno's pictures. The first showed a woman, her buttocks nicely rounded, lying naked on wet sand as the surf broke behind her.

He flipped to the next—a girl kneeling on a fur rug before a bright fire. He activated video, and the fire crackled. She unbuttoned her shirt, revealing the brown areolae and nipples of her full beasts. She shimmied, her breasts jiggling.

The next had a lady in a boudoir, her blond hair sleek. She reclined on pillows, wearing nothing but a feather boa and a sultry expression, her eyes huge and impossibly violet. Come to think of it, the hair wasn't natural either. Probably bleached.

He brought up one image after another, searching for a woman with auburn hair, but the images all proved a disappointment. None could compare to his Angel.

He cradled his gear in one hand, but his narwhal, as Keno had named it, remained unresponsive. If he and Angel were to lie in bed together, her cheek against his shoulder, now that would excite him. Alone, he couldn't do it.

He hailed Keno. *These aren't working.*

You didn't even try.

I did.

I've got more pictures.

An image flashed onto the screen—two men embracing.

Sorry, not my type. Teakh shut it off.

No problem, Keno said. *You have full access to the image library. You're welcome to browse at your leisure.*

Teakh arranged his crutches and stood. *I'll be going to my quarters. Signing off.* He transmitted to open the door and hobbled out.

Hairy stood at the dining room door. "Gimp, we're getting together a game of Justice Poker. We need a fourth."

Teakh thought cards might be a pleasant diversion. He enjoyed watching faces and calculating odds. "Sure, deal me in." He crutched into the dining room. "What are you betting?"

Indirect daylight shone in the room, illuminating the clock, chore roster, and buffet, now vacant exempt for mugs and a samovar. At a card table, Pector passed out pencils and tablets for recording the wagers.

"Sit-ups," Limber said, seated across from Ripple.

"Does the winner or loser do the sit-ups?" Teakh asked.

Pector tapped a pencil. "Depends on if you'd like to do sit-ups or not."

Hairy took a seat, and Teakh sat across from him, partners. Hairy scratched his furry chest. "I've got some great pictures of gals."

"Let's see them," Pector said.

"Not unless you win."

Teakh kept his face neutral, concealing his distaste for girly pictures. He'd already seen enough of them.

Pector flourished a pencil. "And I will make one of my fine lanyards for the winner." He shoved pencil and tablet toward Teakh. "What'll you bet? Pony it up."

Teakh fingered the smooth tablet. What did he have to offer?

No one would want his clothing, and he was loath to lose his knife.

"How about if you get a hot wax from Iris? Get rid of that tuft." Pector thrust out his chest.

Teakh glanced down at the meager hair over his heart. "Not worth the trouble. But I've got a nice signal whistle in my quarters."

"Why would we want a whistle?" Pector said. "Lose the fur."

"Seaguard safety requirement," Teakh said. "Be prepared."

"If we have your whistle, then you're not prepared."

Teakh jotted his wager. "I'll shout real loud."

"So be it." Limber shuffled the cards and dealt.

Teakh fanned his hand, assessing both cards and his playing companions. Hairy sat beetle-browed, lower lip outthrust. Limber fingered his cards, even his hands graceful. Pector held his cards close to his smooth chest, the quirk of his lip smug and serene. Did Pector have a good hand or was he merely sending out false tells?

TEAKH LAY ON his couch in his quarters. He'd lost his whistle and ended up with Hairy's Poseidon-damn girly pictures, as if Teakh didn't already have full access to such dreck.

Founder! Teakh couldn't even win at cards. He'd been hoping for the lanyard. Even the sit-ups would have been better. He sighed and opened Hairy's collection. A woman dressed in shiny black bent forward displaying, through a strategic opening, her cunt. Her black catsuit was so tight, she must have used lube to wedge herself in. She looked back toward the camera, one finger touching her painted lips.

He flipped to the next image. A cold-eyed woman wearing bandoliers crossed over her breasts, her skin marked with blood and bruises. In one hand, she held a whip at the ready. Her other hand was entangled in the hair of a kneeling man.

The images had the same appeal as putrid shark meat. Maybe he'd spent too much time spot-checking videos of dying fish. Just as well. The sordid activity seemed an affront to the memory of Angel.

He recalled her slim fingers lightly playing over his thigh, her laugh—Danna, her laugh as clear as chimes! And her scent, maybe sweet gale or something spicy. Was it perfume or her own divine fragrance?

CHAPTER 08
Gull

TEAKH STRETCHED HIS hamstrings. Behind him, the mirrored walls of the studio reflected Pector's sculpted physique as he also engaged in exercise.

Keno entered the studio, carrying a case. "Gimp, got a delivery for you." Labels on the side declared the contents fragile. "Where do you want it?"

Teakh gathered his crutches and stood. "Up in my quarters." He followed Keno into the dormitory wing and transmitted his door open.

Keno set the case on the floor and straightened. "From your aunt. Is this the ornithopter you requested?"

"Aye." Teakh said no more. Gull was a drone, technically a telechiric robot designed for surveillance. Best to hide that he owned and regularly used such a device.

"May I see it?"

Teakh frowned. Yet he owed Keno for springing him from the brig.

"Just curious," Keno said. "Have you cleared your aircraft with Dojko Seaguard?"

Teakh preferred that the Seaguard knew as little as possible about his activity. He'd learned a trick from the old men in Ralko, a way to access the Sense-net for transmission relay while bypassing normal protocol. He could fly Gull anywhere, local Seaguard none the wiser. "She's harmless. A toy." Most Seaguard boys had some sort of remote-control aircraft. "My hobby."

Keno squinted with one eye. "I'll set my net you're not the sort who has harmless hobbies. I've heard tell of how Seaguard might smuggle small robots aboard a pirate ship to scuttle the vessel. If you've brought such a device into my home, I believe I have a right to know."

"My Gull isn't like that." Teakh opened the case to prove his point. His ornithopter drone appeared to be nothing more than a sleeping seagull—eyes closed, beak tucked under a gray feathered wing—nothing sinister in her appearance.

Keno whistled. "How much did that toy cost?"

All the money that Teakh had owned and then some. He'd borrowed money in his sister's name, passing it off as one of her educational expenses. In ordering his bird, he'd specified a mimic of a seagull, precisely a hybrid of a glaucous gull and herring gull. He used her to investigate fisheries crime. Among the crowds of seagulls hoping to snag a bite of fish, Gull went unnoticed.

"Enough. Don't touch." A careless bump of Gull would send agony through Teakh's body. The bird's pain threshold was set low, lower than recommended, but he couldn't afford repair costs.

Holding Gull's feathered body between his hands, Teakh merged with her. He became aware of himself as Gull with wings tucked over her back and her webbed feet hanging beneath her breast. He shook her tail and eased her wings, packed up too long. He lofted Gull and spread her wings. Gull landed on the window ledge. Through camera eyes, he saw himself kneeling beside Keno—two men in the light of a clerestory window, Keno naked and muscular, the other himself.

Gull pecked at the automatic window opener. Teakh struggled, moving Gull's head sideways to get her beak under the manual release mechanism. Fingers twitching, he fought the urge to use Gull's feather-covered pinions. His own head bobbed along with his bird's. The latch moved. Using Gull, Teakh shouldered the window open and stepped Gull out onto the roof.

A breeze blew from the ocean with the tang of salt, fish, and seaweed. Teakh preened Gull's feathers, smoothing them with her beak, then flapped her wings and resettled. Teakh felt pleasure emanating from his bird. She had suffered no damage in shipping.

Gull sprang upward to soar above the roofs of the village. Beyond the cottages, the water of the harbor glinted in the sunlight. This was what Teakh lived for.

They flew along the waterfront. Seagulls were always on the lookout for food and jealous of rivals. Teakh's needs were different—pocket money. He planned to earn it by finding things out of place, signs that fishermen had under- or over-reported their catch. Perched on a pylon, Gull observed the harbor, the boats in their slips, seagulls squabbling over scraps.

A hand on Teakh's shoulder startled him, bringing his consciousness jolting back to the gym. "Depths! Keno, warn me next time. Will you?"

"Are you flying?" Keno asked.

Teakh perched Gull on one foot, and he turned. "I'm at the harbor."

"You sit like a bird, and you hold the position too long." Keno pulled a throw pillow from the couch and dropped it beside Teakh. "You should sit on this as if meditating. Go on, try it."

How Teakh interacted with Gull was none of Keno's drift.

"Now straighten up here." Keno jabbed a finger between Teakh's shoulder blades.

Teakh slumped, refusing the advice. "How is this going to help with being a stud?"

"The girls will like it," Keno said. "We'll work on it. Your hamstrings are too tight. Your lower back is collapsing. I get it. The way you stand." Keno shook his head. "Shaped like a bird's spine."

Teakh grunted. He and Gull worked together very well. As Gull, Teakh took to the air to fly above the boats in the harbor.

TEAKH STOWED GULL and went into the weight room, where he sat on the floor and commenced his exercise routine.

Hairy hoisted a set of weights onto standards. "Did you hear the one about the stud and the sucky?"

Teakh worked on flexing his foot.

"Which one?" Limber arched into a complex balancing pose.

Hairy launched into the story. "So a stud and a sucky arrive at a biological bank. She's got full breasts." He cupped his hands to demonstrate size. "She's selling milk. So they send her into a booth, and she expresses herself. She comes out and gets paid. The stud comes out after expressing himself. He gets paid too. She says, 'So why did he get more?' 'Sperm donor,' is the answer. So the sucky comes in the next day. Her cheeks are full. She goes like this, 'Mmm mmm.'" Hairy puffed his cheeks and pointed at his mouth.

The men laughed.

Did women actually make money by tricking men out of their sperm?

"You know a person could suckle mother's milk, spit it out, and sell it," Limber said.

"But why?" Hairy asked. "An' you'd have to convince the gal you're a baby."

Come to think of it, seagulls fed their chicks by regurgitating food. Teakh had made a study of gull behavior and customs. He'd once made the mistake of sending Gull into a seagull colony and would never do it again. Gull society included complex etiquette. Woe to the bird who failed to understand gull propriety and decorum.

"Those suckies will do anything," Pector said. "Anything. There was this sucky once... Danna! she was beautiful. She wanted me so much, she'd let me do her any way I wanted. Her mouth, her pussy, and what a sweet ass!"

"So how'd you do her?"

"I stole the collection condom."

The joke disturbed Teakh. As among gulls, Teakh again remained an outsider and didn't entirely understand the rules.

"One came after me," Ripple said. "She was using an artificial vagina. So we go at it. I pull out and nail her right where it's supposed to go. And she was screaming for more."

Pector toweled his ear. "Suckies. You gotta love 'em."

Keno entered the weight room. "Gimp, got some training videos for you."

Pector hoisted two dumbbells. "Stud flicks it is."

"Marriage documentation," corrected Keno. "Only way to keep tabs on the lot of you."

"Oh la la. Marriage. Is that what you're calling it?" offered Ripple.

Pector smirked. "Train him good."

"Don't mind them," Keno said. "We'll watch in my office."

In the office, Teakh settled in a chair. Keno shoved a hassock toward him, and Teakh rested his heel on it. The weightlifters were still visible through the window.

Keno used a remote to darken both the glass of the window and the overhead skylights. In the dimness, the screen on the tilted planning frame glowed softly with a still image of a man and woman entwined.

"Marriage documentation? Or more from that library?" Teakh asked.

"A bit of both." Keno sprawled on the other chair. "Studs at work."

"These aren't marriages."

"Sure, they are. Temporary marriages, but they've still got extensive contracts. Pages specifying who will do what to whom. Video flicks are made showing documentation that the contracts were fulfilled as agreed. Officially the flicks are private, but they get around. Part of the industry."

Teakh grimaced.

Keno laughed. "It's good advertising. We're sex gods, and fans love watching their gods perform. Good stud flicks make a huge difference. Gotta look good on camera and make the woman look even better."

"What do the girls think of such a document being made public?"

"Some are pleased with the celebrity. Others aren't, and that keeps the lawyers busy. Some clients specify that the act remain undocumented. Others keep the flicks along with baby pictures and sonograms."

Keno flicked through clips, commenting and critiquing. "He flubbed that one. Didn't let the camera in. If at all possible, give the camera and witnesses a view of actual penetration. You want to get close, give the woman a good time, but also have enough space that the viewers can see." Keno paused the images. "You've just got to see Limber in action."

Another clip flickered on the screen. Limber kneeled on a litter carried through a crowd by six semi-naked women, his abdomen undulating in seemingly impossible contortions, body writhing as sinuous as a snake. Onlookers screamed in appreciation, dropping clothing and shimmying to a primordial drumbeat.

"Where's the girl?" Teakh asked.

"They're carrying him to their tent. He's their prize."

"For all of them?"

"I don't know the details of the contract," Keno said. "I think they wrestled for him in oil. Or maybe strawberry jelly."

Next up was a video of a boy doing a young woman from the rear, his hand on her shoulder, hips rocking against her haunches. The boy's face was beardless.

"I looked younger than my age," Keno said.

"You don't now."

"Just how old do you think I am?" Keno asked. "Consider, I've established my own gym and developed a reputation as a trainer. The beard helps with making me look less adolescent. And also the training to increase muscle. My clientele at the time was largely virginal. Also moon couples and some mature women with that kind of taste. I liked the moon couples best. They usually know what they want without being domineering. Sometimes I felt I was a girl cursed with a penis. That's why I'm good at training. The men out there don't know what women like. They really don't know."

"But then how could you perform with women?"

"Now that's the trick I want to teach you." Keno leaned forward. "You're like me—genetically programmed to love one person. But genes are a recipe, not fate, not destiny. Just directions for a hormonal cocktail. Pinch of adrenaline. Splash of progesterone. Jigger of testosterone. For you and me, a chaser of oxytocin, the cuddle hormone, lactation and childbirth, the monogamy ingredient. But we don't have to drink that brew."

"Monogamous and homosexual?" Teakh said. "Not that boy on the screen."

"You know what a bull is?"

"Male cow."

"Uncut male cow. Ever seen one?"

"Eaten beef a few times. Odd flavor. A bit like lamprey but richer. Milder than seal."

"Not many bulls around," Keno said. "Farmers use artificial insemination. It's like this—a veterinary assistant puts on a helmet and arms himself with an electro-stimulator and an artificial vagina."

Teakh grimaced.

"You don't want to know what goes in your ground meat," Keno said. "The bull gets restrained in a squeeze chute."

"Good Danna!"

"Some human studs also like restraint. Increases oxytocin, or sometimes adrenaline. Depends on how it's done. With a kind and understanding assistant, the stud enjoys the activity. The assistant might take pride in a job well done. But neither bull nor assistant are enthusiasts for interspecies sex. Left to his own devices, the bull would arrange things quite differently. He still prefers cows."

"I prefer women," Teakh said.

"But present the right combination of stimulants, and it doesn't matter who's holding the sperm-collection device."

"I'm not an animal," Teakh said.

"Don't know about that. But we've got human brains, and we take responsibility for ourselves. Brains are good for playing mind games, tricking ourselves."

"So what's the trick?"

"A lover. When I pleased a girl, I did it for him. Afterward, he would make love to me and tell me how well I'd done. And then—" Kinkill! Keno was crying, his face turned away. "I'm sorry. I get a bit emotional. He died."

"What happened?"

"We weren't married, not officially, but he was working for my clan. A fisherman working for Dojko. He fell overboard. My kin didn't know he was gone for over an hour and gave him up for dead. His body washed up later. In pieces."

"Whose boat?"

"Not saying."

Teakh had lost his mother to fever, yet Poseidon, the inexorable forces of nature personified, had taken her as surely as nature had taken Keno's partner.

Keno spoke first. "Someone following the Noah Code would have noticed he was missing and would have searched. The way you noticed a galley fire and put it out."

"Anyone would have done that."

"On a boat belonging to someone else? For a man who wasn't kin?"

"Observe. Assist the stranger. Be prepared," Teakh said. "The Noah Code."

"Exactly. They say that you and I do this by instinct. It's in our DNA. A man's death is hard on his widow, male or female. That's why we need more people like you. That's your shtick. Your clientele is those who have lost men, and you'll father sons as a memorial to fathers, brothers, and uncles lost at sea."

The proposition seemed overly morbid to Teakh. "I sure can't father sons for you."

"You can father your own sons, men who follow the Noah Code."

"It was an accident." Teakh flicked his leg brace. "A grease fire in the galley."

The Noah Code asked for people to remain observant of the tide and of events around them, and that awareness supposedly helped others. Teakh observed, but he wasn't altruistic. He remained alert for selfish reasons. He was willing to offer assistance when needed, but service to others wasn't his goal. If he was altruistic, it was by accident, nothing more than being at the right place at the right time.

"Doesn't matter." Shyly, Keno glanced through lowered eyelashes. "I can be your lover if you wish. That's what your aunt asked me to do."

"She's a hag."

"She just might be, but we could give it a try."

"You make for one ugly female. "

"We could start with kissing. What do you say?"

"I'm up for it," Teakh said. If he was going to be a stud, he needed to get accustomed to this sort of thing. And if he didn't like it, then he'd know.

"Try closing your eyes," Keno suggested. His hand stroked Teakh's torso, gliding over his ribs, then his hips and down the length of his thigh. The caress was respectful, reverent.

Lips met his, and Teakh accepted, sampling, experimenting. Keno kissed delicately, blissfully, his mouth as sweet and tender as any girl's. A girl with a beard and solid muscles. Teakh couldn't trick himself. He pushed Keno away gently.

Keno laughed. "Ah, yes. Wild Noah to the core. You'll want a woman for that. You're the genuine article. That's done with. We'll tell your aunt that we tried."

CHAPTER 09
Idylko

TEAKH, ONE WITH Gull, flew along the waterfront. His human body, seated on a meditation cushion, remained nearly forgotten. The crispness of the morning invigorated him, washing his mind clean. Dirty pictures were a poor substitute for Angel. Even if he could get off on women displaying themselves, he didn't want to. He wanted to protect them and cover their nakedness. If today's flight went well, he'd send Gull to Idylko to investigate the identities of the three women.

Teakh observed boats making their way to the fishing grounds. He flew along the shore from the harbor to the esskip lagoon, all the while watching to see what had washed up on the morning tide.

He avoided the Dojko men's house located behind the lagoon. The less he had to do with Seaguard, the better. Near the lagoon, a graduated pole, a numbered tidal gauge, thrust from the inlet. Using his implant, he noted the time and water level before continuing along the shoreline.

Driftwood and bright-green kelp lay in rows mounded by the now-receding tide. The inlet waters, glassy smooth, reflected the steep, spruce-covered sides of the fjord.

Teakh landed Gull on a strip of gravel and poked her beak into a tangle of beached flotsam. She sampled a whelk, tasted the seaweed—checking the health of the fjord estuary—and relayed the data to Teakh.

Another seagull flew along the shore, wings flashing white and gray in the sunlight. It descended to the beach and folded its wings then hopped forward toward what appeared to be a dead fish.

Teakh sent Gull nearer, and she responded with hunger and fierce desire; that carcass was hers. She landed, flooded with anger in response to her programming. Screaming, she lunged. She and the bird grappled, open mouths locked together. Gull pulled, the artificial fibers of her neck straining, and the pain radiated through Teakh's shoulders. Determined, Teakh forced himself through the agony and demanded the fish. The other bird released it and backed away. Teakh seized the chance to get a sample for chemical analysis. He sank Gull's beak into the rotting flesh and savored the odor and bitterness of ammonia. His implant readout identified the carcass as herring. Teakh sent disgust, and in response, Gull spat out the fragment. She retreated, allowing the other bird to claim the prize.

Breaking contact, Teakh shook his head, trying to clear his head of Gull's surging passion. He'd have to recalibrate both her pain threshold and emotions before he sent her to find Angel. He became aware of the other men at the gym seated on mats, their breaths even as they meditated.

LATER, TEAKH LAY facedown on a massage bed while Keno smoothed oil onto his back.

"Your shoulders are like a bag of rocks. Relax, will you?" Keno said.

"I'm trying."

"Think of something pleasant."

That would be Angel. He needed an excuse to leave Dojko. Sink Aunt Dyse and her greed, too cheap to spring for a prosthetic splint. Or maybe her intent had been to limit his mobility. Maybe Lord Ralko had refused to allow Teakh to audit catch records just to curtail his spending. Maybe. Maybe. Speculating didn't change his lack of money, his debts, or his inability to travel. Eyes closed, he brought up the ferry schedule.

Keno rested a hand between Teakh's shoulders. "I'm warning you. This will hurt, but in the long run, it'll feel better."

Teakh gasped as Keno drove his knuckle into a knot, the sharp, throbbing pain oddly pleasant. As the massage continued, the pain subsided.

While Keno worked him over, Teakh considered his options. He couldn't fly Gull to Idylko and back on one charge, but he could sneak her onto the ferry. Sending a robot into the territory of other clans without permission was illegal, but not a major problem. By listening to the old men back in Ralko, he'd learned of nearly forgotten codes for relaying transmissions between repeater cells. It helped that Teakh's room in the Ralko men's house had once been a telecommunication closet and retained active equipment. If Gull lost contact, she'd fly a search pattern until she was again in range. That left the problem of recharging.

Teakh decided to take his chances. He'd feel her exhaustion as physical tiredness before she lost power. If nothing else, she could walk into a post office and ask to be mailed, but since Gull was unregistered, she'd probably be confiscated. His shoulders and lumbar tingled as if they'd been iced.

Keno finished the massage, seemingly having taken Teakh's spine apart and put it together again. In his quarters, Teakh sat on his couch and activated Gull. She burst from her niche and flew upward then out the propped clerestory window. A ferry was moored at the quay. He landed Gull on the top deck and searched for a hiding place. He selected a nook under the solarium canopy, out of sight and out of the weather. He flew Gull to it and snuggled in. After tucking Gull's beak under a wing, Teakh left her dormant and set an internal alarm.

SITTING ON A bench beside the lap pool, Teakh prepared to swim. Under Keno's patient tutelage, Teakh's swimming style had rapidly progressed from a dog paddle to a crawl. He now swam laps proficiently, if not well.

An internal alertness, the alarm, startled Teakh. He closed his eyes and gave his full attention to Gull, who peered out from under the solarium roof. The gangway remained deserted, so Teakh sent Gull to perch on the deck. The ferry was approaching the terminal. On the quayside bridgework, men in orange vests and hard hats waited, ready to receive lines thrown from the ferry. Near Gull, a door slid open, and a passenger exited. Startled, Gull took to the air. Teakh flew toward Idylko Village. He planned to trace his steps from the hospital to the cottage where he'd spent a delightful few hours with the three women. At the hospital, Gull alighted on the pavement before the entrance. The double doors remained shut. Cooky was no longer lodged in the hospital as a patient, so Teakh couldn't ask for his assistance in opening the door.

Teakh flew along the path he'd walked with Angel and paused beside the harbor. He didn't expect to find her, but maybe something would jog his memory. He landed on a pylon. The tide had risen. A few men worked on boats. PZ *Idsir* was gone, probably out on her rounds. Otherwise the harbor remained the same.

Beside the lap pool, Teakh removed his brace and rubbed his leg. Teakh would search despite the nearly zero likelihood of locating Angel's footprints or an item she had dropped. He had no other option. Eyes closed, he activated Gull and continued following his route, scanning the pavement, boardwalks, and clusters of houses. He flew along the alley to the cottage where he'd fallen in love. He'd only been with Angel for a few hours, but he couldn't get her out of his mind, not just her richly colored hair but the sparkle in her eyes.

The cottage's back door was closed, and the rubbish bin was closed as well. The windows, shuttered from the inside, yielded only glimpses of a kitchen wall covered with photo-electronic wallpaper. A broom leaned beside the front door, and the stoop had been swept recently. Someone lived there, even if they were currently out.

Teakh landed on the roof of a nearby house. There, he folded Gull's wings, settled her feathers, and turned her head toward the doorway.

His attention returned to his human body, and he opened his eyes to the gym. The pool water reflected light onto the ceiling. Devoting minimal attention to the stakeout, he set his brace aside and lowered himself into the pool. He kicked off the wall with his good leg and started his practice.

While Teakh swam and counted laps, Gull watched for movement. A flicker became two women walking a dog, a terrier. Teakh rested his forearms on the edge of the pool and sent Gull to give the women a flyby. The dog went wild, barking and pulling at the leash, but Teakh didn't recognize either of the women. He returned Gull to her stakeout and kicked off from the wall for yet another lap. He surfaced for a breath, water churning around him.

Other people passed below Gull, but none Teakh had seen before. He hauled out of the pool and went to his quarters. There he sat on his meditation cushion and resumed his watch.

When noon sunlight threw shadows to the north and hunger gnawed at Teakh's belly, a brown-haired woman hurried along the lane. She had the wrong color hair, but could she be one of Teakh's threesome? He hadn't noticed the brunette much. He'd been too infatuated with Angel.

Gull dove and veered away from the woman's head. She glanced up. Teakh's heart hammered. He'd found the brunette.

She went into the cottage and closed the door, so Teakh returned Gull to her roof perch and went to the dining room. The men chattered around him as he ate. He barely tasted his food, all his attention focused on the cottage door, willing it to open. He left lunch early, muttering that he'd complete his chores later. In his room, he once again seated himself on his cushion and waited, but not for long.

The brunette exited the cottage and walked in the lane. Gull flew above and behind her. Maybe she would lead Teakh to Angel.

At the hospital, the brunette opened the door and was swallowed by the building. Depths! Without hands, Gull had no way of operating the door latch.

He sent Gull over the roof, searching for an open window or back door. The brunette seemed to live in the cottage and had some business in the hospital. But it had been Angel, not the brunette, who had initially approached him in his hospital room.

Teakh returned Gull to the front entrance and considered the latch. He jumped, pumped Gull's wings, and brought her weight down on the lever. Her wings beat against the door as he centered her weight, but she missed and dropped to the ground. Teakh tried again, changing his angle of attack. He landed on the lever, depressing it. Wings flapping, human arms twitching, Teakh struggled to swing the door, panting with the effort.

Then the door opened on its own, and a woman peered out. "What the depths?"

Teakh made a dash for the interior, sending Gull scurrying past the woman's legs then flapping upward to the nursing station. Teakh recognized the nurse who'd changed Cooky's bandages. Gull squawked.

"Get it out of here!" the nurse shouted.

Where had the brunette gone? Gull leapt off the desk and flapped along the passageway. As Gull flew, Teakh read door signs: patient rooms, examination rooms, and a lab. He banked and continued along the hallway. Doors opened.

A crowd now filled the hallway, but none of the women were the brunette, or the raven-haired woman, or Angel. Founder it all! Gull was blocked in.

He landed and charged, wings spread, mouth open, head up, squawking.

Legs of the crowd yielded as nurses and orderlies shouted, "Stay back! Someone hail animal control."

Comsets clicked.

A door opened. "What's with all the noise?"

Teakh halted the attack. Excitement thrummed through Gull's body. Reacting to Teakh's emotions, she lifted her beak to the brunette, seeking a red beak spot on the underside of her chin. Kinkill! Gull's programmed instincts were overly realistic.

Discussion volleyed above Gull's field of vision.

"I've never seen a seagull that big."

"It flew right at me near my house," the brunette said.

Gull again lifted her beak in affection, the behavior of a hungry chick.

Another door opened. "What's going on?"

"A seagull followed Jeena. It seems to like her."

Jeena. Savoring the name, Teakh moved Gull closer, nuzzling Jeena's leg. She pushed Gull away.

Someone laughed. "Reez has competition. Tell the bird you're married."

Teakh tried to absorb the implications. Was Reez a man or a woman?

"Get that filthy bird out of here," shouted a nurse. "This is a hospital."

A janitor arrived with a broom. "Someone open a door, will you?"

The crowd backed away. Teakh could see two open doors. The janitor brandished the broom "Shoo! Get going." She swung it at Gull.

Knowing when to call it quits, Teakh sent Gull scampering for the exit. She flew out of the hospital and back toward Jeena's cottage. At her place, a vent window had opened, an automated response to the heat of the day. Gull stood on the brink beside the window opener then dropped into the cottage.

Teakh surveyed the small interior, looking for anything related to Angel. He decided to search systematically, starting from the front entry where rain parkas hung above neatly arranged footwear. Teakh landed Gull and peered into shoes and boots, checking the chemical signatures of residual sweat. Roughly half of the shoes were of a slightly smaller size, and the odor had an acidic tang. None smelled like Angel.

The front room contained a planning frame set near the window, a couch, and two chairs—nothing unusual there. The kitchen wallpaper displayed photographs of Jeena and the raven-haired beauty—Reez?—together or individually: laughing, dancing, embracing. One photo appeared to be a wedding picture, with the two women dressed in beaded bridal caps. Teakh searched for an image of Angel but found no sign of her, as if she'd never existed.

He continued his surveillance, flying Gull through a transom into the bedroom. The bed was unmade and the cuffs gone, but the male nude remained, a small painting about the size of a handscreen.

Teakh recalled Angel adjusting it on the wall. Jeena had complimented her, and Angel had shrugged. "Just a study," she'd said.

Gull perched on the headboard to inspect the painting, but one of her camera eyes nearly grazed the panel; she was too close for a good look. He pulled the picture from the wall and let it fall to the bed, where it landed image down. Teakh went after it. On the mattress, Gull inserted her head and beak under the frame. She levered it over to reveal a delicate painting, the glossy oil marked by the brush strokes which had brought to form a male figure. The man's smooth-shaven and sculpted musculature seemed familiar—quite a bit like Keno, actually.

Teakh noted the signature: Matta Carrie.

The front door opened. Gull sprang from the bed.

"Jeena? Is that you?"

Gull settled back on the rumpled coverlet and stood over the painting.

The raven-haired beauty peered into the bedroom. "Get!" She snatched up a hair brush and flung it. "Filthy bird."

Gull dodged and leapt from the bed. Teakh sent her through the ventilation shaft as the dark beauty fingered the hallway switch pad. The vent window slammed, pinching Gull's tail before she sprang free.

He sent her back to the ferry terminal. Heart pounding, he sat in his quarters. He'd risked Gull for very little information. He'd do the best he could trolling the Network for information on the artist Matta Carrie.

Seated in his quarters, he came up with mostly bycatch about a mythological figure called Mother Carry. She wasn't a woman with a fish tail or wings but the allure of the sea itself, the seduction of wind and waves. A merciful siren, Mother Carry conducted seamen to Paradise, carrying their souls to a place called Fiddler's Green.

Among the mythological references, Teakh uncovered a painter specializing in male nudes, but no images of her work. She sold only originals and strictly on commission, but he located a small photo of the artist tucked into a news article announcing a gallery opening in Fennako City. The photo showed Matta Carrie turned away from the camera, but her glossy hair was a deep reddish-brown.

CHAPTER 10
Money

TEAKH READ BOTH the article and commentary with care. Matta Carrie's show had featured Seaguard lords, or their heirs, in the buff.

"Little better than hired sperm donors," ranted one irate citizen.

Teakh knew how they felt. It seemed Angel had created quite a stir by including a nude painting of the Queen's grandson. Some readers were offended by the impropriety of the display, while others blasted the tradition of arranged marriage.

In comments, a few readers defended the use of the paintings as part of marriage transactions. Seaguard lords had responsibilities to their own clans and so, by necessity, lived distant from their wives. Paintings were offered as gifts to the brides' clans, consolation for his long absences or maybe as part of negotiations. Despite, or perhaps because of, the controversy, Matta Carrie's nudes had become a coveted status symbol.

Teakh scratched his ear beside his neuro scars. If he announced he'd made love to Matta Carrie, he might gain notoriety but not the kind he wanted. And who would believe him anyway? He wasn't even sure Matta Carrie and Angel were one and the same. But she had been drawing during lunch, and in Idylko, she'd commented on the painting above Jeena's bed.

Teakh flopped back on the couch in the gym. He could approach Matta Carrie with a request to paint his portrait, but that would put him in competition with every other man seeking such a dubious trophy. He leaned back against the bolsters and fantasized about Angel painting his image. Better yet, he'd hire her to paint a self-portrait to hang in his quarters. Then he could gaze on Angel whenever he liked. He imagined her naked but for high-heeled mules as she balanced paintbrushes and palette, legs long, hair cascading around her shoulders. His fantasy of commissioning a painting had a small hitch—he had no money. Considering the problem, Teakh went to work out while Gull rode the ferry home.

THE FOLLOWING DAY, he sent Gull out to make rounds of the waterfront. He wished Dojko fishermen weren't so almighty honest and would commit some crimes. He needed cash.

At the small boat harbor, everything was normal—trollers with their tall masts and poles, stern pickers with reels mounted on their decks. Everything was as usual except for a small black rectangle on pier three. No real seagulls were after the palm-sized object, so it couldn't have been food.

Teakh landed Gull and sent her scampering toward the rectangle. He moved her head side to side for better depth perception. The item didn't move and didn't have much odor, so Teakh sent Gull closer. Seemed to be a billfold.

Using Gull's beak, Teakh opened the wallet. It was stuffed with eulachon bills and coho bills too. Teakh's heart hammered. Money. With a little, he could buy passage to Fennako City. With a bit more, he could buy a painting.

Using one of Gull's eye lenses, Teakh looked for identification. BELUGO. Must be Lugo. Teakh knew the fellow— bit of a shine boy, skipper of *Zephyr Winds*, moored farther down the pier. Why did the fellow have so much pocket cash? And why wasn't he out fishing?

Teakh pulled and tugged the billfold to a secure location then headed Gull toward *Zephyr Winds*. The boat was in excellent shape with fishing gear set up for trolling. Knotted coxcombing adorned the rails, and the brass boat davits were polished bright. Teakh felt the thrill of the chase. Maybe Lugo was breaking the law. Teakh landed Gull on the deck and peered at the hatch cover. With a view inside, he might see what Lugo had down below, but Gull had her limitations. He left the boat deck and landed Gull on the water near the propulsor jets jutting from the boat's stern—Evenko make, with a lot of power. The number of fish Lugo caught didn't jibe with the expense of his boat.

Teakh left Gull on standby and rubbed his hands together. Smugglers went for top-of-the-line propulsors. Nothing wrong with enforcing justice, if Lugo was a smuggler, but Teakh had found no evidence of lawbreaking. More likely, the source of Lugo's money was mundane and legitimate— generous kinswomen. Successful women liked to support their male kin in traditional activities.

Such men could afford to be fair-weather fishermen. Teakh sighed. He'd return the wallet, and maybe Lugo would give him a reward.

Teakh hailed Loopy at the Salty Hound for Lugo's address codes, then Teakh hailed the man himself.

Your wallet has been found on pier three. Still there. A gull is standing guard. You might want to feed her a eulachon or two, maybe a coho.

Who is this?

Just a fellow.

Lugo emerged out of his boat.

Teakh used Gull's beak to push the wallet toward Lugo. As he stooped, Gull sprang back, following her programming, sending fear to Teakh. His heart raced.

Lugo opened the wallet and flicked through the sheaf of bills.

Squawk! Squawk!

Lugo glanced from his wallet to Gull. "Seriously? You want money?"

Teakh bobbed Gull's head.

Lugo pulled out a eulachon bill. Teakh overrode Gull's programming to send her scampering forward. He emphasized how much he wanted the money and how good it would taste. Following instinct, Gull seized the bill. Teakh sent her flying to the top of a pylon.

He crumpled the eulachon in Gull's starboard talon. His right foot, confined to a brace, cramped in sympathy.

He eased his toes.

Gull snapped her beak. *Squawk!*

"Another?" Lugo held up the bill.

Gull swooped downward, taking the money on the fly, then landed on the pylon and balanced on one foot.

"Can you beat that?"

Gull glided from her perch.

"Sorry. No more." Lugo closed and pocketed his wallet.

Gull returned home. She came through Teakh's window and dropped the money before he settled her in her charging niche. He smoothed the two bills against his knee. They displaying not the silver salmon of coho bills but hooligan smelts. Sadly, two eulachon was more cash than he'd had in months.

Teakh left his quarters for a training session in Keno's office. Teakh accepted a glass of water from Keno and sank into his accustomed chair.

"How are you coming with that assignment?" Keno asked.

Teakh cradled his drink, the glass cool in his hand. "Quite well."

Keno, seated in his own chair, raised a questioning eyebrow.

"I'm sure not telling you the details." Teakh took a swig of water. If only Hairy's girly pictures excited him, his life would be easier. Expensive taste. That's what he had. Angel was beyond his reach. He sucked on an ice cube.

"Gimp, we've got a problem here." Keno scratched his beard. "We've got little more than a year to get you ready for your first marriage."

Teakh spat out the ice. "Marriage?"

"As a stud, you'll be under contract for temporary marriages. You'll have less than a day to fulfill your obligation to a bride you've never met before. Most studs have assistants, people they trust helping out."

Teakh swirled his water, ice cubes clinking. "What kind of help?"

"Anything you want. Assistants can get a woman ready for you or get you ready."

"I don't want anyone." Teakh took a swig. He wanted Angel, not some hired assistant.

Keno frowned. "Assisting is a difficult undertaking." He

crossed his arms. "So tell me. Can you get an erection, hold it, and ejaculate at the right time? All without help?"

Teakh nodded, but he wasn't at all sure that he could.

"I don't want to send you to your first liaison then find out you can't follow through. How about if I bring in a girl and you show me?"

"When?" Teakh didn't want just any girl.

"This afternoon. I know a gal who's willing to help out with these things. I'll give her a hail."

Teakh collapsed against the back of the chair. "Dyse won't like it."

"Probably not."

If Teakh was going to be a stud, he'd need to perform as one. Might as well give it a try. "No one watching. Just me and her."

Keno held a good poker face, but his eyes gave him away with the hint of a smile. "Trust yourself. It's like swimming."

Teakh grinned. "Give her a hail."

KENO USHERED TEAKH through the front parlor to a room with walls covered in flocked velvet wallpaper—real cellulose, not a photo-digital imitation.

"Tide carry you," Keno said and closed the door.

A woman sat topless on a cot, her robe around her hips. She stood, and the robe fell away from generous proportions: full breasts, rounded belly and thighs. "Darling, I understand you're having a bit of trouble." She reached to stroke Teakh's cheek with a long, manicured nail.

He pulled back. "Not really." With those lush curves, she was attractive enough, but she wasn't Angel.

The woman fluttered long eyelashes. "Tell me what you want."

"I'm supposed to... well..." Teakh's face heated.

"How about if we start by kissing? Would you like that?"

"Well, yeah."

"Like this?" She pressed against Teakh, letting her hand slide down to cup his ass, her soft breasts pushing into his chest. She smelled of talcum powder.

Teakh met her lips with his own. Her tongue invaded his mouth. He backed away, shaking his head.

She straddled one of his legs, rubbing herself against his thigh. "I can talk dirty if you like."

"I'd rather you didn't."

"Do you want to be on the top or the bottom?"

"Top, I guess."

She sprawled onto the cot, knees up, head tipped back. "Take me, darling."

If Teakh didn't follow through, he'd be the laughingstock of the gym. He'd be back to living on the docks with no hope of commissioning a painting by Angel. His penis hung slack, completely uncooperative.

The woman sat up. "Come here." She reached for his gear, her nails long and adorned with sparkly stones. "May I?"

"Oh, yeah."

"Tell me what feels good." She cupped his balls, stroking his penis. "You're a hard one."

Except his penis wasn't. "Let me." He pushed her back onto the bed and used his hand to rub his penis against her opening. He closed his eyes, trying to imagine he lay on top of Angel, but he felt only shame. He'd betrayed her.

"Maybe on the bottom," he suggested.

They rolled, and the woman took over. "So manly." Her hand worked between his legs. Her breasts weighed him down, the odor of talcum cloying and the pressure nearly suffocating.

He coughed. "Get off me."

She sprang away and perched on the side of the bed, her eyes questioning.

Teakh sat up, angry at the whole Poseidon-damn situation. Danna! He wouldn't cry, not this time. In Idylko, lust, grief, and bliss had overwhelmed him. This time was different. "Kinkill!"

"Are you okay?" The woman drew her robe around her shoulders. "Do you want to continue?"

He shook his head. "What will we tell Keno?" The lubber had been right. Teakh couldn't perform.

With a forefinger, she tracked circles on his thigh. "We

don't have to tell him anything."

Teakh exhaled.

"If you want to get together again, just give me a hail." She belted her robe.

Teakh nodded.

As he walked out of the room, Keno was nowhere around, and that suited Teakh.

TEAKH DRESSED AND walked downhill to the Salty Hound. The tavern was filled with Chuck, Jake, a skipper by the name of Nerka, and an assortment of fishermen and deckhands. Teakh sat on a stool and stared at the graffiti cut into the bar top. He ordered nothing, not even water. Loopy glared at him, surely for being a freeloader, but Teakh was saving every eulachon for Angel.

He hadn't been able to perform sexually with Keno's friend, but he hadn't known the woman. The situation had been awkward. Maybe Keno was right—Teakh needed to trick himself into thinking the woman was Angel.

Lugo barged through the tavern door. "Fellows, you're not going to believe this. I lost my wallet."

Slouching, Teakh watched Lugo and the others.

"We believe that," Chuck said.

"I go out looking for it," Lugo said. "And there's this seagull squawking at me. Like she knows what I'm looking for. Pushes the wallet right toward me and asks for money. Clear as anything."

Chuck turned on his stool and raised his beer glass. "Was she talking to you?"

Lugo leaned against the bar. "I could tell what she wanted." He nodded to Loopy.

Chuck laughed. "That wasn't a seagull. A seagull would just take the whole thing and eat it. No asking."

"Well, this one asked." Lugo warmed to his story. "So I pull out a eulachon, and she takes it and asks for more."

"That was a seagull all right." Chuck hoisted his glass and took a swig.

"So I hold up another bill," Lugo said. "And she takes it out of my hand. On the fly. Did it twice."

"What have you been drinking?" Nerka asked, seated at a nearby table.

"Nothing yet," Lugo said. "I tell you, she was that big gull. The one that hangs out on pier four, sitting up on a pylon. You seen her."

"That big herring gull?" Nerka asked.

"I think she's a slaty-back gull," offered his mate.

"I tell you. Not a slaty-back gull, a herring gull."

"Glaucous-winged gull," Lugo said.

"Bigger than that," Chuck said.

Loopy placed a drink before Lugo. "Are you sure it was a gull at all? Seaguard is always using robot thingamabobs."

"Naw. Seaguard don't bother with imitating birds." Chuck laughed. "And don't those things got to be registered?"

"She was a gull," Lugo said. "Yellow eyes. Yellow bill. A red spot on the beak."

"Gotta be Seaguard." Nerka took a swig of his beer.

Depths, taking that money from Lugo had been a stupid thing to do. It was time to get Gull out of the area.

CHAPTER 11
Gallery

DETERMINED TO LOCATE Angel, Teakh crutched uphill to the gym. Poseidon take it all, he was a detective. He'd use Gull to investigate the lead on the art gallery. Sending Gull aboard a ferry to Fennako City would take days, and the same on the way back. He'd have to smuggle her aboard an airplane. If she were caught, there'd be Poseidon to pay. Telechirics weren't allowed on commercial flights, not unless they were bonded and inaccessible to the operator, but Teakh would risk it.

In the morning, after observations and breakfast, he returned to his quarters. He flew Gull out the propped clerestory then westward toward the commercial stratoport in Ordako.

Ordako Bay glistened in the sunlight, reflecting the blue of the sky. Piers, harbors, and dwellings embraced the bay, a narrow but substantial village strung along the shore. A tower built on a hillside rose above the bay—surely Ordako Seaguard traffic control. Searching for aircraft docks, Teakh sent Gull winging toward the waterfront.

A plane roared as it descended, the sound all around Gull. Depths! Gull was in the flyway. If the plane didn't land on top of Gull, the turbulence could smash her. His mouth dry, Teakh sent Gull into a dodge and fled from the descending plane. The backwash caught Gull and sent her tumbling. Gasping, Teakh corrected. The plane passed Gull, splashing down onto the bay. A wave pushing from her prow and her wake rolling, the plane taxied to the terminal.

Teakh sent Gull after the plane. She perched on the terminal roof and watched passengers exit the aircraft. When the terminal door opened, Teakh sent Gull into the building after the arriving passengers.

Travelers shouted and attempted to shoo Gull from the building, but Teakh sent her above their frantic waves. He landed her in the rafters near a flight-status screen. The flight for Fennako City was on time. Travelers settled down to read or play games on handscreens. If he waited with them, he might not get out of the terminal. He sent Gull on another dash out a door and set her on motion detect near pier Bravo.

He was rereading the articles on Matta Carrie when Gull sent an alert. Baggage handlers were bringing out trolleys. Teakh waited until the baggage handlers were nearly finished unloading, then he sent Gull winging past a stooped baggage handler and inside the hold. The hatch closed, and he shifted her vision to infrared. Teakh's heart rate slowed, and he nearly whooped. He'd done it. Smuggled Gull aboard an airplane.

He secured her by wedging her against a dunnage brace. With Gull dormant, Teakh left his quarters.

In the gym, Hairy lifted weights.

"You sure spend a lot of time in meditation." He grunted as he lifted a barbell.

"Part of my routine," Teakh said.

"And you twitch while you do it," Hairy said. "Like a dog dreaming about chasing squirrels."

"Might look strange," Teakh said, "but it's a special technique for increasing libido. I promised my guru I'd keep it secret."

Hairy guffawed and set down the weight. He gave a spastic impression of Teakh, shoulders jerking, fingers twitching. "Oh yes. The girls are gonna love this."

"You haven't met my guru." Teakh continued through the gym to the kitchen for a snack.

HE RETURNED TO quarters and activated Gull. He felt a jolt then another jolt. The plane slowed, water buffeting its hull. The movement of the plane subsided into gentle rocking. The hatch opened, and daylight flooded into the hold. Teakh waited until a baggage handler bent to jot on a noteboard, then Teakh sent Gull flying out over the man's head.

The man looked up, mouth open. "Kinkill! What the depths?"

Gull soared above the bay, leaving the plane behind. So this was Fennako City. Sunlight glanced off the green dome of a monument, high above the harbor and roofs of the palace complex. Other islands glinted with buildings and bridges, sunlight winking off glass.

He set out to make a circuit of the closest island, surely Lawrock. The iconic green dome of the Zenhedron was unmistakable. Gull passed over extensive harbors and docks along the waterfront. On the north side of the island, waves broke against abrupt cliffs. Brightly colored ornithopters rode updrafts, their young Seaguard pilots somewhere nearby. Teakh avoided the children. He'd once played with robotic toys like theirs.

He continued his survey of the shore. Kittiwakes and mew gulls wheeled as they brought food to their young nested in the cliffs. On the south side of the island, he skirted esskip hangars and lagoons then landed Gull on a roof.

In his quarters, Teakh straightened his back and stretched his arms, preparing for his next move. He hailed the gallery. *Art Patron here. May I have directions to your place?*

What are you about? came the response.

I'm here to take a look at paintings, sent Teakh. *I'm needing to know where you're at.*

Well... the woman paused. *Viewing is by appointment only.*

When can you fit me in?

We do not show these paintings to just anyone. Please understand.

He understood. In response to the controversy, the gallery must have changed its policies. Teakh would have to pass himself off as someone important. What the depths? Seaguard lords commonly used telechirics. He'd imply Gull was in Fennako City so Teakh could remotely attend some legislative function.

I'm a busy man. I was hoping to view the art via remote while I have equipment in the area. I happen to have a telechiric in Fennako City.

Seaguard, we appreciate your time.

Good. He had her attention. *He just might be able to pull this off. My sister wants me to take a look at Matta Carrie's paintings.* If need be, Teakh could talk his sister into claiming an interest in art as part of her studies.

Normally your clan would contact us and vouch for you.

My sister wants to have my portrait painted. She thinks it'll improve my prospects. He sent a burst of synthetic laughter. *Frankly, I'm skeptical. I plan to take a look at the artist's work before I agree to sit for the painting.* He feigned irritation over his sister's fictitious demands. *Sink it all!*

Sir, we might be able to fit you in if you're willing to send your equipment immediately.

I can do that, but I'll need directions.

The gallery sent a map with its location and address. Teakh dropped Gull from the roof into the lane between close-ranked houses. A security camera mounted on a cornice swiveled, but Gull shot past before the camera could focus. Seaguard would have difficulty distinguishing Gull from the many other seagulls in the city.

In the gallery district, just back from the waterfront, Teakh landed her on a balcony. The windows of the building were shaded.

Teakh again hailed. *We've arrived and would be much obliged if you'd hold the door open.*

The front door swung inward. A woman, presumably the gallery attendant, stepped out and turned her head one way then the other. She shrugged. Teakh flew Gull from her perch and flashed past the attendant into the dimness of the front room.

Greetings, sent Teakh, his voice issuing from the comset hidden on the woman's shoulder pocket. Teakh bobbed Gull's head in a semblance of a bow.

The attendant stepped back. "Good Danna!"

Please close the door, sent Teakh. *We prefer not to be observed.* He ruffled Gull's feathers and folded her wings.

The attendant shut the door.

Thank you. Teakh twitched Gull's tail and strutted after the attendant, who pushed aside a heavy velvet drape. Teakh followed her into darkness lit only by spotlights which illuminated paintings in gilt frames. The floor-to-ceiling canvases displayed men painted in oil.

"Our Matta Carrie is a real mistress," the attendant gushed, extending an arm. "Such a sense of color and line. And that painterly quality."

What the depths did *painterly quality* mean?

Despite the fancy jargon, the men sure as Poseidon looked like studs on display and not all that different from peacocks. Teakh sent Gull sauntering toward a painting. He swiveled Gull's head to the side, bringing a lens to the signature. Through her vision, Teakh eyed the gilded frame and fluid brushwork depicting a pair of bare feet. A seagull's view brought an unusual perspective to art appreciation. Teakh opened her bill and drew the fragrance of turpentine and linseed oil across her sensors.

Head tipped back, Gull sent Teakh a view of the towering naked man. Precise paint strokes rendered the toes, tickling them into dimensionality. A sensuous brush mark hugged the man's calf and traced up his leg, caressing his hip. Teakh shivered, imagining the touch that left such a path, envying the image of the man. Above the man's hip, glare and the acute viewing angle obscured detail.

Teakh sent Gull scampering away from the canvas far enough to turn and observe it in full. The man's head was turned aside. Neuro scars peeked through his intricately braided hair.

"May I assist you?" The attendant placed a chair in the middle of the room.

Teakh sent Gull fluttering to the backrest, so she was perched at human-eye level. The paintings depicted nude or partly clothed Seaguardsmen, some wearing boots and open life vests but little else. All displayed heroically rendered musculature. They stood against backgrounds of seascapes, foam and breaking waves depicted in luminous details.

Teakh sent, *I understand your show has kicked up some controversy.*

The attendant smiled and folded her hands. "I suppose."

Teakh inspected the seascapes, and in one, he identified Lawrock Island and the green dome of the Zenhedron above storm-tossed seas. The man sharing the canvas with Fennako City sported a beard and wore an open life vest. Teakh pointed with Gull's bill. *Looks like Tristan Bay. Is that one the Queen's grandson?*

The attendant spread her hands, neither admitting nor denying the man's identity. "Every one of these men is a prince or magnate."

Teakh cocked Gull's head. *You're shining me.* If the articles were correct, Angel's paintings were being used to sell Seaguard lords as husbands.

The attendant smiled. "Matta Carrie has her ways."

She sure did. Teakh had made love to her once, at least he thought he had, and now no other woman was good enough. But how could he compete? His grandmother wasn't a queen, and he had no territory or political power. He didn't even have an esskip, for Danna's sake.

He swung Gull's head, scanning the paintings. Each man had implant scars except for…Teakh turned one of Gull's lenses toward the painting at the end. The background wasn't a Seascape either, but an interior with a couch and drapery. The man's posture projected grace and confidence. His physique was more impressive than any of the other men. Depths! What was Keno doing in this lineup?

Well, if Pretty Boy was worthy of Angel's artistry, then so was Gimp. Teakh announced, *We'd like to hire her.*

The attendant laughed. "Hire her?"

My kinswomen and I are impressed with her work. We'd like to engage her services.

"For a commission, an introduction would be in order, someone to vouch for you. But even so, Matta Carrie is selective and makes up her own mind."

Teakh fluffed Gull's feathers. *Would you provide such an introduction?*

"With your permission, I'll inform her of your visit, but as I'm unaware of your clan name and haven't actually met you in person, I can't in good faith offer such a recommendation."

Teakh tipped Gull's head to the side while he drummed

his fingers against his leg brace. Antagonizing the gallery attendant wouldn't help his cause. *Thank you for your assistance. Please convey to the artist my deepest admiration. Tell her the Seaguardsman who accepted hospitality in Idylko sends his regards.*

Teakh made another perusal of the paintings then thanked the attendant again.

She opened the door. Teakh bobbed Gull's head in a bow then sent her flying toward the harbor.

BEFORE GULL HAD even cleared the lane, she received a hail and relayed it to Teakh. *This is Fennako City Police. Please respond.*

Teakh decided to ignore it. A real seagull wouldn't respond, and this was city police, not regular Seaguard.

This is Fennako City Police acting in accordance with Tristan Bay Command. Second attempt to make contact. Please respond.

Depths! If Tristan Bay were involved, he *was* facing Seaguard. Teakh kept Gull flying toward the waterfront anyway. Fennako, either police or Seaguard, might accept that Gull was nothing more than a bird. Surely they sometimes mistook a seagull for a drone.

A flock of bird-sized craft arrowed toward Gull, their wings flashing silver and jade in the sunlight. They sported Fennako police badges, twelve-point stars glinting in silver. *This is Fennako City Police. We are in pursuit.*

The drones might have been ornithopters or propulsor-driven craft, but Teakh wasn't going to stick around to find out. His heart pounding, Gull's wings pumping, Teakh sped toward the harbor. The flock of police drones moved with a living fluidity that could only mean Seaguard control.

Two drones, miniature aircraft with camera turrets, came for Gull, one to the side and the other above, forcing her down. Evasion routine activated, anger flooded into Teakh. Gull came about and lunged. The drones retreated.

Teakh considered his options. He could pass Gull off as a bird, but for how long? Fennako had cameras all over the city, and if they knew for sure that Gull wasn't a seagull, then either attacking or fleeing would get him in serious trouble.

Three drones now came at Gull, and the police transmitted. *Land immediately! Or your craft will be disabled by royal override.*

He was doomed. Disabled by royal override, Gull would freeze in midair, plummet into the lane, and smash against the pavement. There was no bluffing his way out of this predicament. Teakh wiped his brow and landed Gull on a cornice.

Gull here, responded Teakh, trying to control Gull's programmed anger and his own helplessness.

The flock of jade-green craft buzzed over him and turned back to circle. *Clan and registration requested.*

Kinkill! This was Tatumuko all over again. He'd have to tell the truth, or at least something approaching the truth. *I claim hospitality,* sent Teakh.

What is your need?

Teakh had better come up with a good excuse and come up with it quickly. Hospitality could only be claimed if need was obvious or vouched for by an authority, but shipwreck wasn't the only recognized need. Diplomats and traveling students could also claim hospitality, provided the claimant had proper documents.

Student hospitality. I'm helping my sister. It was worth a try. *She's studying art, so I'm visiting art galleries for her.* He imagined himself about six years younger. Police might be tolerant of a well-meaning juvenile, someone too young to be aware of legal ramifications. He wasn't bending the truth all that far. By Fenrian custom, he was still a kid and would be until he reached his two dozenth year.

He hailed his sister. She didn't answer, so he dictated his message: *If Fennako hails, tell them you're an art student.*

A jade-green drone lowered to the cornice, propulsors turned vertically. Its camera turret pivoted toward Gull. *Hold out your wings.*

What?

Now!

Teakh complied and spread Gull's wings.

A proboscis extended from the nose of the police craft. *Hold still.* The snout flicked over Gull's head, along her back, and under her belly, then retracted. *Scan complete. You can fold your wings.*

Teakh did so and settled Gull's feathers.

The camera turret rotated. *That's an impressive ornithopter. Where did you get it?*

Teakh knew this routine. Under a pretense of friendliness, the office would cross-question Teakh.

A gift from my sister, he answered. *Looks just like a real seagull. I fooled you guys.* He hadn't, but he'd pretend cocky ignorance.

Kid, you've violated a whole netful of laws. Use of an unregistered and unmarked telechiric, violating Tristan Bay airspace, and flying in the vicinity of the royal palace.

Uh... oh, sorry.

So tell me, how did you get your 'thopter here?

Maybe the officer was cross-questioning Teakh, or maybe Fennako didn't actually know.

Flew. That could be understood two ways, so it wasn't a lie.

True enough. Your craft arrived aboard a commercial flight. Was your device bonded?

Teakh remained silent.

You sure are racking up the violations. Tell me about the art you've been viewing.

Teakh gulped. *Paintings by Matta Carrie.*

So what did you think of the show?

Odd. Why would police be interested in his opinions? Teakh shuffled Gull's feet. *It's all right. I like the painter, but not so much what she paints.* Depths! He'd let out too much. He should have claimed he liked the style of painting without mentioning Angel.

The police officer guffawed in a burst of electronic laughter. *I'll pass that along. Any favorite paintings?*

*Uh...*Teakh scrambled for words. He sure didn't want to say he liked naked men, because he didn't. He liked how Angel used paint, how each mark on the canvas seemed a caress. *She does waves really well. Nice seascapes.*

The police officer chuckled. *What's your clan?*

That question again, as if Teakh hadn't already claimed hospitality. Good Danna, the officer was sneaky, throwing Teakh off guard before driving at his identity.

Oh, don't do that, Teakh said. *But here's my sister's address codes. Don't let the chief know. My uncle will ground me for sure.*

Set my net he will. The drone went still while the other police craft continued to circle.

Teakh drew up one of Gull's feet and waited. He prayed that police would contact his sister without informing Lord Ralko or Aunt Dyse. The result would be worse than grounding—a Seaguard bulletin. He clenched and unclenched his fists.

The drone's camera turret swiveled. *The gallery backs up your story. We're waiting to receive from your sister.* The drone dropped from the cornice. *We will escort your 'thopter to the station.*

Teakh followed with Gull. The flock surrounded her, forcing her in the direction of the palace complex. They cleared a palace roof and dropped into a courtyard as a wheeling, living cloud. A hatch in a palace wall slid open, and a drone went through the opening. Teakh followed with Gull.

Inside, a woman leaned back in a chair, her booted feet up on a desk, her Seaguardsman's vest unfastened over a green button-down shirt. She'd sounded like a man. Or was she even the same officer? Female Seaguardsmen were rare, and this one was working out of the palace. Who was she?

Teakh landed Gull on the desk and bobbed her head. *Greetings, Sergeant.*

"I suppose that rank will do." The woman removed her feet from the desk. "Let me take a look at your craft." She leaned to the side, and Gull's head followed her movement. "Hold still." The female officer moved closer, inspecting Gull's lenses. "Impressive imitation."

Teakh puffed out Gull's chest. *My sister says Gull is a work of art.* Danna help him, Teakh would continue to pretend naivety.

"Register your bird, or you'll lose her. And your sister won't be pleased."

How'd you figure me out?

"Seagulls don't normally fly out of baggage holds or into shops."

Teakh resettled Gull's feathers. *You saw that?*

"We have a watch on the gallery—necessary security given the nature of the show. We could put out a bulletin on either you or your gull. Your violations are serious and could have endangered the Royal Palace."

I only wanted to see the art show. I don't know anything about the Palace.

"I'm going to let you off with a warning. But next time you visit Tristan Bay, follow the proper procedures." She crossed her arms. "I'm not letting you smuggle that device home. We'll ship it to you, but we need an address."

If he had Gull sent to Ralko, Fennako might contact Ralko Seaguard. But if Gull arrived in Ordako, she'd be in Ordako territory without permission.

Dojko village post office, general delivery. Please, please, don't tell my uncle. Teakh pretended to be an adolescent caught in truancy.

"And the name?"

I'd like to use a pickup number.

"Very well. Understand, your craft will be bonded until arrival in Dojko. You won't be able to use it until then."

Teakh hung Gull's head.

"I think you're a good kid," the officer said. "Keep it that way. Now power down your device. You'll get her back in a few days, no more than a twelve-night."

Honor, sent Teakh and put Gull in dormancy. He'd fouled up this time. He'd very nearly lost Gull, all for a chance to view paintings of naked men.

He stood and hailed Keno. *May I have a word with you?*

Sure, I'm in my office.

Teakh crutched out of his quarters. He came through the office door. "Are you a Seaguard magnate?"

Keno glanced up. "No. Why do you ask?"

"I saw you in an art show in Fennako City. *Magnates: Princes of the Sea.* All Seaguard lords, except for one rather large canvas. Is there something you're not telling me?"

"What were you doing in Fennako City?" Keno pushed back from his planning frame.

"I didn't go to Fennako City. I sent Gull. Why did Matta Carrie paint you?"

Keno straightened. "Probably because she likes me as a model."

"I saw a photo of her. Red hair, brown eyes..." Teakh would

leave out that he'd seen her in person and forgo mention of the tattoo. "Full-sail gorgeous."

Keno laughed. "Deceptive beauty. Best to steer clear of that one."

"But you model for her?"

"Not my type, so I have immunity to her charms. Not that she doesn't try."

"Your type?" Teakh asked.

"If you truly want to know," Keno said with a sly grin, "cheeky fishermen who don't know what's good for them. She has a delusion that all men will fall under her spell if she merely smiles at them."

"Does she...does she do more than that?"

"Do you mean sex? Maybe she will and maybe she won't. She passes herself off as an enigma. Men act like damn lubbers, salivating after her. Steer well clear."

Teakh didn't answer but said, "A portrait by Matta Carrie would help my career—a good investment."

Keno barked a laugh. "You're nearly full of shine. Why this sudden interest in art?"

"My research indicates that modeling for Matta Carrie increases a man's value on the marriage market. I figure it's the same for studs. You could introduce us."

"I could, but I'm not going to feed you to sharks either."

Keno's prejudice was unjustified. "What's wrong with her?"

"It's more you than her. You're Noah, bred for loyalty and altruism—even if you haven't bothered to register your drone."

"Altruism isn't the same as law abiding," Teakh said.

"That may be, but the truth is that as a Noah man, you're susceptible to inappropriate pair-bonding. So am I, for that matter."

Teakh leaned on a crutch. "Meaning?"

"It's like we're wired wrong and can't get out of bad relationships. Some call it hostage syndrome."

"Does she hold men hostage? Really? Beat them?" Not the Angel he knew.

"Only if they ask very nicely," Keno said. "Then she'll cry and kiss the bruises. She knows exactly how to get a man down on his knees and begging for more. No, I'm not bringing you two together. Danna help me."

"I only want one of her paintings."

"I know how the breeders controlled our ancestors," Keno said. "Or tried to. They played with a man's loyalty: cruelty one day, tears and promises the next. Think this through. Don't be a victim of your breeding."

"What about you?" Teakh asked. "Inappropriate pair-bonding?"

"I prefer men. It doesn't mean I act on my urges. I have self-control, and so should you."

"I haven't met her yet."

"Best to keep it that way," Keno said.

But Teakh had met Angel. She could do whatever she wanted with him just so long as it was him she held, not Keno. And not some prince so high and mighty that Fennako Police guarded his image.

CHAPTER 12
Stud Flicks

TEAKH SETTLED INTO a chair in Keno's office. Keno, also seated, pointed a remote. On the screen, Limber went into a backbend, presenting himself for a woman to fondle. Teakh's face heated.

Keno cuffed him. "My boy, you have a lot to learn."

"From this?"

"Limber is a true master," Keno said. "None better."

The image of Limber gracefully inverted into a handstand.

"Show me someone else," Teakh said.

Keno changed to another clip. Two naked women led a third onto a raised platform and arranged her on her hands and knees. The stud watched—oiled and naked except for a gold earring. With a few thrusts, he did the job. The assistants helped the woman to stand and conducted another woman onto the platform. Behind her, other women waited in line.

Teakh gulped and attempted a casual response. "How does he do it? Get ready so fast?"

"An old clip. He was legendary. Not many men can manage it. And we don't do mass insemination like that anymore. But then, maybe it's all an illusion, camera trickery. Here's another from that era."

In a garden, a man lay bound and blindfolded on a bench. A woman stroked his penis, anointing it with oil from a decanter. When his penis rose, ready for action, she kissed it and stepped aside, allowing other women to avail themselves as they pleased, giggling, fondling each other, using him to impregnate their companions as if sharing a delectable treat at a garden party. Through it all, the stud maintained a smile of seraphic contentment. When his member showed signs of becoming slack, his attendant oiled her hands and administered caresses. At other times, she signaled that he needed a rest or gave him sips of juice through a straw.

"And this," Keno said.

A woman lay on a platform draped in sea-green velvet, her knees up presenting her labia nested in soft hair, pink lips open like dark-edged petals displaying their ruffled interior. This time, men awaited their turn—Seaguard men dressed only in life vests and seaboots, heads shaved to show off neuro scars. Their naked reproductive gear was in their hands as they prepped for action.

Teakh's own body responded. He'd stand in line for that woman, but he wasn't going to admit it. "They can't all be the father of her child."

Keno's gaze flicked downward. "Seaguard lords swearing their loyalty to Her Majesty?"

Teakh shook his head. "Like Poseidon!" He refused to be excited by such a spectacle. "Her Majesty Fenna, grandmatriarch of Clan Fennako? Head of the Seaguard?"

"More likely the princess royal. But not the current princess royal. It's an old flick."

"What if one of them is sick?"

"Medicos would have thoroughly vetted everyone involved," Keno said.

A man stepped up to the dais, bowed, and kissed the woman's uplifted pubis, then he stood between her legs and thrust against her.

"The action is hidden," Teakh said. "Did they actually do it?"

"Good Danna! You're observant. Maybe. Maybe not."

"Is that our current queen?" The woman looked a bit like the police officer in Fennako City.

"One of her predecessors," Keno said. "We don't do that anymore either. Seaguard lords still swear allegiance in a similar ceremony, but not for real. The idea is that any one of the lords could be the father of the next queen. Add in the uncertainty of fatherhood, and anyone on the planet could be her near kin. That's the idea anyway."

Teakh feigned disinterest. "Genetic tests will show the real father."

"It's mostly symbolic. Here, take a look at this." On the screen, a woman—maybe the same one—spread her fingers, opening her labia for a man. His penis entered between her middle and forefinger. "Do you see it?"

"Oh yes, she's holding something."

"Female condom. A sleight of hand by Her Majesty? There're a lot of ways to have sex, or look like you're having sex, without pregnancy resulting."

"But why?"

"Social pressure," Keno said. "Social bonding. Call it what you like. A woman could have multiple men acting as father to her children. Or suppose you're a woman and your friends decide to hire one stud for all of you. You like the friends, but you don't like the man, not as the father of your child. If the stud is expensive, you could save the seed from the condom and sell it for some extra money."

"Women do this?" Such a transaction was only slightly more reasonable than succubi stealing the night emissions of teenagers.

"All the time. Men do that sort of thing too. It's the reason the act is recorded. If a question comes up, the videos can be used as evidence. Here."

The screen showed a man and several women. Instead of his penis, he inserted an insemination wand.

"Maybe he couldn't perform," Keno said. "Luckily, he'd prepared with a sample just in case. Or maybe he was bribed to use another man's seed. Maybe the woman bribed him. It all happens."

"Why are you showing me this?"

"Because, Noah man, it's your heritage. Noah believed if his rules were followed, the number of men would be equal to the number of women—no need for studs."

"And the studs don't like this," Teakh said. "They have a good thing going."

"Aye, you got it. Well, the Code didn't work. Why should a stud help out a potential rival? If another man dies, there're more women to go around."

114

"But if the other man is kin or might be kin?"

"And so the game goes. Some women engaged in sex with multiple men to confuse paternity. Anyone might be kin. Other women, eugenicists, decided to breed a better man. As the project came closer to achieving the goal, the breeding stock refused to participate. Problem is, creation of a purebred requires incest. Noah men refused to impregnate their sisters. It got really ugly — Noah men and women using every available trick and inventing new ones. They desynchronized ovulation and spawned in the neap years. Breeders countered, using ever-younger subjects and sterilizing those they deemed unfit. Noah hid their children. The result was two strains: one mostly homosexual, easier to control, and the other wild Noah, the result of generations of trickery."

"What does this have to do with me?"

"You're wild Noah," Keno said. "Your genetic profile, the one produced without regulation—not mine—achieves the initial goal."

"You're all deluded," Teakh said. "My behavior doesn't match my profile."

"If you say so. Eventually Fennako shut down the project. There's less than a half-step from eugenics to genocide. The breeding stock was let go, to love as they pleased and fade into the population."

"Let's see more of those video documents," Teakh said. "The ones with cheating going on."

A passage had opened before Teakh, a way for him to establish himself as a detective. The flicks, regulations, and trickery resembled the ongoing competition between Seaguard and fishermen. Teakh could spot infractions—he had an eye for it. The video documents served a purpose similar to catch records. He could identify studs, attendants, and women cheating in the same way he identified poachers.

"You going to put those tricks to use?" Keno asked.

"Maybe," Teakh said.

What about Jeena, Reez, and his Angel? Given what he'd seen of stud flicks, Jeena and Reez could be considered assistants, attendants who prepared studs or brides for the insemination process. And if Jeena and Reez were attendants, then Angel...but she was an artist and too classy for such deceit.

Poseidon take it all! She'd painted the Queen's grandson.

Keno showed more clips, and Teakh found the infractions, found every one of them. Oh yes, here was another line of business. He'd use his reputation as a stud to leverage himself into the career of consultant, investigator, and professional witness, not as a fisheries detective but as a biological detective.

CHAPTER 13
Sis Arrives

TEAKH WAITED BY benches and lockers in the shelter of the Dojko ferry terminal. Across the lane, the door of the post office opened and a woman walked out, carrying a package. He hadn't received Gull yet. Maybe tomorrow. Today, his sister was visiting.

A green-and-white passenger ferry pulled up to the pier. A gangway lifted into place, and a few passengers exited. Two women together. Probably a married couple. Behind them trailed Teakh's sister, Annon. If Teakh played his cards right, she might help him by commissioning that painting, but then, she might not. She had a way of doing things her own way,

"Sis!" he shouted.

She came toward him, carrying two overnight bags. The hood of her faded student smock was thrown back from straight brown hair. Just a normal young woman from the wrong side of the inlet, Sis had never been given an implant. Her commonplace appearance concealed a keen intellect and a burning drive. Their eyes met, and her face lit with a smile as she rushed toward him.

"You big oaf." She dropped her bags and gave him an affectionate shove. "What's with the broken leg?"

"It's nothing," he said, watching her eyes out of habit. Since she didn't have an implant, they often communicated with glances. He'd become accustomed to deducing her thoughts from subtle changes in her facial expression.

"Nothing?" Her eyes darkened, pupils momentarily wide.

"They're saying you jumped onto a burning ship to rescue some sailors and barely made it out alive."

"Stories have a way of growing." Teakh shrugged. "It's just a hairline fracture. I tripped coming down a ladder."

Her narrow-eyed gaze drilled into him. "What about the job as a cook?"

To those who didn't know her, Sis appeared shy and sweet. Teakh knew better. If she found out about how he'd ended up in the Tatumuko village brig, she'd start telling him what to do.

"It didn't work out," he said.

She laid a hand against his cheek. "I worry about you."

Since their mother's death, it had been just the two of them against the stony insularity of Ralko. They'd always been close. He nudged her hand away and stepped back. No, they were growing apart, had been ever since Teakh had run away to live on the docks.

"About this stud business." Sis put her hands on her hips. "Do you understand what you're getting into?"

He changed the subject. "I'll buy you lunch."

Her eyebrows flicked upward. "I'm buying."

"Suit yourself."

Truly, it didn't matter. Teakh and Sis had always kept joint bank accounts. Lunch would add an insignificant amount to their mounting debt.

They walked along the waterfront, passing the freighter pier and the small boat harbor. Teakh, as always, noted which boats were in and which were out. Looked like Skipper Jake of *Bekra Irene* was tinkering with his propulsors. Seagulls screamed, and Teakh thought wistfully of Gull.

Just back from the waterfront, Dojko women ran housefront businesses catering to mariners: chandleries, bachelor shops, and eating houses. Teakh had in mind a lunch counter overlooking the harbor.

Inside the restaurant, smelling of fried fish, they gave their order. A string of bells at the door jangled as other customers arrived. Sis carried their tray of sandwiches and cranberry seltzer to a table.

Teakh managed two bundles of eating utensils. Setting his crutches aside, he slid onto a padded bench. "What do you know about purchasing art?" He wasn't going to show all his cards yet.

"Nothing." She passed him a salmon burger layered with cabbage and sliced tomatoes.

Teakh lifted the bun and smeared it with mustard. "I've discovered a painter who specializes in portraits of studs and Seaguard lords. Her work is on display in Fennako City. I'd like to get my portrait painted. It'll increase my value as a stud."

"And get you in trouble with the Fennako City Police?"

"Gull was checking out an art gallery," Teakh said. "It happened to be near the palace."

Sis held her sandwich in two hands. "I told Fennako we'd discussed art, but that I hadn't yet declared it as my field of study."

"She's an amazing artist. Worth studying."

At the counter, the server called back to the cook, "Order up."

"Have you taken this up with Dyse?" Sis took a bite of her sandwich.

Teakh shook his head. "I'd like to get the painting done on my own. If it's bad, we won't tell Dyse. If it's good, she'll be happy to reap the rewards. Tell folks you're studying art. We'll call the painting an educational expense." Teakh took a bite of salmon patty and cabbage.

"A thesis in art?"

"Why not?" Teakh set his sandwich on his plate. "What are you studying right now anyway?" Last time they'd talked about it, she'd been considering teaching or social work.

Sis bowed her head. "I don't know. Maybe..." She cast her gaze out the window toward the marina. "But I know one thing—I want out of Ralko. Out of the village and out of the clan. No more begging permission from Dyse or the Ralko dames." She looked him square in the face. "I want our own clan."

Teakh and Sis had long talked of establishing their own clan, a favorite fantasy, but now that he'd met Angel, the dream had an air of urgent reality. He'd have a better chance with her if he were a clan chief.

"You keep talking about this. Could we pull off something like that?" He sipped his cranberry seltzer, acting casual, concealing his hopes.

Sis's smile became shrewd. He knew that look of hers as

she identified a goal and marshaled her crew. More often than not, her crew had been Teakh and his childhood arsenal of robots. He could often goad her in the direction he wanted. Presented with one of her schemes, he'd test for it weaknesses and identify hidden consequences.

"Can't have a clan of two," he challenged.

"I know. I've looked into it. The more women, the better." She flattened her hands on the table, her sandwich half eaten. "Big enough to spread the cost of medical care and retirement."

"So where are you going to get the women?"

"Mama had a lot of friends," Sis said. "More like contacts. I have the names of some of them. We're not the only ones unhappy with our clan."

"I may be wrong, but it seems there're more clanless men than clanless women," Teakh said. Fenria might have had more women than men, but it didn't seem that way down on the docks.

"Aye." Sis nodded. "Clans dislike expelling mothers. It's bad for their kids. Instead they subject us to internal banishment." She took a bite of her sandwich.

Teakh sighed in agreement. "Ralko sure didn't like our mama." He'd spent his entire life in the shadow of her banishment, all because she'd conceived and given birth to him without clan permission. "Listen, if we're willing to recruit men, we've got a bigger pool of possible members."

Sis shook her head. "Men don't count in a clan, not according to Fennako officials. They're the ones who decide if we qualify as a clan."

"Does it have to be that way?" Teakh lifted his glass, bubbles rising through the seltzer. "The Noah Code says to educate your children, no distinction between male and female. I say we make our own rules. We'll include men and children of men, not just of women. So if I have some children and you have some children and we get some others to join us, we have a clan."

Sis's expression softened, once more deceptively sweet. "You're a shiner." She blotted her lips with a napkin.

"I've been called that before. But to recruit members, we

need some sort of draw. If we promise to treat men as equal to women, they might join up. They get tired of being second-class clan members. And think about it—if men and women are equal, my children will be members same as yours. We'll have ambilineal membership. Our clan will grow twice as fast."

Amusement flickered in Sis's eyes. "People can't be in two clans. If children can be members of both maternal and paternal clan, that's what happens. In the next generation, a kid would be in four clans, and her kids would be in eight, then sixteen. Their names would get longer and longer. It would go on that way until everyone was a member of every clan and nobody could marry anyone at all." She dramatically flung down her napkin. "Universal incest."

Teakh laughed, enjoying her irreverence. "Infinitely long names."

She sobered. "I'm thinking you'd better go through with being a stud. It's our best option for both money and for producing children. I'm limited by the number of times I can get pregnant."

"I'd rather be a detective."

She laughed. "Student teacher and fish biter out to found their own clan," she said, once again lighthearted. "Except I decided against teaching."

"Fish biter?" Put that way, his investigations of rotting fish carcasses seemed a poor choice of careers. "Got to have dreams." Truly, their hope of founding their own clan amounted to chasing an ice mirage.

"Student adrift and dockrat. So what will we name our deplorable clan?"

"Sisko," offered Teakh. "Named after our foundress."

"Good Danna, no. At least use my real name, Annon. How about Teakhuko?"

"Teakh-khua-hua? Damn hard to pronounce. How about Noahee?" Teakh stressed the second syllable, emphasizing that it meant father's clan. In the days of Noah, Teakh's name would have been styled "Teakh Noah y Ralko."

Sis's lip quivered with the hint of a smile. "The direct patrilineal descendants of Jamie Noah and Queen Fenna Lee-Smith. If we had patrilineal inheritance, you'd be king."

"Must be some guy around who's better qualified," Teakh said. Like maybe that prince Angel had painted.

"According to the flap about your genetics, there isn't. Genetically, you're the nearest thing to Jamie Noah." She elbowed him. "His heir."

"What does that make me?" He thrust out his chest. "Prince royal?"

She poked him. "Annoyance royale."

"An alternative royal dynasty?" He laughed. "We'll challenge Fennako." Oh yes, with a title, he'd have a chance against Lord Prince High and Mighty. "I think we should take this seriously. About that painting—it'll help with recruitment. Getting it done puts us on par with the royal family."

"Do you really think it'll induce men to join up?"

"No. But my female clients might help us out. I'll get that portrait done so that I can attract influential women who will be mothers to my children, future clan members. What do you think?"

"I think we still have to figure out how to pay for the painting."

"Can't we take out a loan?"

"Let's wait on the art purchase," Sis said. "A clan is an association of parents—no children, no clan. If we're to found a clan, we both need to produce children. I'd better get started." She counted on her fingers. "Not this spawning cycle, but the following cycle or the one after that. I'll need a man."

"That's a cold way to put it. What about love?"

She flicked a lock of hair from his forehead. "Little brother, you're such a romantic. Most guys just want sex, a girl in every port."

"I don't." He'd settle for three as long as one was Angel, but three was enough.

"I'd better start working on it now." She bit her lower lip. "I can apply to Ralko for seed from a shared husband, but I don't want anything from them. Ugh! Dame Ralko's husband. Or I could buy from a donor stud. Hard to tell what I'm getting though. With cover studs, I'd know a bit more, but they cost. The really good ones cost a bundle."

"Aye. They're charging a bunch for me," Teakh said,

unable to resist one-upmanship. Actually, he had no idea of his going rate.

She leaned forward, chin on her hands, sandwich forgotten. "The best option for me? I find a husband, and you marry his sister. They treat us as a pair."

"How about I find a wife, and you marry her brother?" Hopefully Angel had one.

Sis shook her head in uncertainty. "Dyse gave me this." She stretched open a handscreen and displayed the prestigious stud catalog, *Dale's Men.*

Teakh reached for the screen. "You can do that?" Access to such catalogs was strictly controlled.

"Dyse vouched for me, and says if your career goes well, Ralko will pay the fees. I can pick whoever I want. Only problem—Dyse is paying." She grimaced. "And I don't want anything to do with her or Clan Ralko."

Teakh activated the catalog. The screen filled with a man gazing soulfully into the camera lens, the effect similar but not quite as grand as one of Angel's paintings. The accompanying description excluded name and clan, but included everything else: sexual tastes, interests, characteristics, genetic background, and vignettes of personality. This particular man's entry featured musical talent and included audio samples along with photos of the man strumming a mandolin.

"You can search by criteria. Here, bait this way." Sis demonstrated by entering: TALL, DARK, HANDSOME. A listing of studs appeared, accompanied by height, melanin levels, and ratings of physical attractiveness. She laughed and rolled her eyes. "Everything quantified."

"Let me see that." Teakh entered STRONG, HAIRY. By expanding listings and checking pictures, he located Hairy. This time Teakh laughed. "How about short, red-haired, big nose, and left-handed?"

"I'm sure there's one in there."

Instead, Teakh entered NOAH and got one result. An expansion of the entry revealed a somewhat younger Keno, his chin smooth shaven.

So the gym operator was a kinsman of sorts. Teakh rubbed his neuro scars.

Teakh reviewed the accompanying articles, which gave an overview of the Noah Project and touted Keno's innate homosexuality as a desirable feature. "His sons will serve well as uncles, supporting their sisters' children, contributing to their clan, and forming strong bonds with both men in their clan and clan husbands. His daughters will make excellent mothers." Keno was listed as loyal, nurturing, devoted, altruistic, and a swimming coach. He had characteristics described as boyish and pretty. Teakh dropped his finger on a note that Keno was no longer available.

Sis leaned across the table. "Who are you looking at?"

"Acquaintance of mine."

Teakh turned the screen toward her. Keno was older than Sis by about a dodecade, but trim, in top physical condition, and with excellent genetics. Other than Keno's homosexuality, he wasn't a bad match. Best of all, if Sis approached Keno directly, they wouldn't need money from Ralko.

"This? A friend of yours?"

"Do you want to meet him?" Teakh asked. "Maybe you can work something out."

She nodded, eyes bright.

Teakh touched his ear to indicate he was transmitting and hailed Keno. *I have a proposition for you. What do you think of becoming a father?*

Keno laughed. *I already am.*

I mean not just producing children but raising them. My sister and I are thinking of forming our own clan. Teakh took a breath and laid out his proposition. *We'd like to include you as the father of her children.*

Senior clan husband?

That's the idea. Married into the clan but not a member of the clan.

Keno guffawed. *Sure. Come on up to the gym.*

CHAPTER 14
Clan Noahee

TEAKH CRUTCHED SMOOTHLY, keeping a comfortable pace for Sis. At the gym, they entered through the side door. The clank of weights stopped as a ripple of attention traveled through the place. Limber alighted from a handstand, his feet touching down gracefully. Pector struck a pose, muscles bunched, one arm flexed. Hairy shut off the music and stared openly at the young woman in their midst. Danna! Teakh should've brought Sis through the front, not past this gawking audience of naked men.

His face heated, his obvious blush compounding his embarrassment. "Sorry. Keno is this way."

Grasping Sis's arm, he steered her to the front parlor. Sunlight slanted through the window louvers. Tea service and a plate of crackers waited on the table.

Keno stood to greet them, formally dressed in a style resembling Seaguard kit: his boots cuffed at the knees, his vest patterned in Dojko blue and gray. He even wore the required case knife like a badge—attached to his vest handle downward. Teakh doubted Keno's getup had ever encountered seawater. Sis, wearing a faded student smock, paused, hand to hip. She and Keno eyed each other.

Teakh broke the mutual scrutiny with an introduction. "My sister, Annon Noahee."

"Member of Clan Ralko." She shot a glance at Teakh.

He responded with a sheepish grin. He'd be sunk to Poseidon if he'd claim Ralko as their clan, even if technically it was.

Keno bowed, impeccably polite. "Keno Dojko here. Honored." He seated Sis, leaving Teakh to deal with crutches himself. Keno poured tea into translucent teacups painted with roses. Teakh thought the chinaware more appropriate for a clan matriarch than a couple of studs and a student, but it showed Keno's effort.

Keno set aside the teapot. "Tell me about these plans."

Sis ducked her head. "We were just talking, joking around about founding our own clan."

She might affect modesty, but Teakh preferred to be forthright. "My sister needs a husband."

She kicked him under the table.

"Well, you do. You said so." Teakh dove in. "My sister has a subscription to *Dale's*, but I don't want her hiring just anyone. First, how closely are we related? *Dale's* has you down as Noah."

Keno winked at Annon. "Your brother is jumping ahead."

Sis's face reddened. "I'm sorry."

"It's nothing." Keno's eyes shifted, peering at Teakh through dark lashes. "Kissing cousins actually."

Good Danna! Keno was flirting with him. Teakh groaned. How could he have missed this facet of his proposition? Occasionally, a homosexual man married a clan's senior woman but had intimate relationships with one of her kinsmen. Keno was considering not Sis as a partner but Teakh.

"Let's slow down." Sis set her cup aside. "I don't quite understand the situation." She folded her hands in deceptive innocence.

Teakh knew her game of drawing out information. He'd played it often enough himself.

"My brother is out fishing," she said. "Or I thought he was. I find out he's in the hospital, and my aunt's acting like she's won the royal share. Then there's all this nonsense about being descendants of Jamie Noah." She crossed her arms. "Come on. Noah might not have existed at all."

"He built an ark," Teakh said, trying for levity. "Filled it with animals two-by-two and sailed it across the galaxy. How did he get whales aboard a spaceship, anyway?"

"However it was done, they're here," Keno said. "Wild

stories often have a grain of truth. Someone composed the Noah code. His actual name?" He shrugged. "It probably was Jamie. I don't know about the Noah part. It might have been a group of people or even an organization."

Sis set her lips in a firm line. "How does that relate to you and me?"

The drift of this conversation offered more shoals than Teakh cared to navigate, Sis presenting herself as mild, even naïve, while drawing Keno out. Teakh busied himself with his drink.

"It's like this." Keno passed around the plate of crackers. "Fenria doesn't have enough men for each woman to have a man of her own." He set the plate aside. "Once the ratio was even worse—five men only: Henson, Lee, Smith, Jones, and Noah." Keno ticked the names off on his fingers. "Four of them became the Great Studs, the fathers of Fenria." He wiggled four fingers. "Jamie Noah declined to contribute sperm. Instead he remained faithful to one woman and gave us *his* contribution, the Noah Code."

Teakh thought the stories a bunch of shine. "The Jones stud? Is that the Davy Jones who lures women to his underwater lair?" The bizarre and endless lore of Davy Jones combined naval battles, musical talent, and death at sea—the stories almost as strange as the mythology of Noah. "The last ferry to Clark's Village?"

Keno shrugged. "Or maybe that was John Paul Jones."

"Only five men?" Sis shook her head. "I'm sorry. The legend is too much like old stories from Earth."

Keno broke a cracker in two. "Five men or five grand, it doesn't matter. Not even the names matter. Genetic tests show we have only five paternal lines. Those five men might not have lived at the same time. The Great Studs had many children, and their children had children, until the planet was populated with the descendants of Henson, Lee, Smith, and Jones. They're our ancestors even if we also carry some Noah genetics. A stud like Davy Jones can produce grandgrosses of children. If only three live, he's still ahead of the Noah man raising two."

She leaned forward, hands folded demurely, as she challenged Keno. "That's if the prolific stud can convince women to go along with it."

"Aye, that's the hitch." Keno seemed to have misunderstood her implication that he was a con man. Or maybe he hadn't. "Jamie Noah must have figured that if more men survived, women would have a choice, and they'd favor men who'd assist in child-rearing."

One forearm on the table, Teakh said, "I haven't seen you do much child-rearing." Keno could take that comment as reproach or as an opportunity.

He chuckled. "A lot of studs around here could use some remedial parenting. Child-rearing, coaching, and mentoring are all about the same."

Teakh ignored Keno's smoothly delivered barb.

Sis gave one of her deceptively sweet smiles. "Part of being Noah?"

"Possibly." Keno rose to her bait. "Noah's plan didn't work. Altruism as a reproductive strategy requires a critical mass of selfless individuals. Not enough men worked together. So along came the Noah Project, social engineers attempting to artificially increase the number of selfless men."

Sis sprang her trap in mock surprise. "So I take it I'm in the company of the only two selfless men in existence?" She gave a snort of laughter. "If you're anything like my brother, I seriously doubt the selfless part."

"Excuse me," Teakh said. "What about..." He'd extinguished the shipboard fire because Cooky was his friend, not because he was altruistic.

"Two Noah men who sell on the open market," Keno corrected. "I'm not saying we're actually selfless. I've fathered some sons, and there're probably more Noah men hiding out, happily married and raising children."

"But not enough, I guess," Teakh said.

"Aye, the Noah Project also failed. Breeding for men who were monogamous and nurturing, the project selected for feminine characteristics and got me, a monogamous, loving, nurturing homosexual." He bobbed his head in a bow. "And it got you, a man who won't do what he's told. The project couldn't control your phenotype. Men and women escaped, forming relationships and raising children on the sly. Monogamous, generous, loving, and nurturing, but outlaws by nature." He raised a cracker in salute.

Teakh said, "How do you know I don't do what I'm told?"

"You were the one who ran off aboard a junk scow. Noah doesn't follow laws; we make them. Not sure they really want more of us around, but I don't care. May our paternal line win." He clapped Teakh on the shoulder. "You're our newest champion."

Sis furrowed her brow. "Reef your sails there. Half a child's genes come from her mother. If you boys would stop competing for reproductive trophies, we might get something done."

"What do you have in mind?" Keno asked. "If the goal is to increase alleles for altruism, the quickest way to do it is by using studs."

"The two of you? Any man who wants to do it doesn't have the right genes." She wrinkled her nose. "Anyway, all of this about innate altruism is complete shine. You both seem more interested in flaunting your prowess than in the good of others."

"Altruism is a marketing ploy," Teakh said.

Keno leaned toward Sis, his hands on the edge of the table. "So what are you interested in? The good of others?"

"I want to live as I please." Sis straightened her smock. "Without Ralko, or anyone else, telling me what I can and can't do."

"We want our own clan," offered Teakh. "With men and women included as equals."

"An idea worthy of Jamie Noah." Keno put his fingertips together. "And if you lived as you please, what would you do?"

"What I want?" Sis asked. "To band together with others like us."

Keno grinned and slapped the table. "And you claim not to believe in selflessness?"

"I want out of Clan Ralko," she said. "Call it what you like. The Ralko dames are greedy, power-hungry slime eels. If Teakh and I refuse to take their orders, we'll be clanless. No one will vouch for us. We'll be homeless, living on the docks and taking jobs no one else wants."

Teakh reached for a cracker. "I already do that."

"But if we could band together with others, we'd have our own clan." Her glance met Keno's, her gaze direct and piercing. "Do you want to be part of it?"

Keno tossed his head in negation. "I'm willing to help, but not as senior clan husband. You're a fine young lady, don't get me wrong, but we need greater genetic variation and more offspring total. Besides, we might end up with a clan of scheming, homosexual outlaws." He laughed. "Your brother? Now, I'm attracted to him, but he has his own preferences, so there we are."

Teakh sighed. There they were. Sis still didn't have a prospect for a husband, but then Teakh wouldn't have to facilitate her relationship with Keno, which was a relief. Teakh poured himself another cup of tea. What a sister! Danna help the man she actually set out to snag.

CHAPTER 15
Roe Stripping

IN A ROOM behind the kitchen, Teakh sat on a chair and folded laundry. Gull was back in her niche after having been mailed from Fennako City. The police officer had been as good as her word.

Dyse hailed. *I'll be stopping by tomorrow to check on your progress. It can't be said that I don't care about you.*

Teakh folded a towel and added it a growing stack. The gym sure went through a lot of linens despite Keno's promotion of nudity as a way to reduce laundry.

Please think if there's anything you need.

Teakh pulled another towel from the heap of clean laundry and gave it a snap. A napkin clung to the towel. Teakh grabbed the napkin and threw it back into the heap. Maybe he could convince Dyse to pay for the portrait. *Well, actually there is. I've been considering my value as a stud. I've got good genes, but I haven't really done anything. I understand my best option is to present myself as Seaguard. I've located an artist who specializes in painting Seaguard lords. We could commission her to paint my portrait. A painting like that would draw parallels between top Seaguardsmen and myself.*

I don't think so, Dyse said, her dismissal of his proposal infuriatingly abrupt.

Teakh jerked the next towel from the heap. *But she's painted the Queen's grandson. The only man higher than that is the king.*

I don't see that such a painting would pay off. I'll handle the marketing. You work on your comportment.

His hands shaking, Teakh seized another towel. Anything he could say would drag him deeper into the mire. He'd get out from under Dyse the first chance he could get. *I'll be seeing you.* He signed off.

Head down, he plowed through the mountain of laundry, folding towels, washcloths, and napkins until he had neat stacks ready to be stowed.

With the briefest of nods to Pector sweeping the floors, and to Limber washing the mirrors, Teakh went to his quarters. Seated on his mat, he sent Gull out the high window for a flight down to the waterfront.

Soaring over the harbor, he tried to forget about clan and money, and to leave behind his anger at his grasping aunt. He observed, trying to locate lawbreakers. A trawler was moored in the wrong spot. Someone on the *Janey Girl* hadn't properly covered a load of fish offal. Both infractions were too small to be of concern or to pay off.

Ah, but here was something interesting. *Zephyr Winds* was in. Lugo lounged on the stern, his arm around a girl seated beside him. Teakh would have liked to sit just like that with Angel. No question of money or status, just two people in love. He sent Gull down to get a closer look. She perched on a stanchion.

"Well, hello there," Lugo said, legs outstretched. "Nothing missing here." He patted his hip pocket.

Leaning against him, the girl laughed. "Is that a seagull you're talking to?"

"Sure, this one's smart."

"So what's its name?" the girl asked.

"What's your name, gull?" Lugo tossed his head and winked.

Gull retreated with a hop. *Squawk.*

"That's its name," Lugo said. "Right out of the bird's mouth. Squawk."

"I think she means it was a rude question."

Teakh sent Gull flapping back to her station atop the pylon. He intended to avoid close inspection, so he kept his distance.

"Watch this." Lugo produced his billfold and removed a eulachon. He creased it and held the bill high. "Hey, gull!

Look what I got for you."

Teakh scratched his ear. If he took the bill, he'd give himself away, but it seemed likely that Lugo already knew what Gull was.

What the depths! If Teakh couldn't get his own girl, he might as well help Lugo, and he did offer money. On Teakh's command, Gull dove, bearing down on Lugo, and seized the bill.

"Stars!" the girl said. "It must have thought you held a fish."

"Crazy bird, thinking that picture of a hooligan is for real," Lugo said.

Teakh landed Gull on her pylon, crumpled the bill, and stuffed it in her croup.

"The bird eats money." Lugo nodded to his sweetheart. "You try it." He gave the girl a second bill. "Hold it up high."

"Here, gull. Come and get it," she hollered.

Teakh sent Gull diving from her perch to snatch the money then swoop upward. At a height, he dropped the bill, let it flutter, then dove to catch it. He dropped the bill again and caught it. Then he dropped it, turned a somersault, and snatched it a final time.

The girl whooped. "Where did you find this bird?"

Teakh landed Gull on the pylon, two bills now in her croup.

Lugo handed the girl another eulachon, and she held it aloft.

Teakh launched Gull from her perch and came down into a barrel roll to pluck the money from the girl's hand. He finished with a somersault. They fed Gull bills until Teakh had run through his entire repertoire. Teakh landed Gull and, wings spread, bobbed her head in a bow. Lugo and his girl applauded.

And Teakh called himself a fisheries detective? More like a waterside performer. Anything for money. Gull flapped away from Lugo and his sweetheart. Gull came through the clerestory and landed on the couch beside Teakh. He tapped the red spot on her beak, and she coughed up the money, now coated with lubricant. He smoothed and wiped the bills then slipped them into a pocket in his dummy comset.

WHILE ON HIS daily rounds with Gull, Teakh saw a Dojko esskip lift from the lagoon and cleared the breakwater. Dojko Seaguard was up to something. Where was he going?

Gull flew along the shore, watching for whatever had washed up on the morning tide. She soon caught up with the esskip. It was moored to a buoy, canopy retracted. A Seaguardsman dressed in Dojko gray and blue squatted on the buoy's discus float, an open toolbox beside him as he apparently repaired transmitter equipment.

Gull landed atop the buoy superstructure.

"Sink it all! Fratricidal relay!" The Seaguardsman slammed a hand against a strut.

Gull clung tightly as the buoy bobbed and swayed. Teakh felt for the man. No technology was foolproof, and as often as not, a minor repair snowballed into a major project involving multiple attempts to identify and locate replacement parts. With a squawk of sympathy, Gull took to the air and resumed her patrol along the shore. The malfunctioning relay didn't seem to affect normal radio communications.

Sunlight threw crisp shadows, illuminating a mob of wheeling seagulls screeching and squabbling, their wings flashes of white. A gull seized a prize from the beach and broke from the mob. The thief flew away, booty clutched in its beak, only to drop the load. Other gulls swooped in for the plunder. In his quarters, Teakh sat on his meditation cushion, his mind with Gull.

She landed and, wings aggressively outstretched, muscled her way into the fray. Teakh used her size to his advantage, hissing and threatening in a display of dominance. The mob fought over some sort of fish. A bird hesitated, but Teakh didn't. Gull snagged a fish, a herring, and dragged it from the hungry mob, claiming the loot.

With a scream, Teakh warned the other gulls back, but a bird came at him with wings akimbo, beak open in a hiss. Gull met the aggressor. Beak clamped against beak, they grappled in a tug-of-war. Teakh's neck and mouth ached as Gull tussled, pulling and being pulled until Gull's opponent let go, conceding the fight.

Another bird had snatched the herring. Teakh's blood

heated by his hard-won victory, he and Gull went after his second opponent. The thief took one look at Gull and dropped the fish.

Gull dragged the fish behind a protective snag and inspected the carcass. The fish's belly had been split as with a knife. Teakh recorded images. With a quick taste of the rotting meat, Gull tested its DNA: HERRING FEMALE. Analysis of the sample yielded levels of putrefaction. Yet another bird approached and screamed at Gull, making demands, probably to feed her chicks. Gull gave up the carcass. Teakh had the data, and that was all he wanted

He searched the beach for more fish. Fighting off mobs of seagulls, Gull took more samples. Teakh only needed a bite or two from each small corpse. Several were missing their heads, possibly already carried off or maybe removed. A fierce joy filled him as Teakh practiced his chosen profession: robotically assisted fisheries detective. He and Gull were no longer performing dockside stunts or inspecting garbage heaps for improperly sorted recyclables. These herring just might represent a real crime. Danna, he hoped so. He'd be one step closer to quitting the stud business.

He inspected a carcass for injuries to the lips and found contusions on her delicate gills. When fishermen shook a gillnet to remove the catch, the heads of the fish often broke off.

Continuing surveillance, Gull searched for more dead herring, but either there weren't any or the real seagulls had already cleaned them up. Gull landed on an outcropping and preened, checking feathers for damage, removing lingering traces of dead fish. Gull was fastidious. He'd programmed her that way.

Now then, what did he have? How many samples of distinctive DNA? Ten dead herring, all female, all with bellies split. Two with missing heads, and one with gill damage.

Most likely someone was roe-stripping—taking the valuable eggs and illegally tossing the carcasses. Mistakenly tossing them a bit too close to shore. Or maybe that someone had taken advantage of the damaged sensor buoy then had quickly dumped the evidence.

Sinking depths, here was his break. Danna! What luck!

Teakh accessed his records for names of boats currently running gillnets and brought up a tidy list of suspects. He input ambient temperature and putrefaction levels and ran calculations for possible time of death. A comparison of his records of boats still in the harbor during that time whittled the list down. Gull tucked a foot. Teakh eased his human legs and considered.

Roe-stripping and most types of fisheries crime couldn't be done by a fisherman working alone. The crime required cooperation of both buyer and processing house. The buyer might not know what had happened to the rest of the fish, but surely a processing house would notice eggs without fish.

Sad it was, the mamas killed and their bodies thrown away. In a sense, by taking and selling ova, such fishermen acted as succubi. Surely women who stole human semen also had buyers and processors, their product being even more perishable than edible fish eggs.

As surely as roe was preserved in a processing house, the preservation of human sperm was done in a medical lab. His mind worked on the possibilities. Jeena had the means to have taken his sperm. Keno had warned that any penetration not witnessed might not have occurred. Means and motivation. Opportunity. Teakh cut off that line of thought. He had another crime to solve, and if he delayed, the real gulls would eat all the evidence.

Accessing the Network, he checked for local herring openers. There weren't any, which confirmed that the catching itself had been illegal. Teakh rubbed his hands together.

Gull flew to the harbor and alighted on a net reel. Using beak and tongue, Gull mouthed the fiber of the net, testing levels of ammonia to calculate how recently the net had been used. Systematically, Gull moved from boat to boat, working through Teakh's list until he located a net reel stinking of herring blood. Skipper Nerka had made a recent catch.

Gull pecked at bits and pieces of flesh clinging to the fiber. The scraps tested positive for herring, as did the blood. He'd caught Skipper Nerka red-handed, so to speak, or nearly red-handed. Or maybe it was all a red herring.

Teakh sent Gull to the processing house to snoop around

in the alley. What he really needed was to get ahold of receipt records. If he were Dojko Seaguard, he'd just ask, and the processors would surrender the records. He had several options: he could do nothing and the scoundrels would get away with the crime, or he could tip off Dojko Seaguard. If the evidence was solid, Dojko might pass along word of Teakh's reputation, and clans might hire him as an investigator. He'd introduce himself to Angel as a respected fisheries investigator, and she'd ask to marry him.

All of that was his fondest hope, but a long shot. Despite the blood, he only had circumstantial evidence on Skipper Nerka. Most likely no prosecution would follow. Seaguard would watch Nerka more closely. Aware of increased surveillance, Nerka would mend his ways for a while.

No. Teakh would go to the criminal directly and levy the fines himself, leading to nearly the same outcome, except that Teakh would get paid for his work. His actions weren't exactly legal, but they weren't entirely illegal either. Teakh was Seaguard, after all. Methodically, he checked the nets of the boats remaining on his list. After finding no other suspects, he hailed Skipper Nerka.

I'm with the gull, Teakh sent. *It seems you've been feeding her kinfolk some female herring. Females with ova removed. Now we could take this to the authorities. Or you could feed the gull, and we'll let it go. I'm thinking three grand coho would make a nice meal. What do you say?*

IN THE LATE afternoon, Teakh sauntered down to the Salty Hound, feeling pleased. At last he was bringing in some money. Nerka sat morosely at the bar, and Teakh bought him a beer to salve his conscience. Blackmailing his friends didn't sit well with him, even if his friends were poachers.

"What are you about?" he asked.

"Poseidon-damn gull," Nerka said. "She seems like fun with her tricks, but she's one nasty bird, I'm telling you."

"What did she do?" Teakh asked.

"Stole from me. Bunch of eulachon."

"Well then, don't leave it lying around," Lugo said. "Gulls are like that." He winked at Teakh, who gulped his cider to hide his expression.

Later, out in the lane, Lugo asked, "What did you do to him?"

"Nothing." Teakh would maintain the fiction that he and Gull were separate entities, even if Lugo suspected otherwise. Teakh said, "That gull noticed a few things in his operation weren't quite shipshape. She brought it to his attention, that's all. She charges money. You know that. There's none to be made in competitive swimming."

"Fair enough," Lugo said. "Big fish eat little fish. Fishermen get away with whatever we can. It's all part of the game."

"It is," Teakh said, "but let's keep this to ourselves."

CHAPTER 16
Plans

NOW FOR THE real work. Teakh had promised to read Sis's clan proposal, for all the good it would do. With Gull in her recharging niche, Teakh closed his eyes and tried to make sense of densely written frames of legal jargon. If Sis could write and understand this legal stuff, she had him beat. He gave her a hail.

I've got our clan charter here. What's this about universal suffrage?

That means men and single women can vote and hold office, not just mothers, Sis said. *It's what we discussed over lunch.*

What about kids? Teakh spoke with his eyes closed, wishing Sis had a camera as part of her comset.

All of our children will be members, she said.

I mean, can kids vote?

I've been struggling with that. If we set voting age at two-dozen-and-one, we can't vote ourselves. But twelve-and-one seems too young.

How about if we split the difference? Teakh sent a burst of laugher. *A dozen-six.*

There is historical precedence in that. Eighteen in old Earth numbers.

So what happens if we disagree? With only two of us, we'll deadlock. Given that he could be as stubborn as Sis, an unbreakable tie was inevitable. *How about if we include Keno? This time as a member, not as a husband.*

If he'll agree to it, Sis said. *I'm running for the office of grandmatriarch. If you vote for me, I'll appoint you as Seaguard chief.*

Teakh's mind reeled with the sheer hubris of the proposition. He'd be sovereign magnate. *For life?*

That's the way it's written, Sis said. *I can't toss you out unless you're legally incompetent, but you can vote me out of office any time you like.*

What absurd grandeur. Maybe Angel would like it. He tried to make another joke. *Not until we've got at least three members in the clan, so we're even.*

She didn't laugh. *We'll have to recruit more clan members, but mostly we've got to produce kids. Fennako will consider the best interest of children when they decide on our status.*

I might not go through with this stud business. What then? The idea of using children as leverage turned his stomach.

Your children will be clan members regardless of how they're conceived.

Only two people, little money, and no territory. Their plan was an ice mirage. Without more members, he'd be a sovereign chief in name only.

Soon as we're sure of the charter, I'll petition the Queen, Sis said. *The paperwork gets sent in to the Department of Clan and Lineage, but ultimately it's her decision. I'm thinking you should charm her.*

What? She's eight-dozen years old.

You could make her very happy. Sis laughed.

What about me? He sure didn't want to charm a venerable old lady, no matter how august.

I adore kidding you, Sis said. *But think about it. We must convince the Queen we deserve our own clan. I need your help.*

Convince the Queen? I don't know what I can do.

We'll think of something.

Teakh signed off and flopped back on the couch. All his plans ended in the impossible. It seemed as if he were seeking a passage to open ocean. Estuaries and inlets which seemed so promising led to treacherous shoals or dead-end arms blocked by high peaks. What did he have to offer Her Majesty?

He tried to tease out what he knew of her. Hers was an unusual position in that she held three offices: Fennako grandmatriarch, Fenrian queen, and Seaguard supreme magnate. Teakh believed she delegated her responsibilities to her son-in-law, her two daughters, and her grandson, Lord

Tristan Bay, the high and mighty prince who'd posed for Angel. Teakh battened down his jealousy.

This tangle had no way out, not even a free end to start with. He drummed his fingers against his ankle brace. If Angel accepted him, he could approach the Queen through her and the Queen's grandson. But Teakh hadn't been able to get a simple message through to Angel.

THE FOLLOWING AFTERNOON, Dyse again hailed to announce she was visiting and already at the gym. Iris has shared a lovely pot of tea, and she's filling me in on your progress. I'm eager to see how you're doing in person. Come join us in the parlor.

I'll be right there, sent Teakh, feeling no great hurry.

In his quarters, he pulled his old pants from the closet, the ones Angel had repaired. He'd make a bid for wardrobe money. He worked the pants on over his brace then pulled on his old boot and faded life vest. He crutched to the front room.

Dyse sat at the square table with Keno and Iris. Teakh bowed. Iris responded with a nod, and Keno stood.

"There you are." Dyse set her teacup beside a plate of crackers. She scowled. "That's the most hideous vest imaginable."

Teakh could say the same about her robes. The front panel of her getup displayed black-and-scarlet brocade, the colors and style a loud statement of her status in Clan Ralko.

He suppressed a grin. She was playing right into his plan. "It fulfills the Noah Code. Be prepared," he said. "I'd like to talk to you about my stipend." He sat across the table from Keno as if the four of them were prepared to play cards.

"Your stipend?" Dyse said. "But you have everything you need, and you haven't even done anything yet."

"I should look like a Seaguard lord. I can't do it if I'm dressed like a pauper. I sold my emergency whistle." He touched the place on his vest where the standard emergency device belonged and didn't mention he'd lost it in a card game.

"How he presents himself reflects on our reputation."

Iris filled a cup for Teakh and passed it to him.

"What do you have in mind?" Keno asked.

"I'd like a regular stipend." Teakh left the tea untasted. "I'll buy a new vest and boots."

"No. No." Dyse shook her finger. "A man doesn't shop for his own clothing. We'll provide Ralko kit. I'll dress you up as fine as Lord Ralko himself."

Teakh grimaced. He wasn't a child asking permission to buy candy, and Lord Ralko had never been noted for his sense of style. "I have other expenses as well. Good Danna! A man should be able to buy his own underwear and toothpaste. Even as a twelve-year-old busing tables in the Ralko men's house, I was always paid something."

Dyse crossed her arms. "But you aren't working."

"I'm training and doing chores six hours a day. In my time off, I observe the tide and study." Teakh turned toward Keno, pleading with his eyes for support.

Teakh had brought in some money by blackmailing Nerka, but the next time Gull had been scouting the harbor, Nerka had thrown rocks at her. "Thieving, no-good bird! Get out of here, or I'll cook you." Teakh's detective operation wasn't truly paying off.

"Ma'am," Keno said, "if you don't release some funds, he'll figure out how to earn it on his own. And you might not like how he does it."

"Threats will get you nowhere." Dyse removed a handscreen from her front pocket and stretched the frame of the screen open. "Let's be honest. Nephew, you're a smart man. I fear you'll avail yourself of a stipend and not follow through with your training." She made a note on her screen. "If you wish, I'll grant you an allowance, but it will be in the form of an advance. I'm warning you—if you fail to perform as a stud, you and your sister must repay the amount, along with interest. Talk it over with her, and take out any amount the two of you see fit."

Dyse's proposal was no better than the arrangement he already had with his sister, only now he would go into debt in his own name and take her down with him if he couldn't repay.

TEAKH SPRAWLED IN a chair in the office, still wearing his vest and old pants as Keno detailed the responsibilities of a stud. What with documentation, regulations, and interclan agreements, the business resembled fishing. Teakh's wandering mind settled once more on Angel's art, her sensuous brushwork, and her fondness for painting Seaguard lords. If only he were someone within the Seaguard.

"I'd like your advice," Teakh said.

"Is this about that assignment? Or about your finances?" Keno poured a glass of water.

"A bit of both." Teakh preferred not to discuss the inadequacies of Hairy's pornography collection. "I've got something to show you."

Keno indicated his planning frame. "Flash it up."

Teakh transferred the Noahee clan charter to Keno's planning frame. Dense flagtile text replaced the image of a man and women entwined.

"Is that what fills your jib?" Keno set his glass aside. "Looks like a contract. Noahee?"

"We're using that name. It means descendants of Noah. This is the articles of incorporation for our clan. I'm to be Seaguard chief if you and Sis agree to elect me."

Keno whistled. "That'll get you some handsome stud fees."

Teakh grimaced. "Maybe I don't want stud fees."

"How many are in your clan?"

"Three. You—if you'll join—Sis, and me."

Keno laughed and slapped his knee. "Are we trying for the smallest clan on the planet?"

"Sis is all set to petition the Queen."

"You're both shiners." Keno reached for a remote and flicked through the text, scrolling through pages of rights and responsibilities. He stopped on a section describing clan structure. "What's all this?"

"Clan offices and voting."

Keno nodded and pointed with the remote. "It says here that your clan will approve reproductive agreements."

"That's right."

Keno chuckled and tossed the remote beside the water pitcher. "I'd say your sister is aiming to seize control of your stud contracts. You've got a skirmish shaping up: Noah battling the breeders."

"I was hoping you'd agree to join. Sis and I are new to this. I'm not sure we know what we're getting into."

"Can't argue with that."

"Do you think we have a chance?"

"Not really. But I'll give you my advice. Study up on this. Know the law."

"The Noah Code?"

Keno shook his head. "I mean lawyer stuff, precedents, and litigation. Find out if anyone else has tried a clan like yours." He aimed the remote. "For starters, study up on reproductive law." He brought texts to the screen.

"I still have to read," Teakh said. "Texts don't download directly to my brain."

"You're the one planning on being a clan chief," Keno said. "Maybe you'll do better with this than the last assignment."

"I'm working on it." Founder all this complication with clan charters and contracts. What Teakh really needed was Angel, and he was working on that. He'd sent Gull to spy her out.

CHAPTER 17
Angel

G ULL REACHED HER destination in the afternoon, the flight still on time. In his quarters, Teakh sat on a meditation cushion, prepared to track down Angel. He had dragged up the name of another gallery displaying her work, this one in Shellako, a place known more for scenic waterfalls than for fine art. Gull carried a folded slip of paper on her leg, a note addressed to Matta Carrie. If Gull caught the attention of Fennako, Teakh would surely lose her to royal override, but Angel was worth the risk.

When the hatch opened and daylight streamed in, Gull flew out over bright water. The plane floated, snubbed to the dock while handlers dragged baggage from the hold. Shellako Village was strung out along a shore lined with docks, boatyards, and harbor. A steep verdant mountainside rose behind the village, with waterfalls cascading through steep gullies.

Teakh sent Gull flying over the village and located a plaza. He circled Gull over outdoor dining areas then landed on a fountain. Water bubbled from decorative stone and pattered into a catch basin. People dined at tables set out before restaurants. A breeze rippled through the trees, the shadows shifting on composite-stone paving.

Now to find the gallery. Most Fenrian villages lacked street signs. Folks expected visitors to ask directions, and that made for better town security. And to keep robotic seagulls from spying on art galleries. He'd hail for directions, but he lacked an excuse for Gull being in the area. He'd have to hunt for Binnacle Betty's Gallery on his own.

He started his search in the plaza, skirting dining tables as he sent Gull flapping from business front to business front. The diners paid no mind. Among the mostly herring gulls, her glaucous-gull size didn't stand out as all that unusual, or so Teakh hoped.

With Gull's lenses, Teakh peered through windows at goods within: clothing, knitting and weaving supplies, and restaurant tables. He identified the clan hall but saw no art galleries. He expanded his search beyond the plaza to houses with offices in the front rooms, then to the businesses catering to mariners along the waterfront: chandleries, boatyards, bachelor shops, and taverns. At the edge of town, he sent Gull soaring over greenhouses and cottages with chickens and goats in the yards.

In a garden marked off by a picket fence, Teakh spied a rusted sundial taller than a man, the gnomon pole topped by a blue-green glass sphere. He landed Gull on the pole, the oxidized metal rough against her feet. Her shadow fell on hourly graduations welded onto a steel arc. The cottage's wide covered porch sheltered potted flowers and abstract sculptures made of brightly painted steel.

Teakh sent Gull to the railing of the porch to peer through the windows. In the dim interior, he glimpsed canvases on easels, but none of them were framed. No one appeared to be home. The place seemed to be not a gallery but an art studio. The note fastened to Gull's leg chafed, and Teakh adjusted it with her bill.

Leaving the artist's studio behind, he flew back to the fountain in the plaza. Maybe the gallery had gone out of business? But no, the article had been recent. He rotated Gull's head, scanning the houses surrounding the plaza, and spied a gap between two houses. A passageway connecting the buildings arched above the opening to a side court. Teakh sent Gull to investigate.

A shop window inside the court displayed abstract steel sculptures similar to those in the cottage garden, along with wind chimes and whirligigs. A hand-lettered sign in the window gave the name of the shop: Binnacle Betty's Gallery of Arts and Crafts.

In his quarters, Teakh whooped. He'd found it. He landed Gull on the roof of an adjacent building, then he scrambled upright to balance on his crutches and stretch. Now to get inside the gallery. He seated himself again and closed his eyes, all attention on the courtyard as he waited for someone to enter or exit the shop, thus opening the door.

A woman approached, carrying a basket. Oh good, a customer. Teakh sent Gull down to the composite-stone pavement. When the customer pushed the door wide, Teakh sent Gull winging for the opening.

The customer shouted. Teakh banked Gull near a display of knit hats and landed her on a display case. Beneath Gull's webbed feet, silver jewelry gleamed through the glass top. Using Gull's beak, he pulled at the fastener on her leg. He dropped the note on the counter in front of the gallery attendant, presumably Betty. Her short black hair had gray locks along her hairline. Hopefully, given the unusual delivery of the letter, Betty would forward it to Angel. Teakh let Gull spring from the counter and perch on the hat display.

Betty backed away. "What's that bird doing in here? Just look what it did. Made a mess on the counter." She seized a rag and swung it. "Get! Foundered bird."

Teakh sent Gull fleeing to a higher perch on a stand displaying hand-painted scarves. Betty glared at Gull and snapped her rag.

"That's not poop." The customer picked up the slip and turned it over. "It's a note. That must be a carrier seagull." She waved the message. "Addressed to Matta Carrie."

"Matta Carrie?" Betty snatched the note from the visitor. "Cousin Margie's pseudonym."

Margie? Was that Angel's name?

Betty shook a finger at Gull. "You better behave. Shit in my shop and you're seagull fricassee."

Teakh gave a squawk and fluttered Gull's wings.

"What does the note say?" the customer asked.

Betty waved the folded slip. "It's for Margie. You'll have to ask her."

"I don't know why she puts on airs," the customer said. "Nothing wrong with the name Marjoram. It's a pleasant herb." Teakh nearly fell off his meditation cushion. He had Angel's name. But somehow Marjoram wasn't quite as magical as Angel or Matta Carrie. He took a deep breath, calmed himself, and slowed his heart rate.

"A nom d'artiste." Betty sighed. "I don't know how much longer she'll agree to display her paintings with us."

"Oh yes, Margie's paintings." The customer turned to the framed images on the wall.

Matta Carrie's style was unmistakable, even when depicting fishermen fully clothed in coveralls and rubber boots. Painted with sensitive strokes, two men emptied a crab pot, species *magister* by the look of the catch. Clearly Angel was an artist who shared Teakh's passion for species identification.

"They're not bad, I suppose," the customer said.

"I wish she'd paint more seascapes and at a lower price. That's what we can sell." The attendant raised a finger at Gull. "I'm warning you."

"That seagull seems to know what we're talking about," the customer said.

"It had better." Betty pocketed the note. "I'll keep this for when Margie gets back in town."

"I didn't know she was gone."

"She's always off somewhere. She's made quite a splash in Fennako City. Our local girl"—Betty put a hand to her heart—"painting royalty."

The visitor laughed. "And getting love notes delivered by seagull courier."

Teakh blushed and was relieved no one could see it. His message wasn't exactly a love note—more like a carefully worded overture.

"Carrier seagull or not, let's get that bird out of here." Betty stepped around the counter and opened the door. "Get!"

"You're scaring it," the customer said.

"Oh, all right." Betty propped the door open with a bronze starfish sculpture.

Teakh sent Gull winging into the side court. He flew her to the cottage studio and landed on the porch. He wasn't sure it was Angel's place or even if the attendant had been right about Angel being gone, but again he saw no sign that anyone was home. In a nearby yard, a dog snoozed.

In a quandary, he brought his consciousness back to his quarters. Should he use Gull to stake out the studio, which might not be Angel's at all, or should he watch the gallery? What about the ferry terminal and the stratoport docks?

Gull startled, flooding Teakh with her alarm. Something had set off her avoidance routine. He landed her on the roof before identifying the threat. The dog was awake and barking furiously. The issue settled by the dog, Teakh sent Gull flying back to the gallery. The arched entrance to the courtyard offered a more secure location for leaving Gull semi-dormant.

TEAKH TOOK A break to get a snack in the kitchen.

Keno came through the door. "You've been holed up in your room for days. What's with you?"

"Not that long," Teakh said. "I've be meditating, observing my internal tide."

Keno snorted a laugh. "You meditating? So what have you observed?"

Teakh smeared cheese on a round of pilot bread. "Actually I've been working with Gull, doing some research."

"Are you going to tell me about it?"

"I'd rather not right now." Teakh crumbled smoked salmon on top of the cheese. "It's relevant to my stud career, but I'd like to keep it private until I find out more."

"Well, don't be neglecting your training or your physical therapy."

"Aye." Teakh took a bit of the pilot bread and savored the smoky salmon and rich cheese.

THE FOLLOWING DAY, rainwater glistened on the cobblestones and dripped from the roof of the gallery. Teakh sent Gull from her roost to again search for Angel. In the plaza, chairs remained tipped against dining tables. A light misting of rain had settled over the village. Pedestrians carried bright umbrellas. Pinks, reds, and royal blues seemed to glow against the gray mist. He left the plaza area and returned to what he hoped was Angel's studio.

Gull landed on the large sundial. Garden flowers drooped in the rain. The neighboring yard was now vacant of dogs. Teakh sent Gull to search along the waterfront then across the bay to the stratoport docks before returning her to her roost. Still, he saw no sign of Angel. He shook raindrops from Gull's wings then preened and applied oil to her feathers.

In the afternoon, the weather cleared and the sun came out. Waitresses righted the chairs and shook rain from awnings. They set yellow, purple, and pink flowers in vases on the tables.

Teakh continued his search. In an alley behind a restaurant, birds squabbled over a fish carcass. Gull sent him a jolt of excitement. She was programmed to like the taste of fish and when she liked something, so did Teakh. He landed her and made a run at the mob, mouth open, screaming, and wings out. The real seagulls retreated before the bluff. Teakh identified the genus as rockfish, *Sebastes*. He left the carcass to the hungry birds.

A woman laughed. He banked Gull, and there was Angel, eating in the plaza. Quivering with Teakh's joy, Gull landed on a nearby table, wiped her feet and beak on a napkin, then fluttered to Angel's table and landed beside her plate.

She was beautiful! Her reddish-brown hair was held back with a silver clip, her lips glossed with red. Excitement tingled through Gull's body. Depths! She was reacting to Teakh's emotions. Neck undulating, she raised her beak toward the enticing red.

Angel's table companion yelped. "Get! Shoo!"

Teakh startled, losing control of Gull. Gripped by realistic seagull instincts, she reached for Angel's mouth, seeking to tap her teeth. Good Danna! Gull was reacting to the color as if it were the red spot on a seagull's bill. Angel closed her lips and batted at Gull with a wave of her hand.

He forced Gull to move away, stepping her carefully between plates and utensils. Teakh reined in Gull's spiraling

150

attraction and his own excitement. He'd found his Angel. He could watch her forever, the flutter of her fingers, her luscious red lips.

The companion put a finger to her chin. "I think it's taken with you."

Angel set a paper tablet on the table. "Is that truly a seagull?" She scratched Gull's neck, her touch delicate and delicious.

Gull, shuddering with Teakh's pleasure, rubbed against Angel's hand. Angel lowered her head ever so slightly. Losing himself in Gull, Teakh stepped aboard, enjoying Angel's glossy, smooth hair on Gull's webbed feet. The silver hairclip clasped in Angel's auburn tresses was similar to the bracelets on display at Binnacle Betty's.

Angel straightened. "Take a look at this. A seagull hat."

The companion laughed. "How stylish. But what if it poops on you?"

Angel shook her head, and Gull sprang away. Teakh landed Gull beside a vase of chrysanthemums on a nearby table.

Angel straightened her hairclip. "What an odd incident."

"Odd? What a filthy bird. That's what gulls do when they... oh, you don't want to know."

Teakh felt his face heat, his embarrassment acute. Gull had misinterpreted his emotions, or maybe correctly interpreted them, and had acted like a bird caught up in the passion of mating.

Angel's laughter bubbled. "I'm more accustomed to human admirers." She beckoned to Gull. "Let me take a look at you."

Teakh searched for some way to make amends. He spied a floral arrangement. With Gull's bill, he plucked a chrysanthemum from the vase. He flew to Angel's table then dropped the blossom beside her plate.

"Why, thank you." Angel accepted the flower and pulled the stem through her fingers. "May I make a sketch of you?" She set the chrysanthemum aside to sharpen a pencil, leaving peels of wood on her plate.

Teakh held Gull motionless.

Angel's pencil scratched her pad. "Impressive. Quite handsome."

Teakh saluted Angel with Gull's beak.

"Show me your wings." Angel's pencil moved swiftly, darkening the wingtips, capturing the fleeting movement as Teakh extended and fluttered Gull's wings.

The companion stared at Gull. "That isn't a seagull."

"Of course it isn't." Angel kept sketching. "It's a Seaguard telechiric."

She'd found him out, and it was his own fault. In showing off, he'd revealed details of Gull's construction to Angel's expert eye. Danna! What a wily woman. Just his type.

"A drone?" the companion asked. "What's it doing here?"

"Offering me a flower." Angel continued drawing. "When have you seen a drone like this one? It's perfect. Even smells like fish."

The companion glared at Gull. "Why are you spying on us?"

Founder it all, she thought him a complete lubber.

The companion touched her shoulder, activating her comset. "I'm reporting it to the authorities."

"It hasn't done anything wrong." Angel smudged the drawing with her thumb, streaking the wings, lending an impression of movement. "Unless art is a crime."

"That bird made a mess of your hair."

Angel laughed. "It also gave me a kiss and a flower." With her pencil, she scumbled the drawing, darkening the background. "Surely one of my fans."

"If a Seaguardsman likes your paintings, he's queer," the companion said.

"For appreciating art?" Angel worked the drawing. "Then all my fans are strange."

"Shellako Seaguard should be informed."

"'Lord Shellako,'" Angel intoned, "'I'd like to report a strange art patron with feathers.' He'll take it as a joke." She glanced sideways at Gull. "You might want to leave before my friend insults us further or reports you as deranged wildlife. No appreciation of painting or mimetic art." She dashed a final line on her sketch. "Thank you. You're an excellent model."

Teakh raised Gull's beak to Angel one last time and sent Gull springing from the table. He circled Gull above Shellako Village. To follow Angel would be rude after she'd dismissed Gull. Teakh had been rude already, and Angel had been remarkably tolerant.

He hadn't controlled Gull's impulses. If only he hadn't used Gull to sample that fish. Good Danna! A seagull with bad breath! Standing on Angel's head? He shouldn't have let Gull do that at all. Teakh was sunk. Angel or her companion could report Gull to Shellako Seaguard. Worst of all, Angel might never agree to meet with Teakh again.

Sunk! Fratricidal sunk!

CHAPTER 18
Jewelry

NOTHING FOR IT, he'd have to apologize. Maybe a bracelet from Binnacle Betty's? He'd have to make the purchase on the line of credit approved by Aunt Dyse. Angel would recognize the jewelry and know where it had been purchased. She very likely considered the silversmith a friend. Teakh landed Gull on the fountain.

He'd send in an order, but he'd need photographs so he could specify the correct bracelet. He flew into the side court and landed Gull on the pavement. Now to convince Betty to let Gull inside again.

Teakh pecked at the door. Betty, busy straightening the art in her shop, didn't respond. Transmitting desire for the bracelets, Teakh sent Gull into the air. She circled the courtyard and flew straight for her own reflection in the shop window. Gull struck the glass with her chest, the smack painful. The glass reverberated, and Gull dropped to the pavement. Teakh clutched at his own chest until the pain subsided.

Betty came to the door and opened it. "Damn bird! What a lubber!"

Teakh shrugged Gull's feathers into place and strutted past Betty's feet.

"Just where do you think you're going?"

Teakh held up Gull's foot as if it still had a message attached.

"You delivered it." Betty let the door close.

Teakh sent Gull fluttering to the jewelry case. Her webbed feet spread on the cool glass. Teakh considered the bracelets, each a silver cuff gleaming against black velvet. Some were elegant bands of beaten silver. Others were chased with zoomorphic patterns: dolphins and birds roiled together. He admired several engraved with seagulls and brittle stars, wings and arms flowing together, the space between becoming eggs or enclosing cabochons of jasper. He positioned Gull's head and photographed his favorites—the bracelets without the stones, just the interplay of pattern over silver, the engraving dark with silver oxide.

With the photos recorded, Teakh sent Gull from the case and allowed her feelings of entrapment to emerge. Out. She wanted out. Gull beat a wing against the door.

"Oh, all right." Betty opened it, and Teakh flew Gull from the shop.

At the stratoport terminal, Gull landed and tucked her head under her wing. Teakh used his implant to check for flights from Shellako to Ordako. None were scheduled in the next couple of hours. Teakh took a deep breath then composed a message to Betty. He included the photos of his choice of jewelry and asked her to send a gift-wrapped bracelet to Marjoram, the talented painter, along with a note.

Hailing Matta Carrie. Admirer here.

My deepest apologies. I was so taken with your beauty that my gull acted according to her programming in expressing my admiration. I most sincerely hope she did not cause embarrassment. My intentions were only to meet a woman whom I have long admired. I take full responsibility and will correct any errors in her programming.

Please accept this bracelet as a token of my esteem.
Humbly yours. Sending.

Teakh again brought up the photo of Angel's bracelet, a slim cuff of silver with seagulls and starfish. He wrote similar belated apologies to Jeena and Reez and asked that the gifts be sent to them care of Idylko hospital, Idylko Village. The fourth bracelet, larger and in a more masculine style, he had sent to Jamie C/O Salty Hound Tavern, Dojko Village, Dojko Fjord.

He liked to think of his beloved women wearing similar jewelry, linking all of them together, and he'd be able to see evidence of their bond on his wrist, a symbol of his commitment. Now he had to get Gull home.

CHAPTER 19
Baggage hold

TEAKH CIRCLED GULL above the terminal and stratoport docks in Shellako. Two planes floated beside the pier, one craft with passengers loading and a mound of baggage waiting on carts.

Teakh checked his itinerary. He was running late. No time to fly into the terminal. Getting her through doorways had proved difficult and risky. Gull was likely to attract unnecessary attention or get caught inside as she waited for a door to open. A baggage handler hefted luggage into the plane. Teakh waited until the handler stepped away, then he sent Gull through the opening into the hold. As baggage was added, Teakh squirmed Gull out of the way, barely avoiding being crushed by a large case.

With Gull secured against a dunnage partition, Teakh put her on dormant mode and walked to the lap pool. Gull wouldn't arrive in Ordako until after supper. From there, she'd have to fly to Dojko.

Teakh swam, ate supper with the other men, and helped clean up. During evening observances, as the men sat on mats and meditation cushions, their breathing loud and even, Teakh merged with Gull. The hold remained dark, the vibration of the plane steady and unchanging. He accessed the Fennako world clock for the time. Gull's plane was scheduled to arrive soon, but the hum of the plane remained monotonous and unchanging. Maybe the stratoplane had encountered a headwind.

Teakh continued his pretense of meditating until the

closing prayers were chanted. Still monitoring Gull, he stowed his mat and cushion then crutched to his quarters.

Seated on his bunk, he shook his head. According to the ETA, Gull should have already arrived in Ordako, but her view remained dark—unless she used infrared—and the plane hadn't descended. Teakh paced the room, crutches thumping the floor. Gull should have landed by now. Depths! Where in Poseidon's realm was she? When would the plane land and where?

He sat on his bed.

Keno knocked and hailed, *Permission to enter?*

Teakh transmitted to unlock the door. *Come on in.*

"Gimp, did you actually eat anything for supper?"

Teakh's brow ached. "Aye. Some soup."

"You didn't eat all of it, and you've hardly been out of your room. If you're sick, I need to know."

"Why? So you can put me in quarantine?" Teakh flopped against his pillow. He was sick all right, sick with worry.

Keno glanced around the room. "I'm concerned about you." His gaze fastened on the empty charging niche. He closed the door. "Where's your gull?" Keno didn't miss much.

"I've been using her to do some research," Teakh said. Depths! He should've gone inside to check for the correct dock.

"What's going on?"

"I put Gull on a stratoplane." Teakh gripped his hair. "In, uh...the baggage compartment. No ticket." He attempted a smile. "On the way back, I must've put her on the wrong plane. It hasn't landed yet."

"Do you know what flight she's on?" Keno asked.

Teakh rubbed his temple. "Several planes were loading baggage. I sure don't want to notify the airline."

"Just what kind of research were you doing?"

"I've become a patron of the arts. Gull is my agent." Teakh feigned a lightheartedness he didn't feel.

Keno laughed.

"I saw the paintings of Matta Carrie," Teakh said.

"Oh!" All merriment gone, Keno crossed his arms. "So you're still thinking of modeling for her?"

"I was scoping out the prospect."

"Gimp, you have a taste for trouble."

"Could be. Right now I don't care. I just want Gull back."

"Do you want me to wait up with you?" Keno asked.

"I'll be all right," Teakh said. He wasn't, but he didn't want Keno hanging around or asking questions about Gull visiting Shellako and meeting with the artist herself.

After Keno departed, Teakh lay in his berth. He'd set Gull on partial alert, conserving her power.

The light of Luna Minora crossed the floor. Teakh shivered. The superstitious believed Luna Minora to be the moon of chaos and that sleeping in the light of the little moon brought misfortune, but then, Teakh couldn't sleep.

Gull was part of him, as necessary as his hands or his feet. No, even more necessary. Without her, he had no hope of becoming a detective, nor could he consider himself Seaguard in any way that was meaningful. He couldn't afford to replace her. His hard-won neurological pathways would atrophy, a lifetime of training lost, and he'd face years of phantom pain.

TEAKH SPENT HOURS tossing and turning or staring into a hold visible only in infrared before Gull's plane began its rattling descent. In Dojko, the moon had set, and darkness filled his quarters. He yawned.

When the hatch opened, Teakh flew Gull out of the plane, dodging past a lone baggage handler on an otherwise deserted pier. Teakh perched Gull on the canopy of a covered gangway.

Moonlight glowed off snowcapped peaks and glinted off the water, but he didn't know the name of the mountain range or the body of water. Luna Majora was still high in this place, wherever it was. Above the peaks, a pale remainder of sunset lingered in the sky. Judging by the high angle of the moon, Gull was somewhere to the west—a long way to the west.

Lying on his bunk, Teakh stared at the clerestory window and beyond at twinkling stars. In Dojko, the big moon had set hours ago. He made calculations. Good Danna! Gull must have travelled a quarter of the way around the planet.

Teakh launched Gull from her perch and flew along the waterfront, passing above piers and warehouses. At the stratoplane terminal, he could check the posting of arrival and departure times, but there was no terminal. He circled back. The airplane was taxiing away, trailing a white moonlit wake.

What now? He landed on a warehouse roof and considered his options. For the night, he wanted Gull out of sight and out of the weather. Clouds flitted across the sky. How likely was rain? Not knowing where Gull was, he couldn't check the weather report, and he couldn't request such information from local Seaguard without revealing that Gull was in the area.

He sent her to the underside of a fueling dock to crouch on a girder. Gull would be away from dogs and other seagulls. It was the best he could do. With the two moons not yet in alignment, the tide wouldn't rise to the height of Gull's perch. He gave a last look around, tucked her head under a wing, and placed Gull in dormancy.

Exhausted, he pulled a blanket around himself and fell asleep. He awoke to a hail. *Keno here. You coming to morning observances?*

Teakh groaned. *Sink observances.*

And your seagull?

She's not attending.

Do you know where she's at?

An air terminal west of here. A quarter of the way around the planet. Got stratoplane lag. Longitudinal dissonance, that's what it was. *Do me a favor. Let on that I'm not feeling well. Headache or something. My leg is hurting.*

Teakh signed off and rolled onto his side.

Gull became alert by midmorning Dojko time but before sunrise far to the west. A breeze blew brisk and cold. Above Gull, a wheelbarrow rumbled down the gangway, pushed by a man with heavy footsteps. In the soft pre-dawn light, Gull flew out from under the fuel dock. Teakh lay in bed, the bright light of day streaming through the clerestory windows.

Gull soared over cottages of a good-sized village. At a small boat harbor, he searched transoms for clan designation. Most of the craft bore the letters Ultimate, Gulf, Hotel. With Gull perched on the superstructure of a trawler, Teakh used his implant to bring up a registry of clans. Ugashko? Holy Poseidon! He'd never even heard of that clan or their territory. If he mailed her, she could be confiscated on any segment of the journey, but most likely she wouldn't even make it out of Ugashko. The postmistress would notify local Seaguard.

Supplied with the clan name, he checked for direct flights between Ugashko Fjord and Ordako Harbor.

AFTER NEARLY THREE days of travel, Gull arrived at Ordako. There had been no direct flights, so Teakh had perfected sneaking Gull in and out of terminals and baggage holds.

Teakh lay on his bunk. Her power having run down, she was exhausted. Teakh had felt her fatigue as lethargy as he dragged himself through training and chores. He'd slept fitfully, often moving Gull on or off planes in the middle of the night. He still had to hop her home to Dojko. If she lost all power during flight, she'd fall into the ocean to be swamped or eaten. If she lost power while stowed away on a shuttle boat, she'd be mistaken for a real seagull and be thrown overboard to the same fate.

If he went to Seaguard, Gull would be confiscated. Maybe he could get help from another quarter. He sat up and hailed Lugo. He often fished out toward Ordako, and he considered Gull's activities to be, as he'd said it, "part of the game."

Jamie here, sent Teakh. *Got some equipment out at Ordako Harbor. Having trouble recovering it.* Teakh slumped, head on hands.

What kind of equipment?

Teakh closed his eyes. *Big herring gull. You know her.*

That gull? Yours?

She's a drone.

No kidding? Huh. You're Seaguard?

More or less. Mostly less.

Nice gull.

She's run out of power. Nearly run out. I sent her to court my girl and had trouble getting back. Gull is unregistered, so I can't go to Ordako Seaguard.

How did it go with the girl?

Some good, some bad. Can you get to Ordako Bay?

Here's what we'll do. You know that rock out at the mouth of Ordako Passage? If you can get her there, I'll pick her up.

Teakh checked Gull's power level. *What do you have for*

wind speed and direction?

Lugo gave the information.

If the wind doesn't change, she'll make it, sent Teakh, *and be there in about an hour.*

Okay. I'll pick her up there. Tide carry you, Lugo said.

Tide carry. Teakh prayed his luck and the wind would hold. If a Seaguard telechiric were lost, the man's attachment could be transferred to another, but Teakh had no other device.

He activated Gull, forcing her out of conservation mode. She flew slowly with heavy wings. He tried to use dynamic gliding, utilizing subtle differences in wind speed, rising into faster-moving wind then dropping. Theoretically, Gull could travel this way without using any power. Theoretically. Her vision had been reduced to black and white.

The rock appeared, a low jumble of wet stone topped by the bright square of a navigational aid. A wave broke against the miniscule island. Gull eased downward, landed, and hunkered behind an outcropping. Wind blew cold, ruffling her feathers. Clouds lowered, and a patter of rain misted the rock. Gull lost consciousness. Teakh's fingers and toes tingled. A sensation of numbness spread over his body.

Lugo hailed. *I'm at the rock. Where's your gull at?*

Northwest side.

Teakh forced Gull alert.

Can you see her? sent Teakh.

Her cry came out as a whimper. Gull huddled against the cold rock, too tired to even stand. Where was Lugo? Teakh again had her screech to attract attention, but she produced only a weak mew. Danna! What if Lugo couldn't find her?

"Hey, bird! Hey, seagull!" shouted Lugo. He appeared, a rubber boot visible to Gull as he stepped over a rock.

I'm sure glad to see you, sent Teakh.

Lugo picked up Gull and cradled her in a blanket before she lost all power.

CHAPTER 20
Negotiating

TEAKH SWAM LAPS. After nearly losing Gull, his arms and legs still tingled. He wouldn't be hopping planes for a while, not in the guise of Gull.

A hail whispered in his head. *Keno here. Your aunt's waiting in the parlor. You've got a progress check on the calendar.*

Depths! The tide for that meeting already?

Aye. Best come to the front and get it over with. Iris is chatting with her right now.

Teakh hauled himself out of the pool and gathered his crutches. He considered presenting himself naked just to make another bid for wardrobe funds. Nah, too blatant. He went to his quarters for a shirt and a pair of pants, the ones with the mended rip.

Iris and Keno were seated with Dyse when Teakh arrived, the three of them sipping broth and nibbling on crackers and cheese. Iris glanced toward Keno. If the pair of siblings was anything like Teakh and Sis, a subtle signal had passed between them. A handscreen rested near Dyse's elbow, as if for recording wagers. Oh yes, justice poker—the goal was to achieve a mutually agreeable outcome while taking the entire pot.

Dyse leaned back. "Well, well, here's our boy."

Teakh grunted. "What are you about?"

"I understand you've been doing some bodybuilding," Dyse said. "I'd like to see."

Frowning, Teakh crossed his arms. "You want a striptease?"

"I'd like some proof we're getting our money's worth. I

expect you to be ready for the spawn."

"Is that a joke?" Teakh asked. "You're not paying for anything."

"As long as you're here, you're not contributing taxes to clan coffers," Dyse said. "Clan Ralko is losing money."

With a nod, Keno acknowledged Teakh. "We've been working on conditioning, flexibility, and body awareness."

Teakh pulled off his shirt. He sure didn't have the bulk of Pector or Ripple, but he'd give her an eyeful. Water from his wet hair trickled down his back. He brought his hip and leg forward, displaying the rip on the side of his pants.

Ignoring the tattered clothing, Dyse squinted at his chest. "You've made progress, I suppose."

Teakh sat down, facing Dyse.

She tapped her handscreen. "We've got you listed in *Dale's Men* and posted on Kordelko Auctions. We really should have some proof that you behave as predicted. Could you maybe do something altruistic?"

Keno said, "He did risk himself putting out that fire."

The conversation was headed the wrong direction.

"Too bad the injury wasn't worse—maybe a compound fracture. We'll have to make the most of it." Dyse glanced at Teakh. "Go ahead, rescue some schoolchildren from a sinking ship, and some puppies, too, while you're at it. That's what we need. Now about your appearance."

Teakh broke a cracker. "I'm unable to dress properly."

Dyse fluttered her hand as if shooing gnats. "You need better muscle definition or nothing you wear will look good."

She squinted at the patch of hair over Teakh's heart. He covered it with his hand. Pector had been ribbing him about his scanty chest fur, trying to convince him to get it waxed off.

"Bulky muscles?" Keno said. "Teakh shouldn't look like he spends most of his time weightlifting. He needs the appearance of working Seaguard. That's why I have him swimming."

"The wet hair is an interesting touch." Dyse patted her own hair, dyed a conventional dark brown but with the roots showing gray. "If our boy is supposed to resemble working Seaguard, he needs a better haircut, and that beard must go."

She scowled. "Too much like a fisherman."

"Later." Teakh preferred his hair that way. As an ordinary fisherman, he didn't attract attention. But they could argue about his appearance endlessly—she wasn't going to give in. He took a different tack. "How are you doing with my contract?"

"That's contracts plural. You'll have a different agreement with each client."

"But I reckon they're all about the same, and you've worked out what we'll be asking for."

"Aye," Keno said. "She and Iris have been making plans, calculating the optimum number of liaisons."

"You don't have to put it so coldly," Iris said. "We're going for a low number of high-paying liaisons. I believe Teakh will prefer it that way."

"How about if you include me in the discussion?" Teakh said. "I'll decide what I prefer."

Dyse frowned but passed the handscreen.

Teakh read through the proposed contract and dropped numbers into his neuro matrix to make calculations. What with taxes, finder's fee, and compensation to Dyse, Ralko had the largest share of the take. He transferred the matrix to the handscreen and pointed at his meager share. "I don't like it."

Dyse compressed her lips. "You're a rookie."

"I won't be for long."

Dyse drew back, one hand to her sternum. "You're already commanding prices commensurate with fees for top professional studs, experienced studs. The contract is generous. More than generous."

Teakh set the handscreen aside. "After Iris and Keno take their cut, you take your share, and we pay clan fees, there's not much left for me. I'm doing the work and taking on the greatest financial risk. If I borrow money, I pay interest to Ralko." He shook his head.

"You're supposed to be altruistic," Dyse said.

Altruistic? She'd asked him to prove it. He didn't have any puppies available, but if he became a stud, he'd be producing his own children. "Altruistic maybe, but not stupid. I need money to support my kids."

Brow furrowed, Dyse shook her head in confusion. "That's the responsibility of the mothers' clans."

"Put it in the contract," countered Teakh. "My concern proves my worth."

Dyse grunted. "It's not dramatic enough."

"But it is why he's worth so much," Iris said.

Dyse said, "It's why he's so much trouble."

Iris furrowed her brow and touched Dyse's arm. "My friend, set your feelings aside. It all depends on how we trim the sails."

"I wish I'd gone into furniture sales." Dyse exhaled, fanning her flushed cheeks. "Valuable because he wants more money from his customers. It doesn't make a dab of sense."

"He follows the Noah Code," Iris said. "Surely you can't fault him for that."

"Tenth precept," offered Keno. "Educate your children."

"Fifth precept. Respect your elders," countered Dyse.

Teakh inserted himself into the discussion. "And I believe my ancestors were Jamie Noah and his wife Fenna Lee Smith."

Iris pulled a handscreen toward her. "Let's work this out. How about an educational trust fund for each child?"

"But—" If it was in a trust fund, Teakh couldn't access it.

"It addresses Teakh's concern and demonstrates it's for his children, not for him," Iris said, "proving his worth."

Danna! That wasn't what Teakh was after. He needed the money to make an impression on Angel.

Dyse swiped her handscreen away from Teakh. Iris jotted on her handscreen, and Dyse jotted on hers. She said, "An educational trust fund for his daughters."

"My sons too," Teakh said.

"But your sons will be Seaguard." Dyse tapped her stylus. "They don't need more education than that."

"They shouldn't have to be Seaguard." He didn't want them trapped as he was. If he couldn't escape his clan's dictates, he could at least give his sons the freedom he'd never had.

"You're just being stubborn," Dyse said. "Fishermen or Seaguard—what else is there for men to do?"

Teakh said, "If we had the education, we could be

physicians, engineers, even clan matriarchs." He took a breath. He'd stepped into the depths and might as well swim.

"Only a woman can be a matriarch," Dyse said.

"Clan leader then," Teakh countered.

"Educating boys is a waste of resources." Dyse set her handscreen aside. "It's unseemly. They run off to sea, taking their education with them."

"I don't give an eel's rasp what's seemly." Teakh's anger burned through his calm. "Each of my sons gets an education, or I'm not your stud."

Dyse glanced from Keno to Iris. "All right. Requested by our Noah man himself. Education trust funds for both boys and girls."

Teakh shook his head. "Only half of a child's genes come from the father. If we aim for Noah children, the dams must be as good as the sire. What assurance can you give me?"

Dyse chuckled, stylus poised. "You're resuming the Noah Project?" She scribbled. "We'll do it. Breed for Noah alleles. What a status symbol! A clan daughter who qualifies for the services of Noah. Every clan will be after you, the ultimate trophy stud."

Was that how she saw him? He'd only wanted the best for himself and his family.

KENO AND TEAKH returned to studio. Teakh caught sight of himself in a mirror, his beard still scruffy, but his chest and shoulders solidly muscular. Balanced on crutches, he straightened and held his head high, imitating a lord in one of Matta Carrie's paintings. Keno glanced his way and nodded. Flexing an arm, Teakh tried one of Ripple's favorite poses.

Keno laughed.

Teakh dropped his arm. "Dyse is right. I need to work on bodybuilding."

Keno shook his head. "You have muscles from real work. That's good enough."

Would it be good enough for Angel? What did Teakh have to show for himself? He'd nearly lost Gull, and he wasn't much of a fisheries detective. He hadn't caught any lawbreakers in months. "My muscles are from using crutches."

"That, and swimming," Keno said.

"What's the use in that? If I'm going to sell myself as a stud, I've got to be good at something." He wouldn't admit it to her face, but he agreed with Dyse.

"How about competitive swimming?" suggested Keno. "You might surprise yourself. Come along with the team to swim meets."

Well, that did give Teakh an excuse to get out of Dojko.

"You've got grit: shirtless, barefoot, and on crutches, demanding rights for men." Keno laughed.

Teakh doubted it would be enough to impress Angel.

CHAPTER 21
Rescue

RAIN PATTERED ON the high windows of Teakh's quarters, but his attention was with Gull, flying over the inlet as she followed the Dojko fishing fleet. Clouds scudded over gray seas. Teakh enjoyed the routine of using Gull for her intended purpose. He'd selected her species, glaucous gull, for ability to fly in foul weather. In arctic conditions, no gull was better. But he hadn't caught a lawbreaker in months.

Teakh landed her in the superstructure of Captain Jake's *Bekra Irene*. Gull clutched a crosstree spar and surveyed the rigging and the deck below.

Bekra Irene dragged troll lines from her outrigger poles. At the stern, a fisherman in an orange slicker tended the power girdies controlling the lines. Unseen below the waves, the lines drew twirling dodgers and flashers, attracting salmon to baited smart hooks.

Teakh prayed to Danna that Jake was breaking the law by doctoring his hooks. Sometimes fishermen jammed the hook sensors with fragments of a licensed salmon run. If Teakh found *Bekra Irene's* actual catch contained protected species or runs, he'd nail Jake.

But seas were building, and *Bekra Irene* brought in her lines. The wind buffeted Gull as she clung to the crosstree. Rain clouds lowered, and on the deck, the two men stowed gear. Teakh wouldn't send Gull close to identify Captain Jake. Best to keep his surveillance clandestine. A man went into the deckhouse, then *Bekra Irene* came about. Gull flapped her wings, fighting to maintain balance while the boat yawed.

Bekra Irene slammed into a heavy sea, a great wall of water. The wave exploded and broke over the bow. Teakh shivered. As water flooded from the decks, pouring through scuppers and completely over the bulwarks, it washed the man away. Teakh waited for a response from below—a door opening, a slowing of the propulsors—but she continued on her way. The man drifted, a scrap of orange bobbing in the wild gray seas.

He would surely drown or succumb to exposure, but if Teakh reported a man overboard, Dojko Seaguard would identify Gull as an unregistered telechiric. They'd confiscate her, just as Sergeant Fennako had warned. They might even contact Fennako for royal override. Teakh would face years of tingling limbs and phantom pain. As if he'd lost a limb, he'd be crippled.

The flicker of orange dropped farther astern. Teakh couldn't let him die. He hailed the boat. Bekra Irene. *Man overboard. Starboard side. You have a man overboard. Avast! Man overboard!*

No response. Sink it all! Teakh dropped Gull from the crosstree to the pilothouse. She landed on a precarious ledge, the windshield sloping outward above her. A man gripping the wheel looked up, surprise on his face—Captain Jake. Gull beat against the windshield, flapping and screeching.

Teakh transmitted. *Man overboard! Man overboard! Man overboard!*

Jake's marine-com must be turned down or malfunctioning. Teakh lunged Gull toward the location of the unit on the console, driving her beak against the glass.

Jake flipped a switch, and the windshield wipers activated, sweeping across the glass and knocked Gull from her ledge.

The door to the bridge opened. "Go away! Get!"

Teakh lunged Gull at a hanging life ring. She seized its grab line and dragged the ring from its hanger. It thumped on the deck.

"Stupid bird!" Jake picked up the ring.

Damn you, Jake. Teakh took off, desperate to track the overboard fisherman. The shock from immersion alone could kill a man.

He let Gull drop behind *Bekra Irene* to fly above the roiling seas. Maybe the man had a locator beacon. Maybe it was already activated. Teakh monitored the emergency channel and received nothing. If the man didn't have a beacon, chances were that he didn't have a life vest either.

White caps crested the waves, an endless expanse of roiling seas, mountains of gray water and spume. Teakh, the only witness to the accident, hunted for a miniscule speck of orange, the man's hood.

In his quarters, Teakh shivered and slumped on his bunk. Seaguard must be informed. They could bring in esskips and swarms of drones to fly search patterns.

Resigned to losing Gull, he transmitted, *Mayday. Mayday. Mayday. All stations. We have a man overboard. From Dojko* Bekra Irene. *Delta. Juliet.* Bekra Irene. *Delta. Juliet. Bekra Irene.*

This is Dojko Seaguard Command, came a response.

Dojko. Man overboard. He fell from fishing vessel Bekra Irene. Bekra Irene *is underway and not responding to hails.*

Acknowledge. Do you have the victim in sight?

Negative.

Rescue craft deployed. Attempting to contact Bekra Irene.

Fighting a cross wind, Teakh continued his search of the storm-tossed seas. Then he spied the fisherman, drifting passively, only his head and the collar of his life vest above water. Thank Danna, the man *had* worn his life vest. *Victim sighted.* Teakh activated Gull's locator beacon. *Mark my location.*

Was the man dead already? Teakh tilted Gull's wings to circle, screaming as Teakh transmitted her coordinates. How long before Seaguard arrived?

He sent Gull skimming low then plopped her on the water beside the man. Paddling with her feet, Teakh faced Gull into an oncoming wave. It broke, sending Gull topsy-turvy. He righted her and blinked, then peered beneath the man's hood. Good Danna! Chuck! Only the other day they'd been drinking together at the tavern.

Chuck lifted his head, his face gray, teeth chattering, eyes wide.

Squawk! Teakh paddled closer and nudged Chuck, who grunted and lethargically splashed with a hand.

171

Seaguard sent, *This is Dojko patrol leader. Arriving from the southeast.*

Gull sprang from the water, and Teakh sent her soaring upward. He turned her against the wind, fighting to stay in position over Chuck. Teakh blinked to clear Gull's lenses and squinted into the driving rain. *Bekra Irene* had disappeared into the gray fog.

Dojko, sent Teakh, *look for a large herring gull in flight. She's directly above the victim.*

A gust knocked Gull out of position. Teakh fought to bring her around. Wings pumping, he struggled to catch up with Chuck.

A trio of blue esskips skimmed over the waves. *Seagull sighted.*

This was the end of Gull for Teakh. He sighed and wiped a tear from his eye. Chuck would never know what Teakh had given up.

The esskips banked then dropped to the water and slowed. The canopy of an esskip slid open. A Seaguardsman wearing a Dojko-blue life vest and parka stood in the cockpit and held the orange bag of a throw line.

Victim to your ten starboard, sent Teakh.

The Seaguardsman shaded his eyes with his hand. "Hallo! Swimmer."

Chuck raised an arm.

Teakh landed Gull on the coaming of the esskip cockpit. The Seaguardsman glanced toward her, then as the esskip pulsed forward, the Seaguardsman flung the bag. It arced over Chuck, trailing an orange-and-white rope.

"Grab the line!" shouted the Seaguardsman.

Teakh sent Gull from the gunwale to the water to nudge the floating rope toward Chuck. He wrapped a hand around the line, and the Seaguardsman drew Chuck to safety.

Gull flapped her wings and took off. As she flew, Teakh sent, *Hospitality. Request anonymity.* It was worth a try. Maybe the Seaguard would honor his request and let Gull go without repercussions.

WHEN SHE'D RETURNED and glided down from the open clerestory, Teakh stowed Gull and left his room, the shift of his awareness jarring. While he'd been flying, a troupe of men had arrived. They carried baggage through the side door and crowded the entranceway, dripping rainwater. For hours, Teakh had been focused on the wind and waves. Now he was just Gimp, standing in the foyer as a bunch of other studs took up residence in the gym.

A bulky man pounded Keno on the back. "Pretty Boy! What are you about? Ready for the spawn?"

"Randy, you're the same as ever." Keno grinned. "And your revue troupe?"

Men crowded forward even as Teakh shrank back. Maybe he'd go back to his quarters. After the exhausting day, he wasn't prepared to trade boasts.

"They're a fine bunch." Randy slapped his nearest companion on the rump, his gaze challenging Keno. It traveled over Keno's nakedness, who didn't flinch from the scrutiny. "You're looking good yourself." Randy's attention shifted to Teakh.

Keno rested a hand on Teakh's shoulder. "This here is Gimp."

Teakh straightened. Only the day before, he'd received the go-ahead to leave behind the crutches and brace.

Randy squinted, and his gaze dropped in a fleeting glance at Teakh's groin. "Where'd you get that moniker?"

Teakh crossed his arms. "Busted my leg."

"We'll have to give you a new name. Something more fitting for such a manly studlet."

Teakh cleared his throat.

Keno stepped back. "Gimp, meet Randy, Brawny, Solid, and—" Keno stopped at the young man who'd been goosed by Randy. "Welcome. I don't have your handle yet."

"Buttcakes. We're calling him Buttcakes," shouted someone.

Teakh figured he'd come out pretty well with the nickname Gimp.

The troupe lugged their gear into the mirrored studio, taking it over.

Keno stood at the door to his office and said, "Gimp, we need to talk."

Teakh went inside, still dazed by the pounding of wind and waves.

Keno closed the door. "I had a hail from Dojko chief."

Teakh swallowed. "Lord Dojko?"

"He received a man-overboard call."

Behind Keno, a window looked out on the weight room, where studs worked out. Teakh kept his expression bland, but his heart thudded. His day would end with the loss of Gull. He'd be trapped without the freedom to fly beyond the gym.

Inexplicably, Keno's eyes sparkled. "There's been a flurry of bidding over your services. Kordelko Auctions."

What did Gull have to do with Teakh's services? His mind reeled. "I don't understand. There's no bulletin out on me? What did you tell Lord Dojko?"

"That you live here and follow the Noah Code. You've just proved your genetics as authentic. You follow the second precept to assist strangers in need. Apparently Lord Dojko passed that along the Network."

"Chuck is no stranger," Teakh said.

Keno barked a laugh. "He's no stranger because you befriended him. I set my net that you know the name of every fisherman in Dojko."

Teakh also knew their boats, the names of their sweethearts, and what kind of gear each boat was running. "I was hoping Chuck and Jake would break the law, then I'd nail them."

"You had Gull out on patrol. That's what Seaguard does." Keno grinned, his white teeth contrasting with his dark beard. "One hell of a good publicity stunt."

Teakh shook his head. "How do you reckon?"

"It's like this. Seaguard chiefs talk to their womenfolk, the ones who decide on fathers for the next generation of Seaguardsmen. A few of the chiefs are women. You couldn't have planned it better. A few months ago, Lord Dojko received a query from a Fennako Seaguard woman regarding a seagull mimic. The request was from none other than Princess Mareen Fennako, chief of Fennako City police."

Princess? Did Keno mean the Fennako officer who'd controlled the flock of drones? Teakh's face heated with embarrassment over his callow excuses. Princess Fennako hadn't been kidding when she'd indicated her rank was higher than sergeant. Was it possible she was now bidding on his services? He wasn't entirely comfortable with the prospect. "Is this good?"

"Royal interest is extraordinary," Keno said. "You're years younger than the other guys in the gym. After that flurry of bidding, you're also worth more. You could become a target."

Teakh's relief was fleeting. "A target for what?"

"Teasing, hazing, you name it. You've instituted a requirement that a woman guarantee an education for her child. That catches on, and the price of stud services will jump without the studs getting a red eulachon. The fellows just might take a notion to beat the shine out of you. I'm proposing we head off that possibility by sharing a room."

What was Keno's real motivation? He had admitted to a preference for men.

"My contracts shouldn't affect the other studs," Teakh said. "I'm to have an exclusive clientele."

"The fellows won't care. You haven't yet inseminated a single client, but the royal family is scoping you out. You shine too bright—brighter than the moon—and it'll get you in trouble."

Teakh tapped at the scars beneath his hair. "I can protect myself." Using his implant, he could notify Seaguard or call for backup at any time, not that they could be relied on.

"You've made a good impression on Dojko Seaguard," Keno said, "but how quickly are they going to respond?"

Teakh had no intention of whining to Seaguard, either Dojko or Fennako. In seedy waterfront dives, he'd seen his share of brawls and learned the hard way to defend himself. He knew when to transmit for assistance—rarely—and when to slip away before trouble began.

"I want you in my room at night with the door locked." Keno stepped away from the window. "If anyone gives you trouble, they'll have to get past me."

"They'll think I'm your catamite."

"Where do you get these words?" Keno laughed. "That's right, they'll be thinking you're my lover." He grinned his white-toothed smile. "So it'll take them a bit longer to figure out your scheme."

"I'll think about it," Teakh said.

"Would it be so bad?" Keno asked. "I don't snore."

CHAPTER 22
Stud Troupe

A STAGE HAD BEEN set up in the gym and the windows darkened. Teakh entered, hoping to work on his exercise routine.

Music thundered—bump and grind with a heavy backbeat. Colored strobes flashed, illuminating oiled skin taut over rippling muscles. The sound system wailed, "Oh love. Love. Love. Baby, baby, baby."

Teakh backed up, ready to leave. He'd wait on his exercise routine—maybe swim at the rec center instead, but Keno stood beside the door, a bemused smile on his lips. Teakh supposed studs weren't all that different from fishermen, despite their boasting, and he made it his business to observe. Maybe he'd learn something, so he watched the troupe practice.

Randy directed. "Now. One. Two. Three. And turn. All together now. Flex, two, three. And thrust. Thrust. Thrust."

Mirrors reflected the chorus line, multiplying the images of gyrating hips.

"Buttcakes, you're slacking off!" shouted Randy. "Like this." He joined the line, his hips thrusting in time with the others.

A lineup of strutting cocks? Male birds often courted in teams, so why not men? Whatever females found appealing in such spectacles of showy plumage and frenetic dancing was beyond Teakh. The music ended, and the formation broke up.

Randy stepped off the stage and zeroed in on Keno and

Teakh. "We've got the plan. Six studs on stage, flashing lights, throbbing music. The audience screaming. After the show, girls take their pick. They'll be lining up for our services. We have it all set up nice. Private rooms. The clan hires us, so no negotiations and the girls themselves don't pay anything."

"Your choreography has improved," Keno said, as unimpressed as any drab hen turning down a flamboyant suitor.

"Come on, this is the stud extravaganza of a lifetime. The upcoming spawning season is ours." Randy clapped Keno on the back then winked at Teakh. "You want in on the gig? It's quite an opportunity for a young stud."

An opportunity to strut like a blue-footed booby? Teakh kept his opinions to himself.

"Don't be shy." Randy leered. "A fellow's got to practice if he's going to perform. Either sexually or on stage. I can help you out one way or another."

"I've got my own thing going," mumbled Teakh.

"And what's that?"

"I do odd jobs down by the waterfront, and I swim," Teakh said, hinting he was training for competitive swimming and nothing more. "Keno's an excellent coach."

Randy laughed and slapped Teakh's butt. "Odd jobs? Just how odd are you?"

Teakh, hands low, shifted his weight to the balls of his feet.

"Feisty," Randy said. "Like 'em that way."

Keno stepped between them. "Randy, don't mess with this one."

Randy stood toe-to-toe with Keno. "Is that a challenge?"

Keno stepped back. "It's just a warning."

Teakh shook his head. He didn't need Keno's protection.

Keno put an arm around Teakh. "Gimp is here as my protégée. He has potential as a competitive swimmer. Not everyone is training for the spawn."

"For the breaststroke." Randy laughed and made a moue. "I won't mess with him. Not unless he wants me to." He stepped onto the stage. "Fellows, let's give it another run-through."

Keno drew Teakh out of the studio. "Have you thought

long enough about sharing a room?"

Through the closed door, music thudded.

Teakh tilted his head. "What is it with that guy?"

"Well, he's Randy—randy for anything that moves. I believe he enjoys sexual conquest, and he's not very particular. A lot of studs aren't. They think banging each other is part of the business. They call it practice."

"Are they all homosexual?"

"A lot of them don't care about gender one way or the other, so more like over-sexual. If you don't feel the same, they think you're odd. I'm speaking from experience."

Teakh nodded. Across the animal kingdom, those who were different faced pecking, hazing, even ostracism. "What can I expect?"

"Randy is more talk than anything else, showing off, boasting about who's got the biggest sex drive. The other guys? The ones who don't talk? Those we've got to worry about. If you move in with me, they'll think we're practicing sex, and they'll be less trouble for both of us."

Noah had commanded, *Be prepared.* Teakh rubbed his ear. He knew the best way out of trouble was to avoid it. He thrust his chest out, doing his best imitation of one of Angel's Seaguard princes. "You can't resist me."

"Shine off," Keno said, "and go get your stuff. We'll prop the clerestory vent and door transom so your seagull can get around."

"I'm not bringing her into the main gym."

"Good. The less these fellows know about you, the better."

As Teakh returned to the dorm wing, the entire gym still pulsated with male energy: sweat, the splash of men swimming, the clank of weights. He stuffed clothing into his duffle and hauled it and Gull's case to Keno's quarters, a room nearly identical to Teakh's former lodging.

Keno stood beside a berth neatly made with a chenille bedspread. "This bunk is mine." The storage shelf contained an emergency lantern and a screen photo of Keno beside a stocky man. "Take the other."

Teakh tossed his duffle on his assigned bunk and sat on the couch. "I'd say this is inappropriate pair-bonding in action. I'll break your heart."

"Hardly," Keno said. "I'm attracted to you, but remember what I told you about sexual dysfunction, that little feature of ours? For me, there's no sex outside of a loving relationship. I simply can't do it. I value friendship and want to protect you. I'll sing you lullabies if you want."

"No, thanks. I've heard you sing."

For the rest of the day, Teakh avoided the revue troupe. He swam his laps at the community pool and spoke little during supper. That evening, through the walls came the sounds of men rutting, or practicing for the spawning season, as they called it. But Teakh and Keno lay in companionable silence, sharing a room and respecting each other's privacy.

THE FOLLOWING DAY, for a handful of eulachon, Teakh helped Lugo haul fish, then they both knocked off and went to the Salty Hound. Teakh ordered his usual. He and Lugo took a table in the corner, and Teakh settled in for a good session of lie-swapping. A lot of the regulars were there. The door opened, and Jake and Chuck came inside with a cool gust of rain.

"Hey, Captain Jake," called a patron. "Hear-tell either your sailors are clumsy as all depths, or you're the wildest driver on the seas."

Another chipped in. "What were you doing? Leaving poor Chuck behind?"

Jake grunted. "He's alive, ain't he?"

Chuck sat at the bar, a hero for having survived. "I'm telling you a seagull saved me. I thought I was a goner. Then I look up, and there's this seagull circling above me like I was dinner. It lands next to me. I mean right next to me. Biggest gull I ever saw. Thought it was gonna peck my eyes out or something. That damn bird stayed right beside me until Seaguard arrived."

Teakh wished the incident had never happened. It wouldn't have if Jake had turned on his marine-com. He wished Jake and Chuck had finished stowing gear before heading in. He wished that wave had struck at a different angle or a bit later. Or that Chuck had carried a locator beacon. Damn it, why couldn't someone else have been prepared? Maybe Dojko Seaguard could have had drones in place watching for accidents.

"Hey, is that the big herring gull that eats money?" a gruff fisherman asked.

"You mean the one that keeps track of Lugo's wallet?" Another raised his glass to Lugo. Guffaws and bellows of laughter issued from around the room.

"I don't know about that," Jake said. "We were out in Rocky Inlet, and the wind was picking up. I says it looks like a blow and sends Chuck out to batten down hatches. And then there's this son-of-a-lubber bird on the windshield, pecking about hard enough to break steel. So I goes on out and tell it that no seagull is gonna be shitting all over my boat. The son-of-a-lubber starts pulling at a life ring like he's trying to tell me something. I holler for Chuck, and he's not answering. That's when I realized he was gone."

"Jake, my man, you sure know how to tell those whoppers," Teakh said, wishing the incident was nothing more than a tall tale.

"No shine," Jake said. "That bird was talking to me plain as anything."

Teakh took a swig of his cider, wiped his mouth, and said, "Here in Dojko, even the wildlife follows the Noah Code."

"I heard the mayday call," a fisherman commented. "That was no bird making it."

"Maybe it was an angel," Chuck said.

"An angel that eats rotting garbage and craps?" Teakh asked, getting into the spirit of things.

"That one eats money," one of the fellows said.

"And craps," Teakh said.

The fishermen were still laughing when the studs walked in. The place fell silent. No one offered to buy them drinks, not even for Buttcakes and Manly, the newcomers.

Teakh moved his chair to place his back to the studs, not wanting to be acknowledged as a resident of gym. Of the fishermen, only Lugo knew where Teakh lived, and Teakh preferred it that way. The studs remained oblivious of Teakh's presence and of the glares of the fishermen, whose society had been invaded.

Brawny leaned an elbow on the bar and boasted, "I got a girl lined up every month. They're screaming for me. Gonna have to make the spawning season longer so I can service them all."

"But how much are they paying?" Fist asked. "I'm getting top eulachon here. There's a lot to be said for quality."

Lugo stood. "I'm leaving."

Teakh pulled up his parka hood. He and Lugo slipped out the back. The rain had become a fine mist spattering the wet cobblestones. Teakh thrust his hands into the pockets of his parka.

"I hate those guys," Lugo said. "I got one girl. She doesn't pay me. We just like being together. What's wrong with that?"

"Nothing." Teakh splashed through a puddle. "You're ahead of me. My girl..." He shook his head.

"Lost her to one of them studs?" Lugo asked.

"Not exactly."

"How can you stand being around them up at Keno's?"

"I can't. You know where I spend my afternoons." Teakh indicated the harbor with a tilt of his head.

"So why do you stay at the gym?"

"Swimming," Teakh said. "Keno is my coach. I'm gonna take competition as far as I can."

"And still you haul fish. You're Seaguard, and you haul fish?"

Teakh shrugged. "That, and do bird tricks. Me and my clan are on the outs. Got to make money somehow. Competitive swimming sure doesn't pay."

"That was you who rescued Chuck, yes?"

"I'm claiming hospitality."

Lugo slapped Teakh's shoulder. "How about I take you out in my boat? My cousin took off for a few days. Come along as a deckhand. I'll give you a share of the catch. It would keep my girl happy. I told her about you and Gull."

"Lugo, are you going to tell everyone?"

Lugo shook his head vehemently. "Just Rosebay, but she knows already."

Who else would Rosebay tell? If word got around about Gull,

she'd be useless as an investigative tool. If he couldn't spy on Dojko fishermen, he'd have to move his operation. Maybe to Ugashko. Wasn't that the place a quarter of the way around the world?

CHAPTER 23
Questionnaire

TEAKH ENTERED THE gym through the back foyer and slipped into the bunk wing. Weights clanked in the weight room. Dojko Seaguard knew about Teakh's operation, and so did some of the fishermen. How long before the studs knew as well?

In Teakh's new quarters, Keno's berth remained neatly made, but the trainer was elsewhere. Teakh sat on his own bunk, leaned against the headboard, and hailed his sister.

I need your help. I'm planning to do some traveling. By Poseidon, he would get out of Dojko and away from both studs and the local fishermen.

He gazed up at the clerestory windows, identical to the ones in his old quarters, and beyond to gray clouds. If Sis agreed, he could leave Dojko with proper documents—no more passing himself off as either ignorant or clanless.

When have you needed my help for that? responded Sis. She wasn't in a particularly good mood, it seemed.

Teakh did his best to explain. *I don't want Ralko interfering. I'd like to pass off my travels as part of your studies.* Female students engaged in clan-supported research travelled freely. *I'm going to visit that artist in Shellako.*

Is this the painter you were talking about earlier? Sis seemed dubious. *I don't see that commissioning a painting is going to help your career.*

Teakh paced. *This isn't about a portrait.* He kicked at the edge of a rug. *We met in Idylko and hit it off. I need to know if she still has feelings for me.*

Oh, that's what this is all about. My little brother in love, Sis teased. If Teakh admitted to his feelings, she'd pester him for details. *I'm thinking you could tell Ralko you're studying art, and I'm helping you out. Same as we told police in Fennako City.* Teakh glanced at Gull, secure in her niche at the head of his bunk.

But I've never been interested in art, and I don't like lying about it. Good Danna! I was grilled by the Fennako police chief. She even contacted me a second time.

Thanks. Teakh stroked one of Gull's feathers into place. *You don't have to lie, just bend the truth a little.*

This isn't the impression we should be making. We've got to present ourselves as capable of clan administration, not as kids sneaking around and breaking laws on a whim.

Teakh stepped into the bathroom. A ledge supported Keno's razor and shaving soap. *But it came out okay,* sent Teakh. *Fennako chief of police is a princess. Mareen is her name, and she's one of the Queen's granddaughters. She contacted Lord Dojko, who talked to Keno. Keno thinks the princess may be bidding on my services.* Teakh grimaced at his reflection. He pushed a strand of lank hair away from his face and stood up straight, then he paced back into the sleeping compartment.

I told her the truth, Sis said. *We purchased Gull for investigative work and you're a fisheries detective. Your equipment is unregistered because Clan Ralko doesn't approve of your professional aspirations. I also told her about our Noah genetics and how you're listed as a stud in* Dale's Men.

Oh Danna! His cover was blown to Poseidon. *You didn't. I'm sunk.* He'd be known as the stud with the seagull telechiric. What hope did he have of engaging in undercover work? He flopped down on his bunk.

But like you said, it came out okay. Sis sounded so damn smug. *There's no reason to withhold information from the Fennako royal family. They're the ones deciding if we're to be a clan or not. I told Fennako you had Gull in Fennako City for an investigation. And if you want a reputation as an investigator, well again, that's Fennako.*

You did what? Come on. Fennako attention was nearly the same as a bulletin. They controlled the Sense-net and could look in on him through any camera attached to the Network. If they didn't like what they saw, they'd use royal override.

This is your chance to make an impression, Sis said. *Think of me as your character reference.*

I don't want to impress Fennako, sent Teakh, slamming the back of his hand against the mattress. *I've got to find out about my artist. That's why I had Gull in Fennako City. If I can't choose the person I love, what's the point of having our own clan?*

Will you stop being so selfish? You're not the only one trying to gain a little freedom.

I'm not being selfish. Come up with a reason for me to visit Shellako. What are you studying? Every time he talked with her, the subject of her thesis had changed. It might as well be art.

Ralko Education Board thinks I'm studying how to make clanless shelters profitable.

You're kidding. Teakh sent a burst of laughter. *Profitable and clanless don't go together.* Clans received revenue from their members in the form of clan fees.

It's a good excuse for meeting with influential people. I've been contacting Mama's old associates.

Are they still around?

Sure. And they may be willing to vouch for us as a clan. But we have to keep Ralko from knowing our real plans. So if you want to go to Shellako, your stated purpose has to support researching the profitability of clanless shelters.

Maybe shelters could make money by selling art, offered Teakh, trying for some sort of connection.

That's a stretch.

It was. Angel's paintings had nothing to do with poverty. But what could he and Sis possibly tell the education board? He said, *I have firsthand experience with bad hospitality.* There had to be a way to trim this sail. *I claimed hospitality and got thrown in a village brig. That's it— I'll show up in Shellako as a secret charity case. We'll compile statistics on their response.*

Sis snorted. *Statistics on how often you get thrown in the brig? Anyway, Shellako is too small of a sample. And if we're to convince the board, this has to be a real study.*

A full study would take months, even years. *Tell Ralko we're*

developing methodology for a later study. While I'm in Shellako, I'll
drop in on my girl. If we have trouble, I'll give up on the charity case
charade and pull out.

Meet with Mama's friends first, Sis said. *Try to make a good*
impression this time. We need their support.

FIVE DAYS LATER, Teakh debarked from a public ferry,
Gull's case grasped in one hand, a duffle in the other. His
neuro carried a questionnaire and an itinerary of clans and
contacts. Next on his list was Ardeanne Konvai, head of
Clan Konvai hospitality services. As one of Clan Konvai's
matriarchs, she was properly addressed as *Dame.* Sis had
made sure he understood proper protocol.

Teakh checked in at the harbormistress' office as a charity
case and was given vouchers for lodging and directions to a
soup kitchen. He peered into the kitchen and left his baggage
and vouchers at a bunk house. The rooms looked clean, no
sign of bugs or vermin. Teakh gave Konvai good marks.
Dame Ardeanne Konvai ran a tight ship. With the secret part
of his investigation done, he headed to Ardeanne's home and
office. Sis had asked that he interview the dame regarding
administration of hospitality.

Ardeanne met Teakh at her door. An older woman with
soft gray hair and birdlike hands, she invited him inside.
Beyond her foyer, lace curtains fluttered at the front windows,
casting nets of light and shadow over the polished floor. Teakh
glanced at his waterproof boots, visible below his tan pants.
Good manners required he remove his footwear to keep floors
clean. Only Seaguard wore boots inside a private residence.

The corners of Ardeanne's eyes crinkled with a smile.
"Leave them on."

Teakh bowed and nodded, acknowledgement of the honor.

In her front parlor, a tea service waited on a lace-covered
table. Beside the pot, a plate had been mounded with crisp
brown cookies. Ardeanne offered him an oval-backed chair
upholstered in floral fabric. Teakh accepted the chair and sat
up straight. He wanted to make a good impression, but Sis

had told him very little about the dame.

She spooned herbs into a strainer. "To what do I owe the pleasure of your visit?"

"The tide." Teakh gave the polite response, then added, "I'm conducting a survey of hospitality rendered to mariners. I believe my sister sent word."

"That she did." Ardeanne poured hot water through the herbs and let the tea steep. "What about hospitality rendered to Seaguard?"

Teakh evaded the implication that she knew he had an implant. "When is Seaguard in need of hospitality?"

Ardeanne tapped her ear. "You tell me."

He touched his bandanna to be sure his scars were covered. Realizing that this motion only gave himself away further, he resettled his hands in his knee. "What makes you think I'm Seaguard?"

Laughing, Ardeanne held out a plate of cookies—malt crinkles sprinkled with sugar crystals. "You play your part well, but I happen to have known your mother. I also know your services are up for bid on Kordalko Auctions. Doing quite well, I understand."

Yet another person knew entirely too much about Teakh. Had Sis been talking to her? Or had Ardeanne found out on her own? He shrugged and accepted a cookie, neither admitting to nor denying anything.

Ardeanne set aside the plate and poured tea into bone-china cups. "Are you sure that's what your mother would want for you? Maybe you've been told your genetics will save the world. Don't believe it."

Teakh avoided her question with one of his own. "Do you think Noah genetics are worthless?"

"Not at all. I have similar genetic makeup myself." Ardeanne paused, sugar bowl and teaspoon in hand. "Sweetener?"

"Please."

She stirred in sugar and handed Teakh a cup. "Our loyalty renders us susceptible to exploitation."

Teakh had heard this before. He took a gulp of tea and coughed. It was hotter than he expected. He sputtered, "I'm not loyal or altruistic or any of that foundered shine."

"Now who's calling Noah genetics worthless?" Ardeanne filled her own cup. "Why are you selling your services?"

Sink it all, she'd asked a loaded question. He could feign ignorance, or he could be blunt. "I need the money."

She raised her teacup. "How much of that money is for you and how much for someone else?"

Crinkle cookie one hand, Teakh squirmed under her piercing gaze. "I do what I have to."

"I set my net it's all for someone else. I'm quite a bit like you. Your mother showed me another way to help people."

Teakh took the chance to divert discussion away from his career. "I'd like to know about her."

Fine lines formed around Ardeanne's mouth as she pursed her lips. "Your mother devoted her life to guard dogs and to one in particular."

Did she mean Teakh?

She watched him, surely expecting some sort of reaction. He didn't give one, and she went on. "That's what we called Seaguardsmen with no blood kin. Sons of surrogate mothers, they were bred to be brave and self-sacrificing."

"I'm not one of your guard dogs. I have blood kin. As for brave—" Teakh dunked his cookie in his tea.

"Ah, yes. You have a sister, so not quite a guard dog. Often a man such as you wasn't allowed to marry for fear he'd favor wife and children over his duty. It was your father's clan that forbade your parents' marriage." Ardeanne's gaze became distant, her cup held midway to her lips.

Teakh nibbled the damp cookie. She'd summed up his situation—Clan Ralko attempting to control his love life. But his father's duty must have been that of real Seaguard, while his own was impregnation of clients.

"What about my father?" Teakh leaned forward, eager for information that could make his dim childhood memories substantial, but mostly he wanted to avoid talking about himself.

Ardeanne set down her cup. "He was a rescue swimmer, specializing in going into downed craft to extract victims from the wreckage. He died a hero. It was all over the news."

"I don't recall." Teakh had been quite young at the time. He'd witnessed his mother's sorrow but hadn't seen news reports. He'd heard only that his father had died at sea. "What happened?"

Ardeanne shook her head. "A hydrogen tanker ship lost power in a storm, and the crew was trapped inside, the ship listing and about to break up. Your father brought his esskip beside the ship and climbed aboard. He cut into the compartment where the crewmembers were trapped. They all got out, but he thought there might be one more man aboard. While he was searching, the ship listed farther and went down, taking him with it." She bowed her head, a moment of respectful silence and shared grief, then said, "Your parents sacrificed themselves, each in their own way, for what they believed to be right."

Teakh sipped from his cup, carefully this time. He tried not to think of Cooky in a galley filled with smoke, or Chuck drifting in spume and gray waves, or of his father clambering up the side of a listing ship.

A strand of Ardeanne's hair wisped as she sighed. "Someone I loved encouraged me to become a surrogate mother. My sons would be Seaguard, valued members of their adoptive clans. I was deceived, and our relationship ended. I was free to marry someone else whom I truly loved, a woman. Like your father, my sons gave their lives for others. Adoptive clans don't care. To them, my sons were just guard dogs, an expendable purchase. But still, I'm a mother, and I grieve." Her focus distant, she gazed toward the lace-covered window.

He felt for Ardeanne. Teakh placed his hand over hers. It was possible his father had been her son, and they grieved for the same person. "By chance, are you my grandmother?"

She smiled, but her eyes were glossy with tears. "I'm flattered. Your mother helped me find out about my boys. I never should have agreed to give them up."

Teakh offered a napkin, meager comfort, and she blotted her eyes.

Reproductive contracts could be such a sticky tangle. The agreement to bring children into the world often hinged on

190

the agreement to give up those very children, a paradox that he faced himself.

He tried for perspective. "If you had done otherwise, they never would have been born."

Ardeanne folded the napkin and set it aside. "I have no regret for their lives. Only for their deaths." Her gaze became sharp. "I understand you've asked for concessions for your children."

"Who told you that?"

"I've been corresponding with your sister and..." Ardeanne cupped a hand to her mouth and whispered, "It's in your profile on *Dale's Men*. I do subscribe to the service, not that I'm in the market."

"Oh, that." Teakh tried to pass off his actions as inconsequential. "I was trying to talk my aunt into giving me more money. We settled on trust funds for my children."

"An excellent idea. I wish I'd done it. I also understand you're arranging for them to be members of your new clan."

"My sister is writing up the charter."

Ardeanne cocked her head. "A sovereign clan?"

What was she getting at? Teakh chewed his cookie and swallowed. "Only with royal approval. We haven't yet petitioned the Queen."

"So if one of yours wrongfully dies, you can sue in interclan court, bring cases before the Zenhedron in Fennako City."

"True." As a sovereign clan, Noahee would have such a right.

"That'll put teeth in your contracts," Ardeanne said. "I have a proposal for you. Include guard dogs and their parents in your clan. Extend your rights to all of us. You'll have the legal authority to speak for us in court. Your mother would be proud."

"But our clan wouldn't be a clearly defined family." Teakh had planned on including men as equal to women as a way to recruit more members, but Ardeanne's idea left membership open to nearly anyone. "A clan is supposed to be genetically related."

"All humans are kin. It's just a matter of tracing the family tree."

Teakh stared into his teacup. Crumbs and a few fragments

of leaves floated near the surface. He felt the weight of his decision. As much as he liked Ardeanne, agreeing to her proposal might weaken his own position. "I'll consult with my sister."

Ardeanne nodded, seemingly satisfied. "Do what you believe to be best for your children, but remember you're not alone. Now what about this survey?"

Teakh handed over a noteboard, the type of device preferred by Seaguard inspectors. "My sister's research project. We're developing a questionnaire for comparing hospitality programs."

"And how does this further your aims?"

"It's purely an excuse to travel. My sister wishes for me to reestablish my mother's network of associates. We can't let on to Ralko that we're planning to leave the clan. Sis has them convinced we're studying clanless shelters, and I have business of my own in Shellako."

"Dare I ask what kind of business?"

"I've become interested in art. Actually, in an artist. I owe her a visit. Sis and I combined our objectives."

Ardeanne laughed. "Oh, I see. You travel on student hospitality and get lodging for free."

"That's not exactly..." Depths, that was exactly what he was doing.

CHAPTER 24
Angel's Garden

TEAKH SHIFTED IN his seat, straining for a view of Shellako Village over the esskip pilot's shoulder. Ardeanne had arranged for one of her kinsmen to give him a lift. They skimmed past the stratoport terminal. The traffic-control tower jutted above the terminal building and piers.

The craft touched down. Bright foam spraying from hydrofoil struts, they approached Clan Shellako's small boat harbor. Beyond the waterfront, shadows of clouds flitted over the composite tile roofs of Shellako Village. The weather was much improved since Teakh's last visit—so had his method of travel.

The canopy opened.

"Tide carry you," the pilot said. "Give me a hail when you need a pickup."

Teakh jumped out with his baggage. The canopy closed, and the esskip scooted from the dock then sped away. Carrying his case and duffle, Teakh walked up the gangway to the Shellako waterfront. The businesses and storehouses seemed more substantial from a human's-eye view. Sheltered from security cameras by the side of a warehouse, he released Gull from her case. As a charity case, he should ask about shelter, but that wasn't his real purpose, so he hailed Shellako Seaguard for directions to Angel's studio. He claimed to have business with her, and they gave him a map. Teakh appreciated having legitimate documents and access to the Seaguard positioning system.

He studied the map superimposed over Gull's view of the actual waterfront and sent her toward Angel's studio. Gull flew above the branching lanes until she reached the outskirts of the village. There, beneath the marked location, he recognized the garden sundial, its gnomon topped by a glass globe, and the porch festooned with potted plants and brightly painted garden art. He'd been right. The place belonged to Angel.

Gull landed on the sundial gnomon. Sunlight, focused through the ball, fell as a splinter of green light on the rusted steel dial. Angel herself worked in the garden, a basket by her side, a broad hat shading her face. She glanced up, a sheaf of flower stalks in her gloved hand. Teakh's heart beat faster.

He hefted his baggage and hurried uphill from the waterfront. Nearing the last turn before Angel's garden, he slowed to a casual saunter. Best not to appear overly eager. He stopped at her garden gate. "Pardon me, ma'am."

Angel set the cut stalks aside and stood, pruning shears in hand. "What are you about?"

She acted as if they'd never met. Where was that smile he remembered?

Teakh rested his hand on the gate. "I'd like to thank you for hospitality rendered in Idylko."

She wiped her forehead, leaving a streak of dirt across the perfect skin of her forehead. A lock of auburn hair clung to her flushed cheek. "Customarily, hospitality is charity rendered to strangers."

Teakh brought Gull from the sundial to land on his shoulder. "I'm thinking I'm not so much of a stranger."

Angel stuffed the shears into the front pocket of her tunic. "So you're the one who's been spying on me," she accused, but her eyes sparkled with amusement.

"Did you get my messages?" Teakh asked, his mouth dry. Had she been ignoring him, wishing he'd leave her alone?

"You're so sweet." Angel pushed open the gate and whispered, "Best to not talk where the neighbors can see us. Come in." She picked up her basket.

"I can take that." To take it, he set down his duffle and case. He sent Gull from his shoulder to land again on the gnomon.

Angel laughed and pulled off her gloves one finger at a time. "Just put the things on the front porch."

Teakh ran up the steps with the basket. He returned for his case and duffle. On the porch, Angel laid her gloves and shears atop the flower stalks then opened the door to a front room redolent with turpentine.

Inside, Teakh's eyes adjusted to the cool light. Taborets held jars of paintbrushes and palettes. A drape hung behind a tufted divan. Stretched canvas and panels leaned on artist benches and easels or against walls covered with sketches— charcoal and pencil drawings, mostly of naked men but also of seascapes and birds. A backdrop and drapery swags hung behind a tufted divan, the upholstery brown suede. Bolsters, pillows, and furs, piled on the divan, spilled to the floor. A small panel, supported by an easel, depicted a man wearing nothing but a splint.

Angel's gaze followed his. "Oh, that." She flipped a cloth over the painting.

"Just who is spying?" Teakh asked.

"I couldn't resist." Angel dropped her hat on a bench. "Come into the kitchen."

She led him through a second door. Windows looked out on the back garden. Stove, sink, and cupboards formed a galley along one wall. Facing it, on a tall butcher-block table, a pitcher held late-season flowers and branches with clusters of scarlet-orange berries. Two stools waited by the table. Teakh took a seat.

Angel filled a kettle and set it on the stove, then brought out a tin of cookies from a cupboard. "You caught me off guard. I have nothing prepared."

"You're beautiful," blurted Teakh.

Angel perched on the opposite stool, her hands folded on her crossed knees. "Flirt."

He moved the pitcher of branches aside to better see her face.

A smile played over her lips and in her eyes. "So what brings you to Shellako?"

He'd come to see her, but he wouldn't admit it. "I was in the area and decided to drop in. I'm helping my sister in a study of hospitality. I come into a village, request hospitality, and see what happens."

"What has happened so far?"

"I got dumped in a village brig once. I also met a fine woman in Idylko who mended my trousers."

Angel raised her eyebrows. "And you don't tell anyone they're the subject of your study?"

"Exactly," Teakh said.

Her laughter rippled. "You're a shiner."

He put his hand over his heart in mock indignation. "I have a research visa and a questionnaire. I check off boxes, and we compile statistics."

Angel crooked her finger. "You're a wily one. This is rich. You were in Idylko assessing hospitality, and I was assessing you." Her eyes became dark pools of delight. "It's my business to know which studs are on the market."

Teakh sat back, somewhat dismayed. "How do I measure up?"

Angel reached across the table to tap his knuckle. "The issue requires additional research. There's more to being a stud than just genetics." She placed her cool hand over his. "You're about as green as they come. A professional doesn't arrive unannounced at a lady's garden gate."

Teakh set his other hand over hers. "I'm not yet a professional."

"I am," Angel said. "And I can make your career."

He swallowed, his mouth suddenly dry. "Maybe I want more than a career."

She leaned forward. "Just what do you want?"

"What we had in Idylko."

She laughed. "You want to be a perpetual lunch guest?"

"Sure. Just so long as I'm your guest."

"I have high standards," Angel said. "Most of my guests are top Seaguard chiefs."

Teakh's spirits sank. He knew what class of men she painted. He couldn't compete with princes and lords. The kettle whistled, and Angel stood to get it.

"My sister has written up a clan charter," Teakh said. "When it goes through, I'll become a magnate."

"I didn't know you could do that. I thought clans were all

started in the time of Noah." She dropped teabags into mugs and added hot water.

"They come and go," Teakh said. "You just have to prove that you function as a clan."

"You can't be a lord without territory." Angel pushed a mug toward Teakh.

Poseidon, he'd stretched the truth, and she'd caught him. A Seaguard chief wasn't necessarily a lord.

"We'll apply for territory." He accepted the steaming mug.

"I thought every part of the ocean already had a magnate." Angel opened the tin. Inside, butter cookies sparkled with sugar crystals and gleamed with dabs of jam.

Teakh selected a raspberry cookie. "There's more than ocean. Also rivers, glaciers, and the arctic shields."

"You, an ice lord? That seems a bit cold and distant," Angel said. "What can you do right now?"

"Whatever you want." Teakh hoped she'd suggest an exploration of kissing as she had in Idylko.

"Well, your icy lordship," she said, eyes mischievous, "I've still got weeding to do."

Some men would negotiate for kissing, but his offer had been honest. "Then I'm your gardener boy. Sign me up."

"You have the job."

Outside, Angel plucked a garden claw from a basket. "How about if you weed that flower bed?" She handed him the claw. "I'll finish deadheading."

She moved off toward the front of the yard, leaving Teakh holding the claw and wishing the two flower beds weren't so far apart. In his imagination, he and Angel would work side-by-side and maybe drop the tools to get even closer. Oh yes, that's what he hoped for.

He knelt and examined plants, a tangle of green against dark earth. The tall plants must be the flowers and the short plants the weeds. But that wasn't necessarily true. He'd failed his first test, a simple one. If only the plant species were fish, he'd know which to remove and which to leave. He peered at Angel, her head bent as she clipped a flower head.

Teakh brought Gull fluttering down and closed his eyes, focusing on her vision. She cocked her head, moving for better depth perception. Might as well take a taste. Teakh burrowed Gull's beak down amid the rich earthiness of the garden bed and snapped up a thread of green strung with tender leaves. He accessed a plant DNA library: STELLARIA MEDIA, CHICKWEED. The tangle of runners pulled up easily. He examined another plant, and Gull took a taste. The plant was sometimes grown as an ornamental, but other libraries suggested it was a weed. Ah, an excuse to talk to Angel.

He plucked a blossom. "What about the *Linaria vulgaris*?"

"What?" Angel glanced up.

Teakh held out a stalk of yellow flowers. "Are you keeping this stuff?"

"You sure know your plants." She adjusted her hat.

"I've studied biology," Teakh said, feeling pleased. He'd used Gull to taste most every species of fish around, much of it rotten, and a number of fish parasites. He'd leave out the details.

"Pull it." She turned back to her clipping.

Species identification complete, Teakh made short work of pulling weeds. Maybe his next job would be closer to Angel.

She crossed the yard to a small clapboard shed. He tagged behind, appreciating how her hips swayed under her tunic.

"You don't seem to mind getting your hands dirty." She thrust a rake toward him. "Even woman's work? Gardening?"

Was this another test? They walked back to the flower garden, and Teakh drew the rake across the ground, gathering leaves.

"Why shouldn't a man garden or a woman catch fish?" He hoped that was the right answer.

"Some might say that's heresy."

Teakh lifted weeds into Angel's basket. "Noah never said that a woman couldn't fish or that a man had to." He'd best take care. Their relationship could blow up over politics and religion.

Angel fluttered her lashes and let the controversy slide. "What if I like to fish for men?"

What if Teakh were only one among many? "What species of man are you angling for?"

"*Homo mannerly*," Angel said.

Teakh chuckled. "*Homo monogamous*?"

"Depends," she said airily, and Teakh's heart sank.

They separated out the mature weeds, and Teakh carried

the rest to the compost heap in the back.

"What do you wish done next, my lady?"

Angel crossed her arms and pursed her lips. "Let's go for a walk."

"How about to the waterfall?" offered Teakh.

They stowed the rake, pruning shears, and basket, then he brought Gull flying down to her case.

"Why don't you bring your bird along?" Angel said.

"If I fly while walking, I run into things," Teakh explained.

"I could guide you." She linked an arm in his, and they walked down the steps. Gull scampered across the porch, boards rough on her feet, and bobbed her head to Angel, who laughed. Teakh sent Gull darting from under the eaves to circle above the roofs of Shellako Village. A woman in a nearby yard leaned over her fence.

"I believe your neighbor is watching us," Teakh said, his hand on Angel's arm.

"Only one?" Angel asked.

"You were concerned earlier."

"I'll tell them you're a friend who dropped by." She opened the gate.

From Gull's vantage, Teakh saw himself in the lane, strolling with Angel. They walked between houses that thinned at the edge of the village. Gull flew ahead, and Teakh held Angel's elbow, his hand twitching in time to the beat of Gull's wing.

The lane became a road. Gull landed on a spruce tree, and Teakh said, "I'll wait up." He meant that Gull would wait until he and Angel caught up.

Angel understood and leaned into him. "See, I didn't let you run into anything."

He squeezed her arm.

"It must be like flying a kite," Angel said.

"But no strings," Teakh said. The double meaning was deliberate.

The road narrowed to a trail as it followed a stream gurgling over stones. Trees overhung the creek, dropping golden leaves on the water. This was a healthy creek with dappled shadows and deadfall left in place, one with plenty of hiding places for juvenile salmon. Teakh watched for the telltale movement of fry against sun-flecked gravel and in the swirling junctures where the main current encountered backwater eddies. The stream issued from a steep gorge, and the trail diverted away, following switchbacks up a mountainside. Gull flew ahead, viewing foam churning through stone basins. Cool droplets misted below the cascade as it pummeled into the pool.

"I'll keep you warm if you like." Angel leaned her head against his cheek. Her hair, redolent of leaves and garden herbs, tickled his chin.

Teakh enfolded her in his arms. "Let's be like this forever."

She held his hands, her brown eyes limpid. "I won't lead you on. Given what you do and what I do, what chance do we have?"

What chance did they have? "I won't lie to you," she said, and her lovely face creased with anguish. "My career, my reputation, require that I...oh Danna, this is hard...I know many men. They take their clothing off, and I depict every detail. You can't get more intimate than that. They tell me about their lives, their hopes, and their fears."

"How intimate?"

"You're jealous." Angel patted his cheek. "I paint their portraits. I talk to them. And sometimes...sometimes I meet a man who is more than that."

"How do I rate?"

"I've seen your genetic profile and have every reason to believe you're genuine. You won't be happy with me."

"Genetics aren't destiny." Poseidon! He was quoting Keno, for Danna's sake.

"Honestly?" Angel asked. "How will you feel when I'm closeted with a client? Will you wonder what we're doing? Will you trust me? I could love you, but painting is my career, my life. Do you understand?"

"I—"

Angel pressed her fingers to his lips. "Say no more. Love someone else."

Teakh stroked her wrist. "There's no one else for me."

"That puts us in a bind, both of us giving up our careers."

"I'm an expert at identifying marine species," Teakh said.

"I'm a fisheries enforcement consultant. I don't need a career as a stud."

"Just where does that leave me? Do I wait at home, painting innocuous seascapes? You're a stud, the best there is, and I'm a painter, the best I can be. Let's not prolong the agony."

"If we don't try, we won't know if it'll work or not."

She caught her lower lip in her perfect teeth. "I'm afraid..."

"I'm here." Teakh held her close.

THE LACY SHADOW of a curtain shifted ever so slightly on Ardeanne's parquet floor. Teakh sipped tea.

She set aside the noteboard with the questionnaire results. "Now then, about your business in Shellako." She wagged a finger. "Don't be slippery with me. You were up to something."

"My friend does paintings," Teakh said. "Very traditional, all in oil."

"Does this painter have a name?"

"Marjoram Shellako."

Ardeanne tapped a wrinkled cheek. "Marjoram Shellako? Didn't she lose an uncle a few years back? A brother too, I believe. Bad weather, fog moving in quickly. She did a series of paintings about it. Oh yes, uses the name Matta Carrie. Interesting moniker. Seductress of sailors."

"Lucky fellows," Teakh said.

Ardeanne cackled. "I knew it."

"We're professionals," Teakh said. "I'm looking to commission a portrait."

"Is that all?"

"I'd like it to be more," Teakh said, "but she doesn't think it'll work out."

"Poor boy. Your suit came up cold."

"She wants a professional relationship."

"Ah. Love is a shy fish. Make a sudden move, and it's gone. Try to hold it, and love slips from your fingers. Your girl is skittish. How did you go about arranging your meeting?"

"I showed up at her studio. She was gardening," he said.

"And you expected her to be delighted? Dressed in

dungarees and her hands covered with dirt?"

"She wore gloves. And what are dungarees?"

"Denim leggings. Never mind. You shouldn't visit without an invitation. Next time, get one. Even if the visit is regarding business. Especially if it's business."

"We'd met before, and I knew where she lives."

"Properly, the girl initiates courtship and informs the boy's clan of her intent," Ardeanne said.

"I don't want Ralko to know."

"All the more reason to keep this relationship professional. Superficially, anyway. You're not the first to have a relationship on the sly."

"How about if I send her a note and my address codes?" Teakh asked.

"Excellent. Send her an apology for arriving unannounced. Nothing greases the rails of love like a sincere apology. That she didn't toss you out or hail the local Seaguard is a good sign. If she wishes to continue correspondence, she'll let you know. But get going on that introduction by a mutual friend, someone who can assure her of your good intentions. That's where you should set your net."

CHAPTER 25
Beauty Salon

IN THE FRONT parlor of the gym, Teakh awaited Aunt Dyse. He'd returned to Dojko after days of travel, just in time for another of her visits. She wanted photos to post on Dale's Men.

With an armload of packages, she bustled through the front door. "Gorby, bring the rest, would you?" She dumped her load on a table and dusted her hands.

Gorbus followed with even more parcels.

"Return that cart to the harbormistress."

Glowering, Gorbus departed.

Dyse thrust bundles at Teakh. "Hurry it up. Iris has agreed to style your hair." She squinted. "That beard must go. Good Danna! You look like a fisherman."

"I am a fisherman," Teakh said.

"And those pants." Dyse scowled at his mended trousers. "They should be burned."

Teakh set the bundles on a chair and smoothed a hand on his thigh. Angel had done the sewing, but for her sake, he let the dispute slide. He retreated to the dressing room to don the new pants and a long-sleeved undershirt, the type worn under a life vest. So far he had nothing to complain about.

When he came out, Dyse held up a black vest with tomato-red piping—Ralko colors. A pair of seaboots, black with scarlet lining, had been heaped on a chair. Names were withheld on *Dale's Men*, but if Teakh appeared in photos wearing Ralko kit, that fig leaf of privacy would be blown away. Even worse, he'd be branded as Ralko. He aimed to be known as the Noah stud, not the Ralko stud.

"I can't wear that," he said.

Dyse thrust the vest toward him. "I've already had it custom fitted. And we're due in the beauty salon."

Disgusted, Teakh dropped the vest on the chair with the boots. "Then let's go." He'd have to wear something else for the photo shoot. Maybe he could borrow a better-looking parka from Keno or even Lugo.

"Well. Put it on," Dyse said.

"But we have an appointment in the beauty salon," Teakh said. "I'll dress up later."

They went through the passage to the connecting shop. Iris greeted them beside a barber chair with a wall screen and a sink behind her. Nearby, two mirrors flanked a doorway, which opened onto a photo studio. Her work stand held a wicked assortment of curling irons, shears, razors, and combs.

Iris adjusted the chair. "I'm delighted you've made a visit to the salon."

"Take your shirt off," Dyse said. "You'll get clippings all over it."

"And why would that bother you?" Teakh asked, but he removed the shirt.

Iris eyed the patch of chest hair over Teakh's heart. "Have you considered body waxing?"

"Yes," Dyse said enthusiastically.

Teakh straightened his shoulders. "I'm thinking no." He sat and placed his heel on the footrest. He'd never been in a salon before but refused to be cowed.

"Maybe later." Iris draped a cape over his shoulders. "For now, let's consider your hairstyle. Would you call it a pigtail or a queue?" She pulled the twine from his hair, which fell loose in lank brown locks.

"I wouldn't call it anything."

Iris held a comb at the ready. "Well, at least it's not dipped in tar."

Teakh pushed a strand of hair away from his eyes. "Why would I do that?"

Iris laughed and tousled his hair. "Because you're a tar.

Jacky Tar. That's what they used to call mariners. They'd cover nearly everything in tar, including their hair. Relax. We start by washing." She spun the chair.

Teakh now faced away from the sink. A ratchet clanked, and the entire back of the chair lowered as Teakh remained upright.

"Lean back so I can wash your hair," Iris said.

Teakh's head fit into a smoothly sculpted slot, the porcelain cool against the back of his neck, as if he were a sacrificial victim. Iris's fingers rubbed lightly. Water spray tickled his scalp, and Teakh yielded the weight of his head.

"Your hair is unusually dry," she said as she scrubbed. "Swimming does that. How about a hot oil treatment?"

Teakh bolted upright. "No wax, no tar, and no hot oil."

Hovering, Dyse rubbed her hands. "Oh, yes."

Iris patted Teakh's shoulder, encouraging him to lay his head against the edge of the sink. "Don't worry. You can have healthy hair and still qualify as a fisherman. My kinsmen down at the harbor don't care about that sort of thing."

She toweled off his hair. Teakh relaxed as she worked oil into his scalp and chin. She finished by swathing Teakh's head in a turban of clear film and thick towels, then she turned toward a wall screen.

"Queue up," she said, and the pixels of the screen shifted and merged to display an array of hairstyles, all of them a combination of braid rows and shaving. "These are suitable for Seaguard. We'll shave some of your hair to show off your implant scars and braid the rest."

"With gold beads woven in." Dyse clasped her hands. "High-carat gold. We'll let the ladies know you're worth your price."

Teakh slid a finger under the turban, shifting the sweaty plastic. "That'll get me beat up for sure."

"Shift," called Iris. The screen altered to display a single hairstyle, a confection of scars, braids, and gold beads. "We've calculated that this look is the most likely to appeal to your clientele."

"What if I get mugged?" Displaying his scars while working on the docks was bad enough—fishermen would know he was Seaguard and his cover would be blown to shreds—but flaunting gold would invite mayhem. He'd be putting himself above his friends and making himself a target for his enemies.

"They wouldn't dare." Dyse stepped toward the screen. "With this hairstyle, anyone can see you have a neuro. Lord Ralko would receive immediate notification of your death, and everyone will know that."

"Lord Ralko?" Teakh gave a derisive snort of laughter. "If I died, he'd assume my neuro was malfunctioning. I'll be lucky to die. Someone might see fit to rip the antenna wire out of my head without bothering to kill me." The filigree scars on his scalp covered a network of gold wire, the valuable metal unsurpassed for ductility. The beads called attention to what was hidden under his scalp.

"Then you should have a guard," Dyse said. "Maybe Gorbus."

"He'd like that even less than I do," Teakh said.

Iris reached for Dyse's shoulder. "Don't worry. He already has a bodyguard. Keno and Teakh are sharing a room."

Dyse gave a look of exaggerated shock, eyebrows arched, lips puckered. "Just what will that achieve? You need protection during the day."

Teakh nodded. "See. I can't wear gold or display my implant scars."

"Nonsense," Dyse said. "Just stay in the gym."

Teakh nibbled the inside of his cheek. As he saw it, he faced greater danger from the other studs than from the fishermen. Gorbus would be no protection at all.

Iris opened a drawer. "The solution's simple." She pulled out a square of red fabric and flourished it. "Mariners will think you're going bald and trying to avoid sunburn. The studs? We'll let them think it's your new pirate look. So let's talk about your beard."

"I'm keeping it," Teakh said.

"We need smooth shaven." Dyse stroked her own face. "Clean-cut Seaguard."

Teakh recalled the princes in Angel's show. Some were smooth shaven, but even princely Lord Tristan Bay sported facial hair. "A lot of Seaguardsmen have beards."

206

"He's right," Iris said. "A beard and mustache. Well groomed, of course."

"I'm making the marketing decisions," Dyse said.

"But I'm the one living with the hairstyle." Teakh scowled at his reflection in the mirror. "I'm thinking maybe a buzz cut." Such a style would show off his scars when necessary but be easily covered with a bandanna.

Iris patted his turban. "And waste that hot oil treatment?"

Dyse pouted. "If I can choose the rest of the hairstyle, I'll concede on the beard."

"Do you really believe women will like all the doodads?" In Angel's paintings, a few lords had worn braided hair.

"Try it out." Iris wrapped Teakh's head. "If you don't like the braids, we can try another style, even a buzz cut."

"After the photos," Dyse said.

"Agreed." As soon as the photos were done, he'd cut the braids off and sell the beads for cash.

Iris looped and pinned up his locks and set to work with clippers. Teakh accessed Gull. He'd escape the treatment in his mind, but as he flew up to the window and opened the latch, his body twitched.

"Hold still," Iris said.

Teakh sighed and returned Gull to her niche.

With a razor, Iris shaved his neck and the back and sides of his head. "You have handsome scars," she said as she worked. "It's a pity to hide them under all that hair."

She trimmed his mustache with scissors and a tiny comb. Using a bigger comb, she divided his remaining top hair and began braiding. What a tedious process. Teakh thought longingly of the buzz cut.

When Iris had finished, she held up a mirror. The hair on the back of Teakh's head had been cut velvet-short, and the welts of his scars showed through like arabesques in a carpet. She had secured his remaining hair in braided rows, starting at his forehead and finishing in gold beads, each one shaped like a tiny fish, as if his braids were taglines baited and dragged by a troller. Chuck and Lugo would make cracks about luring girls if only he trolled at the right speed. Fortunately, the fishermen would never see the ridiculous hairdo.

"Let's get those photos," Dyse said. "Then we'll pop them up on Dale's."

They went through the door to the photo studio. A white backdrop covered the entire wall. Tripods held lights and a camera. Props waited nearby: a plinth, an old binnacle, a steering helm, and an upholstered bench.

Dyse opened a handscreen. "I've got a list of the necessary shots. First we need you in Seaguard kit. I'll have to go back for your boots and vest."

"I don't want to be photographed as Ralko," Teakh said. "Ralko has never supported me in any way. I'm not Ralko."

"Come now. We raised you after your mother's death, we arranged for your training as a stud. And I bought you custom-made Seaguard kit. Talk about ungrateful." Dyse tugged on Teakh's ear as if he were a seven-year-old she'd caught stealing candy in the village.

He swatted her hand, pushing it away. "If I appear in *Dale's* wearing Ralko kit, people will know who I am. This is another safety issue." Clans registered colors along with designation and name on a publicly available list, but Teakh was grasping at straws. If he were branded as Ralko, he'd be forever associated with them, even after he had his own clan.

"Well then, we'll move on to the other photos." Dyse glanced at her list. "We need nudes and rampants."

"Rampants?" Teakh didn't like the sound of that.

"Erect shots," Dyse said. "Customers like to see if you'll be a good fit."

"So you want me to masturbate in front of you?"

"You're so foundered stubborn," Dyse said. "You don't want your hair done. You don't want to shave. You don't want to wear Seaguard kit. Who made you king?"

Teakh crossed his arms, refusing to answer or argue.

"Hold on." Iris touched a comset in her shoulder pocket. "Let's bring Keno in. He's a good photographer and knows the market. Is that all right with the two of you?"

Dyse lifted her hands in resignation. Teakh nodded, gold beads jangling. Keno would be his backup as Dyse made wretched grabs for money and Iris sugarcoated manipulation as compromise.

A bit later, Keno came through the door, carrying the new boots and vest.

Dyse launched a volley of complaints ending with, "He's impossible." She held out her handscreen. "Here are the photos we need. Tell me, are they unreasonable?"

Keno set the boots and vest on a bench and accepted the handscreen. "Rampants? Aye?"

"How can we sell his services if he can't even get it up for a photo?" Dyse stabbed a finger toward Teakh.

He backed away. "I'm cutting off the braids as soon as the photos are done." He refused to even discuss the possibility of rampants.

"Ladies, please." Keno waved the handscreen. "Teakh and I need to talk."

"Talk some sense into him," Dyse said as she left the room.

Iris followed, and the door clicked shut. Teakh faced Keno in the silence of Iris's place. It smelled of wax and hair pomander. Teakh almost missed the blare of music and the clatter of men working out.

"I don't want Dyse watching," Teakh said. "I want the photos, but not with that black-and-scarlet shine. I should be advertised as Noah, not Ralko."

"If Dyse is the problem, I can take the photos." Keno adjusted the position of the camera tripod. "But we'll have to work with what we've got. Unless you've got Noahee kit somewhere. So which will it be? Ralko kit or nude?"

Caught between repugnant and objectionable, Teakh screwed up his face. He lifted a boot, matte black with the exception of the tomato-red lining. He shook the boot so that the cuff extended, the Ralko colors now hidden as the boot hung from his hand. Worn hip-length, the boots could be from a number of clans. "I might be able to wear these so long as the red is hidden."

Keno whistled. "Mysterious black hip boots. Girls go for that sort of thing, the bandit lover."

"But no rampants."

"When you're ready for those, I'll take the shots. I won't interfere or say anything. Pretend I'm gone." Keno removed the lens cap.

"I'd rather not." Teakh tossed his head for emphasis, beads clattering.

Keno straightened. "What's holding you back?"

Teakh dropped the boot on the floor and closed his eyes. He tried to get ready for the photo shoot by thinking of Angel—that first time in Idylko. She and the other two caressed him, their hands stroking, mouths kissing, taking him, controlling him. He wouldn't cheapen the memory. He opened his eyes. "It doesn't feel right."

Keno cleared his throat. "Rampants are part of the job. Are you capable of performing as a stud or not?"

"Love is—" Depths! Some things were sacred. "There's a woman. I mean, there might be a woman. This isn't fair to her."

"Loyalty! Poseidon damn it!" Keno swiveled the camera. "Inhibited by your major selling point."

"It just doesn't feel right."

"Remember what I told you about bulls? It's all a matter of the right stimulus and a bit of imagination. We could get you drunk to lower your inhibitions, but alcohol interferes with performance. There're drugs which can help you relax."

Teakh shook his head. Only one thing worked for him—Angel. "I've looked into it. I'd like to be assigned a handler of my choosing. That's how it was done with the Noah Eugenics Project."

"That was one of the most ethically questionable parts of that foundered project." Keno squinted.

"But it worked," Teakh said.

"It worked because it was abusive. Suppose you have someone who will do anything for love. How would you control him? The breeders had it down to a science, just how to tie a man in emotional knots."

"But you loved one person and did it for him," Teakh said. "I've chosen the one for me, a woman. I met with her in Shellako. We talked. Matta Carrie. I call her Angel."

Keno's eyebrows shot up. "Oh, really?" He barked a laugh. "You think Matta Carrie will agree to be your girl? Gimp, you sure shine."

Teakh flicked a beaded strand of his hair. "If I'm worth

gold, why not? Let's do the other photos and skip the rampants for now."

"That means you'll have to keep the braids a bit longer," Keno said.

"I'm okay with that." He'd find out if Angel liked the style. If not, he'd change it as soon as he could. He'd have no problem with rampants if she were watching.

CHAPTER 26
Fennako City

O N LAWROCK ISLAND, Teakh and Sis strolled near the municipal harbor, the breeze crisp and invigorating. They'd flown in on different stratoplane flights. Sunlight broke through the clouds and glinted on Tristan Bay. Elated, he strode beside his sister, wearing his new seaboots and Ralko life vest hidden under his old parka and fishermen's bibs. He wore a watchcap and bandanna over his mess of braids and jewelry.

Sis had actually done it. She'd arranged for review of their petition. If it were granted, Teakh would become clan chief. He wouldn't have territory, but one step at a time. His boots crunched on the cobblestone streets. He'd read regulations for clan incorporation. Noahee didn't meet the criteria, not by a long shot. So why had the Queen granted an audience? He thrust his hands into his pockets and hunched against the wind.

They turned into a narrow lane between shop fronts. Window signs advertised goods and services: ships hardware, propulsor repair. One shop displayed electronic posters of men below a sign reading, MADAME X'S MANNERY.

Sis elbowed Teakh. "This must be the place to purchase studs like you. I want to see how this works." She tugged Teakh's arm, and they entered the shop.

Inside, a woman stood to greet them. Shiny black thigh boots encased her long legs, and a tight vest barely contained the swell of her breasts. Behind her, the entire wall displayed the image of a man's muscular torso.

"What are you about?" she breathed, the traditional greeting laden with husky innuendo, but she looked away, flirting or maybe dismissing Teakh as beneath her. Presumably this was Madame X.

"Just looking," Sis said.

"Look all you want. The question is..." Madame X touched a finger to her lips. "What kind of man are you looking for?"

Sis met Madame X's gaze. "What do you have for stud services?"

Taken back by Sis's frankness, he stepped toward the door.

"Insemination. That is what we sell here." Madame X glanced at Teakh. "A wise choice." Good Danna! Did she think they were married?

"He's my brother," Sis said.

Teakh tugged at her arm, but she stood fast.

Madame X said, "Oh. So sorry." Giving her full attention to Sis, she scrolled through photos, giant images of flexing men.

Teakh stared at the toe of his boot and wished desperately that he could be somewhere else. Then his own image came up. Gold was woven into his hair, and his hip boots were matte black, but otherwise he was naked. Sis gasped, her mouth agape.

Teakh slouched, attempting to disguise himself with little more than his posture. He was a fisherman. Nothing more than a fisherman. He pulled his watchcap lower, the wool sliding over bandanna and beads.

Madame X continued extolling his image. "This stud is top quality, genuine Seaguard, and features Noah genetics. You can bid for him on Kordelko Auctions, or for a reasonable fee, I can procure a live sample. Darling, few men can resist me. "

Teakh's face heated, and his ears rang. Madame X was a succubus, the real thing, and trying to sell his seed to his own sister. Madame X turned on her stool, and her eyebrows arched in surprise. She shoved back Teakh's watchcap and bandanna. He caught her wrist and pushed her hand away, too late. His braids tumbled out, beads cascading against his scalp.

Madame X said, "Well, this changes everything,"

"We're going." Teakh grasped Sis's elbow, firmly this time.

"Sir, if you'd slip into the back with me for a quickie," Madame X called from behind him, "I'll give your sister a bargain. Any man she wants at half-price."

The door banged shut as they hurried outside. Teakh stooped in the lane, his hands on his thighs, his face clammy. He coughed, forcing down the sour contents of his stomach. His ancestors had been manipulated and enslaved, tricked into incest in the service of eugenics.

Sis rested a hand on his back. "Are you okay?"

He'd been warned about succubi, but he hadn't expected to be propositioned in such a crass manner in front of his sister. He'd originally thought that woman sexy.

He wiped his mouth and took a deep breath. They were due for their appointment at the Department of Clan and Lineage. He was determined to present himself as confident and well prepared to take on the responsibilities of clan chief. He would put Madame X's proposal behind him.

FOLLOWING AN ELECTRONIC map on Sis's handscreen, they hurried through the twisting lanes to an office in the palace complex. Pausing before the row of business fronts, Teakh removed his hat and bandanna so that his braids hung free over his implant scars. He opened his parka to display the red-and-black vest beneath. It was the best he could do for now. If the petition were granted, he'd have Seaguard kit made in Noahee colors, provided he could afford the clothing.

Using his implant, he transmitted their arrival. *Teakh and Annon Noahee. We've arrived for our appointment.*

Dame Bulla Fennako here. Please leave your shoes in the foyer. Refrain from leaving mud on my floor, she added querulously.

Was this the correct office? Normally a businesswoman would wave through a window or open the door for visitors. Teakh glanced at Sis then opened the door for her.

The foyer contained a polished table with an arrangement of dried flowers but no place to sit. Sis kicked off her shoes and hung her parka on a hook. Hopping on one foot, Teakh attempted to remove a boot, an awkward procedure made even more difficult by wearing them underneath fisherman's bibs. Depths! Would he ever get accustomed to wearing Seaguard kit?

He couldn't take the bibs off without removing his vest.

214

He tottered and caught himself against the wall. There was a sinking good reason Seaguardsmen were allowed to wear boots inside, and Dame Bulla surely knew Teakh was Seaguard.

Giving up on dignity, Teakh sat on the floor to pull off one boot at a time. He stood and hung his parka, then they went into the office.

Dame Bulla faced them across a desk, her lips narrow. "Let's get this over with. The two of you in no way qualify as a clan."

Sis stood openmouthed, and Teakh's anger roiled. He forced out words, tight and controlled. "Why did you have us come here?"

"It wasn't my decision." Dame Bulla held out splayed fingers, enumerating Teakh and Sis's ineptitude: not enough members, no significant assets, and high debt load. They weren't even of legal age.

Teakh clutched at the table, furious that he and Sis had flown all the way to Fennako City only to be told their plans were worthless.

Dame Bulla leaned back, dusting her hands. "However, the Queen has agreed to grant your request on a provisional basis. It's very possible her mental grasp is slipping."

He stared at Dame Bulla. "What are the provisions?"

"The Queen asks only that she is allowed to select the father of Annon's children." Dame Bulla nodded at Sis. "Your name is Annon, correct?"

"Aye," Sis said, her calm remarkable. That sister of his could stare down Poseidon himself.

He leaned across the desk toward Dame Bulla. "So you're saying the Queen will approve our petition if and only if my sister agrees to an arranged marriage?"

"Not a marriage," Dame Bulla said, with a lift of her chin. "Artificial insemination."

Teakh planted his hand on the desk. "No!" He'd just been brazenly propositioned by a black marketeer. If Madame X had succeeded, his own seed could have been available to be used to impregnate his sister.

"It's for your sister to decide." Ignoring Teakh, Dame Bulla laid out the details of the proposal.

He resisted the urge to leave, taking Sis with him, but she

listened intently, asking questions and taking notes. Fennako laid on even more requirements. Noahee wouldn't even be a full clan but a type of club with voluntary membership. It would supplement, rather than replace, its members' matrilineal clans. Teakh focused on taking deep, even breaths. If Dame Bulla had intended to rattle him, she wouldn't succeed. As a good detective, he took part in the discussion: drawing out information, making inferences, considering ramifications. Fennako wanted Sis to have multiple children by the same man, and Teakh pushed for only one child.

When the meeting had concluded, Teakh hauled his boots over his feet and worked the cuffs up over his thighs. He and Sis exited into the lane. The breeze blew damp with a hint of snow, and the sun shone as a blur through clouds.

"It's the same sort of arrangement you're making." Sis walked beside Teakh. "And we agreed men and women are equal."

"It's different," Teakh stopped in front of her, eye to eye.

"Well, yes," Sis said. "I happen to be keeping custody of my children."

Wary of being overheard, Teakh lowered his voice. "They could use my sperm to impregnate you. That's how breeders create a purebred strain."

"How would they get your sperm?" Sis broke off and stepped around him.

"Well..." Angel hadn't taken his sperm. She was too classy for that. He began again. "This whole arrangement is fishier than a tote of rotting chum. Why did Dame Bulla have us thinking we'd been turned down? Why did Fennako purchase our airfare? What in the depths is Clan Fennako getting out of all this?"

Sis's posture stiffened. "The Queen makes this decision, not Clan Fennako."

"Maybe Dame Bulla is right," Teakh said. "Her Majesty is daft. We're not signing until we know what's going on."

"We're not signing anyway until we work out the details and meet with the Queen," Sis said, her whisper vehement.

A mariner in a dark parka approached. With a bob of his head, he addressed Teakh as Seaguard. "A word with you, sir."

With a twitch of her shoulder, Sis glanced sideways, and

they followed the man around the corner of a building.

A woman clad in black leaned against a wall, her vest open and revealing the curves of her breasts. Madame X, spike heel against the masonry, smiled. "My offer still stands." With a hand now bare of the interface glove, she gestured upward. "Security cameras are inoperable here. No one will know."

No one except the man who brought them into the alley and Sis standing right beside Teakh. He forced a smile and remained calm. Too often volatile situations erupted into violence, touched off by hasty words. "I appreciate your offer, but I must decline. We'll be on our way."

The man blocked the alley exit.

"Not so fast." The buzz of an electro stimulator issued from Madame X's hand. "I'm told Noah men like to be roughed up. I can do that for you. With this little toy, I can get a rise out of any man."

Sis launched herself at Madame X, grabbing fistfuls of hair. "Slimy hag!" Screaming, she clawed at Madame X's face.

"Wait! Sis!" Teakh scrambled to reach Sis, but the man got there first.

Arm across Sis's chest, caging her flailing arms, the man addressed Madame X. "What do you want with her?"

Teakh sent a distress signal on the Seaguard emergency channel. Then his own wrath exploded, and he threw a punch, aiming for the man's jaw. Teakh's fist connected and the man crumpled, taking Annon down with him. A second man charged into the fray, and Teakh dodged. Where the depths had he come from?

A comset clicked, and the man on the ground shouted, "We've been mugged."

"I just love it when men fight," Madame X said. "It turns me on. Hold still. We'll finish this up."

She lunged at Teakh with the stimulator. He twisted aside, and the device connected with the man behind him. The man buckled.

"Police!" a voice shouted from the end of the alley.

Madame X bolted, but Sis seized her foot. Kicking and swearing, Madame X attempted to free herself. Sis, her face white with fury, clung like a limpet, oblivious to arriving law enforcement. Danna! That sister of his had no street sense.

"Hands up!" shouted a female officer.

Poseidon damn it! Once again Teakh was in trouble with Fennako City Police, but this time he had Sis along. Madame X jerked free and ran, stumbling in her high-heeled boots.

Sis shouted, "She's getting away!"

"Get down!" bellowed the officer.

The men complied, lying prostrate on the ground, but Sis remained on her knees.

She held up her hands, a strip of black lace trailing from her fingers. "I am down."

Teakh whispered, "Do what they say."

At last, Sis lay beside Teakh. The icy stones of the alley pressed against his cheek.

Why hadn't the police followed Madame X? Or maybe they had; police surveillance cameras might have recorded her identity.

"Put your hands on your head," commanded the officer.

"Hospitality," Teakh gasped. Danna! What a royal tangle. "We claim hospitality," he said more loudly.

Under hospitality, he and Sis could be neither arrested nor released. They'd be held without trial. This wasn't like claiming hospitality in Tatumuko Village, but he had no choice. If Ralko found out where they were and why, Aunt Dyse and Gorbus would come to collect their wayward breeding stock.

"Don't be doing that," the policewoman said. "You'll just be making it hard for yourselves and for us."

The other officer bent over Teakh's assailant, holding a cloth to the man's bleeding nose.

"We're diplomats," Sis said gamely. "I'm clan grandmatriarch. And my brother is Seaguard chief."

"Not likely." The policewoman stooped to frisk Teakh and removed his knife. She next checked Sis for weapons.

Two men approached, dressed in hip boots and gray-green vests, most likely Harbor Patrol. Teakh had hailed them himself. Founder! Now two groups of officers had responded. Harbor Patrol represented Tristan Bay. Fennako police were under the command of Princess Mareen Fennako. Oh yes, Princess Sergeant Mareen had already warned him once.

"What do we got here?" Harbor Patrol asked. "We received a Seaguard distress signal."

"Dockside brawl," the policewoman said. "And this kid is claiming hospitality. He says he's a Seaguard lord."

"My brother was attacked," Sis said, still not playing by the rules.

Teakh glared at her and shook his head. Under the strictures of hospitality, they had the right to anonymity, but they couldn't make accusations.

Harbor Patrol squatted beside Teakh. "Son, I assume you sent that signal. Listen here. It'll go easier if you leave off this hospitality claim. If you were assaulted, we'll have a look at the security cameras and get this straightened out."

"Cameras aren't working," the policewoman said.

"We're diplomats on clan business," mumbled Teakh, repeating Sis's assertion.

"What's your claim number?" Harbor Patrol asked.

Confused, Teakh shook his head.

"At our border, claimants are issued a hospitality number to be used in the place of identification." Harbor Patrol touched his ear as if about to transmit. "You don't have one, do you?"

Teakh grimaced. Seemingly Fennako specialized in bureaucratic complication. Fennako Department of Clan and Lineage had forwarded his airfare and documents without any such number. Teakh had no number, but he did have an implant. On the Seaguard open channel, he revealed his status by transmitting. *Identification given at the border.*

Harbor Patrol straightened. "Excuse me, sir," he said, acknowledging Teakh as Seaguard. He nodded to the policewoman. "This man is Seaguard. We'll look into the hospitality claim."

"Our need is clear," Sis said. "My brother was attacked."

"An authority must vouch for your claim," Harbor Patrol said. "Who approved your entry into Fennako waters?"

"The Queen," Sis said. "We're on diplomatic business."

The policewoman shook her head.

Princess Mareen had been asking Keno and Sis about Teakh, possibly bidding on him. Was she behind this grab for Noah genetics?

Teakh whispered, "Might be a setup, police in cahoots with Madame."

Sis lifted her head and spoke to the policewoman. "Contact Dame Bulla in the Department of Clan and Lineage."

The policewoman clicked her comset and made the hail. "We have two individuals claiming hospitality on diplomatic grounds. One male, the other female, both approximately two-dozen years old. Will you vouch for them?"

"I must consult with my superiors." Dame Bulla's voice was aloof.

Maybe she was part of the conspiracy. Panic gripped Teakh's gut. Keno wouldn't be able to help this time, not up against Fennako. And this time, Teakh couldn't pretend naïve innocence.

"On your feet," the policewoman said. "Let's get you back to the station. Then we'll book you."

A police comset bleated. "Dame Bulla here. These two indeed have been granted diplomatic status. Royal Guard will arrive shortly to escort and protect our guests. Sir, ma'am, Fennako extends our deepest apologies."

What sort of game was Fennako playing?

Royal guardsmen soon arrived in the alley. Their folded boot tops displayed silver Danna stars, and their hair jangled with platinum ornaments, nearly as gaudy as the gold hidden under Teakh's bandanna. These men were under the command of Her Majesty the Queen, nominally anyway. Teakh wasn't sure exactly who they answered to.

A total of seven law enforcement officers now crowded the alley, along with Teakh, Sis, and the two assailants.

"We'll take over from here," a Royal Guardsman said.

Harbor Patrol stepped forward. "With all due respect, hospitality is the jurisdiction of Tristan Bay Seaguard. Harbor Patrol will provide escort."

Amazed, Teakh witnessed two law enforcement agencies dispute for the honor of providing him and Sis with a bodyguard. He settled the issue by accepting one man from Royal Guard and another from Harbor Patrol.

CHAPTER 27
The Queen

AFTER SUNSET, SIS and Teakh sat on beds in their lodging, the walls of the tiny room streaked and peeling. Twilight had softened the grime.

"I'm going to do it," Sis said, hidden in shadows. "If we were a clan, assaulting you would have been an interclan offense, an attack on a sovereign lord. Fennako Police would've arrested Madame X."

"Maybe not." Teakh picked at a fraying sheet. "Consider. Why were the security cameras inoperable? Why did the police let Madame X get away? Why did we have three law enforcement agencies responding and disputing jurisdiction?"

"I don't know."

Teakh shook his head. "I don't know either, and that worries me. Harbor Patrol is Lord Tristan Bay. They handle border security." And Harbor Patrol had received Teakh's distress signal. "Municipal Police is Princess Mareen Fennako. They respond to civil disturbances. Royal Guard might be the Queen or might be someone else." With the elderly queen slipping, power could have fallen to nearly anyone in the royal family. "Don't make this deal."

"But I would like to have children," Sis said. "I do need a man for that. The deal is too good to pass up."

"Find your own man." Teakh's thumb tore through the tattered sheet. "Don't sell your children."

"I keep custody," Sis said. "Anyway, why is it okay for you to sell your children and not for me?"

"I'm not selling my children," Teakh said. "I'm selling my services."

"Well then, I am too. We agreed that men and women would be equal in our clan. I can always bear a child for the Queen then marry whomever I like."

"Do you think your husband will be pleased with that?"

"I might not even get a husband without this deal. What do I have going for me? But if I were a clan matriarch—"

"Then what? You'd have a husband who married you for your status? You're better than that."

Sis drew her feet under her. "What do you think Mama would say?"

"She'd agree with me. Don't do this. Marry a man for love, even if no one approves. Mama and Papa never had clan approval for their relationship."

"And you know how hard that was for Mama," Sis said. "She was an outcast. For Danna's sake, she lived in a bog."

"She did what was right," Teakh said. "And so should we."

"Well, I'm going to continue to negotiate with Fennako." Sis spoke with the resolution of the little admiral who'd commanded Teakh's toy flotilla.

"But we don't have to agree to their terms," he said. "It's a matter of attitude. We've got to act like we have the cards, because we do."

IN THE QUEEN'S antechamber, Teakh tried not to pace. After days of negotiations, they'd finalized the agreement. The balance was good, too good. In exchange for bearing one child, Fennako had agreed to recognize Noahee as a clan and extend partial sovereignty. Fennako would guarantee Sis acceptance into their prestigious law program and would pay her tuition, room, and board. She'd receive a stipend, and Fennako would pay for child support as well as medical care for Sis and the child. Noahee would be able to negotiate contracts, represent members in court, and issue bonds, but wouldn't provide health care or retirement benefits to members.

Teakh had asked for a stipulation that insemination would be done in person. This would guard against illegal procurement of semen and so against incest. Fennako had agreed but countered that there would be no witnesses to the act and that the man would remain anonymous.

The door swung open. A Royal Guardsman bowed and ushered Teakh and Sis into the presence of the Queen, a tiny woman bent with age. She sat wrapped in a blanket with her feet up on a hassock.

Sunlight glowed through rounds of stained glass and fell in bright patterns on a polished wood floor and thick area rug. Molding, carved into flowing curves, entwined windows and walls, as if the wood had become fluid then solidified again in organic shapes, like coral or the bones of a whale.

Annon and Teakh bowed deeply, as they'd been instructed.

The Queen's eyes gleamed, a sharp intelligence within an ancient face. "Come here, let me see you. So this is Annon. Of course you are."

Sis knelt beside the Queen's chair.

Teakh remained standing. "Your Majesty."

"Please call me Grandmother." The Queen smiled. "Now then, you must be Teakh. My, you're a strapping young fellow, and handsome too. A bit like my grandson."

"Thank you, Grandmother," Teakh said.

The Queen smiled at Sis. "And you're a bright girl. Good head on your shoulders."

"Pardon my asking," Teakh said, "but why have you agreed to recognize our clan?"

The Queen folded her age-spotted hands. "Forthright. I like that. I know quite a bit about you, including about that seagull of yours. Get it registered. You'll be getting your own codes soon. You've got daring and initiative, both of you. I like that in young people. You're going to give the breeders a run for their money. Oh yes! I'd love to stick around to see it."

"We're honored," Sis said.

"But why the child?" Teakh asked, standing in his boots on the Queen's fluffy carpet. "And why all this secrecy about the man's identity?"

"Why not? Your niece or nephew will need a good father.

Don't you worry. I've picked out a good man for your sister.
I fancy myself a matchmaker."

"Why keep his identity a secret?" Teakh asked, again
shaking his head, still dumbfounded.

"Politics! I happen to lack absolute authority. Too bad. But
you're smart, both of you, and the man too."

Who the depths was the man?

CHAPTER 28
Drunken Sailor

THE FERRY PULLED up to the Dojko terminal, passing a black-and-scarlet esskip snubbed to a pier. What was Gorbus doing here? Hauling his duffle, Teakh debarked, avoided Gorbus's craft, and tramped up to the gym. He entered through the back door.

"You got a visitor!" hollered Randy.

Keno wasn't in his office, so Teakh hailed him. *What's this all about?*

Your aunt is here asking for you.

Teakh trudged into the front parlor. Keno sat with Dyse, crumb-strewn plates and empty cups between them. He shot Teakh a sour expression. "She's been here for hours."

"Where have you been?" Dyse tapped the rim of her handscreen.

Teakh nodded to Keno and dropped his duffle. "Observing the tide," he said, his answer both polite and meaningless.

Dyse put her hands on her hips, by all appearances an angry fishwife. "You were gone for, what, three days?"

Five, actually, but Teakh didn't correct her.

"Unacceptable." She jabbed a finger toward Keno. "We've entrusted you with our most precious nephew." Blustering, she used the imperial we.

Keno backed up and met with the sideboard. "I've told you before, this isn't the village brig, and I'm not a jailer."

"What's to say he wasn't meeting with some woman on the sly?" Aunt Dyse thrust her finger at Teakh.

He told the truth in a general sort of way. "I was traveling on Seaguard business." He had met with a woman—Her Majesty. Dyse could fuss all she wanted, but in marine matters, Seaguard chain of command took precedence.

"I'll have a talk with Lord Ralko," Dyse said. "Make him understand the situation. We can't have Teakh traveling unguarded, no matter what he thinks of his safety."

"My travel was at the behest of Fennako, not Ralko." Teakh eased his bandanna. Fennako had greater authority than Ralko.

Dyse narrowed her eyes. "Don't slip me a fast one."

"You're welcome to seek verification." With a shrug, Teakh feigned disinterest, as if his business had been of little consequence. If Dyse were to inquire, she'd receive confirmation that his business had been on the behest of Fennako Seaguard but nothing more.

"Never mind that. I know what you were up to. Tracking down that Idylko woman."

How did she find out about Angel?

"She's a confirmed Majora woman, and she has a Minora partner," Dyse said, and Teakh's anxiety eased. Dyse had conflated Angel with Jeena. "Nephew, you're a pushover. A pretty woman comes along, and you're hooked. Not a consideration or thought of why she might be interested in the likes of you. That woman runs a clandestine lab. She was probably looking to steal your seed and sell it. Then she'll dump you without so much as a good-bye peck on the cheek."

Teakh shook his head. Jeena might have run tests without clan permission, but the lab was legitimate. "She works at Idylko hospital. Nothing clandestine about it." If Dyse mistakenly believed Jeena was Teakh's sole interest, he wasn't going to set that record straight.

"Stay away from that woman." Dyse brandished her screen. "If word gets out that you're donating sperm, the market will be flooded with counterfeits."

"The market swimming in semen?" Keno grinned. "Our boy the font of Noah's flood."

Thank Danna for Keno and his efforts to defuse the situation.

"This isn't a joking matter," Dyse said, clearly livid.

"I can assure you Teakh hasn't been off distributing his

marvelous elixir," Keno said.

Dyse sniffed. "It's not what he does that matters. It's what people think he does."

"Teakh knows his responsibilities," Keno said.

It wasn't a joking matter, not to Teakh, not after his run-in with Madame X. He lifted his bag. "I need to get on with my responsibility—training. And most likely Gorbus is getting bored down by the harbor. Don't you have something better to do?"

Keno touched Dyse's elbow. "You are a remarkable woman, so conscientious..."

As Keno laid on the flattery, Teakh made his exit through the central gymnasium on his way to his quarters. Among the weights, a cluster of men had gathered around a tall newcomer clad in full Seaguard kit, seaboots with the tops turned down and a vest with a knife displayed haft down. Kinkill! First Dyse, now a Seaguard officer. Teakh tried to slip past the crowd. He didn't trust any of them, not Harbor Patrol, not Royal Guard, and not whoever this fellow happened to be.

Ripple seized Teakh. "Gimp, come on over and meet Patroller. That's what we call him, because he's Seaguard." Teakh tried to wave him off, but Ripple persisted. "Patroller's got quite the gig. The girl gets tied up like she's been captured by pirates or something. She's all naked and ready." Ripple fluttered his hands, and his voice jumped to falsetto. "'Help! Help! Save me. Someone save me.'" His voice dropped an octave. "Seaguard bursts into the room. 'What scoundrel has done thus?'" He wiggled his eyebrows. "'I'll save you.'" Ripple thrust his hips, then again spoke in falsetto. "'How can I ever repay you, you brave, handsome Seaguard man?'"

Patroller tipped his head back and chuckled. "It's not like that."

"It's not?" Ripple simpered and went into falsetto again. "'Oh no! I've been caught by the Seaguard. I'll never do it again. Hit me! Hurt me! I promise.'" Ripple fluttered his eyelids and clasped his hands. "'If you let me go, I'll make you very happy.'" He swung his hips. "'Come on, big boy.'" He laughed, and the others joined in. "Truly, girls go for that kind of thing. They eat it up."

Patroller straightened his vest. "Well, they do seem to like a man in Seaguard kit."

"It's not just the life vest," whispered Ripple to Teakh. "Patroller happens to be the real thing. It's a nice gig if you can pull it off."

Teakh stared up at the clerestory windows then down at the mat-covered floor—anywhere but at Patroller with his chiseled features, buzz-cut hair, and imposing height. Teakh felt unkempt, sham Seaguard, a freelance detective. Not even that. Teakh spent time squabbling with gulls over dead fish, or fishing, which amounted to the same thing.

With the sun slipping toward the horizon, he skulked down to the waterfront, his gaudy hair covered with both a bandanna and watch cap. In the Salty Hound, he slumped on his stool. He would become a Seaguard chief only if a stranger impregnated his sister. What kind of man was he? Fennako had specified that Sis would meet with the appointed man alone, no witnesses. Anything could happen to her.

Loopy came over, a notepad in her plump hands. "The usual?"

"Better make it a whiskey this time," Teakh said.

"What's wrong, sugar?" Loopy leaned toward him, her lips pouting.

"Everything is wrong." Sure, he'd made an agreement with the Queen, but at the cost of his sister's child. Teakh had been a fool, a sinking fool. Madame X had opened his eyes. If she were after his seed, surely other succubi were willing to jump him as well, including lab technicians such as Jeena.

Loopy placed a whisky on the bar. "Want to talk about it?"

"No." Teakh gripped the tumbler then wrinkled his nose and sipped the contents. The stuff tasted like floor cleaner. He coughed. Moisture beaded on the glass. Nothing for it. He gulped the whiskey. With a mild buzz, Teakh traced patterns on the bar top. If Jeena had taken his seed, Angel must have helped.

The door opened. Lugo entered with a gust of wind and shook rain from his slicker. "Jamie. Say, what's wrong?"

"Don't want to talk about it." Teakh stared into his drink.

On the side of the tumbler, one droplet joined another and slid down to join the puddle forming below the drink.

Lugo leaned against the bar top. "Woman trouble?"

Angel had used Teakh and thrown his carcass away as if he were nothing more than putrefying flesh. "Aye."

Good Danna! He was getting maudlin on only one drink. He struggled to recall Angel in her garden. With his sleeve, Teakh mopped at the rings of moisture left by the glass. Surely such a beautiful woman wouldn't have deceived him.

Lugo gave Teakh's shoulder a shove. "The worst kind. Cheer up. We've all been there."

Teakh hunched and shook his head.

Lugo scooted onto a barstool. "Does it have to do with that stud up at Keno's gym? Has he been after your girl?"

"What stud?" Teakh asked.

"Some fellow stopped by today. Seaguard. And he was complaining about chauffeuring his cousin, who's this prima donna super stud. Getting all the girls. Did he go after your girl?"

"Something like that," Teakh said. Patroller had arrived today, but so had Cousin Gorbus. Most likely Gorbus had been spreading rumors. Mr. Prima Donna was none other than Teakh himself. With a snort of sour laughter, he turned his drink in his hands. If his attempts to get an erection were an indication, he would wash out as a stud. A girl would be tied up, naked and ready, screaming for rescue, and he'd have a limp cock.

"That's the hag," Lugo said. "So you're up at Keno's, swimming. Getting ready for competition to please your girl. And along comes super stud and steals her from you?"

Teakh choked on his drink and coughed. He recovered. "You got it. Lost my girl."

"Hey, Loopy," Lugo said, "another whiskey for Jamie here."

SUPPORTED BY LUGO and Chuck, his stomach roiling, Teakh staggered home to Keno's gym. Nearly at the side door, his stomach heaved. He spewed vomit on the stones of the lane.

"Ah, depths!" Chuck stepped back. "Jamie, you're a mess."

"It's all right," Lugo said.

Teakh transmitted to key open the back door.

There in the back foyer stood Keno, clad in a pair of shorts and nothing else. "Gimp! What the depths is this?" He must have been waiting. Or maybe Loopy had sent word.

Teakh hung off Lugo's shoulder. "Call me Jamie, Jamie Noah." He hiccupped. "Just had a few drinks. Me and the boys."

Keno waved a hand before his nose. "You stink. This isn't like you."

Chuck patted Teakh's shoulder. "Aye. Jamie usually holds his liquor real well."

"That's 'cuz I drink apple juice," Teakh said. "Observe the tide, and you will survive. That's your kin, not you personally. Wish I could just die. Be prepared...assist the stranger in need. Hostis...Hospes...Hospitality...proper treatment of strangers." He hiccupped. "Poseidon gonna turn you into a pillar of salt... Hospital." Angel had found him in the Idylko hospital. He sobbed. A stranger in a hospital. "Honor your father..."

"Hospice," Keno said dryly. "Care for the dying. Let's get you to bed."

"He's all tore up on account of his girl," Lugo said.

Keno sighed then led them into the bunk wing and opened a door. "Bring him in here."

Teakh staggered into the room.

"Say, wasn't Steffin Kosatka your friend?" Chuck asked Keno. The voices seemed distant.

"The room has two beds," mumbled Teakh. "Not sleeping with Pretty Boy."

"Steffin who?" Lugo asked.

"Fellow who drowned a few years back," Chuck said.

And now Keno had a far-off gaze, surely thinking of his dead lover, all bloated, pale, and washed up on the shore in pieces. Frat it all!

"And you're sharing a room with Jamie?" Chuck asked.

"Roommates," Teakh mumbled. He wasn't going to be a replacement for Keno's drowned lover. "Me, I'm in love with a sucky. Angel. Poseidon sink it all! Prettiest girl there ever was. And she's gonna sell my children. Kinkill! This here is Pretty

230

Boy, my gay uncle." He shoved Keno. "He thinks he's gonna protect me, but he just wants to keep Angel all to himself. He thinks he's in love with me. Damn you to Poseidon! He takes his clothes off for her, an' she paints him naked. Sells the paintings to lonely widows and to...and to..." To Jeena and Reez. Keno's picture, not Teakh's, hung above their bed while they made love. Teakh sobbed. "And he doesn't even like girls."

"My kinsman," Keno said dryly. "Honor."

"Kinsman? Then he's Dojko?" Chuck asked.

"Noah," Teakh said. "Told you I'm Noah. I mean Noahee."

"You're gonna be fine." Keno took a firm hold of Teakh, supporting him. He nodded to Lugo and Chuck. "I'll take care of him from here. The lad thinks he's the first person to have been smitten by love."

Teakh sagged against Keno.

"Aye," Lugo said. "Hard the first time, though. We'll be going now. Jamie being safe and all."

The door clicked shut.

"Now get undressed." Keno gripped Teakh's arms and stared him down.

"What're you gonna do to me?" mumbled Teakh.

"Get you cleaned up."

"No!"

"Sink you!" Keno shoved Teakh into the bathroom and pushed him into the shower.

Under a cold blast of water, Teakh stumbled and caught himself against the wall. The spray hissed against his clothing, washing vomit down the drain. His life vest inflated, filling his parka, straining the fabric. He pulled off his parka then fumbled with the fasteners on his vest. His clothing became a wet heap on the floor.

TEAKH AWOKE, TEMPLES throbbing, mouth gummy and foul with the aftertaste of vomit. In pre-dawn darkness, the bedside nightlight glowed, an evil red eye, the light casting Keno's face in lurid shadows.

"Get up!" Keno commanded. "Observe the tide."

Teakh moaned, his body too heavy to move.

"Alcohol excuses nothing," Keno said. "Be prepared. You could be dead. Good thing you were on land with honorable men."

"I want to die. Leave me alone." He pulled the covers over his head.

"Poseidon, no!" Keno jerked the blanket off Teakh, exposing him to a cold blast of air. "You want her to see you falling-down drunk? Think that will impress her? Get yourself together. You revere the Noah Code. Follow it!"

"Sink the Code!" Teakh slid his legs over the side of his bed, sat up, and groaned. The couch, screen, and cupboards seemed to swim, as if darkness were a fluid filling the room.

Keno propelled Teakh into the bathroom. "Get yourself cleaned up."

Eyes bleary, Teakh leaned against the wall. "I did last night."

"Do it again."

Teakh glanced at the mirror. His reflection was hideous, a scowling face beneath braided tentacles. "Stupid hairdo."

Keno tossed him a knit cap, and Teakh pulled it over his ears, covering both beads and scars.

"Drink this." Keno thrust a mug at Teakh.

The dark beverage scalded his mouth. He spat and grimaced. "What the depths is this bilge?"

"Black horehound, nettles, chamomile, and I don't know what else. Drink up."

Teakh choked down the brew and abandoned the mug in the bathroom before following Keno into the studio for morning observances.

Dutifully, Teakh focused on his breathing, then accessed Gull and flew up and out the window, wanting only to escape his aching body. On the roof, he preened his feathers. Head pounding, he flew to the Seaguard lagoon to note the height of the tide. He made only the minimum effort required by the code, then he landed on a pylon and endured.

CHAPTER 29
Hangover

TEAKH SLUMPED, HEAD hanging, elbows on the dining room table. Most of the men ate breakfast. Keno, at the side table, dumped berries into a blender, along with a scoop of something brown.

Pector shoveled down fried potatoes and smoked haddock. The smell turned Teakh's stomach. Pector set down his fork and inclined his head toward Keno. "What're you fixing there?"

Keno stuffed a green wad of herbs into the blender. "Smoothie."

"Looks like a hangover breakfast," Pector said.

"Must be for Gimp," offered Randy. "For hangover, try the hair of the dog."

Teakh groaned. He should've stayed in bed, regardless of Keno. Damn him to the depths. Everyone was watching Teakh as suggestions flew. He stared at the smooth tabletop.

"Put in some vodka," someone said.

"Potato crisps with plenty of vinegar and salt."

"Pickle juice," someone said else, maybe Manly.

"Lima beans for potassium."

The blender whirred. Teakh lifted his head.

"He can get his own." Keno was now adding clabbered milk, and the blender whirled the white stream into a mud-colored vortex.

Teakh nearly gagged and glanced away. "Looks nasty."

"It's good." Keno poured a glass. "Give it a try. I made plenty."

Randy said, "Keno, you made that for Gimp, and you're

not fooling anyone." He laughed. "We've all been there before, and we're glad it's not us."

Randy rested his arm on Teakh's shoulder, and he shrugged it off.

"Let me give you some advice," Randy said. "Studding and drinking don't go together. You may think you're sexy while you're smashed, but you're not. The girls don't like it, and it wreaks havoc with your performance."

"Messes with your sperm count," offered Hairy. "And you can't get it up."

Randy addressed Keno and jerked his thumb toward Teakh. "You going to give him some sort of punishment?"

"I figure he's punishing himself." Keno poured a second glass. "Gimp, you ever gotten drunk before?"

Not like last night. Teakh said nothing.

"So now you know." Keno plunked the smoothie before Teakh.

Teakh took a sip of the swill and grimaced. The taste was like pulverized swamp grass. Oh yes, he'd tasted plenty of that as Gull. He choked down most of the swill then abandoned the glass in the dish bin. He'd make a quick exit.

Keno called out, "I have you down for swimming laps."

Teakh grunted. "I'll do it later at the rec center."

"Right now," Keno said. "Let's get going."

Teakh headed out of the dining room, Keno behind him.

"Exercise," Keno said, as they passed through the weight room. "Best thing for headaches and sorrow. Better than, what was it? Lima beans?"

Teakh attempted a laugh.

"Come on. I even changed the scheduling of the lap pool for you." Keno opened the door to the pool. "Bumped Randy right out of his slot."

"No need," Teakh said. He'd have only have more trouble from Randy.

"Too late now." Keno tossed Teakh a swim cap. "Crawl. A dozen laps. Get going."

Glaring at Keno, Teakh removed his bandanna and worked the cap over his braids. "Sink you!"

Teakh dove into the pool. Enfolded in water, he swam,

tallying the laps on his implant and using it to monitor his heart rate. Maybe Keno was right.

After swimming, the miserable day continued with the noon meal then chores. Teakh hauled dish bins to the scrub closet.

Randy followed him. "What's with the head scarf?"

Teakh set down a bin beside the sink. "I'm a pirate."

Randy sneered. "Who ever heard of a pirate who can't hold his liquor? You hiding something? Or is that a hangover cure?"

"Go to Poseidon." Teakh dumped the dish bin in the sink.

"We'll see about that." Randy whipped off Teakh's bandanna.

Beads tumbled around Teakh's ears, his scars exposed, his Seaguard status revealed. "Ugly hairdo," he said blandly.

Randy swung the bandanna. "Will you take a look at this? Gimp has jewelry in his hair. Gold!"

Forcing a smile, Teakh said, "Gold fish. My head is an aquarium."

Randy snickered. "My little studlet, you're full of surprises."

Teakh leaned against the sink. "You can keep the scarf, but it's not your color."

Randy grimaced and wadded the fabric strip, then he tossed it to Teakh. "Yellow. That's your color."

To the depths with Randy and his juvenile game. Teakh refused to play. "I have dishes to wash." He depressed the lever on the rinse hose and sprayed plates, washing uneaten food down the drain.

TEAKH RELAXED IN bed. The sky above the clerestory window was still pink with sunset. Keno lay in his own berth across the room.

"Have you been with Angel?" Teakh asked. He would be honest with himself. Very likely Angel enjoyed sleeping around.

"Who?" Keno asked.

"Matta Carrie. I mean, besides just for modeling."

"The sea witch." Keno snorted a laugh. "Pretending to be a siren. Oh, she's beautiful enough, but I turned her down."

Teakh's spirits sank. She had propositioned Keno. How

many other men? Teakh swallowed and posed the question he didn't want to ask. "The guys are saying she's a succubus. Is that true?"

"Honestly, I don't know. She cultivates an aura of mystery." Keno leaned on an elbow, his features lost in the evening twilight. "If I were to have a woman, it would be her and not for just one night. But she won't commit for more than that. She's the type who'll break your heart and laugh while doing it."

"I don't care," Teakh said, but he did. "Modeling for her will raise my value. Tell you what—introduce us, and I'll keep the stupid hairstyle." He patted his lumpy bandanna. "If not, I shave my head and leave. I won't be anyone's stud for hire."

"You're threatening?" Keno chuckled. "All because of modeling?"

"I'm telling you like it is. They say a Noah man only loves once, so be it. If she won't have me, then no one will have me."

"You're being silly," Keno said. "Where will you go?"

"Back to what I was doing—fishing. I'm done with women."

"Toss the mawkish theatrics," Keno said.

"Celibate until I die. I mean it."

Keno sat up. "What're you saying? Don't get suicidal on me."

"Who said anything about suicide?"

"You did. Last night," Keno said. "And you weren't drinking for the fun of it. I tell you, alcohol is a nasty way to die. Don't go to sea with a death wish either. Poseidon has a way of granting that kind of thing."

"It was a bender," Teakh said. "Nothing more."

"How alive did you feel this morning?" Keno asked. "Get drunk, drown in your own vomit, and everyone blames the liquor, not the man who got drunk. Not brave enough to face problems head-on and sober."

"I'm sober now, and I'm serious. Without Angel, I can't perform as a stud. It's as simple as that. If she won't have me, I'll leave the gym and save all of us a lot of trouble."

"You're making a mistake," Keno said. "We can solve your performance problems a different way."

"I don't have performance problems. Not with Angel."

"Sink her," Keno said.

Teakh's ire rose. Keno had no business criticizing Angel. "Leave her out of this. I make my own mistakes."

"I'm telling you, she's trouble," Keno said. "How are you going to feel when she goes with another man?"

Teakh frowned into the gloom. Like a compass needle, Keno had homed in on Teakh's desperation. "Maybe she won't."

"Believe what you want." Keno flopped back on his bed. "But remember, I'm here for you. When she rips out your heart and eats it, face it like a man. Don't drown yourself in sorrow and booze."

"I need your help now," Teakh said. "Introduce us properly. Tell her I want to be her model. I'll take it from there."

CHAPTER 30
Artist's Model

TEAKH AWOKE WITH a jolt of awareness. He pulled a pillow over his head, but the insistent urging of his implant repeated, tingling in his arms, hand, and feet. He'd set the foundered internal alarm himself. Then realization struck him. Today he'd meet with Angel.

He sat up. Darkness still filled the room. Keno's alarm clock beeped. Auditory alarms were as bad as the jolting of his implant. Keno's shrill auditory alarm ceased, shut off by Keno.

Teakh sat in bed, thinking of Lugo and Rosebay's wedding of all things. Teakh had stood as Lugo's witness and honor guard as the couple had recited vows before a magistrate and a recording camera. They'd used not the complexities of legal language, but traditional declarations of love. Teakh would have liked such a simple wedding for himself and Angel. If only it were possible.

After Teakh showered, he dressed in Ralko kit, his only formal wear. He secured a bandanna over his braids and wore the bracelet he'd purchased at Binnacle Betty's. Keno would accompany Teakh to Shellako as his chaperone, but this wouldn't be a wedding, merely a modeling session. Teakh sighed. He and Keno left the gym to catch the stratoport shuttle.

THE MORNING STILL fresh, they arrived at Angel's cottage and stepped onto the porch still festooned with garden art.

The sundial cast a shadow on its rusted arc of steel. Only a few bedraggled blooms remained in the garden, along with tall stalks, now smoke-like with fluffy seed heads.

The front door opened. Angel, Teakh's angel, stepped onto the porch wearing a paint-spattered smock, the hood thrown back. Her auburn hair was twisted up and secured with a wooden hair stick, but sweet tendrils had escaped and curled beside her delicate ears. A lump formed in Teakh's throat. He longed to slip the stick from her hair and let the wealth of it cascade free, to nibble at her lobe and caress her cheek.

But without so much as a nod to him, she stepped forward and kissed Keno right on the mouth. "Pretty Boy, so good of you to come."

Teakh clenched and unclenched his fists. How could she ignore him like that?

Angel stepped back, holding Keno's shoulder. "Let me look at you. What are you about?"

Keno inclined his head to Teakh, then Angel stepped around Keno. Mouth open, eyes wide, she put her hand to her heart. "Oh. Oh my! You. And all dressed up." Her eyes sparkled, merriment in their brown depths.

Teakh bobbed his head, the merest hint of a bow. "Do you want me?"

"Oh yes!"

He pulled her against him, and their lips met. Her supple body yielded to him. Their kiss lasted longer than the one she'd given to Keno. To the depths with Pretty Boy!

"It seems you know each other well," Keno said.

Teakh released Angel. "We met under conditions of hospitality." He twisted the silver bracelet encircling his wrist.

Her gaze flicked to the bright band. Smiling, she removed a slim silver bracelet from her pocket and slipped it on.

He bowed. "I trust I didn't offend."

She laughed. "Not at all. A charming hat. And a very nice piece of jewelry." She caressed the incised silver gulls on the bracelet.

Keno shook his head. "What are you talking about?"

"Your friend has an unusual style of courtship." Angel stroked the bracelet. "Unique, shall I say?"

Keno's glance went to Teakh's wrist.

Angel laughed and lightly touched Teakh's hand. "You should have one made for your bird, a wee bracelet."

A leg band for Gull, so he wouldn't lose her. That would be a good idea. "Banded," Teakh said, pleased to wear Angel's tag.

She ushered the two men into her front room, the walls still covered with drawings. Most of the painted canvases had been turned to face the wall. Drapery swags hung behind the divan, which was piled with bolsters, throw pillows, and furs that spilled to the floor. Nearby, a tripod held a camera.

"Please be comfortable." Angel indicated chairs pulled around the tea table.

When they had settled, she lifted the pot by its wicker handle and poured the tea. She placed the pot on the tray. "Now then. About this delectable fellow." Her eyelashes lowered as she smiled at Teakh and licked her lips. "We haven't been properly introduced. Pretty Boy, will you do the honors? What name does he use?"

"Gimp," Keno said, a wicked gleam in his eye. "Gimp, this is Matta Carrie."

Of all the names Teakh used, Gimp was nearly his least favorite, almost as bad a Ralko. Teakh accepted a bowl of tea.

"Is Matta Carrie the name you prefer?" Teakh asked then revealed the extent of his knowledge. "How about Angel? Or Marjoram Shellako? Although I understand your kin call you Margie."

Angel's laugh rang pure. "You do your research." Her eyes sparkled over the rim of her tea bowl. "Is Jamie Noah your real name? Fisherman who accepts hospitality?"

He gulped. She was onto him, and showing that her research may have been as extensive as his. He recovered. "I have several."

"I love a man of mystery. So what shall I call you?"

"Whatever you'd like."

She set her tea aside and dusted her hands. "Noah. Keno told me. And also...well, never mind. You're Noah."

Teakh cradled his warm bowl. "We've chosen the name Noahee."

"I like it, son of Noah." She crossed her ankles. "You're

looking well. Your leg has healed up?"

"Mostly," Teakh said. "Still aches, and there's a bump."

"I'd like to feel it."

Keno's eyebrows rose, but he continued to nibble a cracker.

"The pain?" Teakh asked.

Angel laughed. "No, the bump." Her fingers caressed her own thigh to her knee, and there traced tiny circles through her thin leggings.

"I'll have to take my boots off." Teakh set his tea aside.

"I'd like that," Angel said, her voice husky.

Keno cleared his throat. "Could you two slow down?"

Angel removed the tray, tea service, and remaining food. The tail of her smock swung over as she went through the door into the kitchen. Teakh remained facing Keno over the nearly empty table.

Teakh met Keno's gaze. "Well?" Teakh responded. Angel had flirted but hadn't eaten Teakh alive, or whatever it was that Keno feared.

Keno shrugged. "She's an artist."

Angel returned. "Pretty Boy tells me he's been preparing you, my ideal model."

"I don't know about that," Teakh said.

"Show me," Angel said.

A wave of uncertainty passed over him. Under Keno's direction, he'd practiced holding poses for extended periods, and he'd worked on his muscle definition, his flexibility, and his control, but was it enough? He remained a grubby fisherman trying to impress a woman who normally painted Seaguard princes.

"Go on." She pushed him toward the divan, placed on a fringed carpet.

Teakh's boot sank into the thick pile. He turned toward her, questioning.

"I'd like to do some studies." She moved the camera tripod into position and adjusted the lens. "But first undress for me." Holding a pad of paper, she seated herself at a drawing bench. "Even better, your trainer can undress you, show off his work. Would you mind, Pretty Boy?"

Keno stepped beside Teakh.

"He was just waiting for that invitation," Angel said, inspecting the tip of a pencil. "He likes boys."

"Men," corrected Keno.

"He likes making boys into men," Angel said.

"I like girls." Teakh glared at Keno. He longed for Angel's touch, not the sweaty pawing of his trainer.

"But I promised not to compromise your virtue." She twirled the pencil. "If I undress you, I won't be able to stop. So I'll watch. If that's all right with you."

"I don't see that it makes a difference," Teakh said. "We already—"

Angel put a finger to her lips. "Shhh. Our little secret. Go on."

Keno faced Teakh, one hand on Teakh's life vest.

"So I can see," Angel said. "From the back."

Keno moved behind Teakh, embracing him, cheek-to-cheek, and unfastened the clasps of Teakh's vest, displaying him as if he were a potential acquisition.

The camera clicked, either on a timer or activated by Angel. "Slower." She sighed. "Pretend I'm touching you."

Keno's lips brushed against Teakh's throat.

"Stop right there," she said.

They held the pose as she sketched. When she was done, Keno finished removing Teakh's vest and shirt, and they moved to other poses.

"May I touch?" Angel asked. "I like to see with my hands."

"But you said you wouldn't be able to stop." Teakh leaned toward her.

"Maybe I won't." She pushed him onto the divan and pulled off his boots deftly, as if she frequently helped Seaguardsmen undress.

Teakh shoved that thought aside. She was with him now, and she preferred him over Keno. She smoothed her hands over his arms, his chest, his back. Teakh tugged the wooden pin out of her hair, and the auburn richness cascaded free, the color so dark it was nearly purple in its shadows.

Angel laughed and swung her head, her lips brushing the center of his chest. "You've filled out beautifully."

She continued her explorations, her hands on his abdomen then his buttocks and thighs. Everywhere except the part that most yearned for her caresses.

Keno sprawled on a painter's bench, watching. Sinking voyeur!

"Keno, get out of here," Teakh said.

"He's the chaperone." Angel paused, hand on his calf. "This was broken?"

"Lower, my ankle," Teakh said.

Her hand slid downward, skimming the bone. "I feel it." She bent her head, auburn hair spilling over his feet as she kissed his ankle then his toes.

Teakh gasped. If only she'd kiss some parts a bit higher. He said, "Take off your shirt."

"You're a sassy one," she said.

He spread his fingers. "So I can see you with my hands."

"I'm the one doing the drawings."

"So?" Teakh said. "I want to feel."

She grasped the hem of her smock and pulled it over her head. The motion revealed and lifted her breasts under the thin fabric of her chemise. Teakh reclined into the pillows, bear fur luxurious against his back. Slowly, she removed her chemise, pausing as the silk covered her face, and leaned toward him.

Teakh fondled a proffered breast, palm against her nipple, delighting in the velvety skin, the supple curves. His fingers circled then cupped and lifted the resilient sphere. Alive with the movement of her midriff but nearly hidden by Angel's leggings, the succubus fluttered its wings.

Teakh swung his legs over the side of the divan. He pulled Angel to his lap, and she straddled him. He flattened his other hand against the small of her back. "Does this compromise my virtue?"

Keno cleared his throat. "Maybe we should do some drawing."

"Right," Angel said.

"I like you right here." Teakh held her wrists. "Sink the drawing." He cradled her head and drew her lips to his. She tasted of cherries and apricots.

She giggled. "Pretty Boy is jealous. We'll get back to this." She stood and sauntered away, her hips swinging.

One leg up on the drawing bench, she propped a tablet

on her knee. She sketched, her breasts quivering with the movement of her pencil.

"Stand up," she commanded.

Teakh struck a pose, holding rock steady, yearning for her.

"Pretty Boy must've given you lessons. He knows just what I like."

Her pencil nearly flew as she sketched. She worked quickly, always moving, the mobility of her face as fascinating as the movement of her breasts. She asked for other poses, and he complied, relying on his daily exercise routine for a repertoire.

She turned over a sheet, and it joined the others hanging from her pad. She pouted. "I believe Pretty Boy wants a turn. He's been pacing and twitching, very distracting. How about if I draw the two of you together? Two Noah men."

Keno nodded, as eager as a puppy.

"Pretty Boy," Angel said, "you're lovely tricked out as Seaguard, but you're even better without it."

Teakh grimaced, not sharing Angel's opinion. He'd seen Keno naked far more often than he'd seen him clothed.

Keno stripped off vest, boots, shirt, and pants. Naked and equal, Teakh and Keno stood together, two men in Angel's thrall.

"Go ahead and touch him," she said. "That's what you've been wanting, yes?"

"What about what I want?" Teakh asked.

"I think you'll like it." Angel licked the point of her pencil. "What do you say? It's up to you."

Teakh had never found Keno attractive, yet the delight in Angel's eye turned Teakh on. If watching pleased her, Teakh would do as she suggested. Tentatively he set a hand on Keno shoulder. "Yes."

Keno held Teakh and nuzzled him, muscle against toned muscle, skin sliding against skin, the hair on their chests rubbing, rough against smooth. Angel's gaze, eager and approving, followed the action, shifting between paper and men and back again.

Keno stroked Teakh's shoulders, turning him toward Angel, showing him off. Angel sketched with one hand. With the other, she massaged her bare breast. Caught between repulsion and attraction, Teakh gasped, and his erection rose against Keno's leg. Angel was right. Teakh did like this. The realization disturbed him and so excited him all the more.

"Turn a bit to your left," Angel said. "And Pretty Boy, drop your hand a finger's width. That's good. Now hold it."

His penis aching, Teakh locked his muscles, steady within Keno's strong embrace. Angel sketched fervently.

With a sigh, she set aside her pencil. "I think these studies will work out. You boys hungry?"

"Aye," Teakh said, gobbling her figure with his eyes.

"How about if you come into the kitchen while I fix some lunch?" Angel closed her drawing pad.

"I'm hungry for something else," Teakh said.

"It'll have to wait," Angel said. "We need to talk."

Keno started forward, and Angel gestured him back. "Alone. Don't you worry. We're just going to talk." She pulled on her chemise and smock.

Reluctantly, Teakh donned his shirt and pants then followed her into the kitchen.

Angel placed bread on the kitchen table. She opened a cold cupboard and removed soft cheese and brine-cured salmon, then handed him a jar of pickled nasturtium seeds. "Would you open that for me?" Angel aligned slices of bread. "So tell me, what do you want?"

Teakh poured his frustration into the task and twisted the lid from the jar. He wanted to make love to her right there on the kitchen table. "What do you mean?"

She scooped a spatula into the container of cheese. "I mean, do you want to be a stud?" She spread the spatula across the bread, pushing cheese before the flat blade as if it were paint.

Teakh would take this slow. "It depends."

"If you could do whatever you wanted, what would that be?" She paused, holding the spatula like a scepter.

Teakh rubbed at his implant scars. "Remember what I told you about founding a clan?"

"Oh yes. You aim be a clan chief."

"My sister and I went to Fennako City and met with the Queen. We have approval on a provisional basis. In our clan, men and women will be equal."

"And that makes you what?" Angel's eyes sparkled. "Clan

matriarch?" She laughed. "I'm teasing, of course. How does being a stud fit into your plans?" She cut a narrow slice of onion and placed the translucent rings atop the salmon along with the nasturtium seeds. The sandwich became a palette of pink, white, and green.

"Two ways," Teakh said. "I need money to purchase territory, but mostly I need to increase the size of our clan. As a stud, I can meet with important women."

"And get them pregnant." Angel waved her spatula. "What a scoundrel. Sex and politics."

Teakh gulped. Was he that mercenary and transparent?

She closed the sandwiches and set them on plates, each garnished with lovage, probably from her garden. "So as I understand it, women who hire you are purchasing Clan Noahee membership for their offspring."

"What do you mean?" Teakh asked. "I'm selling my services."

"Ah, but your pricing and contract ensures that only high-status women apply. In a few dozen years, your children will be in positions of power, forming a multi-clan network. Women are buying positions on this network for their children." She tickled his chin with a sprig of lovage.

Teakh hadn't thought about his career in terms of political power. "Uh." He should say something witty.

Angel bit the sprig, tearing the greenery with her white teeth. "What do you want of me?"

"I like you. And, well...I have a little problem." Teakh's face heated.

"And what's that?" Angel gave him a reproving glance.

"I can only service someone if I care about her. And you're the only girl I care about."

She attacked him with the garden herb. "Is that a declaration of love?" She placed the sprig on a plate and set the plate before Teakh. "Poor Keno. Do you know why he agreed to chaperon this modeling session?"

"Because he's a sinking voyeur," Teakh said.

"True enough, but he's also hopelessly in love with you. The only way he can get you to reciprocate is through me. That puts him in a bind. He told me about your performance problems."

"He had no right," Teakh said.

"Disliking casual sex isn't really a problem, not if I help you. I can, but you'll have to trust me. That's why I had you and Keno kissing. You responded well to my little trial."

"Keno warned me about you," Teakh said.

Angel giggled. "He's seething with jealousy, poor fellow. And don't deny it, you're just as anxious about me, afraid that Keno will steal me away. The three of us can work with jealousy. We'll use it to stoke the fire of lust." She caressed Teakh's cheek. "This will be difficult for all three of us though. Have you considered how you'll feel when other men remove their clothing for me?"

"Do you—" He couldn't bring himself to ask if she had sex with them. He couldn't bear the truth.

"I paint male nudes," she said. "Mostly of Seaguard men. They talk, and I listen. You aren't the only man with difficulty performing. Most Seaguard lords are in arranged marriages and serve as shared clan husbands. They're expected to service any clan members who make the request, regardless of their own feelings." She stroked Teakh's shoulder and arm. "They come to me. I paint their portraits, but mostly I lend an ear. I'm discreet, professional, and respectful."

"What about that time in Idylko?" Teakh asked. "Was that professional?"

Angel leaned across the table and tapped Teakh's chin. "For you, an exception. You did enjoy, yes?"

Teakh nodded. "Very much."

"Me too. Very nice."

"Help me," Teakh said. "I'm supposed to be a stud, and women are laying out money for me. A lot of money for something I can't do. I'm a fraud. I'm sorry that's not very romantic, but I'm desperate. Let me be your love slave."

"I know something of Noah men," Angel said. "You are not a fraud. Men such as you cannot engage in casual sex, not without help."

"It's a bunch of shine," Teakh said. "I'm not altruistic or loyal."

"You've been tricked by biology into loyalty," Angel said. "If you've bonded to one woman, that's loyalty. It doesn't matter that it's hormonal, not something you chose. The effect is the same."

"I'm in agony," Teakh said. "I want you. Only you."

"Danna help me. Me too. I want you. We'll turn loyalty back on itself. You'll have sex with other women because I tell you to." Angel kissed him full on the lips, her hand behind his head, her tongue probing between his teeth.

Teakh gasped and returned the kiss, matching her fervor, and the sandwiches lay forgotten.

CHAPTER 31
Photos

SEATED ON AN artist's bench, Teakh enjoyed his sandwich and seaweed salad, but not as much as he enjoyed watching Angel. Eating delicately, she seemed to savor each bite, her fingers light on the bread, her tongue moving under her closed lips. Keno ate heartily, downing a bowl of chowder followed by several sandwiches. Surrounded by Angel's paintings and drawings, they finished up with butterscotch cake.

Angel licked a bit of frosting from a finger. Lowering her eyelashes to Teakh, she said, "I noticed you had photos up on *Dale's*."

"Oh, those." Teakh set down his fork, and it clinked on his plate. Those photos had led to the run-in with Madame X and Fennako law enforcement too.

Angel wiped her hands on a napkin. "I understand you had some difficulty."

Teakh mumbled, "Aye." He didn't want to talk about the assault, if that was what she was referring to.

"He couldn't get it up," Keno said, offering a different interpretation of subject. "That's why there're no rampants."

Teakh nearly choked on his cake. "Not your drift."

Keno shrugged, the gleam in his eye wicked. "He tried. I tried. Nothing."

Why was Keno doing this? It really was none of his business.

Angel laughed. "So what did you boys do?"

Keno said, "Well, we—"

"Oh, never mind. Boys! Trying to do a woman's job." She slapped Keno's knee.

Teakh jerked a thumb toward Keno and said, "He took the photos. That's all he did. I'm okay with photos, but I prefer your help to his."

Angel's laughter rippled.

"His aunt fears you might try to sell his seed," Keno said.

Angel crossed her ankles. "I do that sometimes."

Was she teasing? Teakh put his hand to his chin, fascinated. "Then you are a succubus?"

She flicked a crumb off the tablecloth. "Oh no, nothing like that. Some of my art patrons like a relic to accompany my paintings. Those samples usually aren't active."

Keno's eyebrows went up. "Usually?"

She pursed her lips. "I enclose the material in an ornate box accompanied by documentation. My patrons buy to fill out their collections. It's like model boats or vintage wine."

Teakh frowned, trying to imagine a wine cellar filled with semen. "Disgusting."

"Most relics are," Angel said, her enthusiasm bubbling. "Back on Earth, I understand, they had bloody clothing, even entire skeletons on display. Or fragments of the holy foreskin."

"What's holy about a foreskin?" Teakh asked.

Angel puckered her lips. "It depends on who it belonged to. I'm somewhat of a connoisseur myself."

Keno held up a hand. "I'm Teakh's witness. You may take photos, but nothing else. No foundered semen samples."

Angel stacked dishes on the tray. "How good are you at observing? A little sleight of hand. Do you know what you're seeing?" She sashayed to the kitchen, the tail of her smock swinging.

Keno grimaced. "You wouldn't."

"I like getting a rise out of you." Angel turned at the kitchen door, the tray braced against her hip. "You think only boys can do it for you. Be assured I have no intention of selling Noah seed. Not today, anyway."

Keno shouted after her, "So what about Idylko?"

She peered from the doorway and smiled. "Traditional hospitality. I happen to adore Noah men."

"How many Noah men do you know?" Keno asked.

"Two." Angel returned with the empty tray. "And they're both looking at me." She fluttered her eyelashes. "You wouldn't be my love slave, so I found someone more suitable. He actually prefers women. Imagine that." She sat on the bench beside Teakh.

He put his arm around her. "I prefer this one."

"I'm warning you," Keno said.

"Two for one." Angel snuggled against Teakh, and she smelled divine. "You loyal Noah men sure know how to thrill a woman."

"Toss the flippancy," Keno said.

"You're jealous, both of you, and it's cute." She kissed Teakh, her lips soft against his. "Now let's do something about those rampants. My camera is set up." She tugged at Teakh's belt.

"You can set me up." Teakh stood and tried to remove his pants but knocked over a stretched and primed canvas. He rid himself of shirt and undershorts more smoothly.

"Maybe lie down," Angel said. He reclined on the divan, and she adjusted pillows behind him. "Comfortable?"

His body supported by fur and bolsters, Teakh relaxed, enjoying the view of Angel as she removed first her leggings, then smock, chemise, and panties, dropping them on the floor.

Angel propelled Keno toward the divan. "How about we use this lout as a pillow?"

"Why?" Teakh asked. He'd prefer that Keno leave completely.

"Because I like to punish Pretty Boy. I've been trying to get a sample from him for years, and he won't give it to me. He likes the game."

"It's just that you don't excite me the way a man does," Keno said.

"The way our boy here does. Pretty Boy still likes the game." Angel winked. "I'd be insulted except I feel the same way. So that's why he's going to be on the bottom helping out. You'll both like it. Come on, Pretty Boy, no clothing for this party."

Keno removed pants and shirt and folded them neatly.

251

Angel tugged on Teakh's arm. When he sat up, Keno slipped behind him and kissed Teakh's shoulder.

"Now lie back, and we'll take care of you. Sound good?" Teakh nodded. "Oh yeah."

Keno's solid arm reached across Teakh's chest, urging him to lean back. Teakh yielded his weight. Keno smoothed Teakh's bandanna then kissed his neck.

Her hair cascading over Teakh's abdomen, Angel stooped, and her lips skimmed his thigh. A shudder went through his body.

"You like that?" she breathed.

A delicious rush of pleasure flooded his loins. "More," he said.

"Your little man likes me," Angel said, her breath on his cock.

He thrust his hips upward, giving himself to her as a plaything. Caught between Angel and Keno, Teakh moaned, longing for her to take him in her mouth.

Angel stroked Teakh's shaft. "How long can you hold it?" Teakh gasped. "Don't know."

She swung off the divan, reaching for her camera. "Stand up."

Teakh whimpered, struggling to hold back, despite the discomfort. The photos would boost his career, but more than that, he hoped to please her, to be her love slave if that was what she wanted.

She tapped switches. Lights turned on. Naked and snapping pictures, she backed up for a full shot then close up.

She knelt, photographing from a low angle, then set the camera aside and opened a drawer. "I'll finish you off."

Keno blocked her approach. "No, you won't. I don't trust you. Little sleight of hand."

"Pretty Boy," Teakh said, "get out of the way."

Standing, Angel tore open a package and handed Keno a condom. "For the safety of my two favorite men."

"Is this a trick?" Keno asked, pinching condom between forefinger and thumb.

"No." She took back the condom. "I'll do it." She rolled the rubber in place, her fingers light against Teakh's shaft. "There. All yours, Pretty Boy."

Teakh shook his head. "I want you, Angel."

She pulled Teakh to her and sat on the edge of the divan,

seating him between her naked legs. "I'm here." She nipped at his ear and whispered, "You're my love slave, remember?"

Tight in her embrace, Teakh relaxed. Keno knelt on the carpet and stooped.

"Not going to work." Teakh pushed Keno away and turned to Angel, bearing her down onto the divan.

"On the bottom," commanded Angel.

They rolled, changing positions and pushing aside furs. Now Angel was on her elbows and knees over Teakh, sprawled diagonally on the divan with Keno between their legs.

Jealousy shot though Teakh. Keno had the better position, a view of Angel's glory. Teakh's nose against her arm, he inhaled the wild smell of woman and was completely lost to her. Confined between her and the pillows, ablaze with jealousy and lust, Teakh ejaculated. He gasped, and a shudder went through him. When his penis slackened, the condom fell off.

Angel laid her body against Teakh's, her breasts, arms, and belly soft and yielding. Teakh sighed in contentment.

But Keno held up the condom. "You're not having this."

Teakh grunted. "Good Danna. Not now."

Angel rolled away from Teakh and opened the drawer of a nearby taboret. She produced an ornate box, the metal glowing so yellow it had to be soft gold. "Put it in here. Teakh can keep it."

"I'd rather not," Teakh said, leaning against the pile of bolsters.

"Then can I have it?" Angel snuggled beside him.

"Let's toss it out," insisted Teakh.

She set the box aside and placed a hand over her heart. "But it's valuable."

Keno dropped the condom into the box and snapped the lid closed. "Your stuff could be recovered from the trash. Keep it until you're sure it's not active." He handed the box to Teakh. It weighed heavy in his hand, the heft of lead or of gold.

Angel inclined her head. "Pretty Boy, look at you."

A dribble of fluid clung to Keno's slack cock.

She dabbed it with a tissue, cleaning up the fluid. "And you claim you can't produce. Here." She retrieved a silver box from the drawer and stuffed the tissue into the reliquary.

"So he gets gold and I get silver?" Keno asked.

"And nobody gets bronze." Angel tossed the box to Keno, who caught it. "Isn't it rich? Ambergris is nothing more than well-aged whale shit. Pearls? Oyster tumors." She shook her head. "Those boxes hold enough Noah genetics to produce better than a grand-gross of Seaguard lords."

"Gross being the important word," Teakh said.

Her laughter bubbled. "I rather fancy Seaguard lords myself. One in particular." She tapped Teakh's chest. "Chief."

TEAKH FLEW HOME via stratoplane, confident and happy. His life, for once, was right. With Angel's help, he could be a stud.

Seated in the plane beside Keno, Teakh hailed Angel. *I love you.*

I know you do.

Talk to me. I like your voice inside my head. What are you doing?

Painting your butt. You have a lovely ass, you know, nice glutes. Now I'm getting more paint, adding just a touch of umber and stroking it onto your thigh.

The entire turn of events had come out entirely too well. What had Teakh missed? He felt a vague sense of unease.

CHAPTER 32
Assignation

GULL CROUCHED ON the peak of the gym roof as Luna Majora rose gibbous, the nearly full globe emerging above indigo peaks crested with luminous snow. Inside his quarters, Teakh threw off his blanket and sat up. He couldn't sleep. Tomorrow Sis would meet with a man at a fertility clinic—direct cover, thus fulfilling her contract.

Teakh propped up a pillow and leaned against it. Keno remained fast asleep. A pool of moonlight glowed on the floor, lighting the fringe of the rug. Slowly, ever so slowly, the pool moved. Teakh yawned, settled in bed, and brought Gull inside.

He awoke to Sis's hail, her name repeating in his mind. He groaned. Five in the morning, according to his implant. Not yet morning. He must have actually fallen asleep.

He rolled out of bed and seated himself on the floor. He left Sis's channel open, ready to receive.

I'm in Kasaanko, headed for the floatplane dock.

Acknowledge. Using his neuro, Teakh pulled up a map and marked her location. He waited, calming himself, focusing on his breathing.

"Attending observances?" Keno's spoken question broke Teakh's concentration.

He opened his eyes. "I'm on watch."

"What for?" Keno asked, an inky figure in the morning twilight.

"Sis is fulfilling that damn contract."

"God of the depths!" Keno said out of the darkness. "There isn't a man in this gym I'd send out on a liaison alone."

"I can't forbid her." Teakh had tried, but Sis could be so all-foundered stubborn. She insisted on following the contract to the letter. It had specified no witnesses, not even the traditional honor guard.

"You should have sent Gull," Keno said.

"I offered. Sis refused. I've given her an open channel." Teakh touched his implant scars. "It's the best I can do."

"Does your unit record?" Keno asked.

"Recording now. Both audio and transcript. No video or sensory. Kinkill!" He couldn't get visual or haptic data without Gull, not that it would do much good. Gull would have to bite the man for a DNA test. "Sis says we'll sue Fennako if anything happens to her. I get to sue." A daunting prospect. If she were raped, killed, or abducted, he'd have to singlehandedly take on the most powerful clan on the planet.

The door clicked shut as Keno departed for morning observances. Sis sent updates as she walked through early morning Kasaanko Village. Teakh settled his hands on his knees, again in a position of meditation—back straight, legs folded as Keno had taught. The sky lightened, the high windows shifting from indigo to rose.

I'm at the dock, she sent.

Teakh remained ready with his map, but without permission and updates from Kasaanko, it lacked detail. *Keep me posted.*

No sign of my ride. Wait, I think that's it. An esskip is landing. Fennako colors. Ferry system insignia.

What's the tail number? asked Teakh.

Foxtrot November Eight Six Four.

Teakh used his neuro to make a note.

Gotta go.

Tide carry you. Danna guide you, he sent and meant it. If only the North Star could guide the heart. He checked and recorded the time. How long before Sis contacted him again? That depended on how far she flew. He stood and paced. There wasn't much he could do. In a daze, he went to the dining room, where the studs had gathered for breakfast. At the sideboard, he filled a mug with hot lingonberry juice.

Hairy pushed back from the table and his meal, a slab of smoked haddock and a bowl of oatmeal. "You're quiet this morning."

Because Teakh's sister was getting screwed. Teakh merely nodded. He had no appetite.

After dumping his mug in the bin, Teakh retired to his quarters and hailed Angel. *Sis has gone to fulfill that foundered contract. Alone.*

Damn. I wanted to go with her, Angel said.

I'd like to flense her blubber, Teakh said. *She's the most walrus-headed woman I know.*

Noah, my man, Angel said, *you won't be pleased if I agree with you.*

He wanted Sis to succeed, but this contract was a hag, and she shouldn't have agreed to it. That's what he thought anyway.

When she again transmitted, Teakh recorded the time. Using the speed of an esskip, he calculated the distance traveled and marked his map with a ring centered on Kasaanko. His sister was somewhere within that circle.

I'm walking up from a harbor, she said.

Take a look at boat transoms. I want name, home port, and clan designation.

As Sis read, Teakh located the home port for each boat and marked the map. The common clan identification was Gulf Lima Victor.

I'm going into the clinic, Sis said.

Teakh pinged acknowledgement then ran a search for fertility clinics in villages within the circle. He came up with Galvanko.

With Sis's channel on hold, he hailed Angel. *Sis is at Galvanko Clinic. What do you know about it?*

It's known for medical excellence, Angel said.

Then it's reputable? Danna! He'd feared Sis had been lured into a questionable dive where she'd be forced into sexual servitude.

Aye. It seems Fennako is trying to hold up their end of the bargain despite the nastiness about no witnesses.

Teakh signed off and went to the studio. There he commenced his exercise routine, attempting to focus, to control his anxiety one push-up at a time. Not thinking of his sister as she set aside her comset. Trying not to think of his sister. Poseidon! Even now she would be taking off her clothing. Some strange man entering the room. No! Teakh refused to think of it. In a plank position, he held his body rigid and breathed. He finished his routine and started over.

After an eternity, Sis hailed again. The repetition of her name rang in his mind, her voice shaking with emotion.

Teakh dropped out of a handstand, his skin suddenly clammy. *What's wrong?*

He wouldn't do it. I was ready for him, and he wouldn't do it.

Poseidon-damn lubber! Did he hurt you? asked Teakh.

She sobbed. *It's my own stupid fault.*

Did he hurt you?

She wasn't listening. *I'm not a slut.*

Is that what he said? Damn lubber! No man could abuse Teakh's sister and get away with it. Eyes closed, he ignored the other studs in the studio.

He claimed he couldn't get it up, Sis said, *but he lied.*

If I'd been there, I'd have told him where to go. After all that trouble, the kinkiller hadn't followed through. *Did he hurt you?*

Danna, no, Sis said. *But I was strapped down with these horrid screens in the way.*

Keno had drilled it into Teakh, and all the studs, that the female client was always right. Her needs came first. *Didn't he know what you wanted?*

I agreed and signed a release, Sis said. *It was supposed to be anonymous. But it wasn't. He pushed the screen aside.*

Sue him, Teakh said. The lubber had breached the contract and treated Sis badly.

We talked. He wanted to know why I was there. He thought I was too young. Founder it all.

Teakh took a deep breath. It seemed the man hadn't touched her. He'd merely upset her plans, their plans. *He's right.* Teakh valued his sister more than the prospect of becoming a Seaguard lord.

That's the worst of it, she said. *One chance, and I messed up. He was a perfect gentleman. If only I hadn't been so much of a gold-digging slut. I should have been nicer to him. Now I'll never see him again.*

He doesn't matter. Fennako will have to come up with a different man. The contract hadn't specified which man, only that Fennako would make the choice. Reproductive contracts always left the option of either partner breaking off coitus any time they wanted.

I don't want a different man, Sis said. *He's Seaguard. Tall. Nice eyes. Hazel, I think.*

Realization dawned on Teakh. This wasn't about the contract. Sis had fallen in love with the man, but she couldn't have. People didn't fall in love the first time they met. Angel and Teakh, for example...well, they were an exception.

Did he say he hated you? Pretending to meditate, Teakh kept his thumbs and ring fingers touching.

He told me we'd try again in a more conducive setting. He was just being polite.

Maybe that's exactly what he meant. It seemed to Teakh that she was overacting. *Men are that way. Let him know what you think.*

But I don't have his address codes, and I don't even know his name. How can I?

It must be the Noah family curse, passed down from Jamie Noah himself. Welcome the stranger, sent Teakh, attempting humor.

Sis didn't laugh. *I don't want him to be a stranger.*

Then I'll find him for you. I promise. He'd located Angel. Surely he could find this man for his sister. He considered their more immediate problem. *Where are you staying tonight?*

I don't know.

Keno would probably welcome Sis at the gym, but the other studs would be a problem. What jilted woman would want to be comforted by the likes of Randy and Buttcakes?

How about if you visit Angel? offered Teakh.

But she's your girlfriend.

She's concerned about you and wants to help. I'll tell her to expect you. Teakh checked commercial flight times. *You can catch a plane in Kasaanko, take a hop to Shellako. Get in this evening.*

Too expensive, sent Sis.

She could claim hospitality, but she'd have to demonstrate need, an unnecessary invasion of privacy.

Teakh sent, *If our plans go through, we'll pay off the debt. If they don't go through... what was that about blood from turnips?*

Sis was in over her head, and as much as he hated to admit it, Angel had the experience in seduction and the ways of men that Sis desperately needed. Depths! What would happen if the two women in Teakh's life got together? They might not like each other. Even worse, they might join forces in telling Teakh what to do.

CHAPTER 33
Freeze Off

BESIDE KENO, TEAKH stood on the lagoon breakwater, clad in a swim cap and wetsuit. As swimmers gathered for the race, a raw wind blew, rippling the surface of the esskip lagoon. Teakh shivered and rubbed the gooseflesh of his arms. A snapping line of signal flags spelled out the name of the event—Dojko Open Water Freeze Off—the geometric letters bright against the gray sky. Teakh, Danna help him, would take part in this insanity, an annual winter swimming competition begun years ago on a dare. A race official approached, carrying a noteboard and wearing a green vest, his shaved head crisscrossed by welts. He was clearly Seaguard but not Dojko.

"You Jamie Noah?" The official glanced at his screen then at Teakh and Keno.

"Aye." Teakh straightened the whistle and knife attached to his faded orange vest. He'd won the whistle back in a card game.

The official squinted at his noteboard. "Jamie Noah? Uh huh. You got yourself an ark? Maybe you're Santa Claus too."

Keno jerked his thumb toward Teakh. "That's him."

"So, Mr. Claus, what's your clan?" the official asked, stylus poised.

"Put me down as Noah," Teakh said. Noahee hadn't yet received approval.

"Don't shine me." The official frowned. "We need a real clan for liability release."

"Registration is pending." Teakh gave Noah's original designation, NOAA. "November Ophelia Alpha Alpha."

The official laughed. "That's not a clan. It's a defunct bureaucracy. Are you planning to issue weather warnings?"

"Sure," Teakh said. "Observe the tide. Render assistance to those in need. Be prepared." He shrugged. Good advice regardless of the source.

The official guffawed. "You still need a clan to vouch for you."

"I'm Jamie's coach," Keno said. "Keno Dojko. His release is on file."

"Very well. Hospitality of Dojko." The official jotted on his board. "But you must be in appropriate gear. What do you got?" He glowered and spoke as if Teakh were a fisherman beneath the notice of Seaguard. "Where're your boots, mariner?"

Teakh was a fisherman and proud of it, even if he had an implant. "Don't need them." He slapped his thigh. "Wetsuit. Life vest. Whistle. Knife." He touched the blade strapped to his vest.

The official tapped his stylus against the side of his noteboard. "Comset and locator beacon. They got to be waterproof."

Teakh crossed his arms and sent, *How's this? Waterproof and implanted. I can't lose them that way.*

The official stepped back, his aspect changed. He eyed Teakh. "So what are you? Mariner or Seaguard?"

"Noah," Teakh said. "I observe no difference."

Shaking his head, the official moved on. A raw gust of wind set the flags snapping furiously.

"We'll get you your Noah designation." Keno brandished a marker pen. "November Ophelia Alpha Alpha. That's the code, yes?"

Teakh bowed his head, and Keno wrote on Teakh's cap, the pen squeaking.

The official's voice boomed from speakers. "Ladies! Seaguard! Mariners! We have a blustery day for the dozen-and-third annual Dojko Open Water Freeze Off. We have quite the lineup. Two-dozen-and-four of you have accepted the challenge: swim a mile out to a transmitter buoy then

262

swim back. The water is cold. You'll face swells, chop, and a nice current. A true test of Seaguard skills."

Fishermen, out to prove they were every bit as good as men with implants, shouted and jeered at Seaguard. Seaguard hooted right back. The race gave awards to individuals, but ever since that first dare, the real competition had always been between fishermen and Seaguard.

Teakh rotated his shoulders. He'd worked in the cold often enough, but he hadn't competed in open water. That was Keno's absurd idea.

The official, visible now above the competitors and coaches, stood on a rock. "Two-dozen-and-one of you have elected to swim freestyle, a competitive field. But we have three lubbers believing they can fly the whole thing. That's right, butterfly!"

On Keno's advice, Teakh had entered in the more difficult but less competitive butterfly category, a strategic move. A win, even against only two competitors, would strengthen his portfolio. Besides, camera operators, viewers, and spectators would pick out his style as unusual, and the resulting publicity would gain recognition for his nascent clan.

The official continued. "I'll remind you, we've got cameras and observers out there. They'll be holding you to that agreement. If you come to your senses and crawl, go ahead. We don't want you drowning. But your race will be disqualified." The official finished with, "So may the best win."

Competitors and spectators whooped and shouted. Teakh waded into the frigid bay with the other swimmers. Waves lapped against his foam-insulated thighs. Slippery rocks pressed into the soft soles of his booties. He pulled his goggles in place and adjusted them, then took a breath and immersed himself in numbingly cold water. He checked the sonar function of his neuro. He seldom used it. When immersed, his neuro received vibrations in the water as if Teakh were a fish. He came up chafing his arms, shivering but exhilarated.

Racers schooled in the shallows beside the lagoon breakwater, waiting for the starting gun. He positioned himself at the back of the pack near the woman and a Seaguard man who were his competitors in butterfly. He bobbed a greeting, and they nodded back. Coming out of the start with a different stroke, they would need the extra space.

A man wearing a battered wetsuit and a watchcap entered the water. His life vest inflated with a hiss. Laughing, another man helped him deflate and reset the vest.

"Stupid fishermen," muttered a Seaguardsman. The age-old conflict between Seaguard and fishermen continued.

From the top of the jetty, some men waved to Teakh— Limber and Tunes. Nearby, Chuck and Lugo shouted encouragement. Well, depths! Teakh had about everyone out cheering him on. He waved back.

The official counted down. At the gunshot, the swimmers bolted, a teeming throng of flailing arms and legs. Using his sonar sense, Teakh tracked swimmers.

He hailed Angel. *We're off.*

Staying to the outside of the pack, he marked his two competitors and let the race sort out. He hadn't swum in open ocean before and missed having a lane marker or pool side in easy reach. The cold of the water became merely a notation as he gauged his stamina, predicting how fast he could swim without exhausting himself. He enjoyed the thrill and calm focus of competition. He dolphined and dove, arms sweeping, legs moving as one, the kick of his legs traveling through his body as a wave. In his sonar vision, the ocean extended around him into vast dimness. The sea floor dropped away. Small fish flickered like green sparks among bladderwrack and ribbon kelp.

He was flying, but through the water, not air. The familiarity soothed him with the reassuring rhythm and awareness of his surroundings. He was a gull on the lookout.

Teakh recalled Sis. Once a month, she'd been meeting with the man assigned by Fennako. The designated stud had strung her along, not even trying to get her pregnant. Teakh wasn't sure if he admired or hated the man.

Teakh's female competitor passed him, glowing green in his sonar vision, her butterfly natural and easy, far smoother than his own. He picked up his pace, drafting her, enjoying her technique as much as the reduced drag. She knew what she was doing. His ears above water as he took a breath, Teakh heard the shot announcing the first swimmer had reached the buoy. He continued his flight.

Outbound, they passed the lead swimmer coming the other way, a Seaguardsman with a strong crawl. Teakh distinguished swimmers in a mosaic of senses, hearing as much as seeing. Counting swimmers, he calculated his position in the race.

He and the woman turned the buoy together for the return trip. Teakh hailed Angel without altering his stroke. *At the halfway mark.*

Angel read his split time and added, *You're doing great.*

Boosted by her encouragement, Teakh picked up his pace. He continued listening and watching for the variations in movement which were distinctive to butterfly. Their other competitor wasn't far behind those nearing the buoy.

The butterfly woman was still swimming strongly. Teakh attempted to keep up. He was losing her as she pulled ahead, but he remained in second place in the butterfly division. He kept up his tally of swimmers. Those outbound were now spaced farther apart, their movement noisy and inefficient. Only two more stragglers, and they'd all be accounted for. The second-to-last swimmer moved slowly. The regularity of his stroke faltered then paused.

Teakh raised his head. "Stranger, are you well?"

The man was shivering and his face was pale, but if Teakh stopped to help, he'd lose his position in the race.

"Inflate your vest!" he shouted.

"Can't." The words came through chattering teeth.

Teakh transmitted to activate the man's vest, but he lacked the codes, and it didn't inflate. Poseidon damn! People around him were always getting themselves in trouble: getting burned, falling overboard, and now he had a swimmer who didn't know how to operate his vest. Teakh swam toward the victim and felt along the man's chest for the manual inflation release. With a hiss, the vest inflated.

He hailed on the emergency channel. *Got swimmer floating. Hypothermia. Mark my position.* Swimmers passed as Teakh wrapped his arms around the man, sharing body heat.

An esskip approached, easing in toward them. The canopy

opened, and a Seaguardsman reached with a spar. One arm around the swimmer, Teakh grasped the spar, and they were pulled to the esskip.

"Noah, we'll take care of this," Seaguard said. "Good luck with your race. Give 'em Poseidon."

Teakh lit out, swimming with all his power, fighting to catch his competitors, flying with the speed of excitement and adrenaline.

Nearly to the finish line, he caught snatches of his name shouted in rhythm. "Noah! Noah! Noah!"

Ahead of him splashed the butterfly man. Teakh poured on speed, sprinting for the finish, and they came in nearly together, Teakh only a half-length behind. Gasping, he stumbled into the shallows beyond the finish line.

His male competitor clasped Teakh's shoulders in a rough hug. "Danna, what a race! If you hadn't stopped, you'd have been way ahead."

The butterfly woman grinned.

Flushed with camaraderie and the excitement of the race, he congratulated her. "Ma'am, you're quite the swimmer. Nice technique."

"You're good yourself." She pumped a fist. "Butterfly! We showed them."

The three of them climbed out of the water together, and Teakh felt himself part of a team, an unusual feeling.

COMPETITORS AND SPECTATORS crowded into the Salty Hound. Teakh sat squeezed between Keno and Lugo, the tavern so loud there was no hope of speaking. His body tingled with the warmth of relaxing after hard exercise.

Teakh cradled his glass—beer this time, not apple juice. He hailed Angel and tried to sound sad. *I came in last.*

Don't shine me. Angel laughed. *I watched it all via remote. You came in third and made an impression as the swimmer who calls himself Jamie Noah. I'm so proud of you I'm tickled.*

Teakh sipped his beer. *Keno must have set it all up, hired an actor.* But the symptoms had seemed real enough.

He didn't have to, said Angel. *Every year swimmers get hypothermia or some sort of distress.*

Keno had a sly grin as he blew on the foam of his own beer.

Teakh had signed a liability release. He should have known. *Keno didn't tell me.*

That would have spoiled the effect, Angel said.

Sis hailed next. *Congratulations. I heard race officials gave you a special award.*

Teakh flicked a medal hanging from a ribbon around his neck. *Aye.* Most likely Keno had talked officials into having the bronze medal specially engraved.

We're nearly a clan. Sis's enthusiasm carried over the link.

Is that because I had Noah written on my cap? Teakh quipped.

Aye. You got word out. But that's not all. I've been accepted by Lee-Smith law school. I'm going to be a lawyer.

Was that because of my win? Or did that stud of yours follow through? asked Teakh. Her acceptance as a law student was contingent on pregnancy, and he'd promised not to interfere.

Sort of, she said. *He got me into the program, but we haven't actually fulfilled the contract.*

Teakh took a swig of beer, a resinous lager bitter with the tang of spruce tips. *It's about time he made himself useful.*

Come on, he's a nice guy.

Do you know who he is?

Oh, I have my suspicions, but we intend to follow the contract. It specifies that the liaison shall be anonymous.

He'd thought his relationship with Angel unusual, but he couldn't keep up with his sister and her unnamed beau. Teakh leaned back and laughed, his mood buoyant. The publicity stunt had occurred by chance, but he didn't care. He was surrounded by friends and had the admiration of the girl he loved.

CHAPTER 34
Art Opening

HOOD FLUNG BACK, Angel rushed into Teakh's arms and pressed her body against his. Her hair smelled of autumn. Later. Later they'd fling aside parkas and enjoy themselves. But not in a stratoport terminal with Keno along. The two men had flown to Fennako City for Angel's art opening.

She tucked herself under Teakh's arm. "Did you bring your box?"

Teakh fingered the reliquary in his pocket, tracing the filigree. Such an elegant container for a used condom. He opened his pocket enough to show a flash of gold.

"I worried you'd left it behind. I'll give it back after the show." She nodded vigorously.

Teakh grimaced. "Art is weird."

"Trust me." Angel kissed his cheek, her breath light on his skin. "This show will make your career."

"Teakh's career or yours?" Keno sidled up.

"Both." She cuffed Keno's shoulder. "And it won't hurt yours either. Come, the three of us together." She linked arms with Keno and Teakh.

Leaving the terminal behind, they walked along the waterfront, past moored planes then ferry docks.

Teakh hailed Sis. *I'm here. Just arrived.*

Here in Fennako City?

For Angel's art opening. Teakh kept a hand on Angel.

She nudged him. "Transmitting?"

"Sis," Teakh whispered.

I'm living in the law students' dorm. It's nearly on top of Lawrock.
Teakh sent a burst of electronic laughter. *You're coming up in the world.*

In the company of Angel and Keno, Teakh left the waterfront. To either side, courtyards, cul-de-sacs, and rooftop gardens opened off the lane. Pedestrians teemed—businesswomen and lawyers in hooded robes, others in clothing from outlying areas. Only a few months ago, Teakh had been among the petitioners who flocked to the courts and palace.

What about that stud of yours? sent Teakh. *Is he around?*
I'm not saying.
So he is. Have you got his name yet?
No! That's the agreement. He's the one who got me into law school.
What's he waiting for? Maybe Teakh wasn't the only stud with a performance problem.
It's a relationship. You wouldn't understand.
Oh, I wouldn't? You don't know his name. What kind of relationship is that?
We get together a lot, Sis said.
Then he lives in Fennako City?
It's likely.
Bring him to the art opening, sent Teakh.
We can't be seen together, but I told him about it. I've got to go—a meeting with my study group. They call us the Bleeding Hearts. We're all studying to be human-rights lawyers.
Invite your study group then. A gaggle of young lawyers might be a good group to have on his side.
I did. They're excited to see it.

Angel tugged at Teakh's arm, and the three of them went through a gated archway into a courtyard before a grand hotel. The imposing facade was all glass and tile the color of ice. He and Sis signed off.

In the lobby, water burbled as it flowed down a slab of gray stone four stories tall and lit by an atrium skylight. A concierge greeted them with a bow. Teakh had never been in a hotel like this one. How the depths was a man supposed to behave? Keno, seemingly accustomed to this sort of thing, bowed. Teakh awkwardly followed his lead.

The concierge escorted them to a glass elevator which

whisked them to the top floor. They were ushered into a room all done in white with chrome-and-black trim. A black lacquered headboard gleamed behind an oversized bed heaped with an ivory-colored duvet and pillows. Double doors leading to a sitting room were ajar.

Teakh's battered duffle had been delivered and waited with other cases and bags. He glanced at his boots. All that white carpet and upholstery was likely to get dirty mighty quickly.

"I hope you two don't mind sharing a room with me," whispered Angel. This wasn't a room but a full penthouse suite.

With a wry grin, Keno made a sweeping gesture to the oversized bed. "Too cheap to get two beds?"

"You rascal," Angel scolded. "You just want Teakh all to yourself."

"I must guard our investment." Keno stood behind Teakh. "I'm not letting you undersell us with black-market goods."

"Oh, poohy," she said.

Teakh took her arm. "I'm sleeping with Angel."

She embraced him and fluttered her eyelashes at Keno. "That bed is huge. I'd be cold and lonely without the two of you. Although if you insist, Keno, you can have the trundle bed to yourself. If there is one. Otherwise it's the couch for you."

Keno conceded. "Oh, all right."

"That's settled." Angel dusted her hands. "I have a gift for Teakh, something for him to wear."

Teakh twisted his bracelet.

Angel touched her own bracelet. "Something from me. Go on. It's in the sitting room."

Teakh pushed the door farther open. Seaguard kit had been laid over the back of a chair—shirt, pants, life vest, and parka, all soft gray and dark blue. A pair of seaboots had been folded on the chair seat. Keno and Angel followed him into the sitting room.

"I specified the design and had them made up," Angel said.

Teakh flashed a smile at her. Traditionally only kinswomen provided Seaguard kit. The clothing was custom made.

"How much did you spend?" he asked. The vest alone, packed with materials technology, must have cost quite a haul.

"Never mind that. I'm on good terms with the tailor and the boot maker. We sometimes collaborate."

Teakh drew his hand across a suede-soft boot in amazement. "Is this waterproof?"

"As good as a cold-water immersion suit. Or so claims the bootmaker. I believe her."

Keno crossed his arms. "So you think you own Teakh?"

"His sister approved." Angel held up the life vest. "I present the new Clan Noahee colors."

Keno squinted. "Sure looks like Dojko colors."

"That's the idea," Angel said. "But subtly different."

Teakh grinned. He and Keno would appear to be kinsmen, and it suggested the backing of Dojko. "I'm your man."

WHEN TEAKH CAME out of the bathroom, Angel reclined on the bed, wearing a slip. Keno sat beside her, wearing nothing at all. Keno always slept naked, but seeing him like that beside Angel didn't seem right.

"Come on. What are you waiting for?" Angel pushed the comforter aside, making room for Teakh.

He hesitated. Maybe he should sleep between her and Keno to make himself a barrier, but Keno might like that. Teakh preferred to please Angel.

He slipped into bed. Ignoring Keno reclined behind her, Teakh stroked Angel's silk-covered hip and buried his face in her luxurious hair, inhaling her musk. Teakh trembled with excitement. Danna! He'd longed for this during those hours of practicing poses and swimming laps.

His desire rose until his erect member pressed against her leg, proving that he had no problem performing. His hand glided over her thigh as he lifted her slip. She gasped and clasped him against her soft breasts. He pushed Keno aside and straddled her. She kissed him, her tongue on his lips, and her knee pushed between Teakh's legs.

"Delicious." She moaned.

They rocked together, moving as one. With a sob, Angel relaxed. A moment later, Teakh ejaculated on her satin slip.

"I'm sorry," he said.

"What for?" Angel asked.

"I made a mess."

She laughed. "And why would semen bother me?" She lifted her slip and touched the wet spot to her lips, revealing her tattoo of a winged siren.

"A bit premature," Keno said. "You need more practice."

"Get lost," Teakh said.

"Now, now, boys." Angel rolled to lie equally between them. "Nothing pleases me more than having both of you. Poor Keno. He's hopelessly in love, and this is the closest he can get to you."

"He gets off by watching us."

"Let him." She rolled toward Teakh and stroked his cheek. "If you're going to be a stud, you've got to accept other people watching. You shouldn't go alone to a liaison. It's dangerous. You know how it was for your sister. She was lucky."

Teakh twisted a tendril of her hair around his finger. "I thought maybe you would accompany me."

She shook her head. "Your witness should be a man. It's traditional and creates fewer problems for the clients."

THE DAY OF the opening, Teakh wore the new duds to the gallery. For once he felt proud of his appearance—no more wearing Clan Ralko black and scarlet. Keno dressed as if he were Dojko Seaguard and, like Teakh, wore a gray scarf knotted around his head, raffishly concealing which one of them was actually Seaguard. Angel had clad herself in black leggings and tunic with bronze jewelry.

The gallery was dark inside, except for the paintings lit by spotlights. Some of the canvases were of an intimate size and others floor-to-ceiling. Each of them depicted either Keno or Teakh, or the two men together. A large canvas of Teakh portrayed him wearing only a bandanna and a silver bracelet. When painted by Angel, he sure looked good, better than Keno actually. Around Teakh's image wheeled a flock of birds—guillemot, Bonaparte, and herring gulls. She'd even gotten all the species right.

A placard on the wall displayed Angel's artist statement. What did his beloved think of him? Curious, Teakh read it. The placard explained Angel's appreciation of male beauty and how both Keno and Teakh were direct patrilineal descendants of Jamie Noah. She credited Keno's gym and Iris's salon for body building and grooming. She named Teakh only as Noah and explained that he wished to remain otherwise anonymous. That ploy nicely sidestepped the problem with his clan name. Since Sis wasn't pregnant, Noahee had yet to receive full Fennako approval.

"So if I'm anonymous, how will the show help my career?" he asked.

"Trust me," Angel said so close to Teakh that he could feel their attraction like electricity. "Everyone who needs to know will know."

Teakh looked over each painting. The show started with Keno's portrait and continued to paintings of Teakh.

Keno jerked his thumb toward a scrawny Teakh with crutches and a broken leg. "The before pictures?"

Angel rested her head against Teakh's shoulder. "You've always been beautiful to me. The most valuable jewels are flawed in unusual ways."

"I'm flawed?" Teakh asked.

She kissed his cheek. "A natural pearl, knobby and interesting. You want monogamy, believe in it passionately, but you're selling yourself as a stud." She shrugged and stepped forward, leaving Teakh puzzled as to if he'd been insulted or complimented.

In nearly every painting, Teakh looked directly at the viewer, the effect disconcerting. He hadn't been able to keep his eyes off Angel. Difficult enough to keep his hands off her. Even now, he longed to stroke the swell of her hips.

At the end of the series, an alcove displayed two paintings: one of Teakh, the other of Keno. Each painting was flanked by candles and had a glass case attached to the wall below it. Angel struck a match and lit the candles. In the quiet room, light flickered over the glossy paint, and the air smelled of sulfur and wax. Angel bowed her head, her attitude devout.

"May I have your boxes?" she asked.

Teakh thrust his hand into his pocket for the small box and handed it to her. Candlelight touched the gleaming filigree. She opened the reliquary and set it in the case. With care, she arranged the condom on a nest of tissue.

Teakh scowled, and Angel laughed. "That's how relics are," she said. "Fragments from some mythical holy person." She locked the case with an old-fashioned key and handed it to Teakh.

He pocketed it. "So I'm holy?"

She lowered her lashes. "And I'm an angel, you say." She set Keno's silver box in the case below his image and locked it as well. "Don't worry." She offered the key to Keno. "I've listed the relics as borrowed from a private collection and not for sale."

Keno pointed with the key. "You know those aren't active."

"I'm making a statement," Angel said.

Teakh grimaced. "A collection of used condoms?"

"It's art," Angel said, as if that explained everything.

AS THEIR GUESTS arrived, Teakh stood beside Angel, his arm around her, Keno nearby. She introduced them as Noah men. Teakh had to admit they made quite a threesome, the artist in black with gleaming auburn hair, flanked by her two apparently Seaguard models.

The guests sipped cloudberry wine and balanced plates of smoked sockeye and roe on crackers. Feigning disinterest, Teakh strained to overhear conversations.

"Remarkable," a woman said as she perused the paintings. "The love in his eyes."

"And she's in love with him," her companion said. "She's not even in the painting and you can tell."

"They're both in love with him."

The two women approached Angel. "Nice work. Where do you find such men?"

She gave an enigmatic smile. "They found me."

A crowd of young women came through the door, and one of them waved—Sis with her study group. The Bleeding Hearts had arrived.

"So this is your brother?" a girl asked Sis then covered her mouth.

"We're not supposed to let on who he is," another girl hissed. "Hospitality and all that."

Angel and Sis clasped hands.

"Thank you for coming," Angel said. "How's it going with you-know-who?"

Sis blushed. "Uh, well."

Angel laughed. "Say no more. Enjoy the show."

A woman with a shock of iron-gray hair stood among the students.

Sis introduced the woman. "My advisor, Myrtle Gratianiko, doctor of law. Ma'am, this is the artist Matta Carrie and my brother, who's modeling for her."

"Not supposed to share his name, huh?" the advisor said. "Pleased to meet you." She bowed to Angel then Teakh.

Sis and her friends descended on the appetizers then chatted and laughed while looking over the show, examining images of Teakh's naked body with all its flaws and glories. His face heated. Standing nude before Angel was one thing; inspection by his sister's friends, even if they were law students, was another.

The advisor viewed the show with her hands clasped behind her, looking carefully at each painting.

Angel named other guests as they arrived. "Will you take a look there? That woman is the head of the Breeding Council. They advise clans on the suitability of genetic pairings. Nasty lot."

The breeder became hidden within the crowd.

"Truly," Angel said, "I believe your fans outnumber mine."

"That breeder woman? My fan?" Teakh asked.

"Well, she's not anyone I've seen at an art show before." Angel shook her head.

Sis returned to stand near Teakh. "Angel did a good job with your kit," she said. "It looks nice. I got word out about your show." She departed, accompanied by her friends.

Three members of Tristan Bay Harbor patrol arrived, and one of the patrolmen looked familiar. Teakh stiffened, but Angel's face lit with her bright smile. She waggled her fingers at the man, greeting him warmly.

Teakh assessed his opponent. The man was taller than Teakh and projected an air of command. His kit wasn't particularly flashy but fit him well. His beard had been neatly trimmed. His eyes were an unusual color, not all that different from the gray-green of his kit. Depths! Only a Seaguard lord would have that kind of understated confidence, as if he ruled the seas and expected that everyone knew it. The patrolman bowed to Angel and bobbed his head to Teakh.

"Thank you for coming." Angel returned the bow.

"My pleasure." The man scooped up a glass of cloudberry wine and sipped it as he moved to look over the paintings.

"Who is that guy?" whispered Teakh. "I've seen him somewhere."

"Can't tell you," Angel said with a tilt of her head. "Confidentiality."

Teakh drew back. "You painted him for your other show. I remember now."

Angel stifled a laugh. "You're so cute when you're jealous, but don't worry. He has other interests."

Teakh's glance went to Keno.

Angel squeezed Teakh's hand. "He has a girl. This is rich."

More men in Seaguard kit and a few women dressed in the same style circulated among the crowd.

"Just how many law enforcement officers are here?" Teakh asked.

Angel elbowed him. "These people are here for you. Either that or for your sister, the promising law student. She's made quite an impression."

"For her stubbornness?" Teakh asked.

Angel shrugged. "She's a rising star, the law student out to found a new clan."

A woman emerged from the crowd, her boots and vest gray green without decoration. Sergeant Princess Mareen. Teakh glanced toward a painting. None of the seagulls depicted were identifiable as Gull or even as telechirics.

He straightened his vest. Possibly the princess had been bidding on his services. She was older than Teakh by a dodecade. A handsome woman with dark hair and strong features, she wore no makeup but had that same air of command flaunted by the tall Seaguardsman. Angel might not be the only one with admirers.

The princess approached with a smile for Teakh. "Greetings. I'm delighted to meet you in person at last."

He bowed. "Sergeant."

"You can call me Mareen. I trust your documents are in order this time."

Were legal documents required for art shows? And why was Sergeant Princess treating him in such a familiar fashion? Teakh glanced toward Angel, who was speaking with a group of guests. If the princess wanted to be called Mareen, so be it. She was a princess after all.

Mareen flicked her thumb toward the painted gulls. "I hope you've registered that bird of yours."

Maybe Mareen wasn't interested in his services after all. "Registration is pending," he said.

"My kinsfolk sure can be slow. Tide carry you." She winked and moved off to view the paintings. But in the alcove, she chuckled and turned to grin at Teakh. "Locking it up. Excellent idea!"

Teakh inclined his head. "Angel's the artist." When Mareen had gone, Teakh touched Angel's arm. "That was Princess Mareen Fennako."

"Another one of your fans," Angel said. "You've brought out royalty."

Toward the end of the evening, when the guests had thinned, a woman dressed in dark fur stalked up to Angel. "Are you the artist?"

"Yes, ma'am."

"You should be ashamed of yourself. Blasphemous drivel."

Teakh stepped forward, ready to defend Angel.

"Oh?" Angel squeezed Teakh's hand.

The woman spoke with the fury of a fanatic. "To suggest that Jamie Noah engaged in selfish recreational sex, a hedonist? And you, young man, are a fraud."

A fraud? He'd never been insulted by a woman in quite such a manner. He'd already been caught brawling in Fennako City. If he slugged that woman, he might be hauled in before the police, and he'd be back to calling the police chief Sergeant instead of Mareen.

"Ma'am, you may dislike my art, but don't denigrate this man." Angel rested her hand on Teakh's shoulder. "Noah is truly his patrilineal surname."

"Blasphemers. Noah remained chaste."

Angel's smile was all sweetness. "But wasn't he married to Queen Fenna? And didn't they have children? How else did they found Clan Fennako?"

The woman sputtered. "Fenna was a virgin. She never sullied her pure marriage to Noah with base passion. The great studs fathered her children through artificial insemination. "

"That's an interesting opinion." Angel kept a firm hold on Teakh's shoulder. "Can I bring you a glass of wine and a canapé?"

The woman snorted and, head high, left the gallery. Angel let Teakh go and snickered.

"What's so funny?"

"You. The look on your face. Like a gawping fish." Shaking with laughter, she put her hand over her mouth. "You didn't know what to say. And Noah's pure marriage." Angel doubled over. She wiped her eyes with a handkerchief. "You've noticed Jamie Noah didn't forbid adultery."

"With only five men, he couldn't," Teakh said.

Jamie Noah couldn't have done even half of his supposed achievements. The nonsense about Noah's celibacy and the perpetual virginity of Fenna piled on further absurdity. "I've heard that Noah was actually an organization, not a surname."

"Organizations don't found paternal lines." Angel brushed her lips against his arm. "Your genetics prove your ancestor's existence. Whatever his name, he must have been very much like you. I can't imagine Keno or you in a chaste marriage." She giggled. "And now we're besmirching the reputation of your progenitor? Good Danna! Our ancestors enjoyed sex. Imagine that!"

AT BREAKFAST, ANGEL read the news. "Listen to this." She lowered the screen. "Reviews in *Fennako City Multicast*. Our show is 'a scathing critique of Fenrian society. A deconstruction of the mythos of Noah.'"

"Do you have a political message?" Keno asked.

"Oh, yes! That men are beautiful. I happen to love them— Noah studs in particular. Judging from the bidding on your stud fees and from sales of my paintings, a lot of folks agree with me."

"Do you love Teakh more than me?" Keno asked.

"Go on." She lowered her lashes. "Teakh loves me more than you do."

Teakh took her hand. "Why do you love us?"

She gave him a shove.

"You use the name Matta Carrie, a siren, and you paint men," Teakh said.

"I lure them into my studio. My singing, I'm sure." She warbled a tune.

"There's more than that." Something he couldn't quite name. "You save men. Save their images anyway. Keno told me my clientele will include widows and those who have lost their men. Who did you lose?"

Keno fell silent, his gaze distant.

"Not a husband, that's for sure," Angel said.

"But someone."

"The usual story: my uncle and my brother. A moment's inattention, a line improperly coiled, a stopcock left open, ice on the superstructure, engine failure, a half-filled tank, and the ballast shifts, a hatch left open. A fire in the engine compartment. Should I go on? My uncle and brother went down on the same boat in the same storm. The truth is, no one knows exactly what happened."

Teakh asked, "Do you believe Noah genetics would have saved them?" Maybe she viewed him as a talisman against death.

"A bunch of shine. When Mother Carry calls us, we go. We all go."

"So you took a variation of her name? Matta Carrie?"

"The name of the goddess," Angel said. "It means 'merciful mother.'"

"You pray the sea will be merciful?"

"Stud, you're getting mighty philosophical," she said. "Maybe I'm Calypso or Sedna."

Teakh shook his head.

"Old stories. Come here." Angel leaned forward and traced Teakh's jaw. "Sedna was betrayed and thrown off of her ship. When she tried to climb back aboard, her fingers were chopped off. They became whales and dolphins. That's how the story goes. Sometimes dolphins save drowning mariners. I'd give up my fingers to have my uncle and brother alive."

Teakh held her hand and touched each of her knuckles. She'd lost the men she most loved. Did she fear losing him as well?

"Does it have to be that way?" He kissed the fingertips so often splotched with paint.

CHAPTER 35
Attack

TEAKH FLEXED HIS biceps and studied his shoulders and arms in the weight room mirror. Angel's paintings made him look better than his actual appearance.

Randy came through the doorway, holding a handscreen. "Get a load of Gimpy boy's fees. That's in halibut, not coho, not eulachon."

The clank of weights paused, and men looked toward Randy. Teakh held his pose. He had no desire to see the number of zeros in his stud fees.

Brawny set a barbell in its stand. "You're joking. Gimp?"

"Aye. You been hearing about the Noah stud? It's him." Randy flicked a thumb toward Teakh.

He ducked as if he could avoid the attention.

"That runt? Can't be." Buttcakes grunted as he lifted himself in a chin-up.

"Lookee here." Randy held out the screen. "Says right here little Gimpy is a direct descendant of Jamie Noah. To spawn with our boy, a client must provide genetic profile, family history, and references asserting that she sincerely believes in the Noah Code."

Brawny stood and wiped his forehead with a towel. "You mean he's the slime eel who's making studs pay their clients?"

"The studs don't pay," Teakh said. "The clients put money into an education trust fund." Fear stabbed through Teakh. The studs knew him for what he was—Seaguard passing himself off as a fisherman. Like a flock of gulls, they'd soon pursue the abnormal bird.

"And how does that help studs?" Brawny glowered. "You know what you are? A Poseidon-damn kinkiller. Soon all the women will want trust funds set up, and that money's got to come from somewhere. They're gonna pay less in stud fees just to make up the difference."

"A man should be able to care for his own kids," Teakh said. He'd merely set a new standard. If the fellows couldn't meet it, then they shouldn't be studs.

"Are you saying I don't care about my kids?" Brawny reeked of sweat, his breath like stale cheese as he stood bare chest to bare chest with Teakh. "Hag parasite. Look at him tie himself in knots."

Teakh stepped back. A fight was coming his way. Heart pounding, he snatched at and rejected options. He wouldn't transmit for help, not to Keno, and not to Seaguard, not this time. Danna! This was Madame X and her thugs all over again. He was up against Randy, Brawny, and maybe Buttcakes. The others—Manly, Hairy, and Ripple—could be on his side or maybe not. They'd likely desist.

Teakh smiled, bidding for more time as he accessed Gull, a weapon of sorts. "Is that all?" He flew her from the charging niche in his quarters and out through the transom into the hallway.

Randy slapped his own chest. "Jones here and proud of it. A true son of the forefathers."

Teakh urged Gull onward, flying her along the hallway from the dormitory.

"Noah gave us the Poseidon-damn code," growled Brawny. "Told everyone what to do. Be nice to strangers. Be nice to granny. Be nice. Sink it to the depths. I want to kick some Noah ass." His meaty arm encircled Teakh's neck.

Trapped in a headlock, Teakh jerked his arm free. He struck Brawny's nose with the back of his hand then elbowed him in the gut.

Buttcakes and the others jumped in—to stop the fight or join in, Teakh had no idea. He underhanded a chop to someone's groin and struck the back of a man's knee with his foot. The man buckled and fell, but Teakh remained pinned against Brawny.

Teakh's emotions broke free, and Gull dove, screeching at Brawny, stabbing his face and buffeting him with her wings. Using Gull's talons, Teakh scrambled for purchase on Brawny's naked chest then went for his head. Clutching hair, Gull stood on Brawny's head while driving beak into flesh. Teakh's fear and anger overrode her pain reception; she couldn't be stopped.

Letting go of Teakh, Brawny flailed at Gull. "Get it off! Get it off!"

Gull released Brawny's hair. Teakh screeched, the sound inhuman. Both gull and man charged with wings and arms akimbo. His fists were clenched, elbows out, grimacing, mouth open, braids and beads lashing.

Gull lunged at Randy, going for the nose, and clamped her beak on soft flesh. She tasted the iron of blood. In Teakh's mind, a DNA readout flashed: HUMAN MALE. HUMAN MALE. HUMAN MALE.

Randy shook his head. Teakh lost Gull's grip but reclamped her beak on Randy's mouth. Randy shouted, his words unintelligible as he tore the bird away, lacerating his own lip. Both Teakh and Gull came at him again, striking with beak and fists.

Doors slammed.

"Seaguard here!" a voice shouted.

Panting, Teakh balanced on the balls of his feet, fists at the ready. Gull tumbled, fluttering to the floor. Randy moaned, hands over his face, blood seeping through his fingers. Beak open, screeching, Gull made another run at Brawny.

He backed away, hands before his face. "Fratricidal bird. Kinkill!"

Patroller stood in the doorway to the weight room. "Stand down!" He wasn't exactly Tristan Bay Harbor Patrol, but he managed to project authority even when stark naked and dripping wet.

Once again, Teakh had been caught in a brawl. He took no pride in his fighting style, ugly and scrappy, learned in waterfront dives and perfected among angry seabirds, who grappled beak-to-beak in a fight. Good Danna! Biting Brawny's lip had been a nasty move. Word of the scuffle would get back to Fennako, and where would that leave Teakh and Sis?

But right now, he'd best get Gull out of the way. He sent her flying through the clerestory window to the roof. He shook her wings then folded them and, checking for damage, preened her feathers and removed spattered blood. Heart still pounding, Teakh focused on this simple task.

Patroller stepped into the room.

Randy slumped on a bench. "A seagull attacked out of nowhere."

"Come on, you grabbed Gimp," someone said.

"We were only joking," mumbled Brawny. Blood dripped from slashes on his face, chest, and scalp.

Teakh rubbed his neck, still burning from the headlock.

"Sir," Patroller addressed Teakh, "I heard what was said. Fenna protects her own."

Teakh put a shaking hand to his head. What did the fight have to do with Queen Fenna?

Patroller continued. "You do not insult Queen Fenna in the presence of Seaguard. Or her consort, Jamie Noah. Seaguardsman, are you well?"

Had Patroller just addressed Teakh as Seaguard? Teakh staggered. "Aye."

"As Seaguard, we're obligated to render hospitality to these lubbers," Patroller said.

"I'm bleeding," Brawny said. "Scratched me up bad."

"Someone go get him a cloth." Patroller glared at Brawny. "Fenna spared your eyes. You can be thankful for that."

Clean washcloths were produced, and Patroller directed Randy and Brawny to press them against their bleeding faces. Teakh stood motionless, still dazed. How had the fight occurred? He'd intended to keep his views to himself, his identity private.

"Get dressed, brother," Patroller said to Teakh. "We'll escort the injured to the clinic."

Teakh shook himself and focused on the present. "I'll make the hail." He contacted the clinic. *We have two male patients. A fight. Both aged about three-dozen. One has lacerations on head, face, and chest. The other puncture wounds and lacerations on nose and lips.*

Where are you at?

Keno's Gym.

Stay put. We'll send someone.

"Healthwyv is coming." Teakh scooped up his bandanna and went to his quarters.

Still shaking, he pulled shirt and pants from his closet

and dressed. When had he started shaking? He resecured his bandanna, stamped on his mariner's boots, and returned to the weight room.

Patroller now wore a vest and close-fitting trousers, the type of pants worn under hip-high seaboots. "Gimp, a word with you."

Teakh frowned but followed Patroller into the studio. They stood amidst the mats and towels strewn on the floor.

Patroller tapped his ear. "You got a record of what happened?"

"Maybe." Teakh's neuro kept a log when he was under stress, but he wouldn't admit to making such recordings unless he had a good reason to.

"I'm assuming that bird is yours. Best imitation of a gull I've ever seen. But inside a building and defending Seaguard?" Patroller shook his head.

"Maybe I'm not Seaguard," suggested Teakh.

"Don't shine me. You going to press charges?"

"What for?"

"For assaulting Seaguard in the line of duty."

"Duty?" What exactly had been said leading up to the fight? Teakh recalled that they'd argued about the trust funds for his children.

"He assaulted you as a representative of Noah, the founder of the Seaguard. Seaguard brotherhood won't take kindly to that. The catalogues have you as something like the reincarnation of Jamie Noah."

"Not exactly." Teakh followed the code, but he cared more about his own family than about anything else.

"Well, that's what the boys believe, and that's why they attacked you."

"What's this about Queen Fenna?" Teakh asked. "Come on, some ancient monarch defending me from the grave?" For a man born in the marshes and rejected by Clan Ralko, Seaguard sure had given Teakh a lot of leeway.

"Fenna programmed the Sense-net just like you programmed your bird," Patroller said. "So in a sense, she's still around."

"But the Sense-net didn't defend me. That was Gull."

"It's all about the same. She knows about you. No doubt

about it." Patroller glanced upward as if locating security cameras. "You're the type of fellow she's fond of."

Teakh keenly felt his ignorance. He'd never had an uncle explain the inner workings of the Sense-net. "Fenna, the guardian of children? It's a bedtime story."

"Suit yourself. The Sense-net is still a gal you want on your side, and Fenna has strong feelings even if she's just a program." Patroller ran a hand through his close-cropped hair. "Are you going to press charges? Your choice."

If Teakh pressed charges, the suit would be tried in interclan court, his clan against the clans of his assailants. Clan Noahee wasn't prepared for a lawsuit, not yet. As things stood, Ralko, not Noahee, would represent him in court. Aunt Dyse would ask for fines paid into Ralko coffers, letting Randy and Brawny get off scot-free.

Teakh knotted his bandanna. Forgiveness was in his own self-interest. "Don't think so. Let's check on the injured." He'd provide hospitality, if only to prove his Seaguard status.

He and Patroller returned to the weight room. Brawny, seated on a bench press, held a pad to his bleeding face. Randy wore a robe and blotted at his nose and lips with a cloth. The medical team, three women, arrived.

Randy peeled back the cloth to show his slashed nose and lip. "Bit me. Right on the schnoz and the kisser." With a swollen lip, he gave a stiff smile.

The healthwyv looked toward Brawny. "From him? Is that a human bite?"

"Bird," Randy said. "Poseidon-damn seagull. It got both of us."

The healthwyv raised her eyebrows.

"Attacked out of nowhere," Randy said. "Rabies! A rabid seagull."

"Where's the bird?" the healthwyv asked.

"All taken care of," Patroller said.

She pointed at her noteboard. "Seaguard, it's essential to know if that bird carries an illness."

"The bird in question is a Seaguard telechiric operating on behalf of Her Majesty." Patroller glanced at Teakh. "The instrument is basically clean."

Teakh nodded. Gull's saliva had antimicrobial properties

THE FISHERMAN AND THE SPERM THIEF

to prevent contamination of specimens.

Brawny lowered the cloth. "Gimp is Seaguard? You gonna arrest me?"

"You're not worth it," Patroller said. "You knew he was Seaguard when you assaulted him."

The side door opened. Keno entered and faced the carnage. "What happened?"

"Seaguard matter," Patroller said.

"I come home and two of my men are injured. Don't go telling me it's a Seaguard matter."

"They attacked Gimp," offered Buttcakes. "And a big bird came out of nowhere."

Keno raised his eyebrows. Teakh crossed his arms, his gaze steady, without answering Keno's unstated question.

"Seaguard Network came to his defense," Patroller said. "These men assaulted him. We have records."

"Is that true?" Keno faced Teakh. "If it is, those two are out of my gym."

"You know me," Teakh said. "I'm not saying."

"I also know Randy and Brawny." Keno turned away. "Patroller, sir, I'd appreciate it if you'd give me an explanation in private."

Patroller and Keno went in the office and closed the door. Teakh waited, clenching and unclenching his fists. Keno didn't blindly take directions from anyone, but Patroller was Seaguard. To keep himself busy, Teakh flew Gull back to her niche.

The office door opened, and Keno and Patroller came out. Keno nodded to Teakh then spoke with the medical team about wound care and follow-up.

When the medics had departed, Keno called a meeting in the dining room. Teakh seated himself well away from Randy and Brawny. His hands on the table before him, Teakh figured he'd catch trouble from Keno for fighting, but Teakh refused to accept criticism for defending himself as he saw fit. He hadn't started the fight.

Keno met the gaze of each man seated around the table. "I understand today one of our members was assaulted for his support of the Noah Code. This should not occur among us. I'm inclined to remove the perpetrators from this gym and report them to their clan councils."

"I didn't know," Brawny said

"Didn't know what?" Keno asked.

"That Gimp is Seaguard."

"We've all seen his scars. Men don't get those by accident," Patroller said.

Teakh wadded his bandanna, acutely conscious of the welts on his scalp and the gold beads in his hair. "I have a neural interface. What does it matter? What if I were just a fisherman? What if I were clanless?" He knotted the bandanna over his head and tugged it in place.

"At this gym, we treat others as equals." Keno bowed to Teakh, the sign of respect as disconcerting to Teakh as his exposed scars. With a flourish, Keno produced a bandanna from his pocket and secured the fabric over his head. "Gimp is Seaguard but has asked for no special privileges. I honor him."

A glance passed between Keno and Patroller, who produced his own bandanna. Keno glared at Brawny then Randy.

Good Danna. This was ridiculous.

Keno stood. "Here, we are all sons of the Forefathers. No difference between Seaguard and mariner, Noah and Jones." His gaze rested on Randy.

Randy's eyes moved as his glance went from Keno to Patroller, then he flipped open a napkin and tied a knot at each corner. With a wink to Teakh, he donned the makeshift hat.

The other men followed his example, covering their heads with towels, napkins, and bandannas, hiding scars and lack of scars. Such absurdity, grown men with napkins on their heads.

"I don't recall being assaulted." Teakh kept a straight face as he bowed to Randy then Brawny. "I'm sorry you were injured." Teakh couldn't press charges without involving Aunt Dyse, so he completely let the issue go.

CHAPTER 36
Liaison

I N AN UPSTAIRS parlor, Teakh remained at attention while Dyse and the bride's mother read his wedding contract before a notary camera. Keno stood behind him as his witness. The words droned, the same document read twice, and it was already an inordinately long document.

The bride wasn't present for the legalities. Was she pretty? Was she kind? Teakh was forbidden to know her name or interact with her outside of the bridal chamber. They were not to talk. Even the name of her clan and this village had been withheld.

Strains of music and laughter wafted from the village plaza, where dancers and revelers celebrated the conjunction of the two moons. Teakh and Keno had come from the celebration in the plaza. Each had been pulled into a different exuberant quad of dancers who'd honored them as bridegroom and best man, not just hired studs.

Directed by a magistrate, Teakh averred that he understood the marriage contract and entered of his own free will. He had, Danna help him. Sis had sold herself for the sake of Clan Noahee, and Teakh would do the same.

He wore his best—the seaboots and the blue-and-gray vest given to him by Angel. She'd told him to go through with the wedding. He recalled her breath, soft on his cheek, as she whispered how the prospect pleased and excited her.

"You're my stud," she'd said.

With the legalities finished, senior members of the bride's clan lined up to welcome him. He endured the dry kisses of elderly women smelling of lavender and talc. Symbolically, he was now married to the entire clan.

Keno and the rest of the wedding party followed Teakh in a procession down the stairs and out through a foyer. In the plaza, six women flanked an open litter draped with a velvet throw. The tasseled edge of the coverlet spilled over the carrying poles to trail on the cobblestone pavement. A crowd of spectators pressed around the litter, a chaise lounge on poles.

Teakh whispered, "They're not going to carry me on that thing." Women might mud wrestle for Limber and carry him as their prize, but Teakh would be damned if they did that for him.

Keno grinned. "They're taking you to the bower houses so you can consummate your marriage. It's all part of the show."

"What about you?" Teakh asked.

"I'm walking and making sure you don't get dropped," Keno said.

Teakh hailed Angel. *They're going to carry me.*

Who? asked Angel.

The girl's kinswomen. There're six of them.

Angel's laughter bubbled. *Have fun. And send me videos. I want to see the whole thing. If anyone asks, tell them I'm your artistic consultant. I love you.*

Teakh signed off and reclined on the velvet-covered conveyance. With a drum roll, the bearers lifted him to their shoulders. He clutched the edge of the swaying litter. To the beat of drums, the women carried him through the village as if he were a sacrifice soon to be devoured by Danna, Danna the cruel, Danna the ice-hearted. Or was she Sedna, the bereft?

The procession paused before a row of hexagonal cottages, each with a cupola but otherwise windowless. Teakh had never been inside a bower house, a place off-limits to children and to men other than husbands and designated witnesses. When the litter had been lowered, Keno offered Teakh a hand and pulled him to his feet.

"You next time," Teakh said. "Six strapping lads."

"Bring them on," Keno said.

Leaving the bearers and litter behind, Keno and Teakh entered the bower house through a side door. Windowless walls muted the now-distant skirl of music. The room, with two chairs flanking a table, seemed to be a foyer. Two interior doors remained closed.

Keno flopped onto a chair. "Now we wait."

Teakh paced, unable to sit. He'd been told his new bride was a virgin. He would initiate her into intimate pleasures. But if he couldn't perform, her expectations would soon turn to scorn. He'd be the laughingstock of Keno's gym.

A door opened, and a woman stepped through. Was it her?

Her brown hair had been arranged in a high coiffeur, and she wore a red tunic split at the sides. She was older than he'd expected. Keno put a hand on Teakh's arm.

The woman smiled and bowed. "Welcome. This way, please." Apparently she wasn't Teakh's intended, but an attendant.

The next room contained a bench, dressing table, and clothing rod. Keno helped Teakh undress and don a silk robe, the fabric smooth against Teakh's skin. The luxurious material caught on his rough hands. Here he was, a fisherman all decked out as a premium stud. His stomach fluttered. His price had been astronomical, more than he was worth. His birth had been an accident, his genetics a bloodstained legacy. If he performed, he'd betray his ancestors, who'd held fast to monogamy. If he refused, he'd betray Sis and Angel. But when he entered the bridal chamber and encountered the girl, he'd be on his own.

Under the central cupola, she reclined on a dais strewn with rose petals. The windows had been darkened, and spotlights shone down on her. Her smooth skin glowed with youth and health. She was only a year older than himself, he'd been told. She wore a cutwork nightie, her blushing skin playing peek-a-boo through the openings in the white fabric.

Rows of witnesses were seated before the dais as if for a theatrical performance. He'd emerged from one of two doors behind the platform. The attendant accompanied him to the front of the dais, then she and Keno joined the audience. Teakh bowed to the assembled witnesses, nearly a dozen of them.

He stepped onto the dais and into bright light walled by opaque blackness. The audience and cameras were now hidden in the shadows. Teakh had never before initiated sex. That first time in Idylko, he'd made love to Angel, but they'd never again engaged in full intercourse, and Angel had been in control. If he ejaculated prematurely, she didn't mind. It was a game to her. He'd never been the one in control and never with so many people watching. Both Keno and Angel had explained what to do, how to please a woman.

Taking a breath, he drew on his training and preparation: sessions on anatomy, hours spent developing awareness of his body, and long discussions with Angel about beauty, art, and love. Teakh called Angel to mind, the luscious curve between her waist and hip, the hidden pleasures between her legs. He silently dedicated his performance to her.

Letting his robe drop, he stood naked. Aware of the hidden audience, he moved slowly, giving all a good view. Modulating his movement, he knelt on the bed beside the girl. Her breath caught, and her lashes fluttered.

He smoothed her dark chestnut hair and broke the prohibition against speaking. "You're beautiful. Good Danna, you're beautiful."

She smiled, her brown eyes lively and bright, and he smiled back. She jangled his gold beads with a slim finger. He kissed her plump lips. Her body was softer than Angel's and so innocent. His responsibility weighed on him, excited him.

He lifted her gown, a wide circle of sheer fabric smocked at the shoulders, revealing the soft tangle of hair at her pubis. He tugged, but she was lying on the fabric as if she were a crystal vessel wrapped in tissue. With care, he arranged the lacework, exposing her breasts without covering her face, making sure that she could see and watch.

She placed her hand on his head, encouraging him. He stroked her breasts, licking them, teasing her nipples, inhaling her scent: roses, starch, and linen. But hidden in the sweetness was that wild woman musk—not as spicy as Angel, a little sweeter.

Moving lower, he explored her body, seeing it with his hands, painting her with his tongue. One hand under her hips, he burrowed his nose into the soft hair of her mound. He whimpered, his desire now urgent, but he'd take it slow for her.

He sought her cleft, his fingers exploring her hidden lips and parting them. Using his tongue and his lips, he searched out each fold, the contrast between soft flesh and rough hair.

She arched her back and thrust against him. Mouth open, he sucked gently. He slipped a finger into her opening, feeling the textures of her channel—more texture than Angel—then satin smoothness. He hooked his finger slightly. Keno had told him of an inner area of pleasure. He felt for that spot and was rewarded with gasps.

"Oh Danna! Stop! Stop!"

He withdrew his finger.

"More," she said. "Good Danna, more!"

He spread her thighs and parted her lips, then he straightened, giving the cameras and witnesses a good viewing angle as he slid into her satin-smooth tightness. He rocked his hips. She arched again, her breath ragged. He brought her nearly to climax then withdrew.

"More!" she screamed.

Again, he entered and worked her until she whimpered. Pumping together, their breath rose to a crescendo. Her inner walls contracted rhythmically, and the movement shocked Teakh. That wasn't like Angel. Not like Angel at all.

The third time, he lost control. Sink the witnesses! Sink the cameras! He drove into her, and she arched against him. As she sighed, he collapsed against her.

They lay together, his member still inside her, their bodies still pulsing. He loved Angel. Why had this felt so different, so right? He covered the girl with her gown and lay beside her. And then he knew. He'd never penetrated Angel. He'd made love to an artificial vagina hidden from his view. She'd stolen his seed.

The girl mouthed, "Thank you."

He suppressed a sob and hated himself for being a fool. Angel had betrayed him. Poseidon damn it! What kind of man cries after having sex? And it had been good sex. The best he'd ever had.

The girl's caress lingering on his face, Teakh bolted from the spotlight. In the dressing room, away from cameras and witnesses, he pulled on his pants.

The door opened, and Keno entered, a wicked grin on his face. "You were hot. I was ready to jump your bones."

Teakh stared at his robe flung onto a chair. Chair and robe

blurred. Keno touched Teakh's wet cheek. He knocked Keno's hand away.

Keno laughed. "You're in love. In love after doing it once."

"Go to hell." This wasn't love.

"Women cry during sex all the time," Keno said. "An orgasm was once called the little death."

Teakh fastened his vest. "I'm not a woman."

Keno grinned. "The camera caught you crying. Proof that your emotions match your genetics."

Poseidon damn it! Was that all Keno cared about?

"I had to leave her." He'd never again see his bride, soon to be the mother of his child.

"If you liked leaving, you wouldn't be worth as much." Keno rested a hand on Teakh's shoulder. "That's why I can't do it anymore."

"Angel lied to me." Teakh wiped at his eyes. "She tricked me. Damn succubus. She stole from me. I thought—"

Keno interrupted. "You assumed. You believed what you wanted to believe."

"I thought she loved me."

"As far as I know, she does," Keno said.

Panic rose. Teakh was trapped, in love with a woman who'd cheated him.

"If it makes you feel better," Keno said, "I doubt Angel has sold it yet. She'll wait for the price to go higher."

"Poseidon sink you!" Teakh yanked open the foyer door.

Keno gripped his shoulder. "Observe. Hold fast to the Noah Code."

Teakh pulled away from Keno and shut the door. The words of Noah offered no comfort. No one honored fatherhood, including Teakh. Before he'd even begun as a father, he'd failed.

CHAPTER 37
Gift

BACK AT THE gym, Teakh stripped off his clothing then stepped into the shower. He dialed the water to hot and nudged the temperature higher until the heat stung as the water drummed on his skin. If only he could wash himself clean of betrayal as well, but the memory of Angel remained, the gentleness of her embrace and the sweetness of her laughter forever tainted. He longed for her, but he couldn't go to her even if he wanted to. He had no money for airfare or even for a ferry ticket.

He dried off, sat on the floor beside his bed, and accessed Gull. Pouring his consciousness into her, he sprang for the window and left his body behind. He flew along the shore, on the lookout for fish scraps. Anything to forget himself and Angel. Spread out below Gull, the inlet rippled in gray-green waves. If only Teakh could live forever as Gull and never come back.

But he could not escape.

The door to his quarters opened, Keno invading. He brushed against Teakh's arm. "Gimp?"

Eyes shut, Teakh maintained his focus on flight, the flare of a wing tip, the cant of Gull's tail. "Go away."

"Your aunt is in my front room making a nuisance of herself. You'll have to talk to her."

Teakh tossed his head. "Tell her to sink to the depths."

"You'll have to tell her yourself." A wad of clothing struck Teakh in the head. "Put something on. Unless you want to talk to her naked. If you don't come, I'll bring her up here."

"Damn you." Teakh banked Gull into a turn and flew for the gym. "I'm coming down."

Shaking his head, Keno disappeared out the door.

Teakh brought Gull through the clerestory. He savored the last bit of flight as he glided down to his cot and hopped Gull into her niche.

He yanked clothes from his closet—a pilled sweater and his torn and mended pants. Dressed to match his mood, he stalked out of the room. He entered the front parlor, and Dyse stood from her seat at the table. A crumbled biscuit remained beside her empty teacup.

"What a performance!" she exclaimed. "Your price is going through the roof." She rubbed her hands together, a wicked gleam in her eyes.

"Never again." Teakh stalked forward, his bandanna firmly over his scars. "I'm done with this stud business." He'd left behind a beautiful woman soon to be pregnant with his child. He'd never see her again and wouldn't even know his child's name. And it was all for nothing. Angel, the only woman he truly wanted, had cheated him.

Dyse shook her head. "Don't give me that shine."

"Not shine," Teakh said. "It violates the Noah Code. Honor thy father."

"This has nothing to do with your father. Nephew, we've arranged things quite well. Your children will have good mothers, they'll be educated and cared for, and you've taken a stand for your sons. Work with us. I have a surprise for you."

Teakh's heart sank. This couldn't be good.

"Down at the harbor. Your sister's here."

That wasn't much of a surprise. He'd stopped transmitting after his liaison. Of course Sis would be worried. He didn't want to talk to her or anyone else.

"She came by esskip with a Fennako pilot. But that's not the surprise."

Good Danna! Had his sister's assigned stud done the deed?

GLUMLY, TEAKH ACCOMPANIED Dyse to the waterfront. The weather was too bright for his stormy mood. Sunlight sparkled on the inlet, and the satin flanks of waves reflected the rich blue of the sky. Dyse trailing behind, Teakh trudged down the dock ramp to the small boat harbor. Sis stood on the dock, and an esskip floated nearby. She wore a navy-blue tunic trimmed with white braid and fastened with intricately knotted buttons.

"Teakh!" she shouted.

The craft sure didn't look Fennako, not with that gray-and-white coloration and not with that call sign. NOA425.

Sis shook her head. "I couldn't get the original designation."

Was this craft for him? Poseidon founder it all! What did matter if the designation were NOA or NOAA?

"What's wrong?" Sis searched his face, knowing him too damn well.

He shook his head, unable to articulate the emptiness that filled him.

"We're now a clan." She beamed toward the esskip. "A gift for the new clan chief."

Once the gift would have pleased him. He'd wanted to become clan chief to please Angel and to care for his children, but all that was lost to him now.

"How did you pay for the esskip?" Teakh and Sis had linked accounts. They couldn't afford the *gift*.

"I took out a loan," Sis said. "With your stud fees, it'll be easy to pay off."

Even if Sis intended well, he was trapped, betrayed by everyone he loved. He'd be forced to continue as a stud to pay off the debt. "How much did it cost?"

"Two-dozen g-gross."

"Eulachon or coho?"

"Coho," whispered Sis.

"We can't afford it." He'd never performed sexually without Angel or the thought of Angel. If he couldn't get it up, he couldn't be a stud. It was as simple as that. "I can't accept the gift."

"Dyse told me your first liaison would be difficult. She suggested I give you the esskip as consolation."

"To trap me," Teakh said.

Dyse pushed between Teakh and Sis. "Isn't it wonderful? You can travel as much as you like, visit whomever you want. If you fancy, you can locate your children. I won't stop you."

"It seemed to be a good idea," Sis said. "I commissioned the esskip a year ago. Dyse approved the loan."

Dyse. Of course she did.

"You can return the gift," Dyse said, "but you'll still be responsible for the non-refundable design fees."

No way out. Teakh focused on his breathing, trying to observe the tide within, but that tide roiled and churned.

"We had it delivered last twelve-night." Dyse smiled. "It's been waiting for you."

He tore off his bandanna. "Kinkill!"

He'd return the esskip, accept the debt, and get work as a fishermen or a longshoreman until he could establish his reputation as a detective. He'd clear that debt eventually, along with Sis's student loan and the debts incurred by courting Angel. He'd be paying for both his mistake and the debt for the rest of his life.

Angel was a succubus, always had been. He should have known. Love tangled with shame and regret, his emotions jammed and pulled tight. She might have sold his seed. If so, how would he trace it? Worst of all, Teakh wanted Angel, wanted her still, wanted her despite what she'd done. This anguish tore him apart.

Blocking out Dyse and Sis, he stared at the boards of the dock, one hand to his implant scars. How good was his memory of that first encounter in Idylko? His ankle ached with the lingering pain of the misstep that had landed him in Idylko Hospital. He remembered Angel's laughter, her smile, and the softness of her touch. She wouldn't have cheated him. He knew Angel. What if he were wrong about the theft?

The esskip floated beside the dock. Realization dawned— with the esskip, Teakh could go wherever he wanted. He'd fly to Shellako and confront Angel. Dyse wouldn't stop him.

He looked up and forced a smile. "I accept the gift. Thank you." He'd accept it for now. He could return it after he'd made a visit to Angel.

"I trust our arrangement remains," Dyse said. "You will find it profitable."

As Dyse departed along the dock, Sis stepped close to Teakh. "You can't fool me. What's wrong?"

"The debt. We can't afford that craft."

"Don't shine me. There's something else."

"If you must know... uh... I had a quarrel with Angel." Teakh nodded at the craft's tail designation and changed the subject. The craftswomen who injected the pigment were licensed. "How did you get that call number? Who did you bribe?"

"No one," Sis said. "It's legitimate. We're a clan. I fulfilled the contract."

"It's still bribery." Teakh scowled. Aye, in a sense they'd bribed the Queen, or she'd bribed them.

Sis put a hand over her belly. "It's not."

Good Danna! She *was* pregnant.

"Just where is that man of yours?" The lubber had walked out on her, just like Teakh had walked out on the rose-petal girl.

"He's over at the esskip lagoon with Lord Dojko," Sis said.

"With Lord Dojko?" Teakh wanted nothing to do with the local Seaguard lord or with any member of the Seaguard.

"Well, yes. He had to moor his esskip somewhere. He promised to stay out of the way."

He'd better. Teakh intended to confront Angel in person without supervision by Lord Dojko or anyone else. Teakh turned from Sis and hailed Angel. *We must meet immediately.*

What fun, she said.

This is serious. It's regarding the time we first met in Idylko.

Guess where I am right now? She giggled, but her laughter was strained. *Jeena and Reez are with me. Come join us in Idylko. We'll be waiting for you.*

This isn't fun or funny. I'll be there in about an hour. Teakh wasn't sure exactly how long the flight would take. He signed off and turned to Sis. "Something has come up. I'm going to Idylko."

"What's going on?" Sis crossed her arms and got that stubborn look in her eye, becoming the little admiral. "I happen to be your clan matriarch, and I purchased that esskip for you."

"This is a Seaguard matter. And I'm paying for that esskip."
Sis's eyes were hard, but her voice was all sweetness. "A Noahee Seaguard matter?"

"Actually, I need to speak with Angel to clear up a misunderstanding."

"Then it *is* a clan matter. I'm Noahee grandmatriarch. You need me. I'll pull rank on you."

Good Danna! Barely a clan and already Teakh and Sis were at odds.

CHAPTER 38
Confrontation

SEATED IN THE cockpit, Teakh stretched out the esskip's starboard wing and fanned the pinions, plates rather than feathers. A thrill went through him. When he flew Gull, his mind followed her in flight, but his body remained behind. This esskip offered real freedom. He folded the starboard wing at wrist, elbow, and shoulder. The pinions closed alongside the fuselage, the sensation comfortably familiar.

"Thank you." He turned to face Sis, who was seated behind him and wearing his old orange life vest.

Above the craft, the tail jutted upward, a tall fin with horizontal stabilizers near the top. How exactly did the elevators and rudders respond to his thoughts? He'd have to trust the programming he'd transferred from Gull.

He ran through the preflight checklist provided by the manufacturer, made sure that Sis's harness was fastened, then he hailed Dojko Command. *This is Noahee esskip located in Dojko Harbor.*

Lord Dojko here, came the response from the Dojko chief, his voice synthesized but a good likeness of how the senior man actually spoke.

Teakh fastened his own harness. *Flight plans. Travel to Idylko.*

You got a rating for that craft? asked Lord Dojko.

Teakh hoped the transition from Gull to the esskip would be seamless without glitches in the transferred programming. *Chief Noahee here. Head of Noahee Seaguard.*

Dojko laughed, an electronic buzz. *I reckon you issued that rating yourself. Ever flown an esskip before?*

I'm an experienced drone pilot. The principles of flight remained the same regardless of the type of craft: ornithopter, airplane, or esskip.

Ah, yes. With a large herring gull noted for eating money, brawling, and making man-overboard calls.

Teakh swallowed. Lord Dojko must have known all along. *Honor is yours.* Dojko's laughter chafed. *Still, I'm not about to let an inexperienced lad get in trouble.*

Teakh made a bid for legitimacy. *I'm logging flight time.* Initially, every pilot was inexperienced.

Not with a passenger aboard. Tell you what. We got a fellow here eager to stretch his wings. We'll send him along as an escort.

We'll be fine on our own, sent Teakh.

This fellow isn't the sort who takes no for an answer. You want to fly to Idylko, you'll have to accept an escort.

Accepted, sent Teakh. He could either accept or argue flight regulations with Dojko command.

Stand by, sent Dojko.

Twitching his pinions and rudder, or what he thought might be a rudder, Teakh waited, his craft drifting from the pier. The rudder felt like Gull's tail.

Cleared for departure, sent Dojko.

Teakh activated the pulse jets, a sensation akin to inhaling, but it felt as if his shoulders filled rather than his lungs. He coughed and nothing happened. Then a tickle in his chest spread to his shoulders. With a powerful release, the esskip lurched forward.

"We're off!" Sis said. "Congratulations."

He repeated the procedure, moving the esskip away from the dock and out of the harbor. As he relaxed, the movement smoothed out, as natural as breathing.

In the open fjord, he increased his cadence. With his wings still tucked, he extended his landing skis to rise on step. Water rippled over his landing skis, the sensation as if he were standing barefoot on the waves. With a burst of power, he reached out his pinions and flew, skimming half a wing length above the sea. To his stern, a gray-green esskip sped from the Dojko lagoon.

Teakh watched the craft through his rearview cameras, seeing the esskip from bow-on. The angle obscured the tail number and insignia. Still, the gray-green esskip could only be Fennako, not the craft of some Dojko pilot eager for a jaunt. He made a guess about the pilot's identity. "Your Fennako sweetheart is on our tail."

"We aren't supposed to know who he is," Sis said, confirming part of Teakh's suspicion. "For all we know, he could have borrowed a Fennako craft."

"Not likely." Teakh continued flying. Surely the man was Fennako. "Where have you two been?"

"We had a nice full-moon holiday," Sis said, her voice smug.

She had as much right to choose a lover as he did. Still, this was his sister. Whoever he was, that man had better be good to her.

Teakh concentrated on flying. If he didn't think too much about Angel, he flew without difficulty. But if he tried to piece together how the odd tail of the craft responded to his thoughts, he faltered. He focused his thoughts and entered into flight as if he were a bird.

Leaving Dojko waters, he hailed for permission to enter the next territory and received clearance, along with charts and navigational updates. He timed the pulse of the jets with the movement of his wings—in for speed, out for lift. He was flying smoothly now. He passed floating chunks of glacial ice. Angel would appreciate that shade of blue. She would paint a seascape of glacial ice floating just off that dark headland.

He came around the headland and encountered chop and a crosswind which buffeted his fuselage. He fought to gain altitude, but the wind caught him, and his esskip yawed. Reflex took over. He corrected. A wave caught his wingtip, wrenching his fingers, wrist, and shoulder. His hull hit the water, and the esskip spun broadside to an oncoming wave.

"Teakh!" Sis shouted.

The wave crashed over them, and they rolled. Teakh's world turned over in a blur of green-and-white spume. Lucent water pressed against the canopy, and bubbles hissed against the glazing.

Suspended from the seat by his harness, he shouted, "Are you okay?"

"What do you think? I'm upside down."

He tried to project calmness even while his heart raced and his shoulder ached. "Don't worry. This happens all the time."

Sure, it did—to other pilots. In theory, an esskip could be rolled upright like a kayak. But if he failed to right the craft, he and Sis would exit into frigid water to float among brash ice until the Fennako escort scooped them up.

A man's voice barked from Sis's comset. "What the depths!" Then it softened. "Are you okay?"

"Aye," Sis replied.

"What does that addlebrained brother of yours think he's doing?"

Teakh tried to disregard his sister's upset sweetheart. The craft would float and the cockpit was sealed, so they had enough air for now. He could barrel-roll Gull, and he could perform a flip turn while swimming laps. Presumably the same type of action would right an esskip.

He let his consciousness expand, becoming the craft floating belly up. With a blast of his propulsors, he scooped his starboard wing through the water. Runnels sheeted from the canopy as the esskip rolled upright.

"Not too bad," the disembodied male voice said, "but don't try that again."

Founder the arrogant lubber. Teakh shook his pinions, scattering droplets of water as if from his fingertips. He took a breath, and his racing heart slowed.

"Are you married to that guy?" he asked, not caring if his sister's comset remained open.

"Not anymore. Our marriage ended yesterday when we fulfilled the contract."

"Good," growled Teakh. "I don't fancy him as a brother-in-law. I'd rather think of him as your stud."

"He's not paid. Ex-husband. We delayed fulfilling the contract as long as we could." She sighed. "Married for only four months."

"And you still don't know his identity? How'd you manage that?"

"We never appear together in public where I might overhear his name. And my study group censors news for me."

The man was a public figure. "Then you do know who he is."

"I refuse to know his name," Sis said. "I'm not supposed to. That's what the contract says, so that's what I'm doing."

Teakh felt grudging respect. Sis and her man had stretched out a single liaison into a marriage lasting an entire winter.

"What is he getting out of it?" Teakh asked.

"What do you think?"

The guy had been regularly making out with Sis, but he seemed to genuinely care about her. Teakh resumed his journey, keeping his attention on his craft. The Fennako esskip followed closely. Sis's ex, however, remained silent.

Coming into Idylko, Teakh hailed traffic control. *Noahee here. Destination Idylko Village. Meeting with medical technician Jeena Idylko.* Angel had promised she was at Jeena's place.

Chart updates filled Teakh's screen. *Go ahead, Noahee, you have the codes.*

He soon received another hail. *Harbormistress here. Proceed to small boat harbor. Dock at pier four.*

Good, Teakh wouldn't have to jump his craft over the breakwater into the Idylko lagoon. He'd seen the maneuver g-grosses of time but had never done it himself.

The trailing esskip peeled away. With a flaring of wings and a burst of speed, the Fennako craft cleared the embankment to land beyond in the protected water of the lagoon.

With considerably less skill, Teakh splashed down and glided into the harbor, the location of pier four flashing on his chart. Most likely, Sis's ex had requested different docking sites for himself and Noahee, all to avoid Sis overhearing her ex's name.

Mooring line in hand, Teakh jumped to the dock. He secured the line to a cleat. "Will you be all right waiting? I'm not sure how long this will take."

"I've got studying to do." Sis held up her handscreen. "And someone to talk to." She touched the comset at her shoulder.

Teakh tramped along the dock then up the gangway to the narrow lane leading up from the harbor. His booted feet thudded on the boardwalk, the sound not as staccato as the thump of his crutches the last time he'd been this way. Behind front windows, women glanced up from planning frames.

He ignored them. At Jeena's cottage, he hailed, then removed his bandanna and stuffed it in his pocket. He would present himself as Seaguard with his implant scars visible. Despite his feelings for Angel, he would demand return of his property.

The door opened, and Angel greeted him. "Give me a kiss."

Teakh's resolve nearly slipped, but he shoved past her, refusing her embrace.

"What's wrong?" She frowned.

Jeena, standing in the foyer behind Angel, pushed up her sleeve, revealing a silver bracelet. Reez, with her raven-black curls, stood with a hand on Jeena's shoulder, her bracelet also visible.

Teakh refused to touch his matching bracelet. He stepped into the room without removing his boots, his right as a Seaguard officer and his right after being lied to. "Chief Teakh Noahee to you."

Angel brushed Teakh's shoulder. "I like the shiny new title."

His resolve to behave as a Seaguard officer nearly melted under the warmth of her affection, but that was probably fake as well. He pulled away.

He and Angel sat on the sofa without touching. She fidgeted with the hem of her tunic. He adjusted the cuff of his boots, displaying the Noahee colors on the lining to emphasize his status as a Seaguard officer. Could this be any more uncomfortable? In the kitchen, a kettle whistled. Jeena went to get it.

Angel leaned back, glancing at him through her lashes. The gesture, once so charming, now seemed to be an affectation. "What is this important matter?"

Teakh spoke with as much authority as he could muster. "I'm seeking the return of stolen property."

"I don't understand."

Teakh glanced away, hiding his pain. "That first time we met. You lied and stole my seed. I want it back. I know what you are now—a damn succubus."

"Oh, that." She brushed her knuckle against his cheek. "Danna's truth, I didn't take it."

He glared at her and pushed her hand away. "I thought you cared about me."

"I do care," she said.

Jeena returned with a tray holding cookies and a tea service and placed it on a low table in front of the sofa. "I did."

Blinking, Teakh stared at Jeena. What the depths!

She set out saucers and cups painted with daisies. "When I did your blood work, I was so excited about your genetics, I told Reez, and she called in Angel. Angel's an expert in sperm acquisition—the best—and a good friend."

Angel an expert? Not only an expert, but the best in sperm acquisition. Teakh should have known she was a succubus. Keno had warned him. The other studs had told him. Even Aunt Dyse had been suspicious.

Reez accepted a teacup and smiled at Jeena. "We wanted our children to be half-siblings. We researched insemination studs and liked Keno's characteristics best."

"I tried and failed with Keno," Angel said. "You know how he is."

Jeena passed a cup to Teakh. "I started looking for Noah men on my own, checking DNA when I did blood work."

Had his seed been used? Had it been sold, or did Jeena and Reez still have it? Where were his children?

"That's illegal," he said, struggling to maintain a tough persona while being presented with chamomile tea and barley-sugar crinkles. All while seated in the very same cottage where the four of them had made love. He placed the teacup on the table. "You didn't have permission from me or my clan."

Jeena shrugged and set aside the teapot. "Running tests was a harmless hobby. I never thought I'd actually find a man with a complete Noah profile."

"And one who wasn't gay," added Reez. "Male succubi are difficult to come by."

How could they be so casual about this? Had the three of them planned and practiced their responses? "What you did is criminal. Clan Noahee will prosecute to the full extent of the law."

Teakh would have to check with Sis about that extent, but he would be pushed no further by these conniving women. Jeena blanched, and satisfaction shot through him. He had her scared.

"But I'd rather not," he continued. "Return my property, and we'll drop the issue."

Angel folded her hand over her midriff. "She doesn't have it because we used it."

"All three of us," Jeena added. "We cut it with extra fluid, so we had enough to go around."

Three kids. Good Danna! How could Jeena talk about conception as a technical challenge? He wasn't an experiment! The situation had become a tangled net, tightening around his throat. "You're pregnant? All three of you?"

"We don't know yet." Jeena glanced at the wall calendar. "We used it yesterday. When you were with that girl."

"Wasn't she gorgeous?" Reez gushed. "And you! So were you."

Angel reached for Teakh's hands and clasped them. "We want you to be our children's father."

"We'll raise them proud to be your sons and daughters," Reez said.

"You're a good man. You deserve it," Jeena said.

His charade of the tough detective crumbled. "I don't know what to say."

First they'd stolen from him and now they offered fatherhood and expected him to be grateful. Were they sincere? Or was this a setup? He'd seen too many acts put on by poachers. Aye, Jack Tar and his dondering dandy dickledoo. Why should succubi be any different?

Teakh shook off Angel's hand and bolted for the door. He refused to be a dupe. She called after him, but he slammed the door. He needed time to sort out his warring feeling: anger, betrayal, hope, and, yes, even excitement.

Along the lane, women stood or sat behind nearly every window. The news of his visit must have spread like a shipboard fire. Teakh nodded to each woman as he passed, but his anger grew with each step. They'd watched him before, seen him leave Jeena's place after his seed had been taken. The entire clan must have known the names of Jeena's associates, yet when he'd contacted Idylko hospital for Angel's name, they'd pretended not to know her. The men in the harbor continued cleaning and repairing boats, less curious than the women, or maybe less obvious about their curiosity.

Sis was still seated in the cockpit of the esskip, but she'd removed her borrowed life vest. She glanced up, a finger on her handscreen. "How did it go?"

"Badly." High on a pylon, a camera swiveled. Teakh indicated the camera with a flick of his eyes. "Watchers."

Sinking depths! First the Idylko women and now Seaguard was spying on him. Fishermen as well. He could see at least three of them within hearing distance. The nearest was knotting decorative coxcombing around the rails of a boat, the sort of work mariners did in order to appear busy.

Sis folded her screen and tucked it into her front pocket. "We could talk in the esskip."

Teakh shook his head. "Let them eavesdrop." He'd give Idylko an earful.

Sis climbed out of the cockpit, and they sat on the dock, Sis with her knees together, Teakh cross-legged. His face heated as he explained the deception. Knowing that both mariners and Seaguard were listening, he spoke loudly and clearly. He had nothing to be ashamed of.

Sis shook her head. "I like Angel. Well, I did like Angel."

"She didn't actually lie, but she didn't tell me everything either. Then she went ahead with sharing the sample."

"Do you want my advice as your sister or as your lawyer?"

"Both. Should I prosecute?"

"It's clearly an interclan dispute and belongs in the Zenhedron. I'll be the one prosecuting since I'm Noahee grandmatriarch. How do you feel?"

"This is hell." Teakh clutched his head. "I thought she loved me. I don't know."

A fisherman pushed a wheelbarrow toward them, the wheels rumbling on the decking. Teakh scooted out of the way to let the man pass.

"So what do we ask for in court?" Sis asked. "The Zenhedron is justice poker on a grand scale. To win, we must know what we want and what we're willing to give up."

"Danna! I want..." What did he want? He longed to undo his mistake made in Idylko over a year ago. He should have never left the hospital with Angel. "Angel," he said. He still wanted to be with her.

Sis shook her head. "We don't have much of a case against her."

She'd misunderstood him. He wanted Angel. He didn't want to sue her.

Sis continued, "You gave implied consent by engaging in

unprotected sex. The court will also consider your ongoing relationship. A number of lawyers and judges attended Angel's art show."

A seagull cried, and Teakh thought of Gull and of flying away from this shameful mess.

Sis tapped her upper lip. "We could go after Idylko. It's a stronger case."

Danna! As if that were important at all.

"The entire clan knows," Teakh growled. "They covered for Jeena. Hospital personnel claimed they didn't know Angel."

Assessing the number of listeners, he glanced around the waterfront. The fisherman with the wheelbarrow had gone, but the mariner continued knotting cord. The camera remained motionless. Very likely a crowd of Seaguardsmen watched and had agreed to leave the camera directed at Sis and Teakh.

Sis stood, turned to the camera, and proclaimed loudly, "Collusion. Multiple violations." She enumerated on her fingers, hand held high as if bidding in an auction. "Breaking confidentiality. Illegal testing of DNA. Rape. Theft. Fraud. Storage and distribution of stolen goods. Violations of hospitality. Mistreatment of a stranger. Collusion in crimes against another clan."

"Let's sit in the cockpit." Teakh indicated the camera with a glance. If Noahee pursued this lawsuit, Teakh would have to describe his love life to the Fenrian supreme court, but he wasn't about to let on that he opposed a lawsuit, not with Idylko listening.

Teakh and Sis climbed aboard the esskip and settled into their seats. Teakh shrugged the canopy closed and adjusted the opacity of the glazing. The two of them were engulfed in darkness. "Sorry." He adjusted the opacity to milk white, then he knelt on his seat facing astern.

The sunlight shone through the glazing, bright and diffuse over Sis's navy-blue tunic. Despite her new clothing, she retained her appearance of innocence, with her large brown eyes in an elfish face. He should be protecting her, not sending her up against veteran lawyers and judges.

"I'm not prepared for the Zenhedron," Teakh said. He'd

have to explain his most intimate decisions while standing in the center of an amphitheater, surrounded by twelve judges and grand-grosses of spectators, the proceedings broadcast to the entire Fenrian archipelago, maybe the entire planet.

Sis leaned forward, and hair fell over one of her eyes. "I'm not either. With your permission, I'd like to talk with my advisor and study group."

"The girls from the art show?" Teakh recalled the band of young women eating canapés as they gawked at paintings.

Sis tucked a strand of hair behind her ear. "Our group is assigned to an advisor, one of the best attorneys in the field. This type of complicated custody battle is just her thing." Sis grimaced. "Five clans. Three children."

Teakh toted up clans: Noahee, Idylko, Shellako, Ralko, and Reez's clan, Pontako. He added the clan of the rose-petal bride to make six. Her clan had a stake as well. They'd paid a high price for what other clans had received for free. "Four children."

Sis placed a hand on her belly. "Five. Clan Noahee's status depends on the paternity of my child."

Good Danna! The clan of Sis's ex brought the total number of interested clans to seven. Might as well include Dojko for an even eight. Eight clans with a stake in the outcome. "We are a clan, yes?"

She patted her fabric-covered belly. "It depends on if conception and implantation have occurred. Once we have test results, our status will be backdated to the full moon yesterday. My man and I decided on a paternity test instead of witnesses."

Teakh would prefer that sort of arrangement himself, even if it offered no protection against theft. "What if the pregnancy doesn't take?"

"Then we try again. In the meantime, we can ask Jeena, Reez, and Angel to take emergency contraceptives," Sis said. "Threat of a lawsuit gives us leverage, but if the issue were to reach court, we'd have to ask for abortions or even capital execution, depending on delay. Otherwise the clans might call our bluff. Is that what you want?"

"No. They're my kids. This mess isn't their fault. I don't

want them killed. Surely the court wouldn't allow the murder of children."

"No possible resolution is off the table, even if it's Solomonic," Sis said. "Wise Solomon once resolved a dispute by threatening to cut a baby in half. Custody was awarded to the woman who conceded custody in order to save the child. That sort of bluff happens all the time. And sometimes it's not a bluff."

Teakh considered. His response would be seen by the watchers, including, most likely, Sis's Fennako man. Teakh's attitude toward his children might very well determine if he received custody or not. "I won't risk my kids. No emergency contraceptives. I want to be part of their lives as a father. That's my demand."

"Do you think the women will agree to that?"

"They haven't said otherwise."

"Then there's no need for a lawsuit. We simply come to an agreement regarding custody and formalize it with a contract."

Teakh sighed. Such an agreement wasn't simple, not for him. "The problem is Angel. How can I trust her? I thought she loved me. Now I don't know."

"Can I be frank?" Sis pushed back her hair, which had again fallen forward. "I like Angel. She's brilliant, talented, and kind to a fault, but her business practices are shady. Don't trust her. Have every agreement put in writing, recorded by notary, and certified by video."

Teakh turned in his seat to face his navigation screen and the frosted windshield. Sis had offered a cold-hearted course, a relationship not of love but of rock-hard resolve. Was that what he wanted?

CHAPTER 39
Crime Ring

TEAKH HELPED SIS step from his esskip. How quickly would rumor of the lawsuit travel? Mariners and working women would hail sweethearts, siblings, and spouses with news, possibly beating out Seaguard and the Sense-net for spreading the word quickly.

Teakh hailed Angel. *Sis is with me. I'm coming back to Jeena's place.*

I've been wanting to introduce her to Jeena and Reez, said Angel, her voice unnaturally cheerful.

Stop pretending you don't know what's going on. Teakh kept his tone stony. *Sis is Noahee attorney general. We'll be discussing legal action. Let Jeena and Reez know.* He would be cold but fair, as was Danna of the icy north.

Angel's comset clicked off.

Angel? Kinkill! She wouldn't talk to him.

Sis at his side, Teakh stalked up the ramp. A camera swiveled to follow their movement. Teakh kept his head down as they marched from the waterfront and through the gauntlet of women murmuring behind front windows. Damn them all. His boots scuffed the cobblestones then thudded on the boardwalk. A light breeze blew through the lane.

"This is it." He halted before Jeena's place and hailed. *Teakh here. I'm out front.*

Jeena opened the door. "Come in." She stepped back and looked over her shoulder at Reez behind her in the foyer.

Teakh introduced Sis. "My sister, Annon Noahee, Grandmatriarch of Clan Noahee."

"Grandmatriarch? But you're so young," Reez said.

"And Noahee attorney general, my legal counsel," Teakh said. He entered the parlor, hoping to see Angel. She sat straight as a mast, her face without expression.

"I have tea ready." Jeena retreated into the kitchen.

Angel rolled the hem of her smock between her fingers. He tried to catch her eye, but she cast her gaze to the floor. Reez lowered herself into a chair and crossed her ankles. Teakh sat on a sofa beside Sis. He recalled his first day at school in Ralko village, when the Ralko kids had looked with open hatred at the strange new eight-year-old in their midst.

Jeena returned with the tray and daisy-painted tea set. Barley-sugar crinkles had been replaced with pilot crackers. The tea smelled of mint. This was traditional hospitality and more symbolic than appetizing. Teakh's stomach turned.

"Nice weather," Jeena said, but the attempt at small talk fell flat and attenuated into murmurs.

Sis selected and broke a cracker with an emphatic snap. "We come in search of redress." The room went silent except for the clink of china. "My kinsman has informed me that the three of you are soon to become pregnant with his children. The semen for insemination was acquired without his knowledge or consent and without clan permission. Due to the structure of Clan Noahee, the children will be members of our clan."

Angel leaned forward and spoke to Sis. "But you knew about my relationship with Teakh. You approved."

"That was before I knew about the theft," Sis said, each word as weighty as a dropped stone. "You could have chosen to destroy the sample without using it. You did not."

"But Angel never had it." Jeena set the teapot aside. "I did. We'd agreed to split the proceeds."

Teakh stared at her, his mouth open. Not only had they taken his semen, they'd planned to sell it for money.

"Then we can add another crime to the list," Sis said, striking her pinkie and thumb. "Conspiracy to defraud. You three qualify as an organized crime ring. We will be filing for injunctions against each of your clans: Shellako, Idylko, and..." She glanced at Teakh.

314

Despite his deficiencies, he could at least supply the name of Reez's clan. "Pontako."

Sis went on. "In the Zenhedron, you won't win. I'm well known in the legal circles of Fennako City and by the royal family."

Angel put a hand over her face and whispered, "It's true."

"But we're willing to settle out of court," Sis said and glanced toward Teakh, a signal for him to speak.

He took a breath, steadying himself. Sis had offered to present their demands, but he'd do it himself. He'd take responsibility for his children.

Teakh cleared his throat. "We ask for joint custody of the children. We ask to be included in decisions regarding their education and well-being. My children must be guaranteed an education and profession of their choice regardless of gender. The mothers' clans will cover costs of medical care for the children and for the pregnancies."

"Don't you want more than that?" Angel arched an eyebrow, her lips as soft and inviting as ever.

Teakh turned away, refusing to acknowledge his desire for her. He still longed to be with her, but their relationship was shredded.

"Yes," Sis said. "We want reparation for losses and for pain and suffering. Your actions have hurt my brother deeply. You have also damaged the integrity of Clan Noahee by putting my brother's children beyond the reach of their clan."

"Dyse," Angel whispered, then spoke more loudly. "What about Aunt Dyse?"

"What about her?" Teakh asked.

Angel spoke to Sis. "I understand that Dyse is Teakh's guardian until he reaches his majority at two-dozen years of age."

"I'm now his guardian," Sis said.

"Will it stand up in court?" Angel asked. "We know Dyse is greedy and a real hag-eel. She was his guardian at the time the semen was acquired. Suppose she sets up Ralko as the wronged clan? What then?"

Sis stammered. "Well...uh..."

"I have a proposal." Angel straightened. "Teakh and I get married. May I have your brother's hand in marriage?"

She bowed from the waist to Sis.

"What the depths?" Teakh's heart fluttered, driven by excitement, inflamed with fear and anger. He'd never imagined Angel proposing in such a manner.

"It's simple," Angel continued. "Teakh and I get married and document the consummation. Dyse has no way to prove that the semen was acquired when Teakh was under her guardianship."

The idea was both brilliant and devious. Teakh and Angel would effectively destroy the evidence without harming their child. If she was willing to marry him, surely she cared for him, right? But he'd been deceived before. He reefed his emotions and stayed the course. "What about my other children?"

Reez waved a cracker. "He'll have to marry all of us."

"No," Jeena said. "We're married already. You're my wife."

Reez grinned. "But there's nothing wrong with a partnership between a heterosexual couple and a moon couple. It's traditional. Sis—may I call you Sis?—include it in the prenuptial contract. If Angel approves, Teakh may have other partners. That's how it works for the two of them anyway."

Sis sat open-mouthed, teacup in hand, looking as confused as Teakh felt.

He stood and straightened his vest. "I think we should talk in private."

Teakh and Sis went through the kitchen and into the hallway between the bedroom and bath. Gull had once flown through the roof vents now directly above Sis.

"I knew we'd have interclan custody disputes." Sis shook her head. "I didn't think it would be this big or this soon." She put her arm around his shoulders. "Or so personal. Oh, Teakh. One way or another, you'll have to formalize your relationship with Angel, either through marriage or joint custody."

"I'm fine with three-way consummation," whispered Teakh, keeping his voice down to prevent Angel and the others overhearing, "but not with letting Idylko off so easily. I set my net the clan has done this sort of thing before. Surely they'll do it again."

"You won't fall for that trick twice," Sis said.

"What about other men and their children? In this case, forgiveness is selfish."

Sis frowned. "So what's more important to you: punishing Idylko or protecting your own children?"

Teakh shook his head. "If the clan of the rose-petal girl gets wind of this, and they will, they're likely to sue." As part of the contract, Teakh was required to remain ignorant of the girl's clan, or at least to pretend he didn't know how to find her. "And what about Dojko? Dyse agreed to give Keno and Iris a cut of my stud fees."

"We'll ask for payment as part of the prenuptial agreements," Sis said. "The amount should be large enough to please the rose-petal clan and act as a deterrent, but not big enough to cause Idylko resentment. We'll give Dojko their cut. If we play this right, we'll be able pay our debts and set up an insurance fund against further lawsuits. Everybody wins."

"Everybody?" Teakh considered. The arrangement would formalize alliances with Shellako, Pontako, and Idylko. The solution seemed balanced, except for his shifting emotions. He'd have to tie them down. Angel would have to prove herself before he loved her so blindly again. "Everybody but Dyse."

Sis shrugged. "Even your relationship with Jeena and Reez will be an asset. I'll hazard that Jeena knows the black market. By marrying, you're getting yourself a detective agency. It takes a thief to catch a thief. Isn't that what they say? What does Reez do as a profession?"

"Medical supplies," Teakh said. "She's a sales rep."

"Then she's your black marketeer. You've got yourself an interclan crime ring." Sis grinned and shoved his arm. "Just your thing."

He scowled. For most of his life, Teakh had looked the other way when crimes occurred, or else he'd blackmailed the criminals, serving his own needs at the expense of others. Maybe it was time to change. He'd take control of the situation and no longer be a victim. "We should shut them down."

"But why?" Sis asked. "I say we follow our charter and act in the best interest of Clan Noahee. That's our mandate given by the Queen."

"What about the law?"

"We're now a sovereign clan. We make the laws. The Queen wants us to go after human-rights abuses. We'll be the most effective if we have underworld connections. Do the same thing you've always done—selective law enforcement. It just happens we're legitimate and after a different kind of poacher."

Sis's reasoning made sense. Supported by the three succubi, Teakh would be able to protect and provide for his children. He'd have the cooperation of their mothers, even if they did dabble in the black market, but Teakh still couldn't forgive Angel.

CHAPTER 40
Trust

A MIDST CRATES AND partly assembled camera gear, Teakh took a break with Angel. They'd been setting up equipment for documenting the consummation. They sat on the bridal bed without touching. Keno and Binnacle Betty chaperoned from a respectful distance. Teakh kept one booted foot dutifully on the floor. Absurdly, those asked to witness the marriage consummation also acted as chaperones to prevent any premarital hanky-panky.

All morning, Teakh and Angel had spoken of lighting and camera angles, but not of their relationship or feelings. It was time to change that.

Teakh said, "That first time we met, you could've told me you're a succubus."

Angel's face creased, and Teakh longed to wipe away the furrows.

"I thought you knew," she said. "I assumed you'd made arrangements with Jeena."

Teakh sat on his hand, resisting the urge to smooth those furrows away. "I hadn't even met her."

"I realized that later, but I thought it didn't matter. You had a good time. We all did. A lot of men make a pretense of recreational sex or even of love. We go along with a man's wishes. If his clan finds out, he can claim he didn't know. We protect our clients."

Teakh recalled Angel's first art show, the one with the controversial painting of Lord Tristan Bay. "Sis's man? Is he one of your clients?"

A hint of a smile flicked around Angel's eyes as she leaned toward him. "You're jealous."

"My sister and my fiancée? Sinking yes!" Sis's ex appeared to have effortlessly received respect, power, and wealth which Teakh had struggled for. On top of that, he'd been messing around with the women Teakh most loved. "Damn him!"

Angel vigorously shook her head. "Only for boudoir paintings. I don't have intercourse with clients. It's all simulated artifice. My clients know that."

"I didn't," Teakh said.

He wanted to hold her and tell her how much he loved her, but he'd resolved not to. Even if he trusted her, both Keno and Binnacle Betty were seated in nearby folding chairs. Betty's needles clicked as she knitted. Keno, for the most part, stared at the ceiling.

"A lot of men view succubi as cheap prostitutes and strippers." Angel made a face as if she'd eaten raw cranberries. "You treated us well from the very beginning."

"I thought you were prostitutes." Teakh had at first considered that Cooky had hired the women to remedy Teakh's virginity, but Cooky had denied making arrangements.

Angel said, "And you still treated us with respect."

Teakh wished she'd treat him with respect in turn. "Always."

"I ignored your messages at first. I assumed you'd lose interest. When you didn't, I looked into your background."

A ray of hope broke through his desolation. "Did you like what you found?"

She shook her head, and Teakh's hopes sank. She might have stumbled across his semi-legal activity and his nearly clanless status.

"I didn't believe the hype about innate altruism and monogamy" —she smiled, her expression bright and warm— "not at the time. Then you showed up with your bird telechiric, stumbling all over your webbed feet."

"Gull doesn't stumble."

"Metaphorically. But you apologized nicely and behaved well until you arrived with that cockamamie story about clanless shelters." Angel's grin became mischievous. "So I told you I'd been doing research as well—the truth, more or less. My opinion has weight in some circles. I tried to warn you. I wanted to break off the relationship before it began."

"Too late," Teakh said. "It began the day you walked into my hospital room." He recalled lying in bed, his ankle broken, unable to work as a fisherman and uncertain of his future. She'd walked in and smiled as if he were the delight of her life.

"You're right. I couldn't break it off." She slumped, the light gone from her eyes. "I didn't want to, so I asked Jeena and Reez to destroy the sample. They refused, and I offered to buy them out. They turned me down—they said because I couldn't afford it. Which was true, but I would have come up with something—borrowed money, sold more paintings."

Teakh wanted to believe her. "If only I'd known."

"Jeena agreed to hold the sample in reserve. If I'd told you or anyone else about the deception, she'd have sold immediately. I tried to make it up to you with the art show, my attempt at catharsis. The critic called it 'a scathing deconstruction.' Lubbers. Not a deconstruction but my sacrificial offering, atonement."

"Did it help?" Teakh looked into her eyes. This close to her, he could smell the warm spice of her skin.

"Diluting the semen and sharing it three ways seemed to be a good compromise. If none of the pregnancies take, the sample has been effectively destroyed."

"Do you want to carry my child?" Teakh asked. Maybe she preferred that the pregnancy didn't take.

She nodded. "The code of my heart is yours."

These were the words of the traditional marriage ceremony. Teakh's breath caught. He touched her hand, palm to palm.

"I want to be your wife, not merely your handler or the mother of your child. I suppose I'm sentimental that way." She caught his wrist and kissed his fingertips.

Ignoring the witnesses, Teakh lifted his foot from the floor and leaned to embrace Angel. Binnacle Betty cleared her throat.

Angel's body shuddered and relaxed against Teakh. He wanted to tell her it was all behind them and they'd begin anew, but Teakh had been tricked before. He didn't trust so easily now. He had to speak with Sis, get her advice. He let go and stood. "I'll see you soon."

After leaving the bower house, Teakh, followed by Keno, passed through lanes then a grassy courtyard, returning to the house given over to Noahee. Idylko had provided separate lodging for each of the visiting clans. Inside, Keno flopped on a chair in the parlor. A staircase led upward in the corner of the room.

"Nice," Keno said, one leg over the arm of a chair, "but they've given Dojko an even bigger place. The lads all want to attend the wedding ceremony."

"Do you mean the studs or the fishermen?"

"Both."

Teakh groaned. "I could do without the audience."

"Tough," Keno said. "You just bagged three top succubi."

Teakh hailed Sis. *Keno and I are at the Noahee place. Where are you?*

Upstairs, she responded.

Teakh left Keno in the parlor and joined Sis in an upstairs room with multiple cameras and screens as well as a movable backdrop. A wall screen displayed a woman with a shock of iron-gray hair. Wasn't that Sis's academic advisor? He accessed his implant records and thought *art show*. He grimaced. He'd recorded the date but not the woman's name.

Sis nodded and responded with a repeat of introductions. "Teakh, this is Myrtle Gratianiko. Ma'am, my brother, Teakh Noahee."

"So the fuss is about him?" The advisor crossed her arms and leaned back. "Now, young man, don't get above yourself. No need for an entire harem."

Teakh stepped back from the screen. "I don't have a harem." He wasn't pleased to have a lawyer he'd met only once butting into his private life.

She snorted. "Don't mind me. I'm an old cuss. I'm pleased you've got a name this time—enough of this anonymous shine. We'll do things right."

"How much are we paying you?" Teakh asked. Not only was she nosy, but in in all likelihood, she was expensive.

"Pro bono," the advisor said. "I've got a passel of young lawyers to train. The Queen wants attorneys ready to handle human-rights abuses in the reproductive industry. You, young man, are better than moot court. You'll keep law students talking for a good long time."

Teakh groaned. Now he'd have law students butting into his personal life too. "Pardon me, I need to speak with Sis."

"Well then, I'll ship on out," the advisor said, and the screen blinked off.

Teakh remained standing. "Angel thought I'd agreed to sperm donation. After she found out I hadn't, she tried to recover the sample. I don't know if she's telling the truth."

Sis picked up a handscreen. "I'll need your implant records of the discussion."

"I didn't make a recording," Teakh said. He'd chosen not to.

Sis frowned. "Well, here's what I've got. Jeena and Reez do work in the reproductive industry, but their business practices appear to be lawful. Idylko and Pontako claim the two never intended to sell your semen, and the procurement was a private transaction. But they may be lying in order to avoid racketeering charges."

Teakh said, "If it's all right with you, I'd like to interview Jeena and Reez." His experience sifting through the tall tales of fishermen might prove useful. Maybe the two would corroborate Angel's story. He hoped so.

AT PONTAKO LODGING, Teakh and Keno entered directly into the kitchen. The entire first floor of the house had been given over to food preparation. Pontako was providing catering for the wedding reception, just as Idylko was providing lodging, and Shellako had arranged for documentation and the magistrate. Noahee provided only the groom, but Sis was plenty busy with negotiations. Pots bubbled on stoves with fragrances of chilies and coriander. Women with toasty skin and jet-black hair gathered around a counter piled with cookbook screens.

Teakh introduced Keno to Reez, and they exchanged bows.

Reez wiped her hands on her apron. "We've been discussing kabobs. Should we have scallops and shrimp separately or on the same skewers? What do you think?"

"Ah..." Teakh rubbed his implant scars. "Good either way. I need to talk with you about Angel. Don't bother with tea and biscuits. I've had plenty."

The three of them gathered around a kitchen island. Reez's kinswomen continued chopping vegetables and sautéing spices.

Teakh activated his record function and cleared his throat. "I need to know what sort of agreement you had with Angel that first time we met."

"No agreement," Reez said. "At least not with me."

"But there was an agreement?"

Reez shook her head. "Jeena made the arrangements." She leaned forward. "Now you listen to me. Without Jeena, you'd never have met Angel or become a stud. Jeena discovered you. Does she get thanks or a finder's fee? No. You slap her clan with a lawsuit over a minor procedural error."

"It's not minor to me," Teakh. said "But right now I'm concerned about Angel. I need to know if she's telling the truth. How did you three decide to become pregnant with my children?"

"Jeena and I were planning to give birth at the same time. We wanted you to be the father. Angel insisted we include her in lieu of payment or her cut of the profits. It worked out quite well. Yes?"

Teakh shook his head. "Would you have sold the sample?"

"It wasn't my choice to make," Reez said. "Angel's been either ecstatic or in anguish about that dab of semen. She cares about you."

Nothing Reez had said contradicted Angel's account, but Teakh still hadn't discovered much. He said his good-byes and left to find Jeena.

At the house of the Idylko grandmatriarch, Teakh was ushered through an impressive foyer. Glass mullions in the door transoms scattered light over a polished floor. In a side parlor, tea and cakes had been laid on a lace-covered table. Jeena stood and politely bowed. Beside her stood the nurse who'd changed Cooky's bandages.

324

Jeena directed them to chairs and distributed tea and cakes. "Reez hailed. I know why you're here. Blame me if you like, but not her or Angel."

Ah, so Teakh had found the crux of the tangle, and the threads led to Jeena. It seemed she'd been the ringleader, or maybe not.

"So you agreed to take the fall?" Teakh asked.

"Well... no... uh, yes. Angel wanted the sample destroyed. I didn't and told her so."

"What was your agreement?" Teakh asked.

"Initially, I hired Angel to acquire your semen. I've been in this business long enough to know quality. Many studs market themselves as producing limited numbers of offspring, but I've seen the samples going through my lab. Some of those gents produce more children by artificial insemination than by direct cover. If a man produces a large number of offspring, his children may inadvertently have sex with their siblings. He puts subsequent generations at risk for recessive genetic disorders. I don't want such a man fathering my child or Reez's."

Teakh frowned. "By using my sperm without my knowledge, you subject my children to the same risks."

"You're quality. No doubt about it. After a roll, most men think nothing of their children. A wet spot on the bed, nothing more."

"I don't care about my quality. I care about my kids and about Angel. When did she try to recover the sample?"

"I'm not sure exactly. She hailed me, all upset about how you'd never signed a release. The sample was a gift for Reez. I told her to calm down and not be hasty. We weren't planning to use the sample until a full moon during the spawning tide anyway."

"But you threatened to sell the sample if Angel reported the theft?"

"If she'd reported me, my lab would have been raided. I'd have sold the semen to get rid of it before authorities arrived." Jeena set her lips in a grim frown. "I didn't want to sell."

"It wouldn't have been difficult to hide."

"Possibly, but sharing seemed the best option. Maybe none of us will become pregnant."

Teakh stared at his hands and twisted his bracelet. If he consummated the marriage with the three women, he'd never know if the theft or the consummation produced the children. Did it matter? His acceptance would wipe out their guilt.

CHAPTER 41
Wedding

N ERVOUS, TEAKH WIPED his sweating palms on his pants then thought he shouldn't have. He'd worn his best for the wedding, the Seaguard kit designed by Angel. Keno, wearing Dojko kit, followed Teakh as part of the groom's party which was made up of Sis, Teakh, Keno, Lugo, and Rosebay. The aroma of grilled salmon wafted from barbeques. Kettles of clams and oysters steamed. Guests had spilled out of the hall onto the plaza. Teakh nodded to a Pontako woman setting up tables for the reception as he passed her on his way to the Idylko clan hall.

Randy and Hairy stood outside the double doors. Both men wore head coverings—bandannas this time, not napkins. Randy gave Teakh a thumbs-up. "That's our Gimp. Nail those suckies."

Keno laughed and clapped Teakh's shoulder. "Studs adore suckies, but those ladies are forbidden fruit. If a stud is known to consort with suckies, there goes his career. Except for yours."

Teakh disliked the notoriety but accepted it as good for business. Word about his skill in tracing biological theft would spread. In the eyes of the studs, he'd caught the thieving succubi and made them pay. Studs would call on Teakh's agency for assistance in legal matters.

Teakh's entourage passed through the doors into the hall. Sis led the way, followed by Teakh and Keno, then Lugo and Rosebay. The entire assembly, including cameras mounted in the beams, turned to watch their entrance. The house was packed. Standing guests lined the walls. Women with jet-black hair and dusky complexions, surely Reez's kin, stood companionably with the pale-skinned women of Shellako. And the entire village of Dojko must have turned out for the wedding. All of the men had covered their heads. A sign of respect? It had to be the doing of Keno and Patroller. Even Lord Dojko, standing to the side of the hall, had a scarf secured over his balding pate.

Teakh felt an urge to flee. He'd much rather be alone with Angel. A cluster of Seaguardsmen in Fennako green also stood along the wall. One of them raised a hand in salute, and Teakh recognized the Seaguardsman as a woman—Princess Mareen Fennako. Beside her stood a man wearing Tristan Bay Harbor Patrol kit. Mareen had brought along her brother, Lord Tristan Bay, and he was also wearing a bandanna.

Teakh returned the salute then caught sight of Angel. Standing on a dais at the front of the hall, she wore a gown of copper-colored silk. The split-sided gown clung to her figure and was held in place with lacing that crisscrossed over her thigh, hip, and torso. A curtain of crystal and copper beads swung from her beaded cap and sparkled against her dark-ginger hair.

Teakh went in procession up the aisle and took his place on the dais across from Angel. She shared the dais with the magistrate, a mature woman with gray-streaked hair, who wore a gray-green robe with a tasseled hood. A harmony pipe hung on a cord around her neck. The magistrate lifted the pipe to her lips and blew the two-tone note, calling the assembly to order. The gathering became attentive.

Ceremoniously, she turned to each cardinal direction to invoke the sun, moons, and earth. She addressed Danna and Poseidon as the polestars and asked for their guidance and protection. Facing the assembly, she bowed. "Greetings, my sisters and brothers. We are gathered at this tide for the union of this woman and man, Marjoram Shellako and Teakh Noahee."

The crowd shouted and clapped until the magistrate again blew her harmony pipe and the wedding guests quieted.

"In the beginning," she said, "Darkness loved Light and Light loved Darkness. Striving to come together, they danced the universe into being. Some say that Darkness is Danna and Light is Poseidon, but it could just as easily be the other way. In love, opposites come together in balance and harmony. This is as Noah taught."

Teakh snuck a grin at Angel, and she returned it with a lift of her eyebrow.

The magistrate continued. "Long ago in an archipelago named Greece, a male god threw Danna and Poseidon from the heights. He banished Poseidon to the depths and consumed Danna, making her attributes his own. She was reborn as Athena and gave her allegiance to this new god. Opposites were at odds and couldn't be reconciled."

Soon Teakh would cross the dais to embrace Angel, and they would make their own reconciliations.

"And then an injustice occurred." The magistrate's voice rolled. "A giant named Cyclops, a devotee of Poseidon, attempted to kill and eat a stranger—yes, a stranger to whom hospitality is owed. In retaliation, the stranger blinded Cyclops with a hot stick. Poseidon became enraged. He rose against the stranger and sent him on an odyssey. The stranger became enthralled by the sea witch and couldn't get home to his beloved wife and her kin. They prayed to Danna, and she came to their aid in the form of a man named Mentor, who brought the stranger home." The magistrate bowed her head. "May Danna and Poseidon bless this marriage with cold reason wed to deep, abiding passion."

Angel swished her coppery gown. For Teakh, she was Athena and the sea witch rolled into one. With a lift of her chin, she met Teakh's eye and spoke the opening of the marriage vows. "The code of my heart is yours."

He gave the traditional response. "I will observe your heart. I will observe your passage. I will observe your clan as my own."

They ended the vows, speaking as one. "Tide of the heavens above us. Tide of the ocean below us. Tide within us brings joy."

Coming together, they circled, the rotation symbolic of the swirling of Light and Darkness in the fluid of the universe, until their hands met. Teakh scooped his arm around Angel's

and the careers of all three women: artist, technician, and sales. Consummating their marriage was the most important athletic performance Teakh had ever faced.

The event would be remotely filmed by a Seaguardsman with videography experience. Teakh, eyes closed, checked camera access and saw into the bridal chamber, where Jeena and Reez reclined on a hexagonal bed. Their witnesses sat in a row of four chairs. Two seats remained empty: one for Keno, the other for Binnacle Betty.

Teakh reined in his fear and his excitement. To impregnate all three women, he had to maintain an erection after he ejaculated and make his performance look good at the same time. He had to make his moves between when he ejaculated and when his penis went slack.

Angel hailed. *Ready.*

Ready, sent Teakh.

Cameras rolling, the camera man responded.

From the wings, Teakh watched a camera view. Jeena and Reez embraced, their limbs entangled, raven-black curls beside brunette locks.

The cameraman transmitted. *Enter on five, four...*

Teakh took a long slow breath and let it out, focusing, preparing his mind as if for a swimming race. On *one*, he stepped into the chamber. He smiled at Angel coming toward him, her auburn hair loose on her shoulders, her siren tattoo revealed. She smiled back.

In front of the bed, Teakh pressed against her and nuzzled her silk-smooth hair. He responded to her like no other.

Show her off, sent the camera man. *Turn a bit to your left.*

With a final squeeze, they parted. Teakh caught a view through the camera as it followed the curve of Jeena's thigh, paused on her breasts, then focused on her contented face. Angel knelt on the bed. The camera panned to her then zoomed on her midriff and the rising succubus. Teakh knelt and rubbed his erection against her tattooed guardian.

She bowed her head and trailed kisses down his chest and abdomen. With Angel's love, everything was right. In her presence, his confidence increased, and so did his prowess.

Jeena drew Angel into her arms, and Teakh gave a nod to

Reez, who took her prearranged position on top of Jeena. The three women embraced, stacked one atop the other, Angel sandwiched between Jeena on the bottom and Reez on top. Teakh would have to move quickly. If he ejaculated too early, he risked going slack before finishing. If he ejaculated too late, he wouldn't get semen into each of the women.

He sought out Jeena first, and through the cameras, he watched his entry. The view excited him. He drove into her. She gasped. He withdrew and, trailing fluid, plunged into Angel. She moaned, arching against Reez. Teakh moved to Reez, sliding into her, working slowly and savoring her shaking body until he went slack. Teakh lay with his three brides, kissing them and gathering them in his arms, protecting his women and his children.

IN THE FRONT parlor of a house off the Idylko village plaza, Angel painted a delicate watercolor of Jeena and Reez who were draped in diaphanous fabric. The partners reclined together on a mound of carpets and pillows. Teakh and Angel had set up housekeeping in Idylko so the three women could be together during their pregnancies. Out of concern for the children, Angel no longer used oil paint.

Teakh stretched out his booted feet, enjoying the domesticity of his soon-to-be clan. Their children would be Noahee with duel clan membership. He'd offered Clan Noahee membership to the mothers, but they'd declined. Women customarily did not have sexual relations with men in their own clan. Such restrictions did not apply to same gender relationships. Keno had agreed to become a member. "Why not?"

Eyes closed, Teakh accessed the Network and put in an order for more robotic gulls—a true herring gull, a Bonaparte gull, and a mew gull.

With that done, he placed a small advertisement:

Teakh Noahee. Biological and fisheries detective. Offering video documentation and document review. Combating poaching, smuggling, biological theft, and fraud. No job too small.

With four babies on the way, five counting his sister's child, Teakh reckoned it was time for his investigative business to become more than a dockside show.

APPENDIX
The Twelve Precepts of Noah

THE ORIGINAL PRECEPTS, detailing proper relationships within Fenrian society, were written in an archaic language. The original no longer exists. A number of versions and interpretations are in circulation.

The Noah Code most likely developed from Dane Law and English Common Law, as did the Fenrian Justice system. However, the precepts have significant similarities to the Judeo-Christian Bible, in particular Leviticus 19:33, Luke 10:30-37, and Matthew 5:43.

The Fenrian language has both a singular and plural form of you, an important distinction within the first precept. The precept promises clan survival, not eternal life. Fenrian conceptions of an afterlife remain hazy. They practice a pragmatic religion.

1. Observe the tide and you (plural) will survive.

2. Welcome the stranger. She/he is your true sibling/ neighbor. Honor to those who assist the needy, highest honor to those who render charity to strangers and to those who forgive their enemies.

3. Be prepared.

4. Respect and protect the planet Fenria. She is your mother and your home.

5. Honor those who have gone before you, your father as well as your mother, all of your ancestors.

6. Keep holy the new moon. Allow your sister darkness. Permit no artificial light to outshine Luna Majora.

7. Allow your brother silence. Do not distract him from observance of the tide. Avoid idle talk. Do not boast or gossip.

8. Protect your sister, provide for her safety.

9. Shelter your brother, equip him to face the storm.

10. Educate your children.

11. Educate the children of your clan.

12. Educate the children of strangers. Teach the way of Noah to all.

·

Coming Soon

The Tristan Bay Accord

Parallel to

The Fisherman and the Sperm Thief

ANNON WANTS HER own clan, and she'll do nearly anything to get it, so she makes a deal with the queen of Fenria. In exchange for recognition of Clan Noahee, Annon agrees to anonymous sex with a man who will father her child. The man, however, refuses to impregnate Annon, insisting she must love him first. In clandestine meetings, he goes about seducing her, pleasuring her, and winning her affection. All the while, political factions attempt to drive the couple apart. Annon must trust her man, protect her child, and find her own way amidst the intrigue that racks the Fenrian royal family.

CHAPTER 01
Madame X

O N THE WALLS of the waterfront shop, photoelectronic images of naked men gyrated in a shifting mosaic of brawny torsos, rippled abdomens, and muscular shoulders. I gulped. I was fine with naked men but not with the blatant objectification of their bodies. The proprietress of the shop sat on a stool, her long legs encased in black thigh boots. Her vest hung open, barely covering her nipples. I should have just left the shop right away. Her sexed-up interpretation of a Seaguard uniform offended me.

"What are you about?" she asked of me, ignoring my brother Teakh. Although a member of the Seaguard class, he appeared to be nothing more than a fisherman. His parka and fisherman's bibs smelled of herring but hid functional Seaguard boots and life vest. Teakh preferred not to flaunt his status and wore both a bandanna and a watchcap over the scars of his implant.

"Just looking," I said. Teakh and I had entered the shop after being intrigued by the sign: "Madame X's Mannary." We were both interested in the economics of the reproductive industry.

Madame X, if that was her name, wore elbow-length lace mitts threaded with electronics. "Look all you want. The question is—what kind of man are you looking for?"

Pretending to be a customer, I said, "A father for my child."

"That *is* what we sell here. Insemination. Either natural or artificial." She glanced toward Teakh with distaste. "A wise choice."

"He's my brother."

"Oh. So sorry. What is your price range?"

"Fratricide!" Teakh swore, using the salty language of a mariner. I winced. To kill a clan member, even unintentionally, was unspeakable. "Why don't you let her decide? Show my sister the best."

"Best depends," Madame X said. "A smart woman picks a sire for the qualities he'll impart to her daughter."

"Boys are just as good as girls," I blurted, stupidly displaying my political views.

Madame X's eyebrows rose. "I still recommend a sire who has talents and interests similar to your own. His genetic contribution should enhance rather than detract from yours. So, miss? What is your profession?"

"I'm a student," I admitted. I hated that she'd called me *Miss* instead of *Madame*, even though I was less than two-dozen years old and so a minor.

She frowned. "What are you studying?"

I'd been studying hospitality, part of social services, but I'd had enough of trying to squeeze enough money from Clan Ralko matriarchs to get through school. "I'm to become a grandmatriarch." I wanted to lead my own clan.

"You?" Madame X oozed incredulity. "You're far too young to be a grandmatriarch."

"I'd best get started, then, if I'm going to have some grandchildren to lead."

She laid on the flattery. "So you need a man worthy of fathering a clan. Someone like yourself—a woman of daring, and one who has impeccable genetics. Men like that are difficult to come by, but I know of a stud. Newly available, a rookie." With a ripple of her electronics-clad fingers, she signaled to the wall display, bringing up a photo of a naked man. The back of the man's head displayed the scars of a neural implant. The remainder of his hair had been plaited into intricate braids terminating in gold beads. Depths! The stud on display was my very own brother, Teakh, who stood beside me in stained fishing duds.

I was well aware that he'd been auctioning his services as

2

a stud, but I'd never been confronted with the huge, naked reality of the business.

"Yes. Impressive," Madame X said, unaware she praised the very man she'd snubbed or that she was attempting to sell his services to his sister. "He's Seaguard with a genuine neural implant. Those scars aren't just for show."

Between Teakh's fingers, his face shone scarlet.

Madame X continued her spiel. "He's a fisherman. Can you believe it? Risked his life to save a friend from a burning boat. You just don't find genetics like his on the open market."

While in the hospital, recuperating from injuries sustained in the rescue, Teakh had been discovered to have the genetics of the ideal Fenrian man. Supposedly, he was innately altruistic. I knew otherwise but kept my opinions to myself.

"Men of his quality seldom sell for money but for other coin." She stroked her thigh in promise of sleazy payment. "This man's services are up for bid, and his price is climbing. If you have enough money, you can make an offer for his maiden gig, or I can help you out. Darling, few men can resist me. For a small fee, you'll have his child."

I'd had enough. Paying for stud services was one thing—paying a woman to seduce a man was another.

Madame X turned on her stool, her gaze halting at Teakh. Before either of us could stop her, she pushed back Teakh's watchcap and bandanna. Braids tipped with gold beads tumbled out. He shoved her hand away but smiled.

She licked her lips. "Well, this changes everything. Sir, if you'd slip into the back with me, I can make you comfortable. We'll help your sister. Any man she wants can be hers. The coin? A trifle from you. No one need know but us."

Good Danna! She considered my brother's semen to be coin, a commodity to be traded as if it were salt cod.

Teakh grasped my elbow. Once outside and away from that hagfish, I felt relief. In the lane, we were once again just an ordinary fisherman and a student walking near the waterfront. The breeze blowing from Tristan Bay smelled of the harbor. Houses lined the narrow lane, the ground floors used for businesses, the upper stories reserved for private residences. The digital posters advertising Madame X

Mannary flickered with their promises of sordid wares.

"Succubus," Teakh said.

"You've encountered them before?" Succubi took semen without clan permission, and some men agreed to these under-the-table transactions.

"None as crass as this one." He tipped his thumb to the shop, and I noticed that he wore a silver bracelet, a purchase we could not afford out of our shared accounts.

"You won't fall for that, will you?"

"Uh... well. Depends."

His hesitation concerned me. "You wouldn't."

"Depends on how much I like her."

I shivered. "Don't joke about this." If Teakh gave away his semen, the price of his stud services would drop. He was being marketed as having a limited number of children, thus reducing the risk of incest among his descendants while maintaining a premium price. Even worse, if he took part in off-the-record donations, we'd have no way of tracking his children.

"Not joking," he said.

"Seriously, did you like her?"

"That hag eel?"

We continued to our appointment in the capital city as if nothing had happened. We'd had an unsettling experience and walked away. No harm done. Or so I believed.

THE PEDESTRIAN TRAFFIC in the capital city was made up of more Seaguardsmen—identifiable by life vests and hip-high boots—than I'd expect. Most likely, they were engaged in legal matters related to the Zenhedron interclan court.

We stopped at our destination, a three-story building with opaque front windows. Dame Bulla, our contact, stood on the stoop. She wrinkled her nose and peered at us as if we were some sort of odious flatworms. Of maybe it was the way Teakh smelled. I didn't mind the odor, but not everyone appreciated the tang of the sea.

The foyer of Dame Bulla's modest office had a row of

hooks on one wall but no place to sit. An open door presented a view of gray-green stripes, a wall covering that could be changed on a whim. Dame Bulla's whim today must have been conservative.

Teakh removed his watchcap and bandanna. He stuffed both in his pocket and shook his head, jangling the gold beads in his hair. He hung his parka and fisherman's bibs on the wall hooks. We'd agreed that for the meeting, Teakh would present himself as high-status Seaguard, replete with hip-tall seaboots, their cuffs folded down to display the scarlet band matching the piping on his black life vest. I hadn't designed his clothing and didn't particularly like it.

Dame Bulla served water and a plate of hardtack, minimal tokens of hospitality. The biscuit was tooth-chipping hard, a bit overly traditional in my opinion. Teakh pragmatically dunked his in a glass of water.

Dame Bulla bent over a screen set in her desktop. "You are Annon of Clan Ralko?"

I corrected her. "Currently of Clan Ralko."

She slid her bi-adjustables down her nose. "And this is your brother?"

"Teakh, Noahee Seaguard Chief." I sat up straight.

"I understand you are seeking recognition of a new clan, Clan Noahee."

I attempted a friendly tone. "That's the name we've chosen."

Dame Bulla wasn't moved. "We've considered your petition and have found it lacking. This so-called clan charter contains highly irregular provisions. You intend to allow men to vote? A man may hold the office of grandmatriarch?"

"That's right." I threw down my challenge to matriarchy. "Universal suffrage. My brother's children will be equal to mine."

In most clans, the children of the women became clan members at conception, but not the children of men. That was how matrilineage worked. In our clan, all children would be included regardless of the gender of the parent. Men would also be allowed to vote and to serve on the mothers' council. We would rename it a parental council.

Dame Bulla shook her head. "A man cannot be a matriarch since he cannot, in fact, be a mother."

"He still can be a father," I told her. "We could change the name of clan leader to *grandparentiarch*." Most clans allowed childless women to vote and hold office. Just because they couldn't get pregnant was no reason to deny voting rights. And men still cared about children.

"*Patriarch* would be the correct term," Dame Bulla said. "But you have other irregularities here. You have written that your brother will be Seaguard chief, but he is inactive as Seaguard. It appears that, instead of patrolling, he's been working odd jobs."

"I work in investigation." Teakh left out his sideline of training to be a stud. "With proper equipment, I can hire myself out as a fisheries detective." Fisheries investigation was a proper occupation for Seaguard.

I yammered on, surely talking too fast. "A failure of Clan Ralko. They haven't provided him with the patrol craft necessary for Seaguard work. On approval of our charter, we'll order a Seaguard esskip. He should receive it in early spring." Paying for the esskip remained a problem that I didn't mention.

Dame Bulla pointed to the screen. "I have here that neither of you are older than two-dozen years of age. You're minors, still requiring parental guidance in signing contracts."

I tried to explain. "Our mother passed away and had no siblings. We're wards of Clan Ralko, but we have no blood relationship to the clan."

Dame Bulla pushed at her spectacles. "Receiving legal emancipation is difficult, nearly impossible. Children can't lead clans."

"I've addressed the issue in our petition. Clan Noahee will be our guardian clan. I've found precedent. In the past, minors have served in clan offices."

Dame Bulla remained unmoved. "You do not meet a single requirement necessary to prove existence of a viable clan. What you have is, in fact, not a clan. Our department has been tasked with registering existing clans, not with establishing new ones."

"But," I objected, "our communication with the Queen indicated our petition would be considered." It was all so unfair.

4

"It has been considered," she said. "You lack members, territory, and assets. Furthermore, you carry significant debt."

I continued to argue what was surely a hopeless cause. "We're not without assets. We have valuable genetics. My brother is a cover stud. He commands some of the highest stud fees in the industry."

Dame Bulla, unimpressed, peered over her bi-adjustables. "Has he received payment for such services?"

He hadn't. Teakh's liaisons, up for bid on Kordelko Auctions, received phenomenally high offers, but bidding hadn't closed, and he hadn't fulfilled any contracts. "A Ralko woman acts as Teakh's manager. She won't allow him to marry or to form a relationship with a woman on his own."

"Ma'am," Teakh said, "we aren't genetically members of Clan Ralko. May I explain?"

She didn't answer him, looking to me instead. I encouraged Teakh with a nod.

He said, "Our genetics are the product of generations of breeding. The Noah Eugenics Project aimed to create the perfect man."

The phenomenal prices for Teakh's services were the result of this failed undertaking. In my view, the project was fundamentally flawed, much like long-ago studies that had attempted to define and identify intelligence as IQ and then sterilized individuals who didn't measure up. Defining altruism was as problematic as defining intelligence.

Dame Bulla wrinkled her nose. "And that is you?"

Teakh said, "Not by a long shot. To achieve their goal, the breeders took as their subjects the descendants of Jamie Noah. They believed him to be the ideal altruistic man. They harvested eggs from our women and bred them with the girls' own fathers: incest. This is how a purebred strain of any species is created. Nearly all the resulting embryos carried harmful combinations of recessive genes. Most but not all of these embryos were identified and destroyed before implantation in surrogate mothers. Some remaining flawed individuals were killed before being carried to term. Despite all this, a number of the resulting infants were born with congenital disabilities. These supposedly defective children were killed or sterilized in the quest for perfect genes."

"We need a clan to protect our children," I said.

Dame Bulla wouldn't budge. "Such genocide couldn't have happened. And if it did, it was a long time ago."

Historically, even on Earth, there'd been a link between testing, eugenics, and genocide, along with denial that the link existed or that genocide had occurred.

"It did happen," Teakh said. "If we don't have control of our own marriages and reproductive contracts, it could happen again."

If we didn't take care, I could be tricked into being inseminated with my brother's semen. I said, "And that's why we need legal status."

As Noahee Grandmatriarch, I could wrest control of Teakh's contracts from Clan Ralko, but I had to become grandmatriarch before he produced any children. Ralko had already set the date for his first gig. The timing was critical. If his children were to be born into our clan, I needed to have a say in the terms of their conception.

Dame Bulla said, "With only two adult clan members, how can you raise and educate your children? You can't. What happens if you get sick or—Danna forbid—die? What happens to the two of you when you reach retirement age? You're putting an overly heavy burden on your children."

"If this is your answer," I said, "then why have you agreed to meet with us at all? We traveled all the way here from Ralko and Dojko by stratoplane. Your clan, Clan Fennako, paid our airfare."

"If it were up to me, you'd have remained in Ralko or wherever you're from. But your petition was seen by the Queen. In her doddering old age, she believes your wild proposal has merit. Personally, I'd have tossed this travesty immediately, but the decision wasn't mine to make. She has chosen to grant you clan status on a provisional basis."

The abrupt change of direction left me reeling. If the Queen had approved our clan, why had Dame Bulla withheld the information?

She flicked her screen and read the provisions. "First, Fennako will act as guardian clan. You'll be assigned advisors and accept counsel."

Teakh and I had hoped for sovereignty so that we could make our own decisions. Instead of becoming a sovereign clan, we'd merely swapped oppression by Ralko for the tyranny of Fennako. "Is that really *counsel*? Or do you mean commands?"

Dame Bulla didn't answer. "This is in your own interest. In the eyes of the law, you are minors incapable of entering a contract. The Palace has agreed to treat you as emancipated and is offering you exactly what you need: the wisdom and experience of the Queen's own advisors. You'll still have final say."

"But not unless Fennako approves," Teakh said.

"They do approve. Or so it seems. The Palace endorses your unorthodox proposal of extending membership to the children of men. However, they stipulate that membership shall be voluntary."

"That won't work," I said. This stipulation restricted clan revenue. My concern was for our children. "We won't be able to provide health care." They'd be able to opt out, and we could be left with only the sickest as members.

"Maternal clan will provide health care. All members must maintain dual-clan affiliation. Your clan will be supplementary only, a type of club."

"An association," I corrected.

Dame Bulla pointed to her screen. "You may make treaties, engage in bargaining, and sue on behalf of your members."

What I wanted most was to protect Teakh and his children. That could only be done if I were at the table, hammering out his stud contracts.

Dame Bulla went on. "The Palace asks that you accept, as members, patrilineal descendants of Jamie Noah as well as descendants of anyone in the Noah Project. This meets with your stated objectives."

At the time, I'd assumed that only Teakh had need of such advocacy. Fenrian clans were matrilineal, each person remaining in the mother's clan. Thus it had been since the time of Fenna Lee-Smith, founder of clan Fennako, and her husband, Jamie Noah.

Teakh leaned a forearm on the desk. "What about other descendants of Jamie Noah—matrilineal descendants?"

7

Teakh and I traced our paternal line to the semimythical royal couple. According to tests of Teakh's Y-DNA, his father's father's father had been a descendant of Jamie Noah, although we didn't know the number of generations. In a patrilineal system such as was common on Earth, Teakh might have become king.

Dame Bulla chuckled. "Then I'd be eligible to join your club, not that I want to. Fennako, our clan, consists of the matrilineal descendants of Queen Fenna Lee-Smith and her husband, Jamie Noah. And proud of it."

Her mother's mother's mother had been a descendant Fenna Lee-Smith. Dame Bulla was a cousin of sorts but so distant that the genetic relationship was inconsequential.

She touched her bi-adjustables and read one final provision. "In exchange for clan recognition, you, Annon, must bear children. Fennako will choose the sire."

I felt as if the floor had dropped from under me. I'd been asked to have sex with a stranger. I'd wanted sovereignty, not this invasion into my personal life. To gain freedom for my family, I'd have to throw it away for myself.

Teakh reacted faster than I could. He stood up, in scarlet and black, an enraged Seaguardsman. "Unacceptable! That's exactly what we must stop. We must have the right to marry as we please."

"Men are so emotional." Dame Bulla made a patting motion with her hand, signaling that he should sit down. "You still may. Fennako only ask that your sister produce children with a sperm donor of Fennako's choosing. She doesn't even have to see the man. It can be done by artificial insemination. You two are the last of a breed, your genetics a treasure won through the sacrifice of your ancestors. Fennako is cognizant of the difficulty you face in procuring an appropriate sire. Without the backing of Clan Fennako, you will be unable to arrange for a sperm donor with genetics of suitable quality. Your line will die out."

So now she admitted that genocide had occurred. Surely Fennako hoped to continue the ill-founded eugenics project. For what? Money? Power? Maybe there was some sort of status to be gained by recreating Jamie Noah. I shook my head.

"Go kill your brother!" Teakh's rage exploded. "You, Fennako, should not benefit from the exploitation of our family. This so-called treasure was produced through incest, abuse, and murder."

Dame Bulla's face reddened, but she remained calm. For that, she had my admiration. "You, sir, are benefiting from this treasure," she said with another wave of her hand. "Sit down. I believe you're making money as a cover stud. The proposed arrangement for your sister is little different than the one you enjoy as a stud."

It was different. I would be selling myself in exchange for a clan charter. Teakh was merely selling himself for money.

"She's right." I wasn't being coerced into the contract. "Why is it right for you to sell your genetics but not right for me?"

"Because you're a woman," Teakh said. "The consequences are greater."

Danna! Even my brother Teakh was sexist. "Didn't we agree that men and women should be treated equally?"

"You can't be thinking you'll accept this contract."

Dame Bulla closed the document. "Consider this *accord*. This decision is not one to rush into. Please take a copy of the provisions and look them over at your leisure."

IN THE LANE, a bird fluttered overhead but was gone before I could determine the species.

"Why did she pretend our proposal had been rejected?" I asked.

"She was softening us up," Teakh said as we walked. "Getting us to accept the terms without question. But we can negotiate, and we will. If Fennako won't accept us as a clan, we'll go elsewhere."

There wasn't anywhere else. Only the Queen had the ability to approve the founding of clans. I kept up with Teakh's long stride. "Fennako is the ruling clan."

"Then we'll take control of our contracts in a different way. We're only cornered if we think we are."

9

Those who believed Teakh's top stud fees were due purely to his genetics were mistaken. With no training or legal authority to do so, he regularly attempted to dictate the terms of his services. If I could back him as Noahee Grandmatriarch, he'd be more successful. I tucked my hand under his elbow. "So what's the worst that could happen?"

"The worst? Fennako impregnates you with my seed. Our children, the product of incest, are born with congenital disabilities. Then Ralko pulls their support, and so does Fennako. We're left as clanless parents caring for disabled children."

I stepped in front of Teakh, forcing him to a stop. "How would they get your seed? You're a cover stud. Have you donated sperm for artificial insemination?"

"No. But there's this girl I like. And we... uh, well. There's a possibility she took my... uh, stuff... and sold it. I don't think she did. But it's a possibility. And there's Papa."

"Papa? What do you mean?"

"Do we know for sure he never had any other children? Fennako keeps a sperm bank. They just might have some of his seed on deposit. We don't know."

"But Papa loved us and Mama. Why would he have donated sperm?"

"There's a lot of ways for a man to lose control of his seed."

"What are you thinking?" I asked.

"I'm thinking we specify natural insemination. At least then we'll know that neither Papa nor I have fathered your children."

We could forbid incest in our contract with Fennako, but if we accepted artificial insemination, we'd have no way of knowing if they followed the terms. Fennako could slip in unauthorized semen. I shuddered.

As we spoke, a man in a dark parka stepped out of a side street. "A word with you, sailor. Got a lady who wishes to talk with you."

10

The Tristan Bay Accord

Book three in the Tales of Fenria

Coming February 2017
Online and in bookstores or at **lizzienewell.com**

ABOUT THE AUTHOR

Lizzie Newell moved to Alaska the year of the *Exxon Valdez* oil spill. As she traveled aboard *M/V Columbia* ferry, she fantasized that Prince William Sound was an injured boy.

The image crystallized into a story when she visited Angoon, Alaska, as part of a program to install computer networks in schools. She saw the tide flowing out of Kootznahoo Inlet and knew she must write of a world where tide determines everything.

She lives in Anchorage, Alaska, where she writes science fiction about the planet Fenria. She also crafts drawings, paints, sculpture, card models, costumes, and jewelry related to her fictional world.

She can be found on the web at: **lizzienewell.com**

If you like this book

loan it to a friend
post a review
or purchase other books in the Tales of Fenria
go to website: lizzienewell.com

61163935R00199

Made in the USA
Lexington, KY
02 March 2017